Praise for *Bloo...*

"Irresistibly provocative, BLOOD RED sizzles with raw sensuality and strong, engaging characters. Steam rises from these pages. Savor the erotic journey."
—Patricia Grasso, bestselling Author

"Blazing erotica within an amazing love story."
—Kathryn Smith, bestselling Author

"BLOOD RED is an amazingly satisfying read. From vampire huntress to lover of both Yannick and Bastien, Althea Yates finds the answer to her dreams in the Demon Twins. Wickedly sensual and beautifully crafted, BLOOD RED not only captures the flavor of the early 1800s in England, it captures the reader with its exquisitely drawn characters. Historical erotic romance doesn't get any better than this."
—Kate Douglas, bestselling author of the WOLF TALES series

"Sinfully delicious. Sharon Page is a pure pleasure to read."
—Sunny, author of *Mona Lisa Awakening*

Praise for *Sin*:

"SIN delivers sizzling sex and engaging characters, an erotic romp through Regency England. Irresistible temptation."
—Patricia Grasso, bestselling Author

Praise for *A Gentleman Seduced*:

"Witty, wicked and wonderful."
  —Romantic Times BOOKreviews

"Sharon Page is a lady to watch out for. Her writing style is sharp, sexy and will seduce you from the first page."
  —Just Erotic Romance Reviews

"Sharon Page is a truly delightful storyteller who knows how to make sex not only highly arousing but full of emotion and warmth."
  —The Historical Romance Club

Blood Red

SHARON PAGE

APHRODISIA

KENSINGTON PUBLISHING CORP.

http://www.kensingtonbooks.com

APHRODISIA are published by

Kensington Publishing Corp.
850 Third Avenue
New York, NY 10022

ISBN: 0-7582-1543-6

First Kensington Trade Paperback Printing: January 2007

10 9 8 7 6 5 4 3 2 1

Printed in the United States of America

1

Awakening

The Village of Maidensby, Yorkshire, 1818

"Can you imagine both our mouths on you, love?"

Althea sighed as the seductive male voice whispered behind her. His warm breath danced over the nape of her neck, stirring loose strands of her hair.

A moan spilled from her lips as his big hands closed over her shoulders, slipping beneath the straps of her chemise. One pair of hands—a gentleman's hands, long-fingered, elegant. Hot, slightly rough, and all too real.

How could a dream stir her senses so?

Her dream lover massaged her shoulders and the controlled power in his touch vibrated through her. His fingers stroked the top of her spine. A bolt of desire raced down and exploded between her legs, drawing out a gasping sob from her very soul. A desperate sound. A plea.

For mercy? Or for more?

With a low chuckle, he held her as her legs melted beneath her.

Against her ear, his husky voice promised sin.

"Can you imagine my hands and his worshipping you?"

No. Althea shook her head, and that, too, felt real. No, she could not begin to imagine it. It was too scandalous. Too forbidden.

How could she, a virgin, be dreaming this?

"Then perhaps it is not a dream, Althea. Perhaps it is a premonition."

No, she argued. It is a dream. Only a dream.

His head bent to her neck. His silky hair brushed her tingling skin. She shuddered at the gentle scrape of pointed teeth. But she could not pull away, even as he drew the straps from her shoulders. He'd unfastened the tapes and the neckline gaped at her breasts, exposing them. He tugged it down further and she grabbed at his hands to rescue her modesty.

"No, sweet. Let us enjoy."

Her mouth dry, Althea stared down at her pale curves tipped with puckered nipples, small and pink. Two large male hands framed her bosom, holding the lacy neckline.

She'd never truly looked at her own breasts, not with the interest, the fascination, of these men. She'd never caressed them, never.

For the first time, the second man spoke. "Beautiful."

Her gaze riveted on him. He lounged on a massive bed, shirt open to reveal sculpted muscles, swirls of golden curls and dusky pink nipples. Skin-tight buff breeches encased his powerful legs. His long fingers skimmed over his crotch, stroking the thick curving ridge that lifted the fabric. Her body ached in response. Her heart hammered, lodged in her throat.

His long golden hair fell across his eyes, shadowing his beautiful face. Only moonlight lit the room, glittering as it fell across his dark eyes. In the bluish light, his hair glimmered like moonbeams, but she knew, the way dreamers did, what his coloring must be.

"Aren't they?" Satin brushed her back as the man behind her moved closer. The buttons of his waistcoat pressed into her spine. Althea felt engulfed by him, small, delicate.

But not afraid.

She tried to twist around to see the man behind, but she couldn't. He seemed formed of light and shadow. Only his hands were rendered in detail. The backs traced with veins, the knuckles large, the fingers astonishingly strong, yet graceful. Mesmerized, Althea watched his fingers release her fragile chemise, which dropped to her waist.

She swallowed a cry as those sensual hands cupped her naked bosom. Her tight, swollen breasts fit into his big palms like ripe apples. He lifted them, displaying them to the other man.

"Pinch her nipples," suggested the man on the bed, and he flicked open the first button securing his breeches.

Thumbs tapped her hard nipples, shocking her with jolts of pleasure and agony. He strummed them, and she arched back, thrusting her breasts forward. He wasn't so gentle anymore. He squeezed tight, plucked, pinched, and tugged at her nipples. But she loved every coarse, rough caress. He knew, far better than she, what she wanted. What her breasts enjoyed.

The man on the bed shifted to his knees. His lean, muscular abdomen rippled. Waggling his brows with teasing amusement, he drew down his open breeches to the middle of his thighs, revealing his small clothes. His intimate parts, etched in relief by shadow and silvery light, pulsed as he moved.

Althea caught her breath. Strangely, in this room, with these two men, in this startling, wonderful dream, she couldn't speak. Perhaps she wasn't allowed to—because she should be protesting her innocence. She should be fleeing for safety.

The man on the bed possessed large, beautiful hands too. Hands tugging down his linens, struggling to release his . . .

"His cock, love."

The man behind her arched his hips forward and she felt the ridge, hard as a poker in his trousers, jab against her bottom. His hips swayed, bumping his staff across her derrière.

It must be a dream. It had to be a dream.

The golden-haired man dropped his linens, freeing his cock. She understood the term "rampant rod," which she'd heard whispered by maids. This thing seemed to have a mind of its own. It wobbled, swayed, and grew longer before her astonished eyes. A nest of hair surrounded it, a cap crowned it, and it glistened as though wet. Moonlight played along its length, revealing a ridge along the back that led to a dangling sack that must be his ballocks. The maids called them jewels, as though they were incredibly precious.

Althea couldn't draw her gaze from it as he slid from the bed. As he pulled off his boots, kicked off his clothes. He swaggered toward her, his cock standing proud, straight, and tall, amidst the thicket of golden curls. She could tell he was proud of it, too, and his hand settled around it in a possessive gesture.

Her legs trembled as he gave one long stroke to the base and back up to the tip. Behind her, her other lover arched hard against her, trapping her thin chemise between the cheeks of her bottom as he pushed his clothed cock against her.

It had been delicious to be caressed by one man, but to have two touch her at once was a sensation unsurpassed. Someone tore her chemise away. Ripped it from her and tossed the tattered garment aside. Four hands moved over her skin, hot as candle flames, smooth and sensuous as a silken robe. They didn't touch her between her thighs but coasted flat palms over her dark red pubic curls.

Althea shuddered, caught on a horrifying cusp between fear and unbearable arousal. Their hands were pale, stark against the peach-tinted skin of her tummy and breasts.

As though they'd said, "One, two, three, go," they both bent and took her nipples into their mouths. Her cry rang out into the room. Both nipples in hot male mouths at once. Both nipples lightly scraped by pointy fangs.

As they began sucking in earnest, they took on their own unique rhythms, the contrasts more stunning than having them work in unison had been. Golden hair spilled over her neck and face from both sides. Two hard male members bumped her hips, one nude, the other clothed.

Hands parted her thighs and she whimpered in relief. Their tongues licked her nipples. Their fingers slid between her nether lips. She was slick, scandalously wet and hot. From their groans, she knew the men liked the feel of her wetness on their fingers. Liked the musky perfume floating up from between her legs.

Something built inside her. Althea sobbed with it and began to rock against their hands. Seeking more. Needing more.

"Yes. Yes." Their voices joined, a chorus urging her on. Their mouths moved over her, pleasuring her nipples, her neck, capturing her mouth. With her lids almost covering her eyes, she couldn't see who kissed her where. She gave herself to them, floating between them.

A finger touched the entrance to her bottom and she gasped. Fingers stroked the top of her sex and she screamed. She ground herself hard against their big hands. Harder. Harder.

"Make yourself come, sweetheart."

"God, yes, come for us, love."

She drove relentlessly, gasping, moaning. "Yes, yes, yes." She cried the word over and over in her mind. A frenzy gripped her, possessed her. She snapped inside. Pleasure swamped her like a wave and her body bucked over their fingers. They held her tight, praised her, groaned with her.

Oh. Oh, yes.

Her eyes shut tight, plunging her into a velvety darkness as the throbbing faded into a light-headed joy.

Faintly she heard a wicked voice murmur against her ear. "You have never been bitten, have you, angel?"

Weak, she shook her head. But for their arms around her, she would dissolve into a puddle on the floor. She was powerless. Powerless.

"Can you imagine the erotic pleasure of having both of us bite you?"

No. She tried to fight. To force her arms to hit and her legs to kick. Desperate, panicked, she thrashed against their strong grasp—

Tangled in her sheets, Althea Yates opened her eyes and bit back a scream. Heart racing, she fought the threadbare blankets, kicked at the sheets that held her, and bolted upright.

Cold air washed over her, prickling against her damp skin even through her heavy nightdress. Moonlight splashed in her room. She rubbed her eyes. There was no ornate bed and certainly no men in her room at the Maidensby Arms. Just a small room overfilled by her narrow bed, a battered dresser, a wobbly desk, and a sagging armchair.

Only a dream. Exhausting, terribly scandalous, and all a figment of her imagination.

Althea blinked, almost more surprised to find it was not real than she would have been if it were.

Dear heaven.

Erotic dreams had haunted her for weeks, since she'd arrived back in England, but she'd never dreamed of *two* men before. What did it say about her character that she would visit such a shocking scene in her sleep? And that she had enjoyed it?

It wasn't that she'd never felt desire before. When Mick O'Leary worked without his shirt, she secretly watched him. Half-naked and slick with perspiration, Mick looked elemental. Primal. Sensual. His back flexed in the most hypnotic way as he worked. Hidden by the wide brims of her prim bonnets and her spectacles, she would ogle him, and flutter inside, as though a thousand butterflies frolicked low in her tummy. She would yearn and want and fantasize until she became bad-tempered and cross and made everyone's life a misery.

That was bad enough.

But two men!

Only the most depraved woman should want such things.

What was happening to her?

Crack!

A strong gust rattled her window and Althea's heart leapt to her throat. The curtains billowed softly, even though the sash was closed. Before her startled eyes, a black shape flew at the glass, retreated, swooped again.

She launched up on her knees, ready for battle. The dark shadow slapped the glass again with an angry thwack. Leaves splayed over the small panes. Nervous laughter bubbled up in Althea's throat. Only a tree branch. She sank back down onto her bottom.

Silly goose. Jumping at shadows.

With a sigh, she relaxed and let the sated, languorous feeling steal over her again. She yawned and stretched, reaching toward the low, timbered ceiling with her hands. Her neck gave a little crick and she moved her head from side to side. Physically she was exhausted, but she knew her mind would just not let her rest now.

She was almost afraid to sleep. Each dream became more indecent, more . . . more lewd. And now she was dreaming of being bitten. If she dreamed again and she didn't wake up in time, what might happen to her?

She could hardly wake up a vampire, could she? But she was not certain. She didn't truly know. Perhaps she could.

Better to think about tomorrow. They would open the crypt tomorrow.

Instinct led her right hand to the cross dangling around her neck. Althea stroked it, cupped it in her palm. For more reassurance, she glanced to the narrow window of her room. The curtains were open, as she had left them. They lay still now, hanging against the rough-hewn trim. Garlic flowers lay along the sash. Another bundle of the pungent flowers sat by the base of the door and some were clustered on the rickety table beside her bed.

Accustomed to them, she barely noticed their smell, but she'd seen the maid's nose crinkle in disgust. The first night she'd gone to bed and found all the flowers stripped away. Small bouquets of field flowers replaced them—yellow daffodils, mainly. Firmly, she had instructed the maid not to touch any of her belongings again.

The flowers, the cross, all were to keep her safe from Zayan, but there was something half-hearted in Father's admonishments about protection this time. And she feared that none of these measures would do any good.

In truth, she was afraid to open that crypt. That was probably why she had the dream.

Althea swung her legs around the side of the bed—really more of a cot—until her bare feet brushed the small carpet thrown over the splintery floor.

Her journal sat by her bed, beside a gutted candle in a beaten brass holder. She didn't dare record her dreams. There was almost enough moonlight to read by, but she felt far too restless to do that.

She wanted to . . . to do something. Plucking up her spectacles, Althea slid off the bed and winced as her feet sank into the cool carpet. She padded across the worn, faded wool to her window. A glance told her the catch was still fastened, though she touched it with her fingers to make sure.

She knew to be wary of unexplained urges to walk about in the dark. Knew to resist the call, the lure. But no, whatever it was she wanted, it wasn't to go out of doors.

Wrapping her arms around herself, she refused to accept that what she wanted was to make her dream come true.

A flicker of flame outside caught her attention. Leaning forward until her forehead brushed the cool panes of glass, she could just make out the flurry of activity in front of the inn.

What she had spotted was an elegant carriage drawn by four coal-black horses, almost invisible in the dark but for its burning lamps and the reflections on the gleaming traces. The carriage rattled slowly over cobblestones and came to a halt before the door. Male voices rose in hale greetings and terse orders. A dog set up a howl, answered by others, which sparked a whinnying frenzy as the horses shied. Skittish animals. It took the coachman minutes to settle them. Surprising for animals reaching the end of their travel.

Intrigued, Althea pushed the garlic flowers to the side. She sat on the deep windowsill and curled her legs beneath her to warm her chilled feet. Cold whistled around her and she rubbed her arms through the long, tight sleeves of her nightdress. Cold was supposed to subdue improper arousal, wasn't it?

The gleaming black door of the coach sported a crest, which meant the newest guest was a member of the nobility.

How would a peer feel about sharing quarters with vampire hunters? The lord in question would never know, of course. Sir Edmund Yates was known only as a famous antiquarian. And no one ever suspected Miss Yates, his plain slip of a daughter, was anything more than a glorified secretary. Even Mick O'Leary had scoffed when she told him she was adept with a crossbow and knew exactly how and where to plunge in a stake.

Movement in the yard. His lordship's footmen in livery—silver and pale blue, startling against the dark.

The coach door swung open. In a blur of motion, a male figure jumped down and straightened—a man dressed in head-to-toe black. Althea could barely see him, but the way he moved suggested he was young, strong, athletic.

Heat unfurled deep inside. Goodness, she was incurable. But she wanted a glimpse. To see if his face proved as promising as his form. A tall beaver hat covered his head, but she saw pale blond hair curling into his collar.

Led by servants with lanterns, he strode away from his carriage.

Tudor in vintage, the inn sat right beside the road, with barely a step up to the threshold. To her surprise, the lord paused at the door, then stepped back.

A servant lifted a lantern by his master's side and golden light slanted over austere features, hinting at a strong jaw line, sharp cheekbones, a broad forehead, a straight nose.

Rendered in shadow and light, he made her think of the man from her dream. The mysterious one who stood behind her. He was the one who came to her in all her dreams. Althea knew the sound of his voice, the scent of his skin, the way he kissed, even the way he braced himself on his powerful arms as he made love, but she had never really seen his face . . .

She gave herself a shake. Of course this gentleman was not in her dreams!

The nobleman abruptly pushed the lantern aside and, as though he sensed her stare, he looked up to her window. His eyes reflected a sliver of moonlight, pure silver disks in the velvety dark. Gleaming, mirror-like eyes. Like those of a wolf or a fox.

The eyes of a vampire.

Althea blinked. She looked again, but he had disappeared from her view. She got up on her knees to try to see him, strained to see him. She couldn't.

A vampire lord. Was it possible? Had it just been a trick of the light? Just her imagination playing havoc?

Shocked, she sat back, and thumped hard against the wall of the window alcove.

She slid off the sill to her feet. Her rumpled bed beckoned, but she'd never sleep now. No, she would sneak out to the top of the stairs and have another look at the mysterious lord. Shrugging on her wool wrapper over her shoulders, she caught the sides around her and cinched the belt tight. The trailing hem covered her bare feet and jammed in her slippers as she hurriedly shoved her feet in.

She didn't dare go out unarmed. By her bed, she dropped to her knees, drew out her case and flipped open the lid. Instead of gowns and slippers and hats, her case contained stakes, a crossbow, a small, lethal sword, and crosses. She tucked a thin, pointed stake between her wrap and her nightgown, secured in place by her snug belt.

A thrill of excitement shivered down Althea's spine. Not that she planned to be foolhardy. She knew to be cautious and careful. If he truly were a vampire, he would possess incredible strength and power. But she had a few tricks of her own. And she knew exactly what to expect.

At the head of the stairs, she saw the lord and the innkeeper in discussion. She stayed in the shadows to watch.

His lordship stood with his face away from her but she had a perfect view of the florid features of Mr. Crenshaw. Alarm flashed in the innkeeper's small eyes and he was punctuating his apologies with wild motions of his hands. The gentleman wore a cloak, she noted, which surprised her. Most men favored greatcoats.

The lord brushed his cloak back from his shoulders, giving a glimpse of the lining, black silk embroidered with gold. From the window, she'd created an impression of him—tall, lean, elegant. Now she saw he was taller than she'd guessed. He towered over Crenshaw by at least a foot. His hat brushed the plaster ceiling. And he possessed a broader, more powerful body than she'd first thought. Shoulders as wide as Mr. O'Leary's, Althea noted.

But was he a vampire?

Her breathing quickened and not from fear. Her breasts tingled and her nipples eagerly stood up against her bodice. Already wet between her thighs from her dream, she flushed as more hot moisture bubbled there.

He was facing away from Crenshaw's lamp, his hat worn low, at an angle that shielded his eyes—and that prevented them reflecting the light.

Perhaps that wasn't his intent. She knew nothing of male fashion to know if all men wore their hats in that way.

The lord snapped a question at Crenshaw, his voice deep and low. Fancifully, she imagined his voice sounded like black silk, dark and smooth. But did he sound like the man from her dream?

He wasn't the man from her dream, she told herself sternly.

If only he'd speak louder.

". . . Yates . . ."

Althea stilled at the sound of her surname falling from the nobleman's lips. His lordship knew her father was here? She left the shadows, not caring if the men noticed her. She leaned against the rail, straining to hear.

Crenshaw appeared bent in a permanent bow. ". . . I fear not, my lord . . ."

Was it only that Crenshaw had mentioned her father as one of the other occupants of the inn? To imply that he served distinguished men? Her father might be a great scholar, a star in his own orbit, but a gentleman antiquarian would hardly register in the mind of a peer.

"You fear not?" The dark velvet voice held a razor-sharp edge now.

He did sound similar, but not quite the same. In her dreams, his tone was always seductive and teasing.

"I am afraid, my lord, Sir Edmund has retired for the evening."

"Wake him."

"I've a fine room available for the night, my lord, and in the morning—"

"I've no need of a room. Your parlor will suffice. I shall wait in there upon Sir Edmund."

"But—"

The gentleman swirled around, sending his cape flapping around him. Like bat's wings, of course—and Althea forgot to move back into the gloom.

His dark gaze fixed on her, appraised, then his wide, full lips curved in a smile. She'd once been set aflame by Mick O'Leary's cheeky smirks. Sizzling as those were, they were nothing compared to the controlled fire in this lord's arrogant, confident grin. She was left with the image of wildfire ready to burst beyond control and consume everything in its path.

"I am sorry if I woke you, my dear," he drawled as he ignored Crenshaw to move to the foot of the stair. This put the lantern behind him and plunged his gorgeous face into shadow again.

It *was* his voice! That lazily seductive growl was exactly the voice of the man from her dreams. She heard his whisper again in her head: *Then perhaps it is not a dream, Althea. Perhaps it is a premonition.*

It couldn't be! But she hunted vampires, and she knew that second sight did indeed exist.

Stunned, she stared into his shadowed eyes. No, she wouldn't... couldn't...

Even in the gloom, she saw his brow lift in interest.

She must behave normally—though what could be normal?

A curtsy. He was a lord, after all. Althea dropped, quick and unsteady, aware that she wore her wrapper and nightgown, her ugly spectacles. Her hair was in its nighttime braid and the end curved around the swell of her left breast. Her heart hammered so hard, she imagined the braid was bumping in time with it.

Did he know about the dreams... had he... oh, goodness...?

Legs trembling, she straightened. "You had an appointment with my father, my lord?"

"Not an appointment, no. But I want to speak with him tonight." His large black-gloved hand wrapped around the banister.

Want. He said the word as though what he wanted was never denied.

She couldn't prevent a blush heating her cheeks. In her dreams, she had never denied him anything. So it was not to be a premonition after all. She was not about to let her father, who was so weak and confused these days, confront this vampire. Definitely not when *this* vampire might know about her dreams. "You cannot, my lord. But you can speak with me."

"And who are you, my dear?"

She moved down two steps. The jab of the stake at the bottom of her ribs comforted. "Sir Edmund Yates is my father. I am Althea Yates."

"Miss Yates." He bowed with courtly elegance. As he straightened, surprise lifted his blond brows. "You assist your father?"

"In *all* of his research, yes. And his investigations." She was halfway down the steps now.

"So you know about the excavation of the crypt?"

Her slipper-clad foot missed the step; her heel glanced along the edge of the tread and landed hard on the next one. Of course, she did, but how did he?

Father had spoken of a vampire—an ancient one—one who could only be defeated by the power of the vampire entombed in that crypt. She hadn't understood. They'd never spared a vampire before. Father's answers were vague and told her nothing. He kept so much to himself now, but she'd understood from disconnected snippets that he was hunting the creature he believed was the oldest of the undead. The first. The ghoul from which all others had spawned.

A whisper of fear shivered down Althea's spine.

Could this man be that vampire? This man who had seduced her in her dreams?

No, impossible. Not if he was truly a peer of the realm.

Father would suffer a fit of apoplexy if he knew what she was about to do.

Crenshaw, Althea saw, was following their conversation. If anything, the portly innkeeper looked more confounded. "My lord, do you wish a room then, or do you wish to retire to the parlor with Miss Yates . . ." Crenshaw's reedy voice died away and the man flushed.

Althea rolled her eyes. The innkeeper was mortified because he'd just suggested that the lord and an unmarried woman make use of a parlor alone in the middle of the night. How ridiculous after what they'd done together in her dreams.

But that hadn't been real.

Trembling, she gazed into his lordship's eyes. Seeking recognition? A clue? A hint of desire for her?

Black and bottomless, his eyes told her nothing.

"The parlor will be fine," she snapped to Crenshaw, suddenly tense and irritable. Suddenly fearful she was far out of her depth. Should she turn and run?

Hell and the devil, she planned to hunt vampires! She couldn't cower over a few dreams . . . even forbidden ones.

Softening her voice slightly, Althea turned to the vampire. Her . . . oh, goodness . . . her dream *lover*. "But first, my lord, might I have your name? You have not yet made yourself known to me."

"You do not know who I am?"

She started. Damn shadows. She couldn't read his expression. He must mean that many young English ladies knew who he was. Heaven knew, once seen he would never be forgotten. In her dreams, he had never bothered to introduce himself. She would not let him get away with that now.

"Until one month ago, my lord, I was living in the Carpathian

Mountains and have done so since I was a young girl. So, no, I do not know who you are."

"The Carpathians? But you are obviously English."

How adeptly he kept avoiding the issue of his identity. "And you are—?"

He laughed. "I do love a blunt woman, sweet." The murmured endearment washed over her. Spoken softly so Crenshaw wouldn't hear.

"Then you won't mind answering my question, my lord." Althea moved down more steps. Only two separated them and this way she stood at his height. Now she could see his large black pupils, the smallest circle of colored iris surrounding them. A silvery blue, or was it green? So hard to tell under only the faintest fingers of light. And despite his fair coloring, he had thick, remarkably dark lashes. What her nanny had termed "eyes put in with a sooty finger." Heavy-lidded eyes. His lashes swept down frequently, giving him a lazily cynical expression.

His gaze slid from her eyes to her throat. Her cross was hidden beneath the overlapped lapels of her wool wrapper, but he saw the chain. He smiled. Lifted his brows in a gesture that seemed to say he was awarding her a point.

"No, my dear. I won't mind at all."

He leaned closer, enveloping her in his tantalizing scent. The magical male scent from her dreams. An enthralling mix of sandalwood and smoke, shaving soap and masculine skin. She hungered to move closer, to feast on his smell. She wanted his smell on her, just as in her dreams. She wanted—

He winked as though he knew exactly what she wanted. "I am Yannick de Wynter, Earl of Brookshire." His voice dropped to a low, thrumming whisper. "The man you plan to resurrect tomorrow is my brother."

2

Captivated

So this was the siren who had entranced him in his dreams? Intrigued, Yannick drank in Miss Yates' green eyes, hidden behind utilitarian spectacles, as they widened in charming astonishment. Thankfully she'd never worn those in his dreams. Her dreary flannel wrapper hinted at the curvaceous body which, in his sleep, responded so eagerly. Her skin's perfume—lavender and dewy feminine perspiration—mingled with the alluring aroma of her rich blood. His nose detected a trace of something pungent. Rather like garlic. Garlic?

Yannick choked back a laugh. A vampire slayer's trick. But garlic or garlic flowers had no effect on him.

"You are the Earl of Brookshire?" Miss Yates whispered as her fingers stroked the silver chain around her neck.

The soft, throaty timbre of her voice played its magic. Arousal shot through him and his cock stood up. A flare of heat rushed through his jaw, threatening the explosion of his fangs. Struggling, he controlled it, but they lengthened a little and jabbed his tongue.

"So you have heard of the Demon Twins." He gave her a teasing smile.

He saw her cast a quick, sidelong glance toward Crenshaw. The man had retreated, but Yannick sensed the innkeeper kept an ear cocked to their conversation.

Originally bestowed upon us when we were mortal. All the more accurate now.

He wasn't quite ready to brazenly admit to being a vampire in front of the curious innkeeper, so he chose a more intimate form of communication. He spoke in her mind.

Unfortunately, as a result, Miss Yates' eyes were circles of horror and her pretty mouth dropped open in shock. She yanked the cross out from beneath her clothes and let it dangle before his eyes.

Yannick tormented himself with the irreverent image of her cross nestled in the lush valley between her full breasts, warmed by her pale, satin-smooth skin.

Miss Yates' hair was as lovely as in his dreams. A magnificent color. A deep, dark red. Not auburn. Not quite burgundy, but darker than flame. Though the length of it was tamed in a thick braid, tendrils dangled over her forehead and danced around her cheeks. Nor was she as calm as she appeared—she had tucked her curls behind her right ear more than a dozen times.

So now you understand why I must speak to your father, Miss Yates.

She shook her head and whispered, "How do you do this? Speak in my head."

We have a connection, Miss Yates. A connection through our dreams.

A bright pink flush washed over her lightly freckled cheeks. "Is that why you wish to talk to my father?" Sheer, raw panic flashed in her emerald eyes.

No, sweet. I'm not mad enough to admit to a man who could

destroy me that I've made love to his daughter. Even if only in dreams.

Her response was entirely practical. "Promise?" she hissed.

I am a gentleman. My word can be trusted.

"But you are also a vampire," she accused sotto voce.

Miss Yates was proving to be as stubborn as she could be in his dreams. *Fetch your father, love.*

Her amber brows drew together, implying she had no intention of complying. "Are you here to free your brother?"

"I have not yet decided," he admitted.

"If we have a connection, can I speak in your thoughts?"

I believe it to be possible. With practice. Yannick lifted his brow and winked. *What would you wish to tell me that you want no one else to hear?*

She didn't rise to his bait. "Can you read my thoughts?"

Not yet.

She dipped her shoulders slightly in relief. Once again, her fingers stole to the errant curl by her ear and she brushed it back.

Yannick wanted to see her hair loose. Not tamed and bound in that prim, tight plait.

Yes, that was so much more intriguing—the thought of her hair free, and that ribbon put to more playful use. Wrapped around her wrists, securing her arms to his bed while he explored every inch of her with his tongue.

"You mean," she murmured, "eventually I could read yours?"

Hell and the devil, he hoped not.

"The dreams—"

Not a word about the dreams. You have my solemn vow. But your father is seeking to destroy a vampire with as much power as God, and, for his sake, he must talk with me.

"But are they just dreams?" she persisted softly. "When a vampire visits a victim, sometimes it is remembered as a dream."

Before tonight, I did not know who you were or where you

could be found. Our dreams have only been that, love. Just dreams. Now, go fetch your father.

"*Oh.* Then what do you want to do with my father, my lord?" She spoke in a normal tone suddenly, one as brittle as ice. Her large emerald eyes narrowed, shooting sparks. Warily, he knew he'd offended. Because he'd issued a command? Or because he'd implied she meant nothing more to him than a delightful partner in his dreams?

If only she knew.

If he had a soul, she would have captured it.

"How did you escape?" she whispered. "We know you were imprisoned too."

Behind her spectacles, her eyes glinted with intelligent curiosity, and Yannick couldn't help but smile. Faced with a dangerous vampire, she showed nothing but courage. "I'm not about to divulge all my secrets, love. And there are some things it is better that you do not know."

She fumed in the most adorable way. "I will fetch my father, then, my lord, as you requested.

Miss Yates.

She paused on the steps and turned back. Damnation, he'd forgotten about Crenshaw, who must be wondering why they appeared to be having such an intimate conversation, why she would come back without a word spoken. He was never impulsive. Still, he couldn't let her go without asking.

Yannick had never asked with any other woman. He claimed. Took. Possessed. Made love to them and drank from them and left them. For the poor women, the jades, he left a few coins. For the ladies, he left only the afterglow of intense pleasure.

For himself, he took enough blood to quench his needs. Nothing more.

Let me come to you tonight, Althea.

Do you mean in a dream? She tried to push her thoughts at him. Her forehead wrinkled with the effort, her eyes shut, her amber lashes feathered on her cheeks. And yes, faintly, he heard her.

She was adorable and he found, to his surprise, another warm, genuine smile on his lips.

I want to pleasure you for real, love.

No. But she faltered. Her plump pink lips parted. He waited, waited for her invitation.

No. Please... no. Don't. I won't... I can't... can't do the scandalous things you want of me, my lord.

He flashed her a lusty grin. *Yes, you can, sweet. You are a sensual delight in my dreams. Trust me, Althea.*

I am not that foolish, sir. I have no intention of being seduced, trapped, tricked, or forced into being a vampire.

She turned on her heel, her spine straight, her head high, and she stalked up the stairs. With a flick of her slender wrist, she tossed her braid over her shoulder and it swished over the small of her back, just above the generous curve of her voluptuous derrière.

Yannick turned abruptly to Crenshaw. "I have changed my mind about a room."

Althea's legs shook as she reached the top of the stairs. She did not dare turn and look back. But in the gloom of the hallway, she sank back against the rough plaster wall. She covered her mouth with her hands, smothering a sudden sob.

What did the dreams mean?

She'd been intimate with that... that beautiful blond man in those dreams. With a vampire. A vampire with the perfect features of an angel! From her dreams, she could remember the salty, rich taste of his bare skin against her tongue. Her fingertips knew his textures. She had played in the coarse silkiness of the golden curls on his chest. She had stroked his erect nipples. Even cupped his bottom as he drove... goodness, in her dreams he had been inside her. Deep, deep within her.

And he knew—*he knew*—what she dreamed, what they had done!

How could she bring her father downstairs? Althea did not believe for one minute the vampire Earl of Brookshire would not torment Father and would keep her secret.

But if he truly was the brother of the vampire in the crypt, Father must speak with him. Whether it meant her exposure or not.

Her wrap and the skirts of her nightrail swished about her legs as she hurried to her father's room, but she stopped in her tracks before reaching the door. The earl had come to her in her dreams. He had deliberately seduced her. Until the last dream, she hadn't even suspected he was a vampire.

Of course he must have known who she was. His denial was a complete lie. How could he expect she would believe he did not? The dreams were a trick—to capture her mind and soul, to use her in some way to release his brother—

"By all that is holy—" Her father's panicked cry froze her blood.

A crash echoed from his room. A heavy thud. Furniture overturned? Her father falling? For several thundering heartbeats, Althea couldn't move—then she wrenched forward and raced up the hallway.

"Father?" She reached his door. Thank heavens, the knob turned under her shaky hand. She pushed the door, but before it opened more than a few inches, it slammed back in her face.

"Father!"

Another crash. Althea shoved the door again, but this time it refused to give at all. She kicked it, twisting the knob so hard she thought it might break off in her hand.

Beyond the door, there was silence. "Father!" she cried once more.

Faintly she heard a twang, followed by an instant thunk. The bolt of a crossbow? There was no cry of agony, only an eerie, disembodied chuckle that seemed to come from her father's room and from behind her at the same time. She whipped around, her hand still clasped to the knob.

There was no one there.

Where was Mr. O'Leary? Hadn't Crenshaw heard the crashes? Hadn't the servants?

Desperate, she shoved at the door, her shoulder and hip braced against it. Althea threw all her weight—not much—at it. She screamed, hoping to summon someone. Anyone.

The metal knob turned to scorching fire in her palm. In vain she tried to jerk it again, even as her skin screamed in agony. A revolting stench rose—her burning flesh. With a howl, she yanked her hand back. Sickening pain shot up her arm as she pounded on the door. Dizziness washed over her as her wounded hand struck the wood.

The door thrummed beneath her blows. From the gaps in the frame, a blue light spilled out—a light filled with small twinkling stars. Once in the hallway, they flew at her eyes. Her spectacles protected her, but some struck her cheeks, her lips. Each delivered a sharp, horrible pain, like a bite from small, sharp teeth. Slapping at the door helplessly, she had to flinch and shake her head to avoid the stings.

A black shape enveloped her, pulling another scream from her throat. A huge hand wrapped around her wrist and drew her back from the door. Althea fell against a large, black wall— the earl's massive chest. "You?"

"You are hurt." Raw fury snapped in his deep voice.

"I don't matter. My father is in there!"

Still holding her wrist, he raised his booted foot and slammed it into the door. Before her eyes, the door arched inward and snapped back. With a bang, a large crack shot through the middle of it and it sagged on its hinges but still stood as a barrier.

"Bloody Zayan," the earl muttered.

Althea jerked her gaze to Brookshire's face, swathed in the

pale blue glow. A deep red fire burned in the depth of his eyes and she caught her breath at the sight. He was a demon and she was praying for his help?

But what else could she do? She'd never been so helpless. None of her weapons could help against so much power.

"Get back."

She flinched at his brutal command.

"Back, goddammit."

Stumbling back, Althea snagged a slipper in her hem and tumbled against the wall behind. Her stake bit into her stomach and frantic breathing surrounded her—her own, choked and raw and desperate. The earl lifted his gloved hands, palms facing the door.

A blast of light arced from his hands and the door exploded into splinters. He was definitely no ordinary vampire.

"Stay there," the earl barked as he stepped into a maelstrom of white and blue light. The dazzling stars swirled as though trapped in a whirlpool. They gathered in a large white ball, which raced into the room behind him.

Wresting the stake from inside her wrapper, she got to her feet and staggered to the doorway.

"Miss Yates, you're not to go in there, lass."

A hand caught hold of her shoulder, the instant she recognized the voice. Mick O'Leary! Finally!

Althea twisted beneath his grip and rapped the stake across his knuckles.

"Ow. Christ Jesus!" O'Leary's hand jerked open, giving her an instant to storm forward. As if she would cower in the hallway while her father was in danger! But as she raced into Father's room, she could not see a thing other than spinning stars and flashes of light.

Cries and shouts and thudding boots came from behind her—O'Leary and other servants charging into the room.

"Father?"

"Althea!"

Dizzy with relief, Althea stumbled through the dark room toward her father's voice. But cold wrapped around her, squeezing tight. A slithery cold as though an enormous snake had dropped on her. She slashed blindly with her stake. The tip glanced off an object, and she drove harder, with two hands. She felt it penetrate and pushed it home.

Something exploded behind her and the force shoved her forward.

Warm, comforting arms embraced her. "Althea, my love." Her father's voice, but weak, a mere whisper near her ear. She pulled her head back from his chest, searching through the screaming lights.

"Father, we must get out. Can you move?"

But he didn't answer, and she felt his hands brush over her back in the sign of the cross. He muttered over and over. Latin, but her head filled with a rush of sound and she couldn't understand his words.

"Father, what is it? What are you fighting?"

A clap of thunder burst inside the room and the lights shot away, toward the window. As they moved, they seemed to tug at her, like a ferocious wind that could pull her off the ground. Father's grip tightened and she clung to him, her hands fisted in his nightshirt.

Her ears rang with the screeching sounds of the fleeing lights, and then, so loud she feared her ears would burst, a cry of rage exploded.

Then silence.

In the center of the strange, frightening stillness, the vampire earl stood, fists raised to the sky. A faint green glow pulsed around him and as she watched, terrified, the soft light sucked back into his body and disappeared.

Her father sagged against her. Althea caught him, tried to hold him up. Where was his bed? Moonlight spilled into the room now, and she saw, to her amazement, that nothing appeared out of place—not the furniture or the bed. The earl lowered his arms. He stood in a pool of moonlight, his hair and face as silver as the light, and he looked like a glowing warrior angel.

"What in the name of God was it?" O'Leary's charge toward the window yanked her attention from the gorgeous, shimmering vampire. For the first time Althea noticed O'Leary was shirtless but wore his breeches and boots. Four strapping male servants stood transfixed near the door, gaping in astonishment. Father's coachman and groom—who knew Father hunted vampires—and two Inn footmen, who did not.

Suddenly her father's weight lifted from her. The earl lifted him and carried him to his bed, bending to lay him gently onto the quilt. O'Leary herded the servants out of the room as Crenshaw's voice rose from the corridor. "Mr. O'Leary, what has happened?"

"O'Leary can take care of them. Now, who the bloody hell are you?" came her father's faint querulous voice.

Despite Father's obvious weakness, a warm relief flooded Althea. He couldn't be too badly hurt if he was as crotchety as ever. The earl spoke in a low, murmuring voice, too low for her to hear.

"Brookshire, eh? One of the Demon Twins. So you've come after your brother, my lord?"

"As a consequence of hunting Zayan, yes."

"You've decided to confront Zayan."

"I want what you want, Sir Edmund. To see Zayan destroyed."

Her father gave a short, curt laugh, then a curse she'd never heard him say. "Won't slay him without your brother."

Althea moved forward as her father struggled to sit up. Her hands shook—she knew father had intended to use Sebastien de Wynter as bait to capture his brother. Imprisoned, de Wynter was the weaker vampire. His brother was strong, cunning, a dangerous foe.

To her astonishment, the earl flipped out his cape and planted himself on the edge of the bed. He took hold of her father's shoulders, eased him back. "Lie down, please, Sir Edmund. Let me find where you've been injured."

"I can tell you that. Ribs below the heart. Right arm. Left leg. Some Hellhound came at me first and mistook me leg for his dinner. Then Zayan crushed me ribs and drove his finger into me chest. Burst into me flesh like a blade. His bloody finger! I got a shot off with the crossbow and caught him through the shoulder—"

Althea tumbled onto her knees on the bed, beside her father. She wrapped her hands around his. "Please, Father, don't exhaust yourself." The sight of his face—drawn, pale, his lips blue and trembling—made her heart plummet.

"Drink, Sir Edmund."

Startled, Althea turned as the earl lifted his wrist to his mouth. His fangs now curved over his lower lip and as she gasped, he sliced into his wrist. Dark blood bubbled along the cut.

Althea got up off the bed, stake in hand. "You can't ask him to drink a vampire's blood!"

"My blood heals."

"It will transform him."

"No, love, it won't."

"He's right, lass. It won't." With a shudder her father held up a shaky hand. "Give it to me then, my lord. I've no other choice, do I?"

"I am afraid not, sir. Your heart is slowing now, laboring. It will not survive the strain."

"I never expected to owe me bloody life to a vampire," her father grumbled.

* * *

Althea sank onto her bed and buried her face in her hands. She should have stayed with her father.

Why had she allowed the earl to command her?

Because he appeared to be a hero. Because Father owed his life to him. Because *she* owed Father's life to him.

The heated debate still rang in her head. With the help of the earl and Mick O'Leary, she had gotten her father into his bed, with his blankets pulled up tight. His pulse, which had been thready and weak, began to beat strong and fierce. Color soon infused her father's lined cheeks and he was quickly filled with vigor. Father had fired question after question at the earl, who told Father to wait until he was recovered to have a discussion. Father had demanded his spectacles, then his journal and pen, but Althea had refused that. Raking his hands through his wiry white hair, he'd argued, but had finally capitulated.

The earl did command that they not open the crypt, then left them to deal with Crenshaw. Father had motioned her close. "I know what he says, missy, but we're to open that crypt on the morrow."

For the first time in her life, she had doubted her father. She had taken a deep breath, knowing she must argue, but she hadn't dared upset Father while he was so weak. "He said we mustn't and he appears to want Zayan's destruction, too. I think—" She had broken off as she sensed the earl's return. Heat flooded her body; her skin prickled in awareness. She couldn't meet her father's eyes, terrified he might guess at her reaction. She placed her hand on her father's, relieved at the warmth there.

"You'd best go to bed, Althea."

"I will stay with you, tonight, Father."

"O'Leary can stay." The earl's deep baritone murmured down her spine.

Althea had twisted to face him, catching her breath once again at the power he exuded. "Mr. O'Leary? He is a fine man, but I would not trust him to change a bandage, much less care for my father. And where was he while that . . . that monster attacked my father? Father needs *me*. I intend to stay with him, I will not leave his side."

"Miss Yates, please . . . Zayan will not launch another attack tonight, not with dawn so close."

"True," Father had croaked. "You need your rest, my dear. His . . . lordship—" He broke off to cough. "His lordship is right, lovey. Go to your bed."

The earl had spoken in her head. *Tonight, I need you, love. I need to be with you. I need to watch over you.*

And so here she was, gathering the garlic flowers from the side of her bed to toss them away. Images from her dreams raced through her mind as she unclasped the cross from her neck and poured the chain onto her bedside table, beside her spectacles. Her hands skimming down his bare back. His mouth on her lips, her throat, her nipples. His erection sliding slowly between her legs.

The images left her trembling, hot, wet.

In three hurried steps, Althea reached the window and plucked the flowers from there. She lifted the sash and dropped the flowers into the dark.

A soft fluttering sound—the beat of wings—told her he had come. She stepped back and he flew out of the dark as a black bat. In a blink, the earl stood in the shadows of her room, and stepped into the pool of moonlight. The silvery light rippled over his broad shoulders, across the planes of his chest, down the lean length of his legs. His erection, long and straight, gleamed like a sword.

"You're nude!"

A surprising self-effacing smile touched his mouth. "My body can shift shape, but my clothes do not." He bowed.

She drank in the flex of his magnificent muscles as the earl bent and straightened. His erection wobbled. She tried to draw her gaze away but couldn't help but stare. Curved like a drawn bow, it bumped his navel. Even to her inexperienced eye, his staff was magnificent. She tightened inside just looking at it.

Her cheeks flamed when she finally met his eyes, glittering in the light.

This was her dream come to life. Did she dare let herself experience it?

The Earl of Brookshire held out his hand. "Come to me, love."

With a soft, shy giggle, Althea did, and he cupped her fingers to raise them to his lips, drawing her up against his naked body, against his surprisingly warm flesh. His cock pressed against her belly and she caught her breath.

She would do just a little bit from her dreams. Not everything.

But as the earl's hot mouth stroked over her knuckles, her knees almost buckled. His lips, wet and soft, pressed against her fingers. With a whispered moan, she gazed up into his glowing, mirrored eyes.

It was impossible to guess the earl's thoughts behind his shining, silvery eyes.

At least crinkles at the corners hinted at his delight and Althea smiled in return. A smile that vanished into a startled gasp as he sucked her index finger into his mouth. His tongue twirled around the tip. In her dreams, he lavished such attentions on her nipples. And tonight he would for real.

And heaven help her, she wanted it so desperately she felt she might burst.

Then she flushed, knowing she must do something she hadn't yet done.

"Thank you," Althea whispered, "for saving my father." She had to whisper. Their meeting was illicit, forbidden, but also, the moment was magical, and she was afraid to shatter it.

"Anything for you, love." His lordship caressed her cheek and led her hand to his.

She'd never touched a man this way, and it was beautiful, strangely sweet, to trace the high ridge of his cheekbone, to slide her fingers into his soft hair. Gathering courage, she laid her hand lightly against his face. Touching him helped her believe he was real. His skin was raw silk and his raspy stubble tickled her palm.

His gaze burned into her. "And you, my beautiful warrior, were magnificent. Courageous."

"How did you send such power out of your—"

"Ssh."

"No. I need to know. How did you escape imprisonment when your twin brother could not? What do you truly want?"

"You. I truly want you." He turned his face in her hand and touched his lips to her palm. Dabbed his tongue in the sensitive center.

"Tonight we are just a man and a woman, love."

Althea's legs weakened again. He caught her by her hips, supporting her. He splayed his hand over her lower back. Even through her flannel nightdress, his heat seared her.

But just a woman or not, she needed to know. "What of Crenshaw, the servants, the other guests? How did you—"

"I entered their minds and erased much of what they remembered. They believe your father had a severe stomach upset. Now, sweet, I am beginning to wish I could control your mind with the same ease."

"You can't?"

"If I could, love, we would have been naked, entwined, and screaming in ecstasy long ago."

A jolt of agony shot through Althea's belly at his blunt words. It must have showed plainly on her face because he gave a triumphant grin.

"You have the most tempting mouth, sweet. I imagine that every man you meet hungers to kiss you."

That startled her. She'd never received more than hurried,

chaste pecks from men. Nothing that prepared her for his hot mouth on hers.

He lifted her chin, just enough to allow his lips to slant sensuously over hers. He coaxed her mouth open, the way he did in her dreams. In her dreams, it was so shockingly intimate to kiss with her mouth wide. But the reality was even more scorching and sinful and perfect.

His tongue slid in, filling her mouth with heat and pressure and taste.

She loved it. She pushed forward. Stopped short.

Fangs.

She pulled back.

The hurt in his eyes speared her heart.

Impulsively, Althea arched up and slid her hands around his strong neck. She'd never done this—never claimed a kiss, not even in her dreams. In the dreams, he always took her. She was always the one lured and seduced and possessed.

She had no idea how to kiss.

Pushing aside fear, she let hunger guide her. She moved her mouth over his, pressing hard, then softly, shifting as he did, savoring his mouth. The earl possessed a heat she'd never known, an intimate taste she couldn't define.

His tongue slid in again and tangled with hers. He kissed her until her wits whirled. Until she understood he would kiss her all night. He kissed her as he tugged the ribbon from her braid and threaded his fingers through her hair. Kissed her as he yanked open the belt of her wrapper and slid it off her shoulders. And kissed her hard as he flicked the first small buttons of her nightdress from their loops, exposing her throat, her chest, the upper curves of her breasts.

She gripped his broad, solid shoulders, her tongue now deep in his hot, delicious mouth. She felt the points of his retracted fangs but forced herself not to retreat.

She wanted to show trust . . . even if she wasn't certain she could trust.

Shadows lengthened as the moonlight disappeared, plunging them into a velvety dark. Althea knew the earl could see her, but she was blind and she clung to him more tightly. He pulled her closer, until her breasts pressed against his chest and her hard nipples poked bands of solid muscle, beneath hot skin and coarse curls.

His hands slid down to her bottom. Scandalously, he squeezed generous portions of her flesh with both his big hands and chuckled with masculine pleasure into her mouth.

He broke the kiss just long enough to whisper, "What a perfect plump arse you have," before he captured her mouth again.

Gripping her cheeks, his lordship lifted her, slid his leg between hers, and lowered her so she straddled him.

Oh God, she wore nothing under her nightgown. His naked thigh rubbed her naked nether lips and she blushed as her wetness coated his skin.

He gave another chuckle, this one filled with pride. Just as in her dreams, he was terribly pleased with himself. She was soaking wet, embarrassingly so.

As though he sensed her shyness, he lavished soft, sweet kisses on her eyebrows and lashes, her nose and cheeks, her forehead, her chin, until she giggled helplessly.

He rocked his leg and the pressure felt so good. She let her head loll back as his hot mouth pressed to her throat.

She stiffened and pulled away. "Are you going to bite me?"

Did I ever bite you in a dream?

"No, you didn't but—" Althea broke off before she said "the other man." She couldn't—absolutely couldn't—say out loud that she had dreamed of another man and him.

"No, angel. I'm not going to bite you. But I do want to taste you. Savor every delectable inch of you." His lips skated down her throat, his tongue licked in the hollow. All the while, his thigh rubbed and rubbed. A wicked hunger blossomed there. He made her throb and she felt as though she floated in air, as though she could fly. Shift shape as he did, spread newfound wings, and soar.

But his hand in her nether curls brought her sharply to earth. He'd slipped his other hand into the bodice of her night-dress. He cradled her breast, the heel of his hand pressed to her pounding heart. He stroked her curls, dipping his finger lower, into her moisture.

She should stop. Must stop. Or was it far too late? Would he let her stop?

Angel, I will stop when you wish.

"You read my mind!"

Only the signals of your body. Your tension. The startled look in your eyes. I am your servant tonight, love. I do only as you desire.

His finger stayed at the very apex of her sex. Althea fought the desire to tip her hips up, to coax him to slide his finger inside her.

"I don't believe you!" she exclaimed in a whisper, even though she ached for more.

And why not, my sweet?

"Because you are a man and every woman knows what a man wants. And because—"

What did you enjoy most in our dreams, Althea? What do you want me to do to you?

Yes, she'd done all these things in dreams. But she couldn't tell him. Couldn't say such things.

His tongue dipped into the valley between her breasts. *Did you enjoy my mouth on your nipples?*

"My lord, I—"

"Yannick."

He was speaking aloud, not communicating in her mind,

and she felt strangely relieved. She clung to the safer topic of conversation—his Christian name. "It's French, isn't it?"

"You want a French kiss?"

He was teasing, she knew, but she couldn't imagine what a French kiss would be. "Your name is French."

"My mother was French, love, with an English marriage to save her from Madame la Guillotine. And de Wynter goes back to the Conqueror." His lord—Yannick's leg lowered but he scooped her into his arms before her slippers touched the floor. "And I believe you would enjoy a French kiss."

Only when he laid her on her bed, when he slid the long skirt of her nightgown up to the tops of her thighs, when he bent and touched his lips to her nether curls, did Althea realize what a French kiss was.

This they had never done in dreams. He had touched her intimately with his fingers, with his . . . his cock, but not with his mouth.

"You can't kiss my . . . there."

"Your sweet cunny. Oh yes, I can. And I will. I never did this for you in your dreams?"

She frowned. "Don't you know? Didn't you have the dreams too?"

"I don't know if we had the same dreams, sweet angel." To her shock, he breathed deeply. Drank in her scent. Smiled. "I was most remiss if I never kissed your delicious cunny."

"That's what you call it? That crude word?"

Yannick was on his knees on the floor now, gazing up at her from between her thighs. His pale blond hair spilled over his brow, dusted across his darkly lashed eyes. His fingers stroked her inner thighs and Althea could barely think.

His brow quirked. "What would you prefer, then, love? Quim? Pussy? Velvet glove? Pleasure passage? Silken sheath? Grotto of love?"

"Grotto of—?" She stared down at him in disbelief, then dissolved into giggles.

He flashed a playful frown, screened by her auburn curls. She caught her breath at the intimacy of their teasing. How could she be joking with a man—an earl *and* a vampire!—who had her most private places exposed to him?

He gave an audacious wink. "Women do not generally laugh when I do this."

He traced the tip of his tongue over her curls. Her hands clenched into fists. She almost shot up right off the bed. His hot breath breezed over a terribly sensitive place and she quivered.

Do you wish me to stop?

"Y—Yes."

"Are you certain?" He blew across her nether lips and she knew he would *not* stop. In dreams, he knew to make her melt until she could refuse nothing.

And he was a peer after all. Accustomed to having his own way.

Althea tried to say "yes" once more but her mouth would not cooperate. She truly did not want him to stop. Slowly, she shook her head. Willed the word *no* at him. Gasped in shock as he pressed his mouth tight to her mound.

Oh yes. Yes. She cried it in her head.

As you command, love. He suckled.

She screamed.

3

Ravished

Her cry of pleasure echoed in the small room, igniting his lust, calling forth Yannick's fangs. They extended, lengthening like his cock, until they lapped his lower lip.

With the greatest care, mindful of the sharpness of his curved canines, Yannick flicked out his tongue to brush the very tip of her clit.

"Oooh!" Althea arched beneath him, as though struck by an electric charge.

A knock sounded on the wall, followed by O'Leary's concerned Irish lilt. "Miss Yates?"

She stared down at Yannick, obviously horrified. With his face buried against her wet pussy, he feigned a look of innocence. Then flicked out his tongue and made her scream again.

"Miss Yates?" The rap was sharper, the voice more insistent. Yannick hoped O'Leary wasn't ready to burst into Althea's room.

Althea found her voice. "So sorry, Mr. O'Leary," she croaked. "I am fine. It was only a bad dream."

Oh, am I?

Yannick tangled his fingers in Althea's crisp curls, stroking the satin-soft skin beneath them. Gently, he laid a kiss at the very peak of her vulva, tasting the droplets gathering there. Her quim shone with her moisture, soaked, swollen and ready for him. And her scent . . . his head swam with it. Lush, sweet, ripe.

He slid his tongue down, down until he brushed her clit once more. But this time she was prepared. She fisted her hands in her wrinkled sheets, sank her teeth into her lips, and rode through the explosion of sensation with nary a whimper.

She was adorable. Delightful.

He felt like a devil, stroking the top of her pearl, where it would be far too sensitive for her. Her clit had never been touched and he should concentrate on drawing his tongue along the sides. She was too tense to come this way but he couldn't resist teasing her.

Yannick loved to watch her arch up with each light brush of his tongue. Loved to see her hair rippling about her like a pool of flame. Loved the long, white curve of her neck and the way her tempting throat moved with each whimpered moan.

Magically, with Althea, he could control the urge to bite.

He circled with his tongue and her fingers sank into his hair. As she gripped his head tight.

"Oh, no . . . please, stop."

He sucked once more, lightly.

Her hips launched up at him and with the surge, she tried to break free of his grip. She fought to scramble back, to push away, but he held her thighs and spread her wide.

Althea's eyes went wide, too. Startled. Almost frightened. "You mustn't. It's too much. I can't bear it."

"I'll be gentle with your clit, angel. I promise." Guilt shot through him. He shouldn't have teased. As the man to introduce her to pleasure, he had certain responsibilities.

This time he laved her clit gently, until her tension dissolved and she relaxed into the bed with a throaty groan. For a few glides of his tongue, she lay, passive, lids shrouding her lovely green eyes. Her bosom rose and fell and he heard the softest sighs tumble from her pursed lips, his name carried to him on one.

Her hands covered her breasts. Not in modesty. She fondled herself, gripping and kneading the lush mounds through the bodice of her nightgown.

His fangs and cock throbbed as he watched her through her thick nest of curls.

He could love her this way for hours—until dawn at least.

But soon, she lifted her hips, rocking them against his face. Tentative, as though she didn't understand quite why she needed to move to him. She was so sweet, so new. Was it possible this was her first orgasm, other than those in her dreams? Yannick couldn't remember his first, but imagined it must have been searing. Life-changing.

It was his duty to ensure she received no less.

Her hips became more demanding and pumped harder against his face. He matched her natural rhythm, the flat of his tongue sliding around her hard, quivering clit.

Althea's hand skimmed down across her belly and clutched at the hem of her nightgown. Yannick released her thighs, saw the red imprints of his fingers as his hands joined hers. Small, delicate hands—hard to imagine them plunging a stake into his heart, but he didn't doubt she could do it.

He helped her draw the gown up until it bunched at her waist. He traced her smooth, softly curved belly. Dipped his finger into her small, shadowed navel. Ran his palm along the generous flare of her hips.

Lovely, womanly. And his. His to enjoy, to pleasure, to treasure.

If only for a few nights.

The benefit to speaking in her mind? He could communicate without ever once lifting his tongue from her slick, musky quim.

Gentle enough, love?

"Perfect," she gasped. "Wonderf—Oooh!"

I want to make you come, Althea, just as you do in your dreams. I want to make you come again and again . . .

He cupped her buttocks and lifted her to his mouth. Feasted on her.

"Oh God!"

Her honey dripped from her now and he slipped his thumb into her quim to stir her. Fiery hot and drenched, her walls clutched him tight.

She was pure, utterly pure, giving herself to him.

It humbled him and he was a man rarely cowed.

He withdrew his thumb, slid two fingers into her, reaching as far as her barrier. Her cunny gripped him tight and his cock jolted upward in hope.

Patience.

In defiance, his prick bucked again. His balls had sucked tight to his body, aching along with his heavy erection. Coated with his own juices, the head of his cock already felt filled to bursting, his shaft straighter and harder than he'd ever known it. She moaned and another pulse of blood filled him. Stretched him. Stiffened him. Hades, his cock felt as though it weighed fifty pounds.

Once she came, then, perhaps . . .

Crooking his fingers, Yannick stroked, and searched for the magic places in her walls. He pressed his baby finger to the snug, puckered entrance between the cheeks of her ass. He eased in a hair's breath. It resisted and he didn't try to go further. Instead he teased her little opening until she shuddered beneath him.

I want to fill you completely, love. With my cock, my fingers, my tongue. I want to fill you in every way I can imagine.

Althea sobbed. Her hips banged hard on the bed.

Yes. Pound against my face, on my fingers. Touch your breasts.

Play with them. Squeeze and stroke your nipples, Althea, love. Together, we will take you to heaven.

She obeyed him. One delicate, feminine hand gripped each breast. More buttons gave way in her gown until her round breasts were bared. Firm little mounds, the color of clotted cream, pearlescent and plump, topped by erect pink nipples that he longed to gobble up. Her small fingers touched and explored, uncertain at first, and then finding delight.

Yannick couldn't bear to be left out of the fun. Reaching up, he found the damp, hot undersides of her breasts.

Pluck your nipples, love, but let me touch them too.

He spanned both erect tips with his hand, while his mouth danced over her and his fingers played inside her scalding cunny.

"Oh heavens—"

Her hips drove up hard against his mouth, banging his jaw. He couldn't draw back in time and pricked her lightly with his fangs.

She didn't seem to care. Her body went rigid. Her quim clenched around his fingers, sucked him in, held him, pulsed around him. Her hands clutched her breasts, clawing mercilessly as she bucked beneath him. Tangled hair flew across her agonized face.

Althea looked so beautiful in ecstasy. Crying out for him. Sobbing. Thrashing with it. Taken by it.

God, yes.

A flood of her juices poured out onto his hand. Yannick slid down to bury his face there, to taste and enjoy.

"Oooooh." She flopped back on the bed. Her legs went limp. Her arms dangled weakly by her sides. "Oh, that was so . . . so unladylike. I am so sorry—"

He chuckled and lifted from her, braced on his arms. Althea's lids dipped over her sparkling eyes, lashes lowered, and she let her head drop back on a sigh.

So angelic, even after orgasm.

He bent, kissed her flushed belly. "Sorry? It's delicious, little one. Such sweet nectar. A reward for pleasuring you well."

She opened her eyes and stared down at her crumpled night-gown. "Oh, I must look a fright—"

Yannick laughed—he'd laughed more in this night with Althea than in all the years since he'd been turned. "You look beautiful. Now, move over, love."

"Move over?"

He stretched out along the length of the bed and drew her slender body to him. She tumbled against him in surprise. Plump breasts fell against his mouth, smothering him, and her wet quim landed tight to his stomach. The tip of his cock nudged her creamy folds.

Voice strained, he joked against her warm curves, "I must get you a larger bed, if I am to share it with you." He opened his mouth wide, head down to hide his fangs, and sucked one nipple into his mouth.

The sweetest moans poured from her lips as her fingers dug into his shoulder blades. He shifted his hips, so her soaking pussy brushed his cock. Suckling harder, he shifted to roll her onto her back.

With a soft squeal, Althea fell onto the wrinkled sheets, her nipple—mottled red now, and standing up—releasing from his mouth with a little pop. Thick dark red hair spilled around her and caught the flitting moonlight. He bent to capture her soft mouth, cocking his hips ahead to push his prick an inch within her.

So hot and wet and tight and perfect—

She jerked her head to the side to avoid his mouth, reached down, grabbed his cock. Both her hands closed tight around it and she wrenched it up, up through her cleft as she pulled it away from her quim. It raked her clit and her moan electrified him. Yannick almost burst right in her hands.

"No."

His normally slow heartbeat thundered in his ears. *No? Sweet angel, why not?*

"The dreams," she said desperately. "Why did we have the dreams? Why? What do they mean?"

His hips rocked of their own volition. The motion drew his cock back and forth through her tight grip. His tender skin snagged and pulled with exquisite agony.

Yannick could barely pull his thoughts together, much less send them to her.

I don't know, but I suspect they . . . were to warn us . . . tell us that we are destined . . . destined to have incredible sex.

He truly didn't know. After all, he'd believed he had no destiny beyond the next full moon.

"But you are a vampire," she protested, "And I am a—"

You are a hunter of vampires.

Yannick did not like the direction of this conversation. But she was an innocent, and a little fear and apprehension were to be expected.

You have no need to fear me, Althea. I perhaps have more reason to fear you.

"I am a virgin. And moral. Church-going. God-fearing. I am supposed to be pure. I can't." Compelling and frightened, her eyes stared up into his.

He needed her so much tonight but he wouldn't force her. Or control her. But perhaps, with another orgasm or two he could convince her.

Althea gasped as Yannick moved down between her thighs again. How she wanted it. Wanted more. Wanted him. But she must stop him. He wouldn't pleasure her without expecting pleasure himself, would he?

But in her dreams, she had always awoken before he found his peak. In her dreams, only she found pleasure. The fiery explosions of her body always woke her.

The dreams ... those wonderful, frightening, scandalous dreams. What did they mean?

Yannick found that blissfully excruciating place again with his tongue. But this time, the sensations didn't spear her with shock. This time Althea felt the pleasure take her and she arched at his touch.

She had already sinned, hadn't she? Was this a sin? Or could she pretend that she had not exactly given up her purity? That she was not *exactly* being intimate with a vampire? She'd touched herself—her own breasts—another sin. But with him, nothing felt wrong at all.

His tongue slid lower. He seemed to know exactly what she yearned for. His tongue rippled into her, filling her, and she tensed. Then cried out in pure delight as he plunged his tongue in and out. It was incredible. As perfect as his ... his cock felt in her dreams.

To her astonishment, he withdrew, ran his tongue lower. Oh, how sensitive it was down there!

Then he touched her bottom—the entrance there—with his tongue.

And in an instant, Yannick proved she was not pure and moral at all.

His tongue dabbled and wetted. Oh it was so wrong, but so good. Althea was horrified—but thrilled.

He cupped her derrière with one big hand, lifted, and circled her tingling opening with his tongue. He skimmed his hands down her bare legs. Goodness, no other man had ever seen her naked legs, yet he casually caught hold of her ankles and lifted her legs up.

Soon Althea had her thighs pressed along her body, her calves and bare feet in the air. This way, her intimate parts were exposed to him—her "grotto of love" and even more shockingly, her bottom.

Yannick's strong hands held her thighs as his lips grazed the base of her spine. Hot and wet, his tongue delved in the valley between her cheeks again.

Slid upward, until it dipped into her entrance again, and pushed inside.

Startled, she cried out in her mind. *Yannick. Oh, but you can't!*

He answered, every inch the demon he claimed to be. *Oh, but I can.*

His tongue slid in and out, swirled, and filled her. In and out. Thrusting like he did in her cunny in her dreams.

Althea gasped as his thumb found her nub, as his two fingers slid into her. He spread his fingers wide, plunging them deep.

Someone was crying out. Her cries. But her voice was so different. Strained. Raw. Demanding. *Yes. Yes. Oh God. Oh God.*

Need made her brave and she grasped his hand on her clit, changing his stroke.

Yannick laughed into her mind, a raunchy, coarse laugh. *Yes, angel, show me how to take you there.*

His words were like a spark to powder. She burst. Burst into a million shimmering pieces. Magical and intense, her orgasm tore through her.

Yes, come, my beautiful Althea.

She did, out of control, wild. She barely drifted back to earth before he took her to ecstasy again.

Althea tried to hang on to sanity. Her head buzzed as though filled with bees, throbbed with the pounding of her racing heart. She struggled to open her eyes, to see him.

He was over her, his hand on his cock, and she knew she couldn't fight him if he slid into her now.

Explore me, he urged. *Please.*

He was truly begging. And Althea sensed it was a foreign sensation for him.

She didn't know whether to feel more powerful or more scared. But she touched his broad chest. Hidden by shadow, it was alive to her senses through feel. Beneath her fingertips, his heart beat slow and steady. She ran her palms over the broad, solid muscles of his magnificent chest. Curved her hands to fit over his solid pecs. Toyed with the dusting of curls.

White-blond hair fell over his face as Yannick ducked his head at her touch. Agonized pleasure showed on his aristocratic features. The sight made her tremble. His hand still rested on his cock and she glanced down. He gave his shaft a long, slow stroke.

Her cunny clenched in response.

She flicked her thumbs over his nipples and he gave a half-chuckle, half-groan. They peaked eagerly at her touch and she pinched them, just as he did to her.

"Do you like that?"

My nipples are just as sensitive as yours, sweet.

Althea glanced up, teasingly beneath her lashes. "Would you like them suckled then?"

His sharp intake of breath truly made her feel like a conquering warrior.

Anything you would like, love, I would.

A few hairs tickled her lips as she covered his dusky nipple with her mouth. She sucked, drawing the peak between her lips. It plumped out against her tongue.

She reached down, closed her hand around his wrist . . .

No, not his wrist, she realized. The thick, hard girth she held was his erect cock.

Please, stroke me . . .

"Show me," Althea whispered, "Teach me."

Yannick covered her hand with his, led her hand up and down the long, long shaft. Down to the thick curls. Up to the satiny, straining, wet head. Their hands were soon slick and sticky, working together.

His breathing came shallow, quick, and harder, until he lowered his head to the pillow beside hers and panted against her ear.

Althea moved her hands faster.

Yes, he hissed. *Jerk me like that. Fuck me with your hand, angel. God, God, God, I'm going to explode!*

His coarse, harsh words excited her, and she gripped him tight, rubbed him hard.

His hips jolted forward, his body bucked. His tongue slid into her ear, flicking wildly, as he grunted and groaned. His cock grew huge in her hand and she almost felt something rushing through—

His hot fluid shot out, spilling over her belly. He collapsed, pressing his hips tight, his weight supported on his muscular arms. With his head bowed, he took deep, ragged breaths.

Tentatively, Althea released his cock. She touched his face, stroked his cheek. Yannick lifted his head, gave an exhausted smile, and kissed her hand.

Watching him reach his pleasure had been so beautiful. "Do you . . . do you wish to do that again?"

He laughed. "I'm not as fortunate as you, my sweet. Only one for me."

He caught her in the sweetest kiss. His fangs brushed her lip but she wasn't afraid. Strangely, Althea found the sight of his fangs arousing now, not terrifying. Tenderness radiated from his eyes. She sensed it even though they shone like silvery-blue mirrors.

She drew back and dropped her gaze. Out of shyness? Out of fear? Suddenly, she just couldn't look into his eyes.

Keeping her eyes shut, Althea felt the bed move. He'd left it. Even though she kept still and quiet, she couldn't hear him move about her room. Had he left her alone?

Softness brushed her tummy. A cloth. With it, Yannick cleaned her gently. After, he placed a kiss on her cooling skin and smoothed out her crumpled nightdress. He lifted her as though she weighed nothing and arranged her gown around her, covering her hips, her still-tingly cunny, her legs.

It's almost dawn, love. I have to leave you.

"I know." With her eyes closed, she murmured it sleepily, drifting.

And you need to rest.

Rest, yes, because today they would open the crypt.

Althea prayed he really couldn't read her mind. Prayed he didn't know her father planned to open the crypt anyway. Was Father wrong to do it? Was she wrong not to tell Yannick?

All sorts of thoughts jumbled in her suddenly tired, confused head.

Yannick. How strange that she thought of him by his Christian name. Only hours before he had been, in her mind, a lofty earl or an evil vampire. A stranger but not a stranger. And now he had tasted her in places she had never even dared touch.

If she slept, what would she dream? About Yannick and the other man again?

That snapped her wide awake. She opened her eyes.

He was leaning over her, smiling down at her as he smoothed her hair. With the other hand, he cupped her waist, letting his thumb stroke the underside of her breast

"Before you go," she whispered, "Can you tell me what happened to you and your brother? Why you were imprisoned and how it happened?"

The second brother of the Demon Twins. Was he the other man from her dreams? Yannick's *brother?*

His brow lifted in surprise but she sensed him shut off other emotions from her. "Your father never explained our story?"

"No."

He sat up, lifting his hands from her. Althea felt bereft to have his heat leave. She wanted to reach out and touch him one more time—put her hand on his bare back, or caress his big, naked shoulder, but stopped herself.

I will come to you tomorrow night, Althea, and tell you everything. He stood up from the bed, standing in the moonlight, which seemed more ethereal now, fainter and less distinct.

Tomorrow night might be too late.

But he bowed and stepped back into the gloom, which was gray, not black, as dawn touched the sky.

Tomorrow. Let me explain all tomorrow. But do not let your father open the crypt.

Guilt burned through her and she looked down. She would have to help her father. It was what she had always done.

And she shouldn't trust Yannick so easily. Shouldn't let seduction convince her to throw aside all she had learned. Over a decade, she had seen what vampires were.

He is unlike any other vampire, her inner voice whispered. *He controlled his bloodlust with you. He saved your father. He is different.*

No. She couldn't fall under a vampire's erotic spell.

Althea, my love.

She stilled as his deep, beautiful voice called to her. Was this what the dreams meant? Love? She couldn't fall in love with him. She couldn't.

And what about the last dream? She couldn't love *two* vampires!

Althea looked up to find Yannick watching her. His brows were drawn together, his mouth turned down at the corners.

"I will wait for you tomorrow," she promised. "We won't open the crypt."

His lips lifted. Before she could blink, he vanished. She felt the faintest stirring of the air. The beat of wings. They fluttered over her hand like a caress—as though he was bestowing one last chivalrous kiss.

And then she was alone.

Althea crossed to the open window, shivering as the damp breeze flitted over her naked body. The sky had lightened. Deep purple splashed over the black, glowing with the soft sheen that promised daybreak.

Dawn was so close.

She prayed Yannick found safety.

Yannick closed the lid, crossed his arms over his chest. Her taste lingered on his lips. Her rich scent was on his face, on his fingers, on his slumbering cock.

What *did* the dreams mean? He had never dreamed about any other woman this way. And since becoming a vampire, he had never visited a woman without drinking from her. Nor had he visited any woman more than once.

Fortunately, he had found a maid beginning her day before daylight and had drunk from her. She'd offered him her tits and quim first, but he'd politely declined. He'd left her weak but healthy, with no memory of his bite, and had gone to where his box waited, placed as per his instructions.

Yannick closed his eyes. Drifted into sleep, still oddly conscious. He was even sure his eyes were actually open, yet the scene played out before him.

"Can you imagine both our mouths on you, love?"

He stood behind Althea, his hands on her slim shoulders. She wore a thin, almost translucent chemise. It fluttered with her quick breaths. Her hard nipples poked against the fabric.

He could smell her lovely feminine skin, could taste it as he bent his lips to her neck.

"Can you imagine my hands and his worshipping you?"

What was this? Bastien lay on the bed, grinning as he reached for the buttons of his bulging breeches.

He was to share Althea with Bastien?

Not this time. Not this woman.

But as the dream played out, he felt himself harden, the erection stealing his fading energy. Yannick tried to will it away, but damn his unruly cock, it stood up defiantly. Hell and the devil, it was a curse to sleep while aroused.

Even after all the women he'd shared with his brother, he watched in shock as Bastien stripped naked and approached Althea. Then they caressed her together and all that mattered was her pleasure.

But he'd never shared a woman that he—

Never a woman like Althea.

"Can you imagine the erotic pleasure of having both of us bite you?"

In the dream, his brother's fangs launched out. As Bastien leaned to her neck, Yannick gripped his brother by the hair and yanked him back.

"Don't you want to possess her?" Bastien demanded.

"No. I am not taking her from life. Not just for me."

"For us." His brother's grin widened, arrogant and goading. "For both of us."

His brother laughed and the dream exploded into a blinding white light, then faded into twinkling dust.

Bastien's mocking laugh echoed in his head. Yannick fought to block it out.

Before Althea had come to him in his dreams, he'd planned to let his time run out and evaporate into dust. He hadn't intended to use the incantation and release Bastien—once he was dead, Bastien would be freed anyway. Why in hell would he want to fight for his existence? He'd hidden the truth for ten years—if he continued to exist he would have give up everything. His title. His home. His country. People had begun to notice he never aged. His peers in London already joked that he'd sold his soul.

But to die now would be to leave Althea for Bastien.

He would be dead, so why in hell would it matter if Bastien captured Althea's heart?

Day sleep stole over Yannick, pulling him deeper into darkness. He willed his fingers to move. They responded slowly, several heartbeats after he sent the impulse.

He remembered the way Althea's lashes had shielded her eyes. The way her wide green eyes had darted away as he walked nude into the moonlight. He had caught her expression of guilt. He'd attributed it to a virgin's shyness after tumultuous sex.

Damn, it was because she was lying to him.

4

Resurrected

Touch us, Althea. Stroke us both.

She was dreaming again. In the shadowy bedroom once more, she lay in the middle of the massive bed. Soft lamplight spilled over the crimson bed hangings, flitted along the fluted posts, and danced across her skin. She was naked, her hair loose and fanned over her bare breasts. Althea kept her thighs pressed together and her hand rested demurely over her nether curls, hiding them.

An embroidered silk counterpane stretched beneath her, smooth and soft against her skin. Yannick lay alongside her on the right. He levered up onto his shoulder and smiled down into her eyes as he stroked his knuckles along her cheek. Her nude vampire-warrior. His large erection parried against her thigh. His hair and eyes gleamed bright and silver-gold in the wavering light.

But the sensuous voice had come from her left.

Long golden hair tickled her lips and cheek. Firm male lips slanted over hers from the left while Yannick bent and licked her neck from the right. Yannick's hands slid beneath her left breast and lingered over her heartbeat, but another man's hand nudged his away.

Pleasure shivers tumbled down her spine as their hot mouths claimed both her mouth and her throat. Each man cupped a breast. She sensed the slight differences in their hands. Yannick's rougher, his brother's smooth. Yannick's fingers pinched and teased her nipple, but his brother turned caresses into pain— not enough to make her cry out and fight him, but enough to make her moan in sweet agony.

Althea gazed up into her second lover's mirrored eyes, dark pools of heat and erotic knowledge. She knew he was Yannick's brother, Sebastien de Wynter.

Fraternal twins, she thought, hazily, as his hands skimmed down toward her thighs. Though shadow cloaked them, she knew they were different in looks. Somehow she knew they would be different in the ways they would make love to her.

Stroke us both, Althea.

She longed to. Lust burned in her. She shifted her hips and the sensitive curves of her hipbones brushed against both their naked cocks. *No,* she whispered in her mind. *I . . . I can't.*

Sebastien's laugh was low, wicked. *Sweetheart, don't remain a prisoner of your goodness. Enjoy yourself.*

Yannick smiled at her again but his eyes flicked a warning to his brother.

She's not yet ready, Bastien.

How could she hear words meant for his brother?

Bastien spoke to her. *No one sins in a dream, sweetheart.*

Was that true? She needed to believe it was.

Bold as brass, she reached down and curled her right hand around Yannick's cock. Her brave action surprised her, and surprised Yannick more, judging by his throaty gasp. She clutched the familiar thickness of his shaft and let her fingertips stroke the velvety length to the firm, full head. Touching it made her wet and achy, made her heart pound in delight.

Just your touch makes me want to explode.

She felt the tension in Bastien as Yannick moaned.

Her left hand crept down. She wanted to pretend she did not control it. Her fingers danced over the very tip of Bastien's cock. Touched his sticky wetness.

Yes.

His cock was different too. Slimmer—for her fingers met around the base of his. Longer? She couldn't be sure. A fuller head. She couldn't resist peeking—first at Yannick's and then at his brother's. In the shadow, she couldn't see much. Only that both were as individual as the men who possessed them and that both were beautiful.

Even in the gloom, she caught the expression on the twins' faces. A trace of uncertainty. A worry that she might prefer one to the other? That one was better?

Both of you are perfect. She tried to stroke them both at the same time, in the same way. But she couldn't. She reached the taut head of Bastien's cock first, and squeezed tight. His head dropped back; his lids plunged down to shield his glowing eyes.

Oh, yes, angel. You're going to make me come.

Come. The word they used for pleasure.

Cupping the firm, wet, hot head of Yannick's cock, she squeezed them both. Two hungry male moans echoed through the room. Echoed through her head, her heart, her quim.

She stroked faster. Clumsily, but they didn't seem to care. Yannick moaned. Deep, hoarse, almost desperate. Bastien panted over and over. *Fuck, fuck, yes, fuck me.* They kissed her lips, cheeks, the rims of her ears, the length of her throat with their mouths wide open. As though they starved for her.

Yannick's cock swelled first, growing so thick and large she could barely drag her fingers along it. His hips bucked forward, his head bowed, and he cried out. Breathtakingly vulnerable. White, hot come shot out across her hand.

You always did lose control first, Sebastien crowed, then he cried her name and came too.

"London?"

Althea stared at her father in astonishment. Their carriage swayed as it lurched up the hill to the churchyard and the case on her lap slid across her knees. She tightened her grip on the handle. She didn't dare let it fall.

Seated across from her, with the view ahead, Father leaned on his walking stick.

"Yes, missy, London. It's too dangerous for you here, lass. And you deserve the excitement of London."

The excitement of *London?* How could London compare to the adventure of hunting Zayan? *And the adventure of bedding two men,* whispered her naughty internal voice. "What excitement?"

"You are a young lady. Balls. Dancing. Gentlemen. The sort of things that young women fancy." His blue eyes twinkled behind his spectacles.

"But I don't fancy them. I am doing exactly what I wish to do."

"Your mother would have wanted to see you do those things."

Oh no, he couldn't make her feel guilt that way—she didn't know what Mother would have wanted. Three when her mother had died in childbed with her second child, Althea could barely remember her. The only portraits stayed at Kenworth House, their English home that she rarely saw. Only a tiny miniature was with her to remind her of Mother's vivacious smile, her vibrant auburn hair, her lively green eyes, and the love and joy she radiated.

"But she let you continue to hunt vampires because she knew how important it is," Althea reminded him. "She let you follow your heart."

"And my sweet Anne would have me head if she knew I had

let you do it." He stretched out his leg, wincing, and rubbed his thigh through his breeches. "You're a distraction to me, lass. I can't be worrying about your safety—"

"And when have you ever needed to do that? I'm well able to take care of myself."

Father leaned back against the seat as the coach took a dip to the right and rattled through deep ruts. "The truth then, lovey? I want you to find yourself a husband. Give me grandchildren. I fancy myself as Grandpa."

Her heart dipped as abruptly as the carriage. Marriage? She couldn't marry! A husband would never accept a vampire-hunting wife. The brief time she'd spent in London had taught her two things. Gentlemen expected a wife to be proper and docile, preferably a pretty china ornament. And twenty-three-year-old bluestockings in spectacles, with only modest family connections and no fortune, did not catch the attention of gentlemen.

Althea opened her mouth to protest. But a soft light sparkled in her father's eyes—dreamy happiness at the thought of grand-children. No doubt her father envisioned sitting beneath an apple tree and bouncing a hearty boy and pretty girl on his knees.

Her thoughts whirled like the swirling lights of last night. Her father longed for grandchildren. But what of her hopes? Did she want children? She'd always thought she should en-deavor to rid the world of evil before bringing children into it, but that was, of course, impossible.

Would it be worth giving up her dreams, giving herself in marriage, to have children?

How could she give herself in marriage now?

A guilty flush swept her face and she couldn't stop it. Her fingertips tingled as though they still touched the velvety steel of Yannick's and Bastien's cocks. Deep in her soul, she heard them moan again. Her body tightened instantly, hot and yearning. Her nipples puckered beneath her plain gown, her gray pelisse. Her quim throbbed like a second heartbeat.

Would this always happen to her now?

She turned to the window and watched the small village of Maidensby slip below as the carriage climbed to the church grounds.

She did see Father's point. Flooded with thoughts of touching and stroking Yannick and Bastien, she couldn't think of anything else. Naughty, sinful dream memories controlled her. How exciting it had been to feel them both in her hands. To know they were both hard for her. She loved thinking about their cocks, their hard, powerful bodies, their silvery eyes glowing with sexual hunger. She loved remembering how time had stood still, how nothing else had mattered but pleasure.

She couldn't even concentrate on hunting. She wanted only to dream of sex.

Stop it immediately, Althea warned herself. She dragged her thoughts from the shadowy bedroom of her dreams and looked out at the world around her.

Pale sunlight struck thatched roofs and shingled ones. Sheep ambled through newly green fields. The carriage climbed, passing a gnarled farmer driving a herd, passing two young ladies in bonnets, mud splatters on their hems, large bouquets of spring flowers held in gloved hands.

An idyllic place to hide a vampire. A place where she had no right behaving like a . . . a strumpet.

"Althea, pet?"

Her father's tentative, gentle voice struck her like a rap to her knuckles.

She turned back, eyes watery. What could she tell him? "But I can't leave you in the midst of this fight."

"I'll survive it. No fears there." His smile radiated confidence, but her stomach lurched with the rocking carriage this time.

She took a deep breath. "But this is what I want."

"You don't know that, pet. I never gave you a chance to have a normal life."

"But balls and London and society would never feel normal to me." How could she give up hunting evil for such an insular, unimportant life?

And she didn't belong in polite society. She'd allowed Yannick—a vampire—to take scandalous liberties. Liberties she had very much enjoyed. And while gentlemen of the *ton* might do such things, unmarried ladies certainly could not. How could she endure bland kisses when she dreamed of wild sex with two vampires?

Out of the carriage window, she spied the tall stone posts of the church gates.

"London soon would, lass. And surely you must want to marry." The twinkle deepened.

They passed the first of the headstones. The old ones, one hundred, two hundred years old, were worn and faded, many split and broken. The carriage rattled on gravel as they passed stone crosses and a large crypt. Large oak branches stretched over the old graves, and a breeze sent shadows dancing. Flitting ghosts, she thought fancifully.

Althea's heart danced as wildly as the shadows. Mystery and adventure surrounded her. She was about to take part in a ceremony that should be impossible. She was about to raise the undead.

How could a stuffy ball ever compare?

She stroked the small case she held. "The truth is that I don't want to marry. I want to pursue vampires."

"And I want to sleep easy, Althea. You're to marry."

Suspicious, Althea stared at her father. "You haven't already chosen someone, have you? You wouldn't do—"

The carriage lurched to a halt.

"Of course not, pet." The door swung open. Sunlight spilled in, tinted with the heady scent of spring pollen, filled with the ruckus of birds. "But I've engaged a lady to help in your search."

As he struggled to stand, Althea launched up and grabbed his elbow to assist. "What lady?"

"The wife of my old friend, Sir Randolph Peters, a fellow of the Royal Society."

Horror and embarrassment wrapped icy fingers around her heart. "A matchmaker?"

Father glanced at the ground, a clear look of guilt shrouding his blue eyes, but before he could say a word, Mick O'Leary leaned in the door. "Are ye ready, sir?"

Loud protest would have to wait. She wouldn't humiliate herself in front of Mr. O'Leary. She bit her tongue and helped her father to the folding stair. But in a low and determined whisper, she set down her position. "No, Father. I don't want a match. And I'm not going to London."

With a grunt, Father stepped down, favoring his uninjured leg. "Oh yes, you are, lass. Indeed you are."

As Mick O'Leary led the way down the rough path, Althea brushed at a bee that buzzed around her bonnet. Her case bumped against her thigh as she followed Father, Mr. O'Leary, and two of the workmen carrying the large trunk.

Once she would have breathlessly watched the movement of Mr. O'Leary's muscles beneath his linen shirt. This morning all she could think about was Yannick . . . and touching both him and his brother in her dreams . . .

Loose stones rolled down the path as her half boots skidded along and mud splattered her hem. She heard her father muttering, reviewing the incantation he was to use to break the curse. Would it work?

They reached the bottom of the hill, the sod torn up where the men had dug up the old stone tomb. Mortared bricks had filled the doorway the day before. The men had labored since dawn and now enough brick was knocked out to allow entrance. Light glowed from within.

"The case, Althea."

He meant to make her wait outside. "I am going in."

Mick O'Leary grinned. "It's dirty in there, love, and smells none too fresh—"

Her gaze shot sparks at the dark-eyed Irishman. "It's not as though I've not done this before."

He held out his bare, callused hand. "Then let me help you, Miss Yates."

"O'Leary . . ." Father warned.

She stomped toward the opening, fed up with them all, gripped the bricks to her side and hoisted herself in.

Lantern light lit the large space and played along the smooth stone walls, tooled into the rock that formed the hillside. The air in the crypt was still, dank, but no longer stale. Fresh air flowed in from the breach made in the bricked entrance. There was no stench of decay—the bodies in the sarcophagi were not dead and decomposing.

Several hundred years ago, the tomb had been built, buried with earth and sod and apparently forgotten to all but legendary vampire hunter, Lord Devars. The peer had used it in the last century as a place to bring and destroy vampires.

And Zayan had known of its existence.

The search for this hidden crypt had been exciting, even though it consisted mostly of reviewing yellowing records and worn maps. She remembered the thrill in her heart when Mr. O'Leary's shovel had hit the walled-up entrance.

The light played along the smooth tops of the stone sarcophagi. A dozen filled the gloomy, musty crypt, arranged in neat rows.

"Cavern of the Vampires." Father's voice held breathless excitement—like a boy with a new pony.

The workmen climbed into the opening, carrying several wooden stakes sharpened to killing points. Nausea roiled in her, sudden and weakening. Her legs almost gave way and she rested her hand on the nearest stone slab for support.

Of course they would kill all the vampires but the one they wanted. But were they all ghouls, or were they men of charm and beauty, like Yannick? Were there other vampires like him? Was his brother also like him? Not just a creature driven by bloodlust?

She felt a stare and whipped around to see Father studying her intently. His gray brows drew together.

Could he guess she was weakening towards a vampire?

Oh no.

And she wasn't. Not really. She still knew that vampires were evil and must be destroyed. Of course, she still knew that.

To cover up, she walked along the row, touching the fronts of the stone coffins to hide her unsteady gait. Her fingers traced chiseled dates and names. Anthony Austen 1612 (d) 1705. Francis Smythe 1512 (d) 1705.

The third from the last was the oldest but the letters were still crisp. Stephen of Myrlyn 1100 (d) 1706.

The date of creation as a vampire. The date of destruction. These vampires had already been destroyed.

Zayan was estimated to be two thousand years old, but to see the evidence of Stephen of Mrylyn's long existence sent a shot of pain through her heart. To walk the night for over six hundred years!

In six hundred years Yannick would still walk the earth, while she would be long buried. Long turned to dust. Long forgotten.

Guilt slid through her like poison through blood. She'd lied to Yannick. She'd looked away from his penetrating, glowing eyes to hide her lie, but still she feared he knew. But that didn't matter because he would know for certain tonight. What would he do?

Would he come to her in a rage or would he not come to her at all? Which did she fear the most?

The next coffin made her want to cry. It was not dated as the others, with the date of the transformation to undead and the date of destruction.

William. 1700–1708. IN HOPE OF ETERNAL SLEEP.

An eight-year-old vampire?

Heart in her throat, she moved on and stared down at the front of the last coffin. Blank. Her fingers, in brown kid gloves, skimmed over smooth, cool, white stone. A hum began beneath her fingertips. A soft, light vibration that strengthened and took on a rhythm. Low and steady, with long gaps during which her heart seemed to beat a hundred times. A vampire's heartbeat.

"Which is the one we want, sir?" O'Leary asked.

She knew even as her father spoke.

"The end one. Where Althea is standing."

She glanced up. O'Leary strode toward her carrying a long iron bar and a second lamp. Her father stood in the far corner—near the entrance, with the young, brawny workmen. One pushed with another bar and stone grated over stone in the far corner, setting her teeth on edge.

"Burned to ashes," her father announced, his voice matter-of-fact.

Had even eight-year-old William been destroyed that way?

As O'Leary reached her side, Father called out, "Don't be so blasted impatient, O'Leary. Put the bloody bar down for the moment."

Despite his wounded leg, Father reached them in a mere moment. Again her father stared at her, as though he knew she could feel the presence of Sebastien de Wynter inside the coffin. Her hand still rested on the lid. Energy seemed to pulse into her hand, up her arm. She couldn't move her hand away.

Though she was certain, she found it all so impossible. "How did Zayan bring him in here? The entrance looked untouched for a hundred years. So did the hillside. Did he truly pass through earth and brick to bury Sebastien here?"

Father gave a curt nod. "He could do that. Or he could open the entrance with a wave of his hand and seal it up afterward with mere thought."

"How is that possible?"

"How is it possible that the dead walk, love? Just because we can't understand, doesn't mean we can't accept the existence of such power. And that we can't recognize how dangerous it is."

Father pointed at her case. "Lay that on the next coffin, please, love, and open it."

She had only seen inside it once, just the briefest glance. She'd caught a glimpse of gold fashioned into a thick, flat necklace of some sort. As she flipped up the lid, she saw two such necklaces sat within, surrounded by a sand that was made of small pebbles of silver and gold. Two necklaces.

Shocked, she turned. Father was laying out strings of dried herbs along the white lid in a crisscross pattern, like a diamond-paned window. He was chanting and she knew she couldn't interrupt him now.

"*Avia aura. Avia solari. Avia noctus.*"

The words made no sense. Not Latin or English or any other language Althea recognized.

As he spoke, he touched each side of the coffin, walking slowly around it. "*Aura se selen. Aura se nordum.*"

Father lifted a hemlock branch, whittled to a sharp point, and traced the shape of a cross from the foot of the coffin to the head and side to side.

"*Bey ara nonum.*"

He traced a circle over the pattern of herbs.

"*Ecta enta aura. Ecta enta decum.*"

Father lifted his head. "Open the coffin."

5

Liberated

"His eyes are open." A woman leaned over his coffin. A woman who smelled of lavender and spring flowers, of fresh-baked bread and country air. Rich and throaty and soft, her voice was pure femininity and his body, even though inert, responded. His instant erection was insistent, demanding, but he was damnably incapable of movement.

"Yes, but he can't see," an elderly male voice answered.

Not true. He could. Not well—his eyesight was still weak—but enough to detect soft, pretty red lips. Red hair, too. A dark and beautiful color like rich, intoxicating wine. Tendrils dangled over her alabaster skin. Golden light glinted over her eyes, shielding them. She wore something over them. She pursed her tempting lips to blow one curl away.

Althea. He knew her name from his dreams. A lovely name for a lovely wanton.

Bastien de Wynter tried to follow Althea, his savior, with his gaze as she moved but he couldn't. Warmth began to prickle through his long unused limbs. A surge of triumph rushed through him. Damn, he'd wiggled a toe.

He smelled daylight. As a nocturnal creature he knew the difference between night and day in the way the air tasted on his tongue, in the way it filled his nostrils, his lungs.

Damnation, was he going to be toasted by daylight after a decade of hell?

He listened intently for an answering heartbeat. A slow, almost silent one to match his own.

Nothing.

So where was Yannick? Still buried somewhere in England? How in hell, then, had Althea awoken him?

She returned and leaned over him. Once more his long-denied senses gorged on the sweet aromas of fresh bread, rushing blood, feminine sweat, lavender, and wildflowers. Before he'd been entombed, he'd never let a night go by without burying his face—and his teeth—into a woman's perfumed skin.

Yes, sweeting, lean a little closer.

In his dreams, she bewitched him. Wrapped her sweet innocence around his heart and drove him mad with need and lust. For ten years he'd been unable to move but his mind had been alert and aware every night. Goddamned agony . . .

He ached to touch her now, but he could not move more than his toes, his fingertips, the muscles of his face. His lips twitched. He blinked.

Had she seen?

No, she had her attention fixed on her hands and the object she held there. Those plump little breasts amply filled her tight-fitting bodice. With fetching sweetness, they rose and fell beneath the beige muslin.

Zayan had buried him naked. He saw her gaze flit down his body. Felt it pause at his crotch. On his cock, which was not immobilized.

Her eyes widened behind the lenses of her spectacles.

Touch me, darling, please. He wanted some of that lush

spring scent on his flesh. Needed her touch on his long-unsatisfied prick. But she looked up.

Cool metal touched his skin at the top of his chest, below the hollow at the base of his throat. His skin began to numb. What in hell was she doing?

Her fingers slid up his throat.

Vulnerable. He had never felt so damned vulnerable.

If he were to die, he wished he could have buried himself in her. Wished to heaven he could have fucked her. In his dreams, she'd given him the promise of dark erotic depths in her soul. He wanted the chance to unlock them.

Numbness spread over Bastien but fire flamed where her fingers touched him. Her gaze locked with his as she brushed back his hair and exposed his neck.

Althea's fingers shook as she flicked Bastien's long hair back from his muscled neck. In the lamplight, the thick, silky strands glowed as golden as the collar she'd laid at the base of his throat.

A blush beat in her cheeks, in rhythm with her heartbeat. A heartbeat that hammered as loud as a war drum. That thundered like bolting horses.

Shivers of desire raced down her spine at the touch of her gloved fingers to his cool, perfect skin.

Only an innocent woman must place the collar around a male vampire's neck. Which made capturing a female vampire even more difficult, as finding a virgin male—

"Hurry up, lass."

"Jesus, he's as hard as a bloody iron bar." Mick O'Leary's coarse comment rang in her ears. In front of Father, O'Leary, and the workmen, she struggled not to look down at Bastien's erection. But the image remained from moments ago, seared in her mind.

Of course it looked just as it did in her dreams. Not an exact match for Yannick's, just as in her dream. Erect, it curved like a bow, the heavy head hanging against his rippled abdomen. It looked almost weaponlike—dangerous and rampant and lusty. His skin was pale, his cock paler still, but blushing pink at the straining head.

She mustn't look.

Wetness gathered between her thighs. Her drawers soaked through, and the lace-trimmed slit became sticky.

Out of the corner of her eye, she saw Father drape a cloth over Bastien's prominent erection. Sparing her the shocking sight.

Yet last night she had run her clasped hand along the length of that cock and squeezed the head until Bastien had begged beside her ear. Until he'd cried out her name and—

Stop. Stop. Stop.

Yes, she'd dreamed of Bastien, but she'd been intimate for real with Yannick. Closing her eyes, Althea quivered, remembering Yannick's tongue circling her . . . her most sensitive place. His tongue filling her bottom. Plunging. His mouth on hers, on her breasts. The way he'd looked when he smiled up from between her thighs.

Stop!

Throat tight, she leaned right down and pushed the collar into place, beneath Bastien's Adam's apple. It fit so tightly she couldn't make the clasp meet. She must bring the two ends together but they fell short.

She pulled tighter.

Had his eyes moved?

Her breasts brushed his chest as she bent as close as she could. As she balanced on tiptoes to lean over more, her tingling nipples pushed against her snug bodice as though straining to reach him. She bit back a moan just in time.

"What's wrong, lass?" asked Father.

The ancient collar, the only one—or rather one of the only

two—in the world, was too small. But she would be damned if she would admit in front of Mick O'Leary that she couldn't even do such a simple task.

Or would the collar not close because she was no longer innocent? Her maidenhead was still intact, but she hardly felt innocent now.

It unnerved to have his eyes open and watching, sightless though they might be. Lifting one hand from the collar, Althea stroked her fingertips over his eyelids and closed them. The way one did with the dead.

But he wasn't dead and her body knew it. She throbbed now, between her legs. She ached to bend down and take his mouth with hers in one of the delicious, wide-open, hungry, devouring kisses from her dreams.

Shame burned through her.

How could she want such a thing with him after what she'd done with Yannick? Yannick might come to her tonight—

But, heaven help her, she flamed with need and desire now.

Trembling, she tugged hard on the collar's ends. Warm now in her hands, the metal stretched as if by magic. The collar snapped into place. The jagged ends joined with a click and a surge of power that jarred her wrists and racked her shoulders.

She had to close her eyes again because looking at Bastien's beautiful face made her fear she might kiss him. He was a handsome prince captured by a magic spell and she was about to awaken him.

He truly was handsome, she mused. Long golden hair swirled to his shoulders. His brows matched, golden too, straight but slanted upward at their ends. Unlike Yannick, his lashes were fair. Thick with a distinct curl, they lay along sculpted cheeks. A full mouth, softly curved. Would it taste of warmth and man and sin as it did in her dreams?

What was she becoming?

A moral woman couldn't want two men. A good woman

mustn't love more than one. She couldn't—*couldn't*—let herself feel this desire for Sebastien de Wynter.

"Good job, lass," came Father's cheerful voice by her ear. Althea's heart jolted at his praising tone. At the word *good*. Guiltily, she stepped back without a word and wrapped her arms around her chest as Father and the two workmen drew a shroud over Bastien's naked body.

"Now, we'd best take this one back," Father instructed, "and find the other."

"You can't capture the earl, Father." Althea glared as Father knelt before Yannick's door and slid a thin metal pick into the keyhole.

"Course I can, pet. And I need both twins to slay Zayan."

"He saved your life." She tried to speak calmly, emotionlessly. She tried to hide the thunder of her heart.

"He's a vampire." Father wiggled the pick. "Blast this thing. Never works."

Was that a creak? Althea spun on her heel. Expecting a maid on the stairs, or another guest, she hissed, "Stop. Stand up."

He did and linked his arm in hers to make it appear they were merely strolling down the hall to their rooms. Several anguished heartbeats passed.

"No one there, love. You're jumping at shadows."

She held out her hand. "Let me try the pick, then. Your fingers—"

"Nothing wrong with my fingers."

"I can see how swollen they are, Father. Please let me try."

Father refused to admit that he suffered with rheumatic hands and legs, but he surrendered the tool. Althea rolled the knurled handle between her fingers. She slid her spectacles back up her nose as she shifted her skirts and knelt at the door. Another skill she must perfect. "All in the feel," Father had said. She wriggled the tip forward and back, up and down, testing resistance.

At the satisfying click, she grinned. Success. Followed by a jolt of conscience. Was she truly going to snap the second ancient controlling collar on Yannick?

He knew what she was. He'd come to her bed knowing what she was. *I am a vampire and you are a hunter of vampires.*

She pushed open the door, slowly and quietly. "I believe we can trust the earl, Father."

"I've never trusted a vampire, Althea." Censure snapped in his tone. "And you've no cause to start."

But she did.

Just as she stepped toward the threshold, Father grabbed her arm. "I'll go first, love."

Which gave her another moment to struggle with guilt and confusion. Yannick was a vampire. No doubt lying in his coffin, arms folded neatly over his chest. She must remember that first and foremost he was a vampire and she a slayer.

"Bloody hell, I don't think he's here."

Ashamed at the relief bubbling through her like champagne, Althea stepped in. The room given to Yannick was not the inn's best, but it was much larger than hers, though the big bed and bulky furniture made it just as cramped. No coffin could be seen, and it could hardly be hidden. The bed was untouched. Father even checked beneath the bed, lifting the worn coverings as he dipped a knee and groaned. She jumped forward to do it instead, but stopped. It was obvious nothing was beneath the bed but dust.

Oh, thank heavens. For a while longer, she didn't have to choose between the man she desired and the career she was determined to have.

"Blast." Father sank down on to the edge of the bed. "I've tried to coax, bribe, or trick his whereabouts out of the servants.

Thought he might try the obvious. Where better to hide than the room in which he's supposed to be?"

He tapped his walking stick on the plank floor. "So I wonder where his lordship's hidden his coffin?"

Sunlight reflected from his spectacles as he gazed at her. Althea shook her head. "I've no idea. The stables, possibly?"

"I expect he's using a box and not a coffin, since I do believe his servants have no clue as to what he truly is. Though no one seems to have seen a box large enough to fit a body, and he's not a small man."

Oh, no, he definitely wasn't small.

"What about the churchyard?" He wouldn't steal a coffin, would he? The thought, a brutal reminder of what he was, made her shudder.

"Clever idea, lass. We'll try that."

From her window, Althea spotted the procession of lanterns as O'Leary, Father, and the workmen fanned out across the stretch of meadow.

She pushed up the sash, letting in the scent of rain and mud. Rain had swept in on the heels of the sunset. A torrent at first, now a drizzling mist, it was enough to soak her hair, face, and hands as she leaned out to watch. The lanterns dipped out of sight in a small valley, then flickered as the men passed between dark trees.

She dropped back into her room, brushing at the droplets on her hair. Moistened by the rain, her nightrail clung to her breasts, almost transparent over her hard nipples. Her bed was turned down, inviting her to crawl in and grow warm again. And beneath the bedcovers, the second controlling collar waited.

She sank down on the bed and laid her hand over the bump under the sheets. Would Yannick come to her tonight? He must know she'd betrayed him. If he came at all, it would be likely to feed from her. To destroy her in cold, vicious vampire rage.

If she snapped the collar around his neck, she would be saving herself. If she staked him, it would only be because he was going to kill her.

She could justify betrayal in the name of self-preservation.

She flopped back on the bed, sinking into the lumpy mattress.

In all likelihood, the collar would do nothing to control Yannick at all. Bastien was free and it was her fault, all because she was no longer completely pure. All because she'd been too much of a coward to admit her sins.

She swallowed hard, her throat tight with guilt, remembered O'Leary's shocked cry. "Christ Jesus! 'E's gone!"

In the middle of buttoning her pelisse, Althea had jerked up. Who was gone? What was O'Leary shouting about?

Her feet had flown over the rough planking and she reached the door at the exact instant O'Leary and Father emerged from Bastien's room. Father carried the thick shroud used to cover Bastien and protect him from light. The sun had just set.

"How in hell did he do it?" O'Leary roared.

Father's left hand strayed to the corner of his spectacles and he adjusted them on the bridge of his nose. He frowned down at the shroud. "My first guess would be that the twin helped him. But it makes no sense. How could the twin remove the collar? Unless—" Father shook his head. "No, it's impossible. It's only now dark."

In one mortifying instant, she'd guessed the probable answer. Bastien had escaped because she wasn't an innocent. That was the reason the collar must not have worked. She must tell them. But her tongue had moved uselessly and she couldn't utter a word. What difference would it make to confess? The damage was done.

It had been so easy to justify silence. It was so easy to justify betrayal.

"There's no need to go up to the crypt then, tonight." Father had raked his hand over his jaw. His shoulders had slumped with his failure.

Admit what you did, she'd urged herself. But instead, she'd bitten her lip.

Father had turned to O'Leary, his back to her. "They'll have to hunt. The newly resurrected one will need blood desperately. So, we'll need more men to hunt them. Blast, it means letting the entire bloody village know who we are."

Althea had walked around to be a part of the conversation, finishing the last buttons on her pelisse. "I will get the crossbow." But could she use it? On Yannick? O'Leary would without a second thought, but she couldn't. What was she going to do?

Father had held up his hand, the shroud balanced over the other. "Oh no, lassie, you are to stay here. In your room."

Now she understood. He'd deliberately excluded her from the plan. And she was forbidden to leave her room? "That is ridiculous. I am perfectly capable of protecting myself while we hunt." This was her mistake. She needed the chance to set things to rights.

"I want you in your room where you will be safe."

"I *must* go! These village men have no experience and most of them will be drunk. And what about the collars?" She took an unsteady breath. Very likely she couldn't put the collars on. She should suggest they find a truly good and innocent woman.

"Well, one wasn't successful, was it, lass?"

She hoped neither man noticed her blush of shame. "How else will you subdue them?"

"Arrows tipped with a mild curare mixture. Even on vampires, it acts to paralyze. We need them controlled before you attempt to put on the collars. I'm not taking any risks—not now we know they don't behave as I expected."

Curare? On *Yannick*? She had launched forward and caught

Father's arm. "No, it could kill him!" The heart continued to beat even after poisoning, but the paralysis caused breathing to stop, and that meant death. She'd read papers from the Royal Society on it. It was damned risky.

He had stared down at her, his gaze surprised, and she prayed her heart wasn't showing on her sleeve. But dear God, she couldn't let them risk destroying Yannick.

Father had frowned. "Not to worry, lass. I am the expert here. Experiment shows that curare does not kill vampires—in the right amounts—due to their slower breathing rate and the enhanced strength of their muscles." He had patted her hand. "I don't intend to kill him, lovey, not even by mistake. I need him."

Now, alone in her room, Althea stared up at her dark ceiling. *Don't come, Yannick.*

Though what was worse? If he stayed away and risked being poisoned? But if he came to her, he would force her to choose.

She shouldn't have any doubts at all. As a slayer—a hunter— she should disable him without even a qualm. A hunter couldn't afford to dwell in emotion and doubt.

What was that? The beat of wings? A whisper of sound different from that of rain striking leaves.

Neck arched, ears straining, she waited. For long moments. Long enough that her back grew stiff and her shoulders twitched from the tension in them.

She should be relieved he wasn't coming, but instead, she felt sick deep inside. She dropped back on the bed and closed her eyes.

Angel . . .

Her lashes flickered. She must have fallen asleep. The weight of the blankets lay along her body. Was he truly here? Was she dreaming?

She opened her eyes to pitch dark. With no moon, there was

no light at all—even the lamps in the inn's yard had been extinguished. Only the brush of air, the beat of large, graceful wings, told her he was there.

While he could see her and didn't need light, she did. Althea sat up. "Yannick?" She reached for the table beside her, to light her stump of a candle.

But before she found the flint, the bed dipped with his weight beside her and fingers twined with hers, stopping her from striking her light. Long, elegant fingers. Cool.

"Yannick." She whispered it again, a smile on her lips. A welcoming one that she truly felt even as her other hand searched for the collar. He was but inches away and she sensed him, but she couldn't make out more than a dark shape.

He caught her by the elbow as she touched the collar. Strong hands grasped both her wrists, not hard, not rough, but she couldn't twist free. His scent washed over her, male skin touched by fresh rain. He lifted her hands over her head. She gasped as he eased her onto the bed.

No, love. Bastien.

6

Falling

Bastien tightened his grip on Althea's slender wrists as she struggled beneath him. In the dark, to his vampiric gaze, her face glowed, a delicate, pale oval. Vibrant wine-red hair streamed across her pillow. Emerald eyes flashed fire at him.

"Let me go!" Her bare right foot slammed into his shin. She followed with a kick and her left foot dug hard into his naked hip. He winced at the thud against his sensitive bone.

He ran his thumbs along the insides of her wrists. "I won't harm you, sweetheart."

The stubborn, willful wench arched up against his weight and strength. And gained an impressive inch off the mattress. "Then let my hands go."

Admirably feisty. Bastien gave a cheeky grin. "Let me enjoy you like this for a moment more."

Althea dropped back, lips trembling. But not on the brink of tears. More likely in anger. A flush colored her soft, satiny cheeks. Though she had little hope of fighting her way free, she twisted her wrists in his grasp.

He'd always loved a feisty wench. And after ten years of enduring living death, he craved this one.

"What do you want from me? Blood?" She spoke without a trace of fear, her voice soft, throaty. Lavender and meadow scents surrounded him, along with the tang of her excitement. And that intrigued him. She wasn't afraid.

"I'd never drink from my savior, sweetheart." Even as he made the promise, his fangs throbbed.

Savior softened her expression. The exertion had only heightened her fetching blush. Her firm, round breasts quivered with the quick breaths she sucked in. With her arms raised, her breasts stretched up toward his lips. Her nipples, plump and hard, tented her filmy white nightgown.

"I don't believe you," she whispered. Even cool and doubting, Althea's voice purred, feminine and silky. Naturally so. She wasn't attempting to flirt or seduce.

"I opened my eyes to see a goddess, love. At first I thought you were another dream. That you couldn't be real. Sweetheart, I would never hurt the angel sent to free me."

Her wrists stilled. She stopped fighting. "Why would you, a vampire, believe an angel had been sent for you?"

"No man looking at you would think you any other than an angel, my darling." He released her wrists. Later, when she trusted him, he would introduce her to the games he most enjoyed.

She pulled her arms down to her sides. "You dreamed about me?" One hand slipped furtively under the tangled bedcovers.

So, she hoped to distract. What did she have there? A weapon? Faster than she could blink, Bastien flicked back the sheets.

"Another collar? How did you plan to put it on, sweeting?" He winked. "Did you plan to climb on top of me and pin me down to do the deed?"

Straddling her hips, he twined his fingers in hers and pulled her hand away from the metal circle. He kept his weight balanced on his elbow and his knees dug into the woefully saggy mattress. "Sorry to disappoint, Althea, but that collar does nothing to me."

"Then Ya—his lordship didn't free you?"

"No, sweeting." Bastien had sensed Yannick's presence since rising with the night. But he was free, gloriously free, for the first time in a decade, and he'd had other things to do with his first night than spend it with his saintly brother. His damned saintly brother who was willing to let him rot in a crypt rather than free him. How long had his twin been free? Had the lovely Althea freed his twin first?

Althea frowned, perplexed. "So you removed the collar yourself, Mr. de Wynter?"

"Mr. de Wynter?" Turning another question onto hers, he lifted those delicate fingers to his lips. Dropped a light kiss on their tips. The scent of her sang to him, a siren's call. Ah, he adored the scent of a gently bred woman. So subtle and clean. How he loved to drink in those light, floral perfumes as he bent to sink his fangs into a maiden's pretty neck. "Call me Bastien, sweetheart. I never stand on formality with women I make love to."

Though his hand held hers, she tried to pull away. "I'm not going to—"

She didn't finish but she didn't need to. Jealousy stabbed in his gut. Sharp and quick, like the flick of a stinging whip. She had been about to call his brother by his first name. Had Yannick already made love to *his* savior?

"Did you free my brother?" he asked, his voice soft and seductive.

She shook her head. "He was freed almost immediately."

Bastien fought to control his anger. How in Hades had Yannick got free?

"Dreaming of you kept me from going mad, Althea. Don't

leave me." He shoved the collar from the bed. As it hit the plank floor with a soft thunk, he rolled onto his back on the bed. With a gentle tug, he pulled Althea to sprawl over him and he groaned in pleasure as her sweet weight landed. Quick as a wink, he grasped a handful of plump derrière and squeezed. "It was torture to waken at every sundown, unable to move. Not even enough to blink my eyelids. I thought I was to spend eternity that way. Do you know how magical it felt to look up from that damned tomb and see you above me?"

Her palm splayed flat on his chest. "But—" She stopped. "You saw me?"

"Yes, I could see you. Gazing down on me, as radiant as sunrise—and, yes, hell, I do remember sunrise."

She looked doubtful, but he meant every word. God, to be awake again and to be with her for real. He fisted his hand into all that lush, thick, soft hair. Pulled her down to his mouth, one palm full of soft bottom and the other full of fragrant, silky hair.

The way to seduce Althea was through her mind. Stoke her forbidden fantasies until she burned with need.

He felt her shift and buck up against his clamping hand.

He let her go, praying she wouldn't leave him altogether. His heart thudded and since he'd become a vampire his heart never raced. Alive or undead, he'd never been so tentative with a woman. They always fell so easily under his spell. He would charm and seduce, enthrall and flatter. Often all he had to do was command a woman to get into his bed. But he was uneasy here. Her loyalty to Yannick was a tangible thing that he could almost taste.

Something dropped from her nightgown and struck his cheek. A cross, dangling on the thin silver chain encircling her neck. Bastien shifted, catching the warm silver cross on his tongue. He suckled it lightly, until she yanked it back. In the dark, he saw her look of horror.

But she didn't leave the bed.

"Damn, but you are a true beauty," he breathed. She ducked her head at the compliment and it seemed to trouble her more.

Her fair brows drew together. Her lashes dipped over her eyes. "I shouldn't."

Bastien was used to wiping clean a woman's guilt. "Because of Yannick?" He cradled her cheek to reassure her. Heat—a flare of it, a spark like a strike across flint—leapt through his hand at the touch. "I know I've shared you with Yannick in the dreams."

She blushed prettily beneath his fingers, a flush he could see easily with his predator's vision.

"What did Yannick do to you, sweetheart?"

"I cannot say."

He caught her delicate chin between forefinger and thumb. "I've been in the dreams, Althea. And I've done unspeakable sexual things. You can't shock me."

She tucked her hair behind her ear but the thick mass spilled forward again. "No, I expect I cannot. But it's . . . it's private. And intimate."

He gave a wicked grin. "Ah, but I always share women with my brother."

"Always?" She stared, eyes wide open. Even in the dark, they sparkled. Though he couldn't see the exact color in the dark, he knew they were the green of the rain-soaked lawns surrounding Inglewood. Yannick's home now. His no longer.

With a fluid movement, he sat up also, so he could cradle her from behind. Althea squirmed for a moment as he lifted her and settled her voluptuous bottom between his parted thighs. His erection bumped her spine through her nightgown. "Aye, always. Which means I've often seen him perform."

She didn't resist as he cupped her slim shoulders. "Now, what does Yannick do to please a woman?" he mused. "What have I seen him do?"

She gasped at that.

Gathering her hair in one thick mass, Bastien lifted it, flicked his tongue along her bared neck. Sweet and salty, touched by feminine perspiration and lavender-scented soap. He traced his way up to her ear. "Did he use his prick?"

He nipped her earlobe gently with his front teeth. He wrapped his arms around her and cradled her tight to him, where she belonged. Her heartbeat raced against his naked forearm.

"Please—"

"Or his mouth?"

"Don't."

"There's no shame, love. There's pleasure in talking about sex." He nibbled her ear, rewarded by the arch in her back, the soft moan whispering from her lips. "An aphrodisiac, as it were."

"And there's no shame in telling me what Yannick's done, love. You're destined to be shared by us." For now at least.

He felt her shudder through his body, recognized it for what it was—a barely restrained surrender to arousal. She liked to talk about sex.

Her head tipped up and she turned in his arms. "What if I do not believe in the notion of destiny? Perhaps I believe I have a choice in this. What if I choose one of you instead of both?"

Bastien skimmed his hands up higher and cradled her breasts. Her heart thudded with life and desire against his palm. "Then choose me, angel."

Heaven help her, Althea thought, the choice was no longer easy. Just like his brother, Bastien had appeared without a stitch—she knew that because his warm, naked skin pressed against her. In the dark, with no moonlight, she couldn't see him, but she knew his long, bare legs stretched on either side of hers. Muscular, naked arms surrounded her. His broad, bare chest was a solid wall behind her back.

This shouldn't feel so intimate. He'd escaped confinement,

for heaven's sake, and was likely dangerous. Anticipation shouldn't be alive in her. Her skin shouldn't be on fire everywhere that his body touched hers.

And the way he spoke, his voice hoarse and ragged as though he truly yearned for her, made his words both a plea and a confident command. How could he sound both brash and vulnerable? But his vulnerability spoke to her heart.

Did he really think of her as his savior?

What about Yannick? Her heart had soared with him last night, had clenched in fear with worry that he might not find safety. Her foolish, traitorous heart could not flip its allegiance from one man to another so easily, could it?

No, what she felt for Bastien wasn't at all the same. It was sympathy and sorrow and concern. Nothing more. Even though he'd been in her dreams, seductive and skilled and gorgeous. It couldn't be more.

But Bastien's mouth was wet fire along her neck. Burning oil flaming across water. "Choose me," he repeated, tempting as the devil.

She caught hold of her senses. "I'm a vampire hunter. I won't choose either of you."

His strong arms tightened, clamping her against his solid body, trapping his thick, erect cock between her spine and him. It felt enormous and rock hard, prodding her back. And strangely, his snug embrace made her feel safe, even though she should fear the strength inherent in his strong, hard body.

He was so different from Yannick. His chest smoother, his legs and arms leaner. His longer hair, gold, tangled with hers as he kissed her neck. But his voice and Yannick's were so very alike, so much so that she quivered in shock each time he spoke. But they must be different, she guessed, in other ways. Yannick exuded both the arrogance of a peer and the gentleness of a loving man. Bastien had wistfully called her his savior, but he chuckled wickedly as he traced his fangs softly along her neck.

Her nerves tensed and shrieked in panic. When he suckled her shoulder at the neckline of her nightdress, with soft lips and wet tongue instead of fangs, relief slammed into desire, and she swayed at the combination.

Bastien held her up. He filled his hands with her breasts, squeezing them through her crumpled muslin nightgown.

"So you want us to slay Zayan for you and then you'll kill us?" His voice was a gravelly rasp.

She flinched. She didn't know. Didn't know. "How did you know that's why you were . . . resurrected?"

"I could hear every word you and your father and that Irish bloke uttered, lass."

"I thought you couldn't—"

His fingers plucked her nipples and she jumped at the sudden, delicious pleasure. Her bottom thrust back against his erection.

"Do you understand, Althea, why Zayan imprisoned me?"

She shouldn't enjoy his touch on her breasts. She mustn't. "Because you could kill him. I understand now that you and . . . and Yannick must be together to destroy him."

"Wouldn't it have made far more sense just to destroy one of us? With one or both dead, Zayan need never fear us." He straightened, lifting his lips from her neck. But his hands stayed on her breasts. Each massaging stroke sent a jolt of need down to her quim. She was wet and hot, but lust was all mixed up with fear.

She managed to twist around, but in the dark she could not see his face. His breath whispered over her cheek. Even to her whirling brain, his words made sense. Why had Zayan spared them?

"I've no idea why he didn't kill Yannick." One hand dropped to rest over her belly. Fingers began bunching up the gown. The hem slid up in front. Bastien murmured in his deep baritone, "But Zayan didn't kill me because we were lovers once."

She must have misunderstood. "*Who* were lovers?"

"Zayan and I." A trace of jaded amusement flitted through his words.

How she wished she could see in the dark! She tried to turn more, following the sound of his voice. Her hand bumped his lean, hard thigh.

How could he have been Zayan's *lover*? "But you are both—"

"Vampires?"

Her chest tightened around her heart. "Men."

"But men can be lovers, my sweet. You must know that."

She knew it happened somehow. And that it was considered a sin. But the shocking image of another man touching Bastien took root and refused to vanish. A man's large hand touching as she wanted to touch. Stroking a broad shoulder. Splaying across his chest. Would a man kiss another man's nipples the way she'd kissed Yannick's? Would a man explore his lean hips, his long legs dusted with golden hair? Would a man touch his cock?

"You are curious, aren't you? Imagining what two men do together. How two men make love."

Knowing Bastien could see her, Althea shook her head—an outright lie. She did want to know. She *yearned* to know.

"Did you love him?"

"Ah, sweetheart, I suspect you are really more interested in the sex."

"No," she lied again. But she was curious. Did men kiss the way a man and a woman did?

She remembered the dreams. Bastien's mouth slanting over hers, tongue skillful in her mouth, luring her to sin.

How could Bastien be of that persuasion and still come to her in her dreams, kissing and caressing her with such intense desire?

"It can be highly erotic to make love to one's own sex," he promised.

"It is supposed to be a perversion."

His laugh was the devil's song, wicked and tempting in the velvety dark. "But I enjoy perversions, love."

Not like his brother at all! For all Yannick was sensual and skilled as a vampire, he'd been tender and sweet about seducing her. With Bastien, she feared she might emerge from the night without her soul.

"But, in truth, Althea, nothing people do together in bed in the name of pleasure is a perversion." He brushed a hot kiss to her cheek and she quivered at the surprising sweetness in it. But at the same instant, his hand delved beneath her nightgown and stroked her bare inner thigh. "After all, there's no shame in having both my brother and me take you to ecstasy. You deserve to have us both enslaved to you."

No, this couldn't go on. Althea pushed hard against his spread legs, seeking to escape.

"Stay with me, sweetheart."

Again she heard the soft plea and again it lured her to stay.

"Can you imagine making love to another woman?" he whispered. "Kissing her plump breasts? Taking her taut, thick nipples between your lips? Tasting and touching her as you would love her to do to you?"

His hand cupped the mound between her legs. "Scorching and soaked, aren't you, sweetheart? I suspect you are like me in your soul, Althea. Wicked and sensual. I suspect you too would love to watch women have sex together."

His hips rocked back and forth. The tip of his hot tongue played over the top of her spine. "I love to watch women suck other women's nipples, and smile with delight at the sound of another woman's moans. Women so enjoy exploring another lass' breasts. A woman with ripe, small breasts loves to lick a great big pair of tits, and a woman with large breasts is most curious about a slender, wee thing. It's so arousing to watch them hug and their breasts squash together, nipples rubbing." He strummed his thumb over her left nipple, as though to make his point.

"I can't imagine watching such a thing!" But his fingers found her clit in her wet folds. "Oooh!"

Stars exploded in the dark as he rubbed. She really must . . . must . . . stop . . .

"You forget I've been in your dreams."

How did he make the word *dreams* sound so deliciously sinful?

"Dreams that kept me alive." He rubbed until she was boneless, whimpering.

"Now, what else do two lassies like to do in bed?" Bastien mused. "Women do so love to plunge a rod into each other's pussies. I had two such lovers who enjoyed giving me a lusty show—they loved to fill every hole they had with long, thick ivory wands. They would suck each other's nipples as they slid the wands into each other's quims, working them until their juices flowed as fast as their moans. Then one bent over on all fours and the other slid a dildo right up her snug little bum. Right to the hilt."

He wanted to shock her. He must. Why else would he be so . . . so blunt, so crude? Shame on her, but his story had her heart pounding and not entirely in dismay.

"They were on the brink of orgasm just preparing each other. The first woman slowly slid the last wand up the other's voluptuous arse, stuffing her full. They then brought me into the fun, and sat at my feet to lick my cock and my balls. They bounced up and down a few times and both erupted into screaming climaxes."

Althea couldn't breathe for the guilt and the shock, but her orgasm didn't care about shame at all. His fingers brought her close . . . so wonderfully close . . . She drove her fingernails into his thighs. But he eased the pressure on her and let her slide back from the brink.

She didn't dare protest. Didn't dare.

"Before I met Zayan, Yannick and I spent many nights at brothels, enjoying such displays."

Yannick did such things? Of course he did. He'd made love to her in dreams with his brother.

Bastien whispered silkily, "But when Zayan turned me, he brought me into a dark, erotic world I quickly became addicted to. Have you ever tried opium?"

Startled, she shook her head.

"Sex can be like that. Addictive, until you are a slave to your craving. And, of course you require more potent doses."

"What—" She shouldn't encourage him, but curiosity—and her throbbing clit—begged her to ask, "What is a more potent dose?"

"Have you ever wondered how a whip would feel against your bare bottom?"

"Dear heaven, no!"

"Or ropes tied around your wrists, leaving you the slave to a gentleman's every wish?" He arched his hips, pushing his cock against her. "The exquisite pain and pleasure of devices clamped to your nipples? A judicious spanking with a riding crop?"

Her head reeled at his words, her quim throbbed. "You would hurt women so?"

"Didn't your experiences with my brother give you some taste of the agony that accompanies pleasure?"

He rasped his finger over her clit, hard and demanding, and she fought a scream. It was so unbearable.

Give me more. Please give me more.

Just like Yannick, Bastien took her to an edge where she feared his caress and craved it too. Maybe she did understand, just a little.

Bastien's touch on her intimate regions became feather-light. Tormenting her. Leaving her panting, hungry, and pressing forward to seek more.

He didn't intend to take her to a climax? Only to tease her in this unbelievable way? "I wouldn't want real pain," Althea said quickly.

"Many do not. But in that dark, sexual world, the submissive and the master learn to trust. I was taught that the true conquest is to lure the submissive into exploring further. Accepting more. Forcing would only cause true pain—though some women enjoyed the game of a dominant man inflicting his will and desires."

"I wouldn't."

His laugh teased against her ear. "In truth, what I enjoyed most was the complete focus on the sex and the game. I don't live to inflict pain. I've known pain. I don't enjoy giving or receiving blows that are truly vindictive or cruel. But when I was immersed in the games—nothing else existed in the world but the power and the creation of punishment and pleasure. I would spend days in a lavish dungeon, with bound, voluptuous slaves, acting as a depraved and decadent king. And spend hours devising ways to tie up my dutiful servants. To wrap them with ropes and chains so that their every struggle would heighten their pleasure."

Despite herself, she whimpered. Aroused, frightened, stunned. *I've known pain.*

He laughed again. Rougher. "So you see. Very addictive."

"Do you wish to do that with me?"

"Only if you wish to try, love."

She shook her head "But what pain have you known?"

"Much. And very little love, sweet angel. What I saw in your eyes as you looked down upon me in my coffin was the most tenderness I've ever seen."

"I don't believe that. You exaggerate."

"It's God's truth, Althea. I've been whipped within an inch of my life by the man whose seed spawned me."

Before she could say a word, Bastien's fingers parted the

slippery, hot folds of her quim and slid inside. His hand lovingly cradled her breast.

No, no, she couldn't let him do this. She tried to push his hand away and he withdrew, resting his sticky fingers at the apex of her sex, within her curls.

"But in your dreams, didn't you enjoy having two men make love to you? After all, that way your pleasure isn't limited to the skills of one man."

"Love is more important than skill!"

"I would love you just as much as Yannick would, and very likely more, my dove."

Could a vampire love her? No, it wasn't possible. They didn't have souls. He was using the word to lure her into sin. She needed to understand more of his relationship with Zayan.

"Did you love, Zayan?" she asked again. "Did . . . did you kiss him?"

"On the mouth, yes. On his cock, too."

Goodness! She thought of Yannick's tongue gliding over her intimate regions. "Did you kiss his—"

"His where, love?" His fingers dipped between her lips again. She flushed in the dark. She was wet and bubbling.

"Mmm," he murmured as his finger slid in and stirred her. "Did Yannick kiss you in other places than your lips and your sweet sex? Your nipples, I'm sure." He gently pinched the one he held. "For I'd love to suck these plump cherries into my mouth. And where else?"

She couldn't speak as guilt and need clashed.

"Somewhere scandalous then," Bastien continued. "Did my dear brother put his tongue in your derrière?"

Any doubt that he truly did share women with Yannick vanished. How else could he know so exactly what his brother had done? But still she did not answer. Even if she'd wanted to, she couldn't force a sound out of her throat.

"Yes, love. Men do that too."

The sudden image of Bastien and another man doing such things should horrify. Instead she squirmed at the stab of desire.

Althea gulped. Afraid of herself, now. She was glad he was behind her, where he couldn't read her face.

"When men make love, they use their mouths and cocks. Even their toes. And they love to have their nipples sucked, their mouths deeply kissed. You know, of course, that when a man and a woman kiss, his erection often presses against her eager quim, a promise of the fun to follow. When men kiss, their cocks parry like swords and the sensation thrills just as much, I assure you."

Another image burst into her wanton mind. Of two men with hips tipped together, fencing with their erect members.

"And men love to have their cocks sucked. Another man's mouth is as warm and accommodating and skilled as a woman's."

His casual words shocked her. "You mean that anyone would do when . . . when you're aroused."

"No, sweet, I don't mean that at all. And before Zayan, I would never have touched another man. But once Zayan made love to me, took me in his mouth, penetrated me, I was addicted."

Bastien bent over her—she couldn't see him, but sensed him there.

His lips covered hers in a kiss, hot and soft, tempting hers to part. His fangs grazed her lower lip. Sparks shot from her lip to her quim and she moaned into his open mouth. He tipped her back and she lost her balance, suspended almost magically by his hand on her breast, his mouth on hers. His tongue slid in, teased, filled.

His voice slipped into her mind. *But in our dreams, little dove, I fell in love with you.*

She fell completely into his kiss.

"What in bloody hell are you doing?"

7

Tickled

Yannick's harsh voice broke the spell. Althea pulled hard away from Bastien and slid from the bed. She tried to land on her feet but they gave way beneath her.

Yannick caught her before she fell. He gathered her up in his arms, engulfing her against his naked chest. Her lips brushed the whorls of his hair. She fit tight against his body, her belly a cradle for his erection, and she breathed in his scent—the trace of sandalwood on naked skin, the tang of his underarms, the rich, primal aroma of his naked male parts. She hadn't heard him—she'd been so caught up in Bastien, she hadn't even known he'd arrived.

Two questions hammered through her head.

Why had he come to her?

How much had he seen?

"I—I—" She tried to think of an explanation. There wasn't one, of course. She'd been kissing his brother. Worse, she could smell her own arousal, and she didn't doubt Yannick could too.

He must hate her completely. Her betrayal was so absolute.

Bastien's shocking words came back to her. *I always share women with my brother.*

Perhaps in dreams and perhaps in the past, but Yannick sounded none too happy now. Her face flamed with shame. She stuttered a few more hopeless vowels. Until she realized Yannick's furious glare focused on his brother and his arms were gentle around her.

"I seem to remember that this is the part of the dream where I suggest you pinch her nipples." Bastien's voice, insolent and mocking, came from her rumpled bed.

Yannick's grip tightened. "What did y—" He stopped, as though seeking control. "What did he do to you?"

She guessed he had been about to demand what she had done, how far she had allowed Bastien to go. "Nothing," she said. Which wasn't true. Yannick must know it. He had seen Bastien's hands—one on her breast, one between her thighs. He'd seen their kiss.

"I . . . I let him. Touch me. Kiss me."

Her mattress shifted with a creak. "And no reason why you shouldn't, sweet angel. Why so possessive, brother? You know she'd love to be shared by us. She is a uniquely sensual woman."

"I'm not," she protested in little more than a hoarse whisper. "Not that sort."

"But we know that you are, Althea," Bastien insisted, "and between us we have more than enough experience to judge that."

Goodness, could they see aspects of her soul that she didn't even know herself?

A spark flared near her bedside table, revealing a large masculine hand, the lean, graceful bones of a strong wrist, a powerful forearm. The hand moved to put the light to the wick, which caught, then glowed. "It is not fair that you can't see too, little dove."

As the flame grew, devouring the wax, the light accentuated Bastien's flowing golden hair, his well-muscled torso. The glow slid along his hip, touched the top of his lean leg, gleamed along the length of his large, erect cock.

"So." He clapped his hands together and his member wobbled with his enthusiasm. "Let the games begin."

"No." Yannick spoke the word with all the arrogance of an earl—thy will be done.

Bastien frowned. "In my dreams, we shared. Did you have some with the lass alone?"

Yannick merely smiled. A conceited grin that Althea guessed would anger Bastien.

And it did. Bastien's silvery eyes reflected the flickering candle flame, and sparks glinted in the soft dark. "No wonder you didn't rush to free me, you bastard."

"I had other reasons for that, Bastien." Only the faintest whisper of light struck Yannick's white-blond hair. His lashes were lowered, changing his eyes to shimmering half-moons.

"You didn't free him from the collar, did you?" she breathed up to Yannick.

"Collar?"

"A device she hoped would imprison us, dear brother." Bastien wore the smug smirk now. "She had one waiting in the bed for you."

"Though I must admit," Bastien continued, his deep voice silkily dangerous, "the thought of wearing a collar that made me her slave does intrigue. What did you plan to do with us both at your mercy, sweet? Sit first on his cock and then on mine?"

"Bastien," Yannick warned, but she felt his erection buck against her backside. Apparently, Bastien's words excited him.

"I had hoped to entice you both to slay Zayan."

At the word *entice*, a crackling energy surged from both men and she felt it.

"Did you indeed?" Yannick murmured. He cupped her breasts, still swollen from Bastien's attentions. Her nipples immediately hardened and poked into his palms.

She couldn't see Yannick's face, but she suspected he'd directed a look of triumph at his twin.

Who crossed his arms over his magnificent chest. "Did you plan to *entice* us at the same time?"

"I doubt she did," Yannick challenged.

"You mean to ask the poor sweet to choose?" Bastien flopped back onto her bed. It squawked in protest as over six feet of solid muscle landed hard upon it. "No, you didn't, did you? You intended to take her for yourself, without even allowing the young lady to have a say. Arrogant sod. So what about her dreams then, Yannick? Not going to let the little sweetheart live out her dreams?"

His legs dangled over the sides of her bed, bare feet on the floor. He reached down and pushed his fist behind his cock, to lift it upright. It didn't stand straight, but listed to the left. Just as she'd seen it in dreams, his member possessed a thick head, wider than the top of his shaft. Perhaps that was why it tipped over, top-heavy.

"Don't ask her to choose, Yannick," Bastien cajoled. "Don't be so bloody selfish. You know as well as I how much pleasure a woman receives from two lovers. Of course," he added, "when I put the idea of making a choice to her, she said she'd choose neither of us."

Yannick's brow merely lifted. His expression appeared carved in granite. "What else did you expect? She destroys the likes of us. She planned to imprison us, use us, then kill us." His hands squeezed tightly over her breasts on the word *kill*.

A protest died on Althea's lips. What Yannick described was exactly what she must do.

But Bastien laughed, the devil's own chuckle. "She's a determined one, though, I must admit. Strong-willed."

She was anything but. "I am here in the room, I might remind the both of you. Don't speak of me as though I'm not."

Yannick brushed a kiss to the top of her head, but she no longer trusted pretty gestures from him. She didn't doubt he was angry and she didn't doubt an angry vampire could kill her in a heartbeat. Not when he feared his survival was at stake. Her stomach churned—her betrayals now put her at risk.

"But," Yannick continued, speaking over her head, "Even knowing that she'd happily put a stake in my heart, I still want to make love to her."

"As do I. But then men are doomed to think with their pricks."

The entire tenor of the room changed. The brothers looked at her, not at each other. She saw Bastien's intense gaze and felt Yannick's. Camaraderie replaced dispute, and she was certain the brothers had shared a wicked smile over her head. It was as though she'd stepped into one of her dreams where both men were relaxed and delighted with the idea of sharing her, as they coaxed her to accept it.

Her head was spinning. First her guilt and fear over Yannick. Then her disturbing lust for Bastien. And now, they planned to . . . planned to—

She'd thought she'd shared a special intimacy with Yannick but she saw now that it couldn't have been the same for him. He lived a scandalous sex life she couldn't even begin to imagine.

Yannick nudged her toward the bed. Althea let her feet obey his wish.

Bastien knifed up to a sitting position, eyes smiling, lips on a level with her approaching crotch.

"I imagine she tastes delicious?" he asked.

"Ambrosia itself," Yannick promised.

"But you didn't taste her most precious nectar?"

"No, and you won't tonight."

Bastien flicked back his long hair over his shoulder and

leaned forward until his chin rested on her right thigh. He bunched up her skirt, lifting and lifting her hem. The heavy cotton skimmed her knees. He reached the spot where her inner thighs touched.

"We want to fulfill your every fantasy," Bastien whispered, then ducked his head beneath her skirt.

She squealed as his hot mouth closed on her quim, as his tongue snaked out.

"Patience, brother," Yannick warned and his powerful arms scooped her up and away from Bastien's mouth.

His mouth took hers, claimed it. Ruthlessly, he kissed her, plunging his tongue inside as though to remind her to whom she'd belonged first.

Afraid she might topple, she wrapped her arms around his neck. She couldn't resist threading her fingers into his white-blond hair, savoring the silkiness against her bare fingers. Before last night she'd never touched a man's hair and, heaven help her, she still felt possessive about Yannick's. His hair was for her to touch and stroke.

He wasn't mindful of his fangs this time. They pricked her lips and tongue. Scratched her lightly, but she tasted a drop of her blood.

She drew back. "I wanted to wait—"

"I know," Yannick whispered against her lips.

"I waited for you tonight. I didn't think you would come. And Bastien did instead."

Why she was trying to explain, she couldn't imagine. She was a vampire hunter. It didn't matter what she felt for him. It couldn't matter.

Yet here she was, gathered in the arms of a vampire earl, as he kissed her senseless in front of his naked brother.

She clung tighter as Yannick moved them to the bed. Her skirt flowed off her thighs, leaving most of her legs naked, and the cool air washed over them.

Then a warm hand stroked the length of her shin. Bastien's hand. It couldn't be Yannick's.

"Such delicate, tiny feet." Bastien cradled her right foot. With a chuckle, he ran his thumb along her sole. Ooh, how it tickled! She laughed, squealed, and tried to pull her foot free.

Yannick laughed and her heart soared at the deep, sensual sound.

"Drop her on the bed, brother. I fancy sucking her pretty toes."

As Yannick let her tumble onto her mattress, Bastien stretched out on her narrow bed at her feet. Candlelight highlighted his long stretch of back, the twin curves of his firm derrière, left his legs in shadow where they hung off her mattress. He gave a wicked smile, fangs gleaming, then he closed his lips around her big toe.

Yannick knelt at her feet too. An earl at her feet. Two gorgeous demons at her feet.

She pinched her arm through the sleeve of her nightdress, just to be sure she wasn't dreaming. No, awake without a doubt.

She shivered with anticipation as Yannick lifted her foot and his parted lips neared. Althea never would have dreamed that toes could be so erotically sensitive.

And it wasn't so sinful to let them kiss her feet.

Her toe disappeared into Yannick's warm mouth and he watched her, silver eyes filled with sensual intent. She'd intended to flash him a smile, but her face contorted as pleasure arced and her moan spoke of pure, delicious agony.

Perhaps toes weren't so innocent after—

Oh!

They sucked and massaged and stroked and teased. Yannick stretched out as Bastien had done and her wavering gaze flicked from one man to the other. Both so beautiful. Both nude. Two broad backs. Two perfect, muscled bottoms. Two giving, skilled mouths.

How wonderful this was.

She closed her eyes.

Someone stopped sucking. "Do you think, brother, she's remembering the dreams?" Bastien. "Remembering our mouths on her nipples. They're hard and plump, now. Two sweet breasts. One for each." Bastien kissed each of her toes in turn. Combined with Yannick's suction, it was a mad flurry of sensation.

She didn't dare open her eyes. As though darkness absolved her of sin.

Oh, yes. She wanted it so.

"Which of us sucks you best, love?" Bastien again. Asking her a question she couldn't begin to answer. "Which of us should earn a place at your breast?"

Her lids shot up. She was supposed to choose? Both men still lay at her feet. Two gorgeous, naked male demons looking like innocent pups.

Don't try to choose if you can't, sweet angel.

The first time Yannick had spoken in her mind tonight. The intimacy of it made her sob.

But I intend to pleasure you best and win, because I have an unfair advantage. I know the sinful pleasures that you enjoy. If you don't let Bastien force you to prefer one of us to the other, we can put our mouths on both your delicious quim and your sweet ass.

Althea whimpered at the thought.

"Yes," she whispered. "Please." Lust spoke for her. She wanted them both so. Her heart raced, just as it did in her dreams. Her quim ached in need.

Do you want us to kiss you that way? To fill you with our tongues? To make you come again and again with our mouths? Together? Do you truly want this, sweet?

Yannick was giving her a choice. Not luring her and seducing her into sin as he did in her dreams. She had one last chance to claw her way back to propriety. Her gaze met his eyes, pale as two moons, sparkling like close stars. *I'm lost*, she whispered in her head. *All sense is gone. It must be wrong to crave . . . but I don't care . . . I've always been so good. My moral compass . . . it's broken now. Fractured. Yannick, please, I don't know—*

They both rose over her, light and shadow. Their taut, muscular arms crossed over her as they braced themselves. How they both fit on her bed, she didn't know. Their long legs tangled with hers. Her wet toes prickled as cool air wafted over her feet.

"Kiss me," Yannick whispered. His pale blond tresses shone like silver. His lush black lashes made his eyes dark, mysterious wells.

"No, me first, my love, for I love you the most," Bastien urged. His long, thick hair dangled over his face, glinting gold.

Yannick's hot mouth pressed to her cheek. Bastien's touched her earlobe on the other side. Sharing wasn't so simple at all. If she chose one to kiss, would she hurt the other?

She twisted and claimed Yannick's mouth. He was the man she'd shared the most special intimacy with.

Thank you, sweet angel. He kissed her hard and deep, teasing with his tongue.

Fingers clasped her chin and drew her mouth from Yannick's. Bastien's lips slid over hers. Back and forth they kissed her, taking turns. And while one twin claimed her lips, the other suckled her neck, licked her cheek, nibbled her ear.

But Bastien cradled her cheek and gazed deep into her eyes. *Let me make love to you first, little dove. Let me be the first to fill you with my cock.*

Bastien—

It's her choice, brother. Being eldest doesn't count here.

8

Captured

Bastien groaned as his finger parted Althea's sweet, sticky nether lips. But his fingers tangled with his damned brother's.

"You are both going to put your fingers . . . in me at once?"

Well, she'd thought of the one act he'd never done. While making love to a woman with Yannick, they always ensured they rarely touched. They were brothers, after all. And there were some sins that even he wouldn't embrace.

But Yannick would not back down and neither would he. Side by side, their index fingers slid into her. Bastien felt her hot fleshy walls, his brother's bony digit. Damnation. Were it not for Yannick, she'd be gripped snug and tight around him.

She cried out in excitement and surprise and her feminine squeal sent another pulse of blood flooding to his cock. Already it stood up like a Maypole—just waiting for a maiden to dance around it.

His tastes didn't normally run to innocents, and he knew for a fact Yannick had never deflowered a woman. Though in the ten years he'd been imprisoned, and Yannick, blast him, had roamed free, who knew what his brother had done.

Free. While he endured hell.

But revenge lay at his side, gazing at him with wide green eyes while he plunged his fingers in her boiling core.

Her hips rocked now, as both he and Yannick slid their fingers in and out. Desperate panting filled the small room—his, his brother's, and hers. And each moist plunge of his fingers filled the room with more of Althea's heavenly perfume.

Jesus, this was more than revenge. More than stealing the wench his brother desired.

He didn't know if he could continue to exist without hearing her breathy moans, holding her in his arms, sharing her ecstasy.

He might share her tonight, but by moonrise tomorrow, he'd have her heart for himself alone.

His fingertips reached her maidenhead, beside his twin's. In unspoken agreement, they drew back. He teased her slick lips, savoring her "ooh." Ran his wet thumb over her taut little clit.

"Oh! Heavens!"

Bastien's cock bucked at her cry. Given that he could tie up a woman and tease her for hours, or endure such torture himself, he was amazed at how desperately he wanted to slide inside Althea. If his balls grew any tighter he might start howling. And one more sweet feminine cry and he might embarrass himself.

Ten years of imposed celibacy must be to blame.

One of them would have to go first.

Those green eyes speared him, hazy with lust, wide with trust.

Had he ever been the first to have a woman, to take her before Yannick?

Not once that he could remember. Most women flocked to his brother's title and wealth, before discovering how he could pleasure them. And the ones he had alone . . . they existed in a dark world that Yannick never entered.

Bastien lifted to mount Althea, to situate his hips between her silk-soft thighs, but Yannick grabbed his shoulder and pushed him back.

She kept me from going insane, Yannick. She's precious to me.

He saw guilt flicker over his brother's face. *And to me, Bastien.*

So what are we to do? Duel for the right to take her virginity? Since we can blow each other away with impunity, what will be the measure? The ball closest to the heart? Bastien pressed close to Althea and claimed her lips, catching Yannick unprepared. He flicked the buttons of her nightdress free, revealing porcelain skin, inch by inch.

There's no way this can be decided without a battle. He laid bare her breasts, peach perfection, and bent to nip the succulent treat, the way he'd once tasted summer's first fruit. *I'm willing to earn the honor of being the one she chooses.*

He could share if he had to, but damnation, he wanted to be her first. Adorably sweet, she arched beneath him as his teeth bit gently into her plump flesh. He caught hold of her hand and led it toward his cock, on the verge of exploding just at the thought of her graceful hand wrapped around it.

"I can't."

What?

Althea shook her head and Bastien saw the tears sparkling in her eyes. "I shouldn't. I mustn't. I thought I could, but I can't. Not with you both. It's too . . . wrong." She struggled to pull her hand free.

Oh bloody hell. Bastien groaned as he let go of her wrist. Why did she have to possess such power of will? Such bloody goodness?

And in a heartbeat, Yannick rolled close to her, captured her mouth and embraced her. *It's all right, sweet angel,* Yannick reassured.

Pain flared as she responded to his brother's caress. One brother, apparently, was acceptable. Two . . . she was not quite ready for two.

Her arms had hooked around his brother's neck. That one night Yannick and Althea had shared—the intimacy they'd built—was something he could not combat.

"I want . . ." she whispered, "I need . . . I thought I could."

"But you aren't ready for two lovers?" Yannick asked.

"I shouldn't even be ready for one."

Her lashes dropped and she coyly glanced at Yannick. Shyly she whispered, "Last night was so wonderful and beautiful. I know it's ruined now—"

It isn't, Yannick promised.

A stake to the heart couldn't hurt so much. But what good would it do to protest? Or beg? The key to winning her heart wasn't to force himself on her.

Bastien hated to admit defeat, but he kissed her hand. *You've chosen, sweet.*

Sitting up, he swung his legs off the bed, pausing just one moment. He wished she would touch him, stop him, tell him she wanted him to stay.

He waited but all he felt across his skin was the whisper of the breeze that carried the rain.

He stood.

Why his bloody twin?

Bitterness twisted in his gut. Why in Hades did she choose Yannick? Bastien had been the one on top in the bloody womb and what did it get him? Out second and always second.

"I'm so sorry," she whispered.

He'd sauntered nude through hundreds of bedrooms—thousands. Always cocky. *Always* welcomed. Now, naked in front of Althea, Bastien understood vulnerability. But he grinned, his old, wild grin and let his fangs show—the entire sharp, curved length of them.

Next to the bed, where his brother and his lovely angel lay, Bastien bent in a courtly bow.

He shifted shape and the pain of the change raged through him. His entire being screamed and molded and rearranged. Hell, he almost enjoyed the agony.

Goddamn, he didn't care if he exploded into so much dust this time.

But he wasn't so lucky. He took flight with the flap of large wings and soared out of the searing pain. His bloody heart still ached.

He swooped across the room and flew out into the wet embrace of the night.

She darted through the slashing rain to the shelter of the oak. Her small hands held the hook of her dark cloak in place as she hopped the deepening puddles.

Sheltered beneath the spreading branches, he drew hard on his cheroot, let the aromatic smoke float out into the night air.

The girl's thrilling excitement flowed to him in waves, so palpable he could almost taste her emotions. As she neared, he saw the ripe, pink flush to her cheek. Heard the seductive patter of her heart and pumping blood.

He smiled down at her as she reached him, a coy, teasing expression now on her face, as though she hadn't sprinted across a soaked field to get to him. She let the hood drop back, exposing chestnut curls bobbing around her white throat. A village girl, sparkling with country vitality. Large brown eyes met his for a saucy instant.

"Well, where's me greeting for all the trouble I've put myself too?"

With a shrug, he crooked his finger.

Her sharp chin jutted forward and she tossed her curls, but she sashayed to him, wide hips swaying. She tugged the tapes of her cloak so the neckline widened and the brown wool parted to reveal a tight white gown, bodice cut low to display her ripe, creamy mounds.

His fangs pulsed. His cock went stiff.

"Ye like them, do you?" she purred.

He tossed away his smoke.

The girl gasped as he gripped her back and drew her tight to him. Those plump tits squashed against his chest. He shoved back her cloak and grabbed two handfuls of arse through her muslin skirts.

"'Ere now," she protested, but she wriggled hips and breasts against him and her breath came in harsh little pants.

Clutching her generous rump, he lifted her until his straining cock wedged in the valley between her thighs. He thrust against her, leaving no doubt as to what he planned.

And the silly fool, who should have slapped his face and run a mile, responded to his harsh motions. She squealed and acted indignant, but the scent of her honey surrounded him. The arteries along her neck pulsed.

He wasn't even going to bother to fuck her.

He lifted her and shook her, like a ragdoll, so her head lolled back with the sudden shock.

"Now that's a bit rough," she exclaimed, but he ignored her and sliced his fangs into her neck.

Her scream pierced the night. The little hellion fought him, shoving with desperate hands, kicking with wild feet. He held fast, fangs buried deep. The blood burst into him, rich and thick. Coppery, tangy, yet sweet.

Her struggles faded. She whimpered, the sound almost lost in the rain.

Ah, bella, *you taste so good.*

After so many centuries, pleasure still surged as he claimed her. Took her.

Her hands fell limply on his biceps now, clinging as she

clung to life. Her legs no longer held her up and he shifted one hand up to her back to keep her throat to his mouth.

"No ..."

Ignoring her, he drew back and let some of her pumping blood spill down her slim neck. It pooled into the hollow of her throat, then poured free. Thin red rivers soaked into her neckline, trickled in the dark valley between her breasts.

The smell of her blood would bring him.

"I hurt."

Yannick couldn't help but smile at Althea's simple statement. *It's the agony of being aroused and unsatisfied, angel. The hurting is part of the pleasure.*

Beneath him, she frowned. "Is it? Must there be pain to be pleasure?" Her hands stilled on her buttons of her nightdress.

He was lying almost half over her now, levered up on his arm. "What's Bastien been telling you, angel?"

"About whippings." Althea tugged at her buttons.

"No, let me," Yannick murmured and gently eased her hands away. "What did Bastien say about whippings?" He tried to keep his tone neutral as he unfastened the rest. Most likely Bastien had discussed erotic whippings, not sadistic ones.

"He asked if I thought I would enjoy the flick of a whip against my bottom."

The image scorched him. Damnation, what in blazes was wrong with Bastien? What was wrong with *him* that the idea excited him?

"And he told me about how two women make love," she continued, wrapped in virginal white muslin and dripping innocence. "And how two men would do it."

She might hurt, but he was in agony. Pure agony. Ten years of imprisonment had not improved Bastien's morals. The first thing his twin did? Described sodomy to a sweet angel.

Her small white teeth sank into her lip. "The way he ex-plained it . . ."

"It excited you?"

Her pretty pink flush answered him.

"Have you ever made love to another man?"

Goddamn, this conversation was killing him. His loins tightened so sharply it felt like he'd been run through with a sword.

"No, sweet, in that arena, Bastien has far more experience."

"Do you mean to imply you have some?" But she didn't ap-pear shocked, merely curious, as she tugged at her skirts, lifting her hips to draw them up. "I want it off."

So did he. He sat up and lifted her too, and pulled her night-gown over her head. Her breasts bobbed as the cloth lifted and released. Just as sweet and delectable as in the dreams. Last night he'd felt them, watched her grope them, but hadn't gotten the chance to savor. Now he did. They pointed toward him, firm and round, tipped with excited pink nipples.

The gown sailed to the corner of the room where he'd thrown it, leaving Althea naked. Her hands went to her breasts, half-cupping and half-hiding. She was creamy, satiny perfec-tion. Graceful shoulders. Full breasts spilling out of small hands. Feminine belly and hips. Her legs were together, tilted to the side, hiding her auburn curls from his view.

Control stretched thin, Yannick moved over her and eased her down onto her back. Supporting his weight on his elbows, he pressed his body over hers. Skin to naked skin.

She slapped his hip. "No, tell me. Have you done something with another man?"

"Not deliberately, love." He grinned down at her. "In or-gies, in the tangle of bodies, I might have bumped a cock or two, or grabbed the wrong arse. But women have always been my preference. And you, angel, are the most delightful woman I've met."

She cocked a dubious brow. "So you weren't Zayan's lover?"

"Zayan?"

"He didn't kill you. He imprisoned you and I want to know why."

Naked and beneath him, she was boldly making demands. His grin grew larger. "I'll explain, sweet. Just not right now."

She reached up and slid her hands along his shoulders, awe and pleasure in her eyes as she stroked. For an inexperienced woman, she knew how to touch, knew how to make a man melt.

"But it is true that you always share your women with Bastien?"

Her husky voice rippled through him. How in hell did he answer that question? "Some women, yes."

"But not always."

Yannick shrugged. No, hell, he had shared every woman. Even the one he once believed was to be his alone. "Yes," he admitted, looking down into her shining emerald eyes, "I suppose Bastien is correct."

His story came spilling out and he couldn't believe he was telling her. She'd somehow seduced it from him without saying a word. Just by beneath him and gazing up at him with that curious, accepting, concerned gaze.

He was a vampire. A demon. The horrifying undead. And he couldn't resist falling under Althea's exquisite spell. Her nether curls were a warm, damp nest for his hard cock, and her breasts pushed against his chest. Lying over her, he bent, suddenly shy, and whispered against her ear, unable to see her eyes. Her hands slid around his back, and her touch spoke to him.

"We'd shared women since we first began stealing away to the haymows with country lasses. But when we reached fourteen, our father took us to a brothel. He thought we should learn our technique from an experienced courtesan, not enthusiastic dairymaids. The madam chose to tutor us herself, and brought us into her bedchamber together. As the eldest, I . . . had the first turn. In front of Bastien."

"At fourteen?" she gasped. Her lips grazed his neck and she brushed a kiss there. Her hands tightened on his back.

"In my father's world this wasn't so strange. He took part in orgies often and had fornicated in front of most of his friends. I was aroused but nervous and determined not to make a poor showing. I tried to last as long as I could. And she was a lovely woman, with large breasts and long shapely legs."

Her hands slid off his neck, where they'd been stroking. "Oh, I see."

Mistake. Damn, he knew better than that.

"Not anywhere near as lovely as you, sweet. But, to a boy . . . well, alas, I came in a half-dozen strokes. Being younger—by a quarter hour—Bastien always competed with me. So he rode her harder and longer than I did, hanging on to his climax for dear life. Watching my brother reach orgasm . . . knowing what he was feeling . . . listening to her grunt and moan beneath him . . . I was excited again and did my damnedest to outdo his performance. And of course he had another try. By the end of the night, the poor woman had been battered senseless. Though she seemed delighted by us. And then she drew us both down to her breasts by the scruffs of our necks. Together we licked and sucked her nipples. I was the first to slide my fingers into her. Bastien was furious I'd beaten him to it, so he played with her bottom, which made her squeal in ecstasy. And then we made love to her together, both buried inside her. After that night, all the courtesans wanted to have the both of us together in their beds. Which led to our nickname."

"The Demon Twins," she said hollowly.

"You are the only one I truly haven't wanted to share." That was the truth. He hadn't been exactly heartbroken over losing the woman he had planned to marry. He'd been enraged out of embarrassment, and fed up to discover that once again a woman wanted him for his title but had fallen in love with Bastien.

"Why not?"

He lifted his head to gaze into Althea's questioning eyes. "I don't know."

She touched his lips and a fetching smile played on hers. "Thank you."

She was a mystery, this lovely woman. How could an admission that he didn't know please her? He went to kiss her curved lips but she suddenly squirmed down beneath him. "What are you doing?"

She gripped his waist to wriggle lower.

"Sweetheart—"

Her tongue touched his stomach, skimming down the hollow there that followed the shape of his muscles. The tip dipped into his navel. At her hot, wet touch, all his blood rushed down to his loins.

"Roll over," she commanded. "I can't reach you like this."

"As you wish, angel." Obediently, Yannick fell over onto his back, only to discover he was on the very edge of the pitiful mattress. His foot shot out to catch him, striking the bare board floor. His right shoulder wasn't even on the bed but before he could move Althea rolled up beside him. Candlelight sculpted her into a goddess as she moved up onto her knees. All that tumbling hair shrouded shoulders and bare breasts. Corkscrew curls bounced over heavy-lidded, sultry green eyes.

For all his experience, he caught his breath like a callow adolescent as she leaned over him and her breasts swayed. He felt like an innocent himself as she brushed her long hair back from her mouth and held it clasped in her hand.

As her wet, parted lips neared the head of his cock, his heart hammered and raced like a mortal's. Need and raw hunger burned through him.

"Are you certain, love?" Lord, he wanted it but she was an

innocent, not the usual experienced lady proud to demonstrate her skill, hoping to capture his interest with a talented mouth.

"I want to give you a French kiss." Her amber lashes lowered. "I loved it so when you did it to me."

Her answer stole his breath. She wanted to show him the pleasure he'd given her. She wasn't thinking of seducing him for gain—she just wanted him to know delight.

She was a treasure. Unique.

Her lips were almost upon him. Even the whisper of her warm breath over the head shot lust through his cock, his ballocks, up his spine.

Did she no longer despise him for what he was?

Hell, he did. With brutal clarity, Yannick realized he couldn't let her give this to him. It meant too much to her. She cared about him, and he was a goddamned vampire destined to die. "No, sweetheart, don't."

"Don't?" Her eyes were all innocence.

He groaned as she licked her lips.

"Don't . . ." The last of his moral fiber dissolved. She was too tempting. Too beautiful. An angel he didn't deserve.

"Don't try to take it all in, sweeting. It's most sensitive around the head and you needn't take me in any farther than that."

"Indeed." Althea brushed back her wild hair again, like dark red velvet in the soft light. Her fingers brushed his pubic curls as her hand wrapped tightly around the base. "But wouldn't you like me to try?"

9

A French Kiss

Zayan heard the rhythm of wings and grinned in triumph. Anger and jealousy, the easiest emotions to evoke and the most potent, crackled in the night. Small stars gathered around the swooping bat. The blue lights darted and spun about, playful and ecstatic. His angels, drawn to the demon who had returned, whom they had long missed.

Zayan bent to the swooning girl in his arms and drew his tongue through the blood on her throat for one last taste.

Wings beat over his head, pausing over his offering.

For Bastien, would blood be more persuasive than sex?

The blue lights converged and shaped into sparkling females—demonesses made of stars like constellations in the heavenly skies.

Giggles and squeals surrounded Zayan as the demonesses took on human form. Long curling hair of every shade bounced in the night air, bewitching hips swayed, bare breasts jiggled.

"Bastien has returned," one squealed. Esmee, the youngest, with pale blonde hair. Another clapped her hands. Several joined hands and began to dance in a small circle.

Not for you tonight, little fairies.

Their fangs gleamed over pouting lips. Glowing red eyes narrowed. "Why ever not, master?"

Zayan waved his hand, irritated, and at his unspoken command they dissolved into stars again.

They lifted to the sky and flew with the bat.

Come to me, Bastien, he willed.

The air grew still before him and darker, as though all light and life were sucked from the spot. Even the rain ceased to fall there.

Only he could see the transition from creature to man. The twisting and stretching of dark form to flesh, the shriek of pain never heard by human ears.

"You wanted me, Zayan?" Cocky and arrogant and just as he remembered him, Bastien stood before him. Naked, beautiful, and thirsting for revenge.

It took him almost no conscious thought to control a spell, and Zayan lowered the intensity of the control he held over Althea's desires as he crooked his finger at Bastien. Tricky indeed, to leave his Trojan horse—Althea—open to just enough temptation to entice the twins, but not enough that she surrendered easily.

Battling over innocent Althea had divided the twins, just as he'd known it would. It made them foolhardy and stupid, the way mortal men became when they fought to spill their seed in a woman.

Bastien flashed his fangs. His legs were slightly spread, body coiled in attack stance, envy and rage pouring off him. "Go to Hades."

"Do you plan to send me there, Bastien?"

Faced with Yannick's long, swaying cock, Althea had no idea what to do. His prick should fill her with awe, or fear, or lust, but she couldn't help but think it looked adorable. Even in her dreams, she'd never been close enough to bestow a kiss. It stretched eagerly toward her mouth and looked rather earnest. The head was silky and taut and even possessed a beauty spot—a darker bronze-brown dot near its rim. At the very tip, clear liquid bubbled from a little eye.

So curious and amazing.

And when she glanced up at Yannick to see his expression, she giggled. He folded his arms behind his head. Excited and proud.

She traced the prominent veins with her fingertip. Her other hand rested at its hilt and encircled the shaft, though her fingers and thumb didn't meet.

A kiss. She could start with that. And a lick. Bastien had talked of women licking his cock and his ballocks.

All she could do was try.

She braced one hand on his slim hip, stuck out her tongue and touched him.

Ooh. Silky and smooth. Flattening her tongue, she roved over the head, and tasted the tang of his fluid, sticky on her tongue. Swampy, slightly sour.

Parting her lips, summoning the courage she always believed she possessed in spades, Althea slid her mouth over him. The hot, velvety skin of his cock filled her mouth. To her surprise, she discovered he truly tasted delicious.

"God your mouth is so hot and wet," he moaned. Warm and gentle, his hands slid along her back.

In answer to his loving caress, she cupped his ballocks. At once she understood why they called them balls. Within the soft sac, two firm eggs scurried from her touch. Cupping her palm, she held them delicately and explored the slightly reddened and bumpy skin. She toyed with the long hairs. Though he was white blond, the thick curls between his thighs were a dark gold.

She looked up. Caught Yannick staring at her, breathless

agony on his handsome features. Shy but pleased, she lowered her lashes.

"But you don't have to take me any deeper if you don't want—"

He broke off and another deep, rumbling moan rewarded her tentative suckling at the head. She saw his point. How did one take more into one's mouth? But she knew—from chattering maids, of course—that men liked to thrust deep when they made love.

Presumably he would like to be deep in her mouth.

Eyes shut tight, tense, she lowered upon him. Too far. Gagging, she lurched back.

A hand cuddled her nude bottom. "Are you all right, love? You don't have to do this."

She brushed at her tears. "I think I know what I did wrong."

"Sweetheart!" He laughed.

Then spluttered as she pursed her lips and took him in once more. Swirling with her tongue, she explored the plump curves of the head. His hips bucked as she flicked across a taut piece of skin that joined the crown to the thick shaft.

Now she felt bold. Daring. Why couldn't she improvise? Play? Perhaps he might not be impressed or well pleasured, but she had to learn at the beginning, didn't she?

Althea ran her tongue down the shaft and back up. Then tried the same trick with him inside her mouth. With a quick dip, she reached his curls with her lips and backed off before she could choke.

Perhaps she wasn't so bad at this after all. He was certainly moaning.

She sucked so hard her cheeks hollowed. To tease, she let him free so he fell out with a twang. "No, no," Yannick groaned in agony.

So she gobbled him up again.

He groaned and moaned and massaged her head. His arm

was tense. She sensed he really yearned to force her to take him deeper, but was trying to fight the need.

Her quim was soaking. Pleasuring him was surprisingly arousing. She gloried in the feel of him swelling more, growing even larger and harder and straighter. She fondled his balls. She wasn't afraid to be adventurous and she ran her hand over his firm, round buttocks. Goodness, they were rock hard. She dipped her fingers into the hot valley between his cheeks.

"Althea, sweetheart—"

He liked that, did he? She had no idea it could be such a delight to touch a man's buttocks.

Feeling confident and naughty, she drove her fingers into his cheeks, like a cat stretching its claws, and pulled him up to her to suck him deep.

"Althea, my wicked huntress, you have to stop."

Yannick caught hold of her chin and tried to coax her to stop. But the minx bobbed her head up and down on his throbbing cock.

It should be easy to hold on to his control, but innocent enthusiasm was more erotic than calculated skill. Sweet sounds rose from her throat, muffled by his cock. Happy little cries. Appreciative groans. She was moaning as though he was pleasuring her. A slurpy pop resonated as she backed off too far and released him. His balls clenched at the sound.

She scrambled back and took him into her hot mouth once more.

Her hot, sopping pussy rubbed and rocked against his thigh.

"No, Althea, you must stop," he begged through clenched teeth. "I'm going to come."

The saucy smile she gave him around his cock almost made him explode.

Sobering thoughts. He needed sobering thoughts, or he'd embarrass himself and damn well disappoint her.

Couldn't be anything more sobering than imminent death.

Yes, think of death, sickle in hand, bony fingers tapping impatiently, waiting to finally take him.

There'd be nothing to take though. If Althea didn't stake his heart first, he might survive to the rise of the full moon. When, if he didn't destroy Zayan, he'd end up as just so much dust. With no soul to carry on either upstairs or down.

Sobering indeed, but his cock was still as rigid as a blade, as impatient as an over-shaken bottle of champagne about to lose its cork.

He was pleading now. "No, sweet. Our fun would be over then. For a while, at least." He tugged gently at her chin. "Come up here."

"But you made me come with your mouth. Wouldn't you like the same?"

"You must know that men rarely have the luxury of many orgasms, angel."

She climbed up over him. Like a cat pacing in a spot of warm sun. "You can't . . . come more than once?"

"Ah, I can. Vampires can. But I fear your mouth would give me such an explosion that I'd not come to life again for a long while. We'd have to be patient and the sun might rise before I do." He crooked his finger. "Let me taste myself on your lips, angel."

Her sleek legs straddled his hips and he savored the sensual picture she made. Even in the dark her lush coloring was a treat to his vampiric vision. Long burgundy-red curls dangled over him, almost touching his chest. Passionate emerald eyes shielded by a thick fringe of lashes. Moist pink lips.

He'd condemned himself to death to have her.

Damnation, it was worth it.

Althea lowered and Yannick sank his fangs into his own lower lip as her hot weight settled on his shaft.

She kissed him, openmouthed and bold. She tasted of his cock.

Now. He needed her now.

She drew back, whispered against his mouth, "I need you."

Yes, angel. I need you now or I'm going to explode. Die. Burst.

I know, she moaned into his thoughts. *Me too.*

With infinite care he lifted her and tumbled her so she lay beneath him. God, he was so ready.

He had to shove hard on his cock to bend it down. The sensation was excruciating pleasure. Once he touched his tip to her bubbling entrance, he'd be lost.

He took a long, slow breath.

But in making love to her, he was going to hurt her. Should he take her now, while her lust drove her, while her need was so great? Or make her come a few times? Relaxed and sated, she might not grow anxious when he had to break her barrier. What made it easier for a virgin?

Her hips arched up to him. "Please."

Make her come, urged an inner voice. *You can't go wrong making her come.*

Two bolts of light shot from Zayan's upraised hands and smashed into his shoulders. Bastien staggered with the force but found his footing. He clenched his jaw against the pain. Being speared with a burning lance wouldn't hurt so much. Hell, he knew that for a fact.

Smoke curled up from his shoulders. He spared them a glance from the corner of his eye. His flesh was singed black.

In front of him, across the stretch of green common, the few lights of the village wavered and danced. Dazzling blue stars swooped around, nipping at Bastien's naked cock. He flicked them away.

He stood, unsteady, refusing to drop to his knees even as the pain surged through his bloodstream. His brain screamed with it. Over the shrieks tearing through his gray matter, he laughed. "Can you not do better than that?"

Another bolt—the two green streaks merged into brilliant red. He danced aside, but the missile followed and caught him on his left side. Below the heart but he heard his ribs snap like kindling.

His footing gave way and he couldn't stop his plunge to the ground. One knee hit and he fought to steady himself. Goddamn, he didn't want to bow down before Zayan.

Zayan's large, long-fingered hands lifted again. Red light flared from them, giving a hellish glow to Zayan's aquiline nose, the cliffs of his cheekbones, the full, firm curve of the master's mouth. The light barely touched the deep-set black eyes. The whites glowed though, rolling in the dark to follow him.

"Nice fireworks." Bastien shifted with care as his ribs began to knit. He felt the hum. The heat.

He knew the next blow would come low, directed at his head. For all his mocking, he wouldn't be able to shift shape fast enough—

The bolt of green energy sizzled beneath him as he launched himself in the air. He landed hard on his feet, but his muscles took it, shuddering. Instinct sent his right hand up into the air. He caught Zayan's red bolt in the center of his palm. It drilled into him, shoving his arm back so hard that his shoulder separated.

He almost retched with the shock of the pain. Hades!

Through sheer will, Bastien forced his shoulder to snap back. The click vibrated through his skull.

He couldn't fight by absorbing power. With Yannick, he could strike down Zayan. Alone, he could only struggle to survive, but after a decade imprisoned, he'd be damned if he just rolled over and let himself be scorched into oblivion.

Behind him the swooning girl lay in the dirt. Not a maiden.

His heightened sense of smell caught the whiff of another man's semen upon her. And the rich scent of her spilled blood curled up like the smoke from his wounds. Tempting him. Maddening him.

He wasn't an animal, to be betrayed by his lowest instincts.

He focused on Zayan. Triumph burned in his maker's black eyes. A feral smile tore apart the beautiful lips. Lips he'd kissed. Lips that had slid tight along his shaft, spurred by lust, passion, and need.

The long black hair, thick and straight, stirred about the pale, coldly handsome face.

Bastien shot a bolt of his own, directed at that smirk. Laughing, Zayan opened his lips and swallowed his power. The white throat glowed with blue light as the bolt shot down.

"Delicious."

Bastien lifted his hand to throw another, but his power did not obey his command. His skin sizzled, his muscles contracted, and nothing came. The first bolt had drained him too much.

Bastien tried to jump, to keep moving so he was not such an easy target. His weakened legs collapsed and he stumbled in the wet, uneven mud.

Zayan's eyes gleamed with satisfaction. "Your magic only feeds me."

A hand reached around Bastien's throat from behind, and nothing but the ancient oak stood before him. Zayan had jumped behind him before he'd even blinked. Long fingers closed tight, crushing his larynx.

He swung around. Drove his fist hard into the jaw of his maker.

Imprison me for ten bloody years—He struck the bone with a satisfying crunch.

You would have preferred destruction, my friend? Zayan's hand closed around his fist and yanked his arm down. Having thrown all his weight behind the swing, Bastien dropped to his knees. He sank in the muck.

To the hell of lying entombed like a true living corpse? Yes. He slashed at Zayan's wrists with his fangs.

A brilliant white flash exploded behind his back with the force of a cannonball. Zayan released his arm and he fell on all fours like a dog. And like a dog, he roared up, fangs bared and went for the throat.

The points ripped into the neck he'd once kissed. Before he could drink, before he could sink in deep, he sailed through the air and smacked the ground with a splash and a thud.

Zayan's broad, powerful body landed over him in a crouch. Slammed down by his maker's large hand, Bastien gulped for air. Zayan yanked a hank of his hair, forcing his head to the side. Baring his throat.

Even knowing he was about to die, Bastien couldn't stop his body from tightening with desire as Zayan's body covered his. Zayan's knee lifted and pressed against his balls. He tensed, waiting for his maker to drive his knee in, waiting for the pain.

Instead Zayan moved his knee teasingly, rocking it back and forth, and the threat stiffened Bastien's cock even more. Having his balls shoved upward was as torturous as having weights suspended from them. How many times had he been forced to submit to that erotic punishment for Zayan?

A humiliation that made him eager to attach the same weights to a submissive jade's erect nipples.

Hades, here he was, expecting to get both his balls crushed and his throat ripped out, and he couldn't resist calling up memories of pleasurable mastery. Of the last mistress he'd kept before he'd been entombed and how she had enjoyed such torture. How fascinated he had been when he discovered she had pierced her nether lips where he could hang weights or apply chains. He'd enjoyed shackling a woman's pussy to her bedposts.

He glanced up to see Zayan grinning at him. His gaze locked with Zayan's inscrutable black eyes.

His maker inclined his head. *I can see inside your thoughts, my friend. And indeed, I remember the girl with the pierced labia.* Zayan's right hand, fingers tipped with long, clawlike nails, scraped over Bastien's pecs. He felt his skin part, his blood well.

Interesting that you think about sex now.

How do you think I passed ten years of hell?

The two sharp tips of thumb and forefinger nails dug into his nipple. *I know how it was that you spent those hours of awakened imprisonment. I know of what you dreamed when you slept.*

Do you, you bastard?

I could not destroy you ten years ago. Zayan plucked at Bastien's erect nipple, twisting it with his fingers. Bastien dropped his head back, swallowing a moan. Balanced on long, lean legs, his maker reached down between their bodies. Bastien hated showing his arousal, but he couldn't control the groan that slipped out as Zayan's fingers wrapped around his naked cock.

Why didn't you destroy my brother?

A protected one? I think not. Fangs glinted, lips parted, and Zayan's long, pointed tongue flicked out to lick along his neck.

Bastien closed his eyes at the familiar, sensual stroke. Warm and wet, the tip stroked his artery up to his ear. Lust scorched a path down to his heavy cock, jacking it up off his belly. Zayan squeezed his knob hard and the knee shoved up, bunching his balls into a taut, smooth bulge.

He was about to die and what his goddamned body craved was a good hard fuck.

"Protected?" he rasped, as Zayan's tight grip dragged at his foreskin. What the hell was he doing? Why did it damn well matter why Yannick was alive? And why he was, since he wasn't going to be that way for long. But he had to know—

what made Yannick protected? He hadn't wanted his brother to be destroyed, but why, once again, was Yannick privileged when he was not?

Zayan rubbed his cock in a rhythm that sent the last of his blood draining from his brain. His maker's canines pressed against his neck, framing his pulsing artery.

Bastien knew what happened when a vampire drained the blood of another vampire. Ecstasy for the one with the fangs in the flesh. Agonizing destruction for the one giving up the blood.

After a decade of hell, he was going to die a torturous death.

"Yannick!"

He grinned into Althea's musky pussy as he rasped her hard clit with his tongue. Cradling her plump bottom, Yannick pinned her to the mattress with his mouth.

"But don't you . . ." She moaned. "Don't you want to . . . to make love to me?"

Yes, after you come for me. Once or twice.

"Twice!" Her hips arched up to his mouth. Her fingers raked through his hair. At her firm, massaging touch against his scalp, shivers raced down his spine.

Or more.

"I couldn't have more!"

Are you giving me a challenge? To prove to you how many orgasms you can have?

"I'd be afraid to give you a challenge," she whispered.

Simple words, but so intimate. Two nights together and they spoke as friends. Yannick had never felt so close to another woman. Yes, he'd bantered with other women, paid them compliments, flattered them, and made love to them. Learned their desires, their needs, the triggers to make them explode.

But he'd never felt this tug around his heart with any

BLOOD RED / 125

woman but Althea. Never felt his heart pound so hard while he made love. He'd never opened his heart to a woman.

He devoured Althea's sweet pussy, not caring any more about technique. All he wanted was to taste her. Savor her. Bury his face into her soaking cunny until he couldn't see, couldn't think, couldn't smell anything but her desire for him.

Against his cheeks, her inner thighs were hot silk. With a low, sensuous moan, she hooked her legs around his back.

Her heels rubbed hard into the base of his spine, slid down to caress his ass. His balls tightened at the pressure against his cheeks.

For an innocent, she was incredible. So innately sensual. Her hands and feet skimmed over his body, exploring, apparently enjoying. Throaty moans wrapped around him. Hers. And his. He moaned into her cunny.

He had to make her come. If he didn't, he was going to lose control.

"Yes," she hissed.

Yes, love. Come for me.

"A little harder. Just a little harder—"

He obeyed, but not enough, for she ground her hips into his face. Althea took control, clutched his head, and held him tight to her. He couldn't breathe and didn't care.

"Yes, yes, please." She banged her head back against the mattress. Fierce and wild. For a moment he stopped. He'd never had a woman go so wild beneath him.

She pushed hard on his head. "Please."

Yannick grinned and sucked hard on her clit. Delighted. Amazed. Now he saw the fierce vampire slayer inside the proper young lady.

She shoved her fist into her mouth. Her teeth sank into her knuckles.

Oh yes, angel. Let yourself burst.

She came. Lurched back and forth as the spasms took her. She sobbed and whimpered and the quiet sounds were more intense than a scream. She was pleading for mercy against the pleasure taking her. Pleading to heaven above.

He wasn't going to last to make her come twice with his mouth.

He rose over Althea, marveling at her beauty. Long lashes curled against bright pink cheeks. Beads of sweat dazzled on porcelain skin. Ethereal delight played on her face.

Her pussy pulsed against his cock, the muscles trying to draw him in. He remembered Bastien's mocking words from the dream: *You always did lose control first.* And when the tip of his cock parted her wet, slippery lips, he prayed the dream was no premonition, that he wouldn't burst too soon.

Her hands gripped his hips. Pulled him down so he slid in an inch. "Please."

Yannick took a ragged breath. *We have to take it slow, angel.*

Sweat broke out on his brow as he slid deeper. Her passage spread for him, just enough to cling tight to him. To hold him snugly in scalding, creamy fire.

He rocked his hips, withdrawing back to her entrance, pushing forward in her steamy core.

She arched back. *Yes.*

In the dreams, Bastien had gone for her throat. He couldn't do that. Couldn't forcefully turn her. But could he make her want to become a vampire? Capture her heart, make her desire him for eternity?

He could not give her eternity. But God, yes, he wanted to capture her heart. And his own pounded at the thought. Never had such a need taken him before sex. The curve of her throat was a mere inch from his fangs. All he had to do was bite—

Her trusting eyes gazed up at him. "I just feel like . . . like I want you deep inside. To fill me. Now. I think . . . I've heard . . . it's better if you just . . . um . . . plunge in."

Plunge in? He couldn't stop himself now—

Pain lanced through his body, so sudden and shocking that he cried out.

"Yannick?"

Althea's eyes widened with fright, but he couldn't answer her. Couldn't speak. Burning pain hit him everywhere.

I'm going to die.

The thought wasn't his.

"What's wrong, Yannick? What happened?"

He heard her terror. Of course, she'd be scared and horrified. He'd been about to make love to her. Now he was fighting the pain racking him. Struggling not to cry out.

Take my blood then. Get it the hell over with.

A cold emptiness gripped Yannick's heart. His back felt cold. Wet. As though he lay in a bath of ice water.

Before his eyes, Althea's face blurred. He fought to see her, to focus on her wide eyes and her moving lips. From the corners of his eyes, a searing white light blossomed. No matter how hard he blinked or shook his head, the white patch grew, like spreading water. Until Althea disappeared. His eyes were wide open but he couldn't see her anymore.

"Yannick! Please!"

He could hear her but as though she was far away. But he knew she was yelling at him, not caring if everyone else in the Inn knew he was in her bed.

All she worried about was him.

He was touching her, but the sensation of her warm skin against his fingertips faded. Numbness slid upward from his fingers, leaving him disconnected. Lost.

Yannick? Yannick?

Not Althea's soft, pretty voice. The desperate rasp in his

head belonged to Bastien. He heard his twin's thoughts. Tasted anger and fear, felt them run hot in his blood.

He knew what happened when a vampire drained the blood of another vampire.

Instinct sent him lurching back. Dimly he felt his pulsing cock leave Althea's heat. Had he left the bed? Was he standing? Where was he?

"Althea?" Yannick couldn't even hear his own voice. Could she?

Darkness. The night sky. The hiss of rain. Mud. The thick stink of mud surrounded him. Rivulets of rain ran beneath his soaked and frozen body. Voices approaching. Somewhere the glimmer of lamplight, rising and falling with men's steps. Boots slopping in mud. Weapons—hefted as men marched.

He turned his head—or maybe Bastien turned his head. A girl sprawled by him, her skin stark white. A white bodice was pulled low over voluptuous breasts. Stained dark. Soaked with dried blood. Blood covered her neck and shoulders like a shawl. The eyes—open? Sightless? Closed.

"Yannick?" Althea's voice pleading. He reached out to her.

Hit a hard chest. Satin beneath his fingertips, smooth and shimmering. And blood-red.

Raven's blood. The rage in London. An accented voice. Deep and throaty. Elegant. Mocking.

With a sucking drain that left his head pounding, all his thought focused on his cock. On a hand stroking the shaft.

Althea? Hoping to rouse him by sexual pleasure?

A *large* hand. Big fingers. Sharp fingernails.

He opened his eyes wide, but all he could see was white and dark. Golden strands drifted across his eyes. He focused hard. Hair. Fair hair.

Not Althea's. Nor his.

Bastien's.

Bastien? In his mind, Yannick shouted his brother's name. Again and again.

He'd never connected with Bastien like this. They were twins, and had always possessed a special bond. Even before he became a vampire he could seem to speak to Bastien through their minds. But he'd never seen through his brother's eyes before.

He moaned. No, Bastien moaned. A hoarse shudder of sensual need and anger at his weakness. Yannick felt a weight on top of him, felt breath puff over his neck. Starched collar points grazed his skin. Male scents surrounded him—the unique aroma of another man. Clean skin. Cedar imbued in the dress clothes. A trace of sweat. The tang of leaking fluid soaking into small clothes.

The coppery promise of fresh blood.

He had a man lying atop him. A man playing with his—no, Bastien's—prick. Long black hair spilled over his cheeks and mouth as the man licked his neck.

Zayan. In his guise as a man. The only clue he wasn't human was the long fangs Yannick felt pressed against his neck.

He was trapped deep in Bastien's mind. Joined with his twin, he felt his hand slide down, just the way Bastien's was doing. As though, like Bastien, he had managed to reach between his body and Zayan's and grip the vampire's erection through perfectly tailored trousers.

Zayan's guttural groan echoed in his mind.

The connection was too deep. The bond too strong. He needed to force his mind to step back. To see his surroundings.

He must break the link to have a chance of saving Bastien.

But against his fingertips, Yannick felt the resistance of fabric. Sharing Bastien's thoughts, he ripped the placket wide and dug in his hand. His fingers scraped along the long, erect shaft as he shoved in. Until he was buried in Zayan's linens past his wrist and his fingers were wrapped around Zayan's balls.

Hairless and smooth. Freshly shaved and done with lather and a goddamned straight razor.

Bastien's voice, awed, heavy with lust, rippled through Yannick. He followed Bastien's stroke, the hot weight of Zayan's rigid pole lying across his palm. He couldn't break the link. Not with his emotions—fear, fierce arousal and hunger—so deeply entwined with Bastien's.

He was wanking a demon's cock. And enjoying it. An answering stroke slid along his own prick, as real as though a hand played with him, and his head swam.

The tips of Zayan's fangs teased along the length of his windpipe. Teased him with death.

"I'll make you come first," Bastien's voice rose in challenge.

Even facing destruction, his twin had to jeer. Dread gripped Yannick's pumping heart. In their mortal lives, he'd seen Bastien insult his opponent on a dueling field until the man was in uncontrollable rage. More than once. Bad aim, shaking arms, and sheer luck had kept Bastien alive past his twenty-fifth birthday.

Yannick tensed. The fangs would plunge. Linked mentally with Bastien, would he feel the pain? Would he experience destruction?

"Yannick! Yannick! What's happening to you?"

A hot mouth surged against his, a wet tongue delved in. Silky curls danced against his chest. Lavender and roses flooded his senses.

Althea.

Relief swept through him as he tasted her sweet mouth on his. He had to break free—

Bastien's voice pleaded in his mind. *Yannick. Don't leave me.*

10

Possessed

Althea wrapped her arms tight around his strong neck and kissed him as hard as she could.

Yannick! Please, please, please talk to me! Respond to me!

If this didn't break the spell, then what? Her arms ached from shaking him. He was so large, so muscular and heavy, she could barely budge him. Even while she'd rained stinging blows on his chest, he'd stayed lost to her.

His large, black-lashed, silver eyes stared directly at her. But didn't see her.

Yannick, come back to me. Hold me. Kiss me back.

She pushed hard against his chest. Her breasts pressed flat against hard planes wet with sweat. She ran her hands all over him. Slippery moisture coated him. Goosebumps also.

Her body wouldn't warm him. Not enough.

He stood at the window, facing the night sky beyond. She'd raced around him to plant herself between him and the window. Afraid he'd fly away.

"Zayan." The name tumbled from his lips in a raw whisper.

Zayan had possessed his mind?

How could she break him free?

First, she wanted to drag him from the window and back to bed. Though she hated to let him go, she had no choice. Praying he wouldn't shift shape, she untwined her arms from his neck and dropped down from her tiptoes. Cold, wet air poured in through her open window. Turning on her heel, she leapt to it and shoved down the open sash. Across the common—an endless sea of formless black—she saw small dots of light.

Father and his hunters.

The window crashed into place and she turned the lock.

Even if Yannick became a bat, he couldn't fly through glass.

But would he destroy himself trying? Would he beat against the pane, unable to stop?

No, she'd prevent that somehow. The vow gave her a burst of courage as she swung back to Yannick.

What was he doing? Startled, Althea watched as his hand slid over the sculpted muscles of his stomach. She stared, strangely hypnotized, as he took hold of his erect member and roughly massaged the head. In a heartbeat, desire rushed back through her. Her legs shook with it, ached with it. He touched himself more harshly than she'd ever dare. Her breath caught.

Until she saw his eyes. Wide, unmoving, unblinking.

She grabbed his free hand and tried to move the unmovable. She'd have better luck trying to pull a reluctant horse.

She tugged hard.

He lurched forward, took a step, and she sobbed at her success.

Another step and another.

"Althea."

Her name again. He was whispering her name again.

Yannick, yes, it's Althea. I'm here for you. She pulled hard. Her calves hit her bed at the same instant Yannick's weight moved once more and she toppled. Her free arm flailed and she caught a glimpse of his expression before she plunged backward onto her mattress.

Surprise, concern, and a sudden relief flashed across his gorgeous features. Then his shin collided with the bed frame with a loud crunch and he fell too. One arm swung wide. Even his cock seemed to lurch to and fro.

His weight hit her and all the breath left her chest.

"*Urgh!*" She gasped.

He shifted immediately, lifting his massive chest. She sucked in air.

Thank God. Thank God. Thank God he was back.

Or was it God she should thank? Yes, it must be. For Yannick was not a vampire as she knew the creatures—

"Althea, angel, are you all right?"

He was worried about her? That was his first thought? With her throat so tight, she couldn't answer. She clasped her hands to his cheeks.

She wanted to hold him tight as though that would protect him.

"Zayan was inside your mind, wasn't he?"

He caught her hands and lifted them. He had her arms stretched up above her head and she was completely imprisoned by him. Her heart beat in a frantic rhythm and she squirmed beneath him. Being a captive was indisputably exciting.

"No, angel," he said, his voice heavy. "My mind was linked with Bastien. And Zayan caught him."

She was instantly sobered and ashamed. "Did he . . ." She couldn't bear to ask the question, to find out. This was entirely her fault. If she'd let Bastien stay . . . By defying the dreams, had she sent Bastien to his death?

And because it was her fault, she must face the truth with courage. "Did Zayan destroy him?"

Yannick released her hands and moved off her. "I don't know, sweet. You broke into the connection."

She covered her mouth in horror. "Oh! I'm sorry, I—"

He gave her a tender smile as he sat up, nude and glorious in the sputtering candlelight. "I'm relieved you did. I don't know what would happen to me—to my mind—if Bastien were blasted while we were connected by the link."

"He could be dead."

Yannick stood still for several moments and her heart sank to her toes.

He shook his head. "No, he's not dead. We're twins and even if we aren't linked, we can sense each other. It's like a second heartbeat inside my chest. I know he's still alive, but his mind is closed off to me."

"Why? What does that mean?"

He raked his hand through his white-blond hair. "It might mean that he's deliberately not opening his mind to me. Or that he is too weak to. Or that he's shifted shape."

"But you can sense him?"

"His life force, yes. Which means I can sense where he—"

Yannick had to break off. The connection flooded back to him with such force he had to put his hand against the wall to stay standing.

Once again he could see through Bastien's eyes.

A manor house, completely dark. Weathered stone and grimy windows and a sagging portico, all buried within a riot of trees and shrubs. The door, a massive slab of oak, hung open and the inside was as dark and quiet as the outside, but he sensed life within. Mortal heartbeats, slow, steady breathing, and pumping blood.

The vision faded and the connection broke. He searched again, reaching out through the dark, but nothing came back to him.

"Is he telling you something? Can you hear him again?"

He looked back at Althea, sitting up now, nude and delectable on her meager, tousled bed. Her eyes were wide with concern and fear—for both him and Bastien. She reached out and touched his naked back.

Sourly, he wondered if Bastien had decided to joust with Zayan just to disrupt his night of pleasure. In their mortal lives, Bastien would have been willing to take a ball in the heart if it would have hurt, irritated, or goaded him in some way. Bastien used to joke that his lordly brother would be the one to shoot him—over a woman. And when they were both dead drunk, there were a few times when his twin had come bloody close to goading him that far.

He'd always stopped before he pulled a blade or a pistol, even if Bastien hadn't.

Tonight was no different.

Shyly, Althea covered her breasts and the sight of her hands on them was pure temptation. "Yannick?"

Her legs parted slightly to display her thick, burgundy curls, topped by glistening droplets of her honey and his saliva.

Yannick took a ragged breath, which only filled his lungs with her scent.

Control. He needed control. But lust raged through him with a force he'd never known.

"I saw—" Damnation, his voice was shaking. Even when he'd been whipped, he'd never let his voice shake. "I saw through his eyes, pet, which means he still lives."

She brushed some of that tumbled hair back from her face. "Thank heaven."

"Indeed."

Leave her? Was he mad? *Crawl back into that bed, spread her legs, and bury your poor, aching prick in her to the hilt.*

The urge rose against his will. His cock and balls hurt like the devil. As for his lengthened, throbbing fangs—shots of fire rang through his jaw and reverberated through his brain. His body screamed for satisfaction.

Frustrated sexual excitement did not sit well with a vampire.

One last little taste. Just one. Of her lips, her nipples, her wet quim. He didn't care which. Or a sampling of all three.

One taste or three wouldn't satisfy him and well he knew it. Give in and he'd find himself in her bed at sunrise, with his brother lost to him.

Would Bastien save you if you were in his place?

Likely not, but Yannick sighed from deep in his chest as he got up from the bed.

He'd saved his twin's arse more than a dozen times, yet he'd never gotten more than anger for his trouble. Not even grudging gratitude. Each time he hauled Bastien from disaster, his brother only found worse trouble.

Smugglers. Duels. Opium dens. And finally vampires.

Stay with her.

He couldn't. And Althea was swinging her bare legs over the side of the bed. "I am going to come with you."

"No, you bloody well are not."

With a groan of heartfelt pleasure, Bastien sank back into the tub. Steaming water lapped at his naked chest and the curls plastered against his body. The trailing ends of his hair lay slick against his back.

The claw-footed porcelain tub was so enormous he could submerge himself completely if he wished. He tipped his head back, resting his neck on the smooth rim. Shut his eyes.

Where in Hades was Yannick? Ignoring him and fucking the lovely Althea, he'd wager.

He groped for the soap on the small table by the bath.

Behind him the door creaked open. Bastien cracked open an eyelid. Sparkling blue stars spun into the room. The glittering lights pirouetted and dipped and darted in an ecstatic dance.

The bedchambers of Zayan's manor held lamps and candles, but none were lit. No light came in through the windows, although the drapes were wide. Rain drummed against the glass and the thick cloud blocked out all moonlight.

The blue stars circled his tub.

"Come to give me a last night of carnal delights before my execution?"

Melodic voices danced through the quiet dark. "We wish to help you bathe, master."

The stars exploded in a shimmer and the force set his water sloshing over the edges.

Six nude demonesses appeared, standing in a ring around the tub. Head tipped back, Bastien took in the delightful view. A dozen pert breasts surrounded him. A dozen long, lovely legs led up to generous bushes of blond and dark curls. Six pairs of reflective eyes flashed at him and six lush mouths pouted, wet, moist and inviting.

But his cock, immersed in the hot water, stayed limp and uninterested. All the women were beautiful, three blonde and three dark-haired, but not one could compare with Althea's sparkling innocence.

Still, he gave each a welcoming grin and stretched his arms out along the edges of the tub, cake of soap in hand.

"Esmee." He crooked his finger. Esmee possessed the most voluptuous figure of them all, with enormous breasts, a nipped-in waist that he could span with one stretched hand, and generous hips.

She dropped an obedient curtsy that set her breasts jiggling. "My lord de Wynter—"

"Not *lord*, sweet demon. That's my brother."

"You are *my* lord," Esmee cooed as she lowered to her knees at his side. Her blond, curling hair dipped into the water. Her large breasts dangled over the tub's rim. As she leaned forward, the mounds plumped against the porcelain, then spilled over, plopping into the water. She gave a little squeal that he answered with a rough laugh.

"And am I to be the fortunate one to wash you?" she purred.

Steam swirled around her, veiling pale breasts and erect nipples, golden ringlets and her pretty face. The illusion of comely sweetness was marred only by fangs and glowing red eyes.

Bastien lifted his leg and propped his foot on the wet rim. "*You* may start."

Disappointed female sighs echoed in the room but he couldn't flatter himself. Each alluring demoness was a succubus. Each craved his semen and his blood with equal enthusiasm.

Esmee began to move down to the end of the tub.

"No. Don't move beyond the reach of my hand and face your bottom toward me."

She did so, wriggling her voluptuous arse all the while. Her soapy fingers slithered over the sole of his foot, her touch skilled and loving. No mortal man could resist her.

Female moans rose in the air as he gave Esmee a slap upon all that plump flesh. She shoved her bottom back toward him, so he could cup and caress.

The moment he lifted his other foot, a dark-haired, dark-eyed beauty took her place on that side. Lithe and slender, she possessed taut, small buttocks, temptingly pert. A joy to spank, he decided, as his palm smacked with a satisfying clap.

He lightly spanked their bottoms with the flat of his hand until their pale cheeks flushed pink. It took a fair bit of coordination but he slipped both his hands down at the same instant and parted heated, sticky lips. Plunging two fingers in their wet quims, he stroked their anuses as best as he could with his thumbs.

They sighed and moaned and rocked on his hands.

But he watched with dispassion. With a sense of distance he could not seem to overcome. His cock should be so erect it stood up from the water like the fin of a shark. Instead it had swollen somewhat but it was still floppy and stirred with the moving water.

The scent of female excitement filled the room and Bastien couldn't draw breath without flooding his lungs with it. Soft sighs and whimpers came from every direction and he detected the distinct sucking sound of fingers ardently playing with soaked pussies.

For ten years, he'd lain in that coffin, unable to move. But his cock had not been dormant. Each night it had stood up to attention. And he hadn't even been able to move his hands to attend to it. Given an abundance of willing female flesh on his first night of freedom, his cock should be making a better showing.

Never in his life had he experienced a recalcitrant member.

And he didn't just risk disappointing the excited demonesses. If he were unable to satisfy them, they'd tear at him with their fangs. Still weak from Zayan's blasts, he wouldn't be able to fight them off.

Was this his maker's plan? Destroy him through an orgy? He laughed at that. A fitting way to kill him.

Facing only a few more minutes of existence, he needed a plan. Instead, he thought of Althea. In Yannick's arms. Crying out in pleasure at his brother's thrusts.

His semi-erect cock wilted to a sorry state.

Blast.

He remembered Althea in his arms, her plump bottom squashing his cock—which had then been impressively rigid. Memories flooded. Lavender on her soft skin. The smooth, pale beauty of her throat. Pretty breasts straining at her maidenly bodice. The silky texture of her nether lips. The rich, unique color of her pubic curls.

His cock returned to half-mast.

Althea. He called her name in his mind, but was given no answer, of course. *Little dove.*

Althea was lovely, but her true allure was within. The breathy way she responded to his sensual scenarios. How desperately she tried to be shy and maidenly, even when he could smell her desire and hear the frantic rush of her blood.

His blood shot down to his cock with the speed of horses leaving the starting line at Newmarket.

Finally, he sported a satisfactory erection, and before it could betray him by slipping away, Bastien rose, water sluicing off him. Esmee clasped his hand and the dark-haired demoness took tight hold of his forearm and they almost dragged him from the bath. Propelled forward, he swung his leg fast over the side and staggered out. "Patience, ladies."

The others ran to him, three carrying thick towels. He'd not been rubbed down so vigorously since he was a boy in the nursery. One dried his hair with diligence until the long strands were in a tangle around his head. And those without towels explored his clean, slightly damp skin with eager hands.

A demoness took his now hard cock in between two palms. Another clasped his balls. And one dropped to her knees behind him and flicked her tongue around the rim of his clean anus.

He should be mindless with the need to fuck but he wasn't. Damn. Abruptly, he grabbed the one who held his cock—a vixen with wide eyes that glowed red and a shroud of straight brown hair. Without words, he splayed his hand over her bare, smooth back and pulled her to him. His cock had softened ever so slightly, so he was forced to take hold of it to guide it to her.

Her arms shot around his neck. Other hands tweaked his nipples, toyed with his ballocks, teased his arse.

Bastien closed his eyes to block out fangs and hellishly bright eyes and imagined Althea in his arms.

A loud clap broke into his fantasy, just as he touched the tip of his prick to her wet pussy lips.

"Enough, my beauties. Leave him for me."

* * *

Althea struggled into her gown. "Oh no, Yannick. I am going with you."

"Bothersome thing!" she snapped at her dress. She was standing on the hem, which made it nigh on impossible to tug the thing up high enough to slide her arms in the sleeves. She shoved her spectacles back up her nose.

"No, you are most certainly not. I can find him much more quickly if I shift shape."

Althea saw how fortunate it had been that she'd closed and locked the window. Yannick wasn't able to shift shape and fly directly out into the night. He had to wait at least long enough to stalk to the window and struggle with the lock.

Of course, he was much stronger than she was and he forced the lock open with a loud scrape. He reached for the sash, then turned back. "You will only be an encumbrance."

"Well, by all means, you should hurry to your destruction! How do you plan to fight Zayan if you are alone, my lord?"

Her angry demand served its purpose. Instead of changing shape, Yannick paused. His dark brow rose over suddenly piercing silver eyes. "My lord?" he repeated.

"Well, you are a lord, aren't you? Decreeing to me, chock full of noble arrogance! I shan't stand by and let you face that monster unarmed." Her fingers fumbled with the buttons, and she left a few at her stomach and a few at her neck unfastened. Since she was nude underneath, she displayed quite a bit of bare skin, but the pertinent ones were done, at least.

"And what do *you* plan to throw at Zayan?" he asked.

The condescending tone of his regal voice set her teeth on edge. "You threw your power at him, but it didn't stop him. My stake drove him back."

In blind haste, she stuck her feet into her half boots—the wrong ones, of course. Not bothering to kick them off, she ducked beneath the bed and pulled out her valise.

"You are the bravest woman I have ever met, Althea, but your stake did naught, love. Zayan retreated for reasons of his own."

"The scream he let out when I plunged it in still rings in my ears."

Yannick stared at her case as she tossed it onto the bed. "He can't be destroyed like other vampires." He spoke slowly, as though considering. Then he looked up and she flinched at the fury in his fierce silver eyes. "Was your father going to have you help him go after Zayan? Did he intend to put you in that much danger?"

"I hunt vampires. I am not afraid to face Zayan."

"You bloody little fool." He crossed to her in an instant and caught hold of her wrist. Tight enough to hurt. She refused to wince but she tried to wrest free.

"Do you want the truth? *I* fear Zayan. How could your father put you in such jeopardy? And how could you go throwing yourself into danger that you don't even understand? You've not got the sense you were born with."

The insult stung. So this is what he thought of her? She stopped struggling and gaped at the unyielding planes of his face. He had no respect for her as a hunter at all. He thought her nothing more than a foolish woman. Adequate to lie on her back and please him.

"Father planned to send me to London."

"London would be an excellent place for you."

She chose to ignore that. "To find a husband. Which, even if I had the desire to do it, I certainly could not now, could I? Not after what I've done with you."

He ran his hand—the one not gripping her wrist like a vice—over his strong jaw. "You *are* still a virgin."

She had a free hand too and she put it to good use. Her slap to his cheek rang out in her room. Her hand stung from the blow but she forced herself not to wince. And the moment her hand had bounced back, she'd regretted what she'd done.

He hadn't even flinched, of course. Not that she'd expected him to. Her goal had not been to hurt him. It had been to communicate what she couldn't think of words to express.

The pain at his casual dismissal of what she'd begun to feel for him.

At least he let her wrist go. Even by candlelight Althea could see her palm was pink—a match to his cheek. But she ignored both and pointed at the case. "Open that and choose your weapons."

"This is mad," he snapped, but he crossed to her bed as she exchanged boots and hooked the laces around the eyes as fast as she could.

"Locked." He cursed and she left her bow to attend to that, but the arrogant wretch broke her locks before she could produce the key.

"If I chase around the countryside with you, I'd have to dress," he pointed out, rifling through her stakes and her folding cross bow. "More wasted time."

"Arguing is significant wasted time." She tied hurried bows in her laces.

"I doubt any of these will stop Zayan."

Althea plucked the controlling collar from the floor. It hadn't stopped Bastien. She doubted it would be effective against a vampire infinitely more powerful. And she was likely not pure enough to use it. But it might slow Zayan down once he was wounded, and she couldn't discount any weapon out of hand.

Ingenuity and quick thinking played a most important part in vampire hunting. "And why do you need to dress?" she snapped as she gathered her hair into a messy bun at the base of her neck.

"We'll take all of your bloody weapons. Wait here, you

exasperating wench." And with that, Yannick stalked out the door.

Naked.

Into a public hallway.

Well, she had in essence dared him, hadn't she?

There were no horrified shrieks from women or startled shouts from men. As she closed her case—leaving the now useless locks open—she heard a door slam.

Would they find Bastien still alive? Were they too late? Was she utterly mad to race headlong into danger?

Father would kill her once he knew. Fortunately for her, she thought wryly, she would very likely be dead already.

Her door burst open and Yannick stood there. Blond hair disheveled, face set in barely restrained fury. Clothed, though he'd done it as sparsely as she had. Wrinkled trousers were stuffed into boots. His shirt flowed loose beneath his cloak.

"Are you ready?" he barked.

Althea lifted her valise and stormed toward him. "Of course, my lord. Lead the way."

11

Entombed

"I can feel a pulse, but it is terribly weak. Can you help her?"

Despite their argument, Althea felt deep relief as Yannick squatted down at her side, large and dominant and strong. He laid his fingers against the girl's throat and Althea moved hers to allow him access to the pulse.

She couldn't help but shudder. Dried blood coated the girl's throat and chest. A dark rusty stain covered most of her bodice.

"Is it too late for her?"

Yannick dropped one knee into the wet earth and bent close to the exposed bone-white neck. "Her wound was closed—the lick of a vampire's tongue will seal a wound."

"Was—was it Bastien, do you think?"

Yannick sat back and raised his wrist to his mouth.

"You will feed her your blood?"

"A little. It will give her more strength to mend. Lying in this wet field has done nothing to help her, but my blood should protect her from fever."

Sheeting rain pummeled through Althea's pelisse and soaked into her bonnet. Her skirts sunk a little lower into the mud, but she didn't care. The poor girl. She couldn't be much more than sixteen. Her breasts, accentuated by the clinging bodice, were lush and mature, but her face appeared so young. Bow-shaped lips and a tiny upturned nose. Baby-fat cheeks. She wore the soft, trusting expression of sleep.

Why hadn't Yannick answered her question? "Was it Bastien?"

Yannick opened the girl's mouth and smeared his blood over her tongue. "He wouldn't waste her blood like this."

What a gruesome thought. "She can't drink, can she?"

"Once she's had a taste, I will let it run into her mouth. I have to be careful—don't want her choking on it." He glanced up. "Don't worry, angel. She won't die. She'll be courting danger again in no time at all."

When their eyes had met, all her remaining irritation had melted and her heart had skipped several necessary beats. But at his words, her anger rose all over again. "It is hardly her fault that a *vampire* attacked her."

Her tone, of course, held every condemnation for his kind.

But he just smiled, showing fangs. "She's a country lass. A vivacious vixen from the looks of her. I expect she came out here to meet a man for a tumble and got something quite different than what she bargained for."

"I don't understand. You mean a man—a mortal man—did this to her?"

"No, I believe Zayan did this to her."

"Yet he didn't drink her blood."

"She was his bait, angel."

"How did you know to look here?"

Absorbed in his task of squeezing his blood into the poor victim's throat, he didn't answer. She tried not to shudder as she watched. The thought of his blood flowing so freely made her head dizzy. "How did—"

"I heard you, sweeting." His voice swept over her like the

icy winds of the Carpathians. "What are you implying by that? That I did this?"

"No. I never even considered that." She truly hadn't and the idea struck her as horrific.

"But now you are thinking it is a perfectly plausible idea, aren't you?"

"No. I imagine if you had done this—which would have been before you came to my room—she would be dead."

"True enough," he allowed and his voice thawed. "I saw the common here through Bastien's mind. Enough detail to recognize the spot."

He drew his wrist from the girl's mouth and Althea saw the girl's throat move slightly, with the distinct motion of swallowing. Then again. The chest rose and fell with stronger determination.

Althea sat back on her heels with a sigh of relief.

Yannick unclasped his cape at his neck. "To wrap her in. Hers is soaked through."

Her heart quickened at his concern, his kindness to this poor victim, as he cast his cloak onto the ground. But he must do this too when he fed.

"You're thinking that I do this when I feed, aren't you?"

She gulped as he spoke her exact thoughts and wondered how horrified she looked. "I . . . I've never seen you drink blood."

"I do, I promise you. But I've never killed for it." Yannick scooped the girl up so gently he seemed more of a knight in shining armor than a demon. He laid the girl on it and wrapped the cape around her.

Althea helped swaddle the girl's legs. "Now, we need to get her to inside. To the Inn, do you think? I've no idea who she is or where she lives."

He nodded. "Could you—no, you can't move her alone, can you?"

"You want me to take her to shelter while you pursue Zayan alone." Blast him, he was determined to be rid of her. Was it truly only for her safety? Or because he didn't believe she was capable of hunting vampires? Pride pricked, she demanded, "What if you take her to the Inn and I pursue Zayan?"

"And I don't doubt you'd do it, feisty wench. But how would you know where to go?"

"You could tell me, my lord, couldn't you?"

To her surprise, he gave a rueful chuckle. "I'm not exactly certain. I can see a manor house, probably once the home of a baronet. Badly in need of repair."

She had only been in Maidensby for a few days but had taken care to learn what she could about the small village. "Chatham Manor is nearby. I've never seen it, but I do know that the family died out. And the house has just been let."

"And how did you learn all this?"

She preened at the admiration in his tone. "Chatter amongst the maids at the Inn yesterday as to the appearance, age, and financial situation of the new tenant." She stroked the girl's cold cheek. "It must be Zayan."

"So where is it?" Yannick straightened so he was looking down on her. Rain pelted into his hair, his white shirt, his trousers.

"We are at an impasse, aren't we, my lord? You can't leave this poor child out here, and you need me to show you to the house."

He slicked back his dripping hair. "You could run back to the Inn and get help."

"And calmly inform Crenshaw the girl was bitten by a vampire?"

"Why not? He must wonder at the real purpose of your father's late-night procession."

"I suspect the whole village does," Althea said. "But I am going with you."

"You're soaked through," he pointed out as he dropped to one knee again. She could barely see him, even so close, but she heard the squish of his boots in the mud as his wet hand cradled her chin. "You need to get inside and warm up."

Her wet, bedraggled bonnet stuck to her cheeks and cold rivulets poured over her lips. When she parted her lips, her teeth chattered. "You're drenched yourself."

"But it won't kill me. I won't develop a fever."

"Well, you can just feed me your blood and protect me, can't you?"

She heard his breath catch.

"What? You can, can't you? You've fed my father and this girl. Why wouldn't you feed me?"

"I would, sweeting. To save your life." He raised her by her hand and she shook out her wet skirts. "And I don't need you to lead me to Chatham House. I can hear Bastien, which means he's alive and he can tell me where he is. Now get your lovely backside down that hill and to the Inn."

She had no choice but to obey his rude, condescending command. Not unless she risked letting the poor girl die. Perhaps he was deliberately making her annoyed with him so she would willingly let him go to his destruction. She couldn't be truly angry at him, not when he'd saved the girl's life. Beneath the nobleman's arrogance, beneath the predatory nature of the vampire, was a kind-hearted man.

And she couldn't let him face such danger alone. But he wouldn't be alone; he would be with Bastien and together the Demon Twins could defeat Zayan.

She had to believe that, but she desperately needed to kiss him before he left. She wanted to hold him tight, touch his face, memorize its every plane. For just a minute, before he had to go.

But as Althea arched up on tiptoe to reach his lips, she saw him stare over her head. She spun around to follow his gaze and spied a lantern at the very top of the common. A lantern that suddenly began bobbing toward them. Father, possibly, or O'Leary or one or more of his workmen. It was true that Father had abandoned discretion by rounding up workmen to aid in his hunt. She suspected most were drunk by now after downing spirits to keep them warm and occupied. The moving lantern did seem to weave back and forth—as though carried by a shaking arm on an unsteady man.

She caught hold of Yannick's arm and heat surged through her at the contact with his solid, muscled arm, even through his soaked coat and shirt, even though she was frozen stiff.

He looked down at her, so close they could kiss if she just stretched an inch more, but she flinched at the low chuckle she heard. How could he be amused by vampire hunters? Even though Father wouldn't hurt him, a dozen drunken uncontrollable louts with axes and shovels could kill him.

"You must get away," she urged. "Go now." A plan began to form. She knew exactly where he was going; she could return to the Inn, then follow.

Yannick's long-suffering sigh broke into her thoughts. He cupped her chin and tipped up her face. Rain splattered her cheeks as he searched her eyes with his silver gaze. "I can guess the plans running through your mind, sweet angel, and I fear that the only way I can feel you are safe is to keep you in eyesight at all times."

"Then take me with you," she breathed with triumph. Then guilt and compassion surged. "But what about the girl? We—I—can't leave her."

He smiled. "A quick entrance into the thoughts of those men will bring them here to help her. We can escape now and leave her to them."

"But—"

"I can also erase their memory of us."

"Perfect." Althea moved back to allow him to concentrate,

though she missed the comfort and the intimacy of having his hand cradling her face. She waited. Was he doing it?

An urgent demand that he hurry up formed on her lips but died as he took a long stride forward and caught hold of her by her shoulders. Every time he touched her, her skin sizzled. Not just where he made contact but everywhere. And most especially between her thighs.

"But, before I do this, we have to strike a bargain." His voice was deep, low, serious.

"A bargain? Of what sort?" Immediately her thoughts flew to an erotic bargain.

"You must listen to me, Althea. And obey me. I demand that you obey me and do exactly as I ask."

His commanding tone once again set her bristling. "I have many years of experience slaying vampires, I might remind you, my lord."

"I do not care if you've had twenty centuries slaying vampires." He started off toward his black gelding—one of his carriage horses, saddled for their search. The horse nickered as his master's hand slid over his nose, turning his head in pleasure at the caress.

She hoisted up her skirts and strode to Yannick's side. "I've been helping my father hunt the undead for longer than you've been one, my lord."

The horse gave a gentle whinny and flicked his head, sending his midnight black mane dancing about his graceful neck. She never expected a vampire to have such a gentle touch with animals.

With a tug, Yannick undid the loose knot, slid the reins off the branch. "Althea, I don't doubt your skill. Or your courage. Or your quick wit."

In one fluid motion, he settled his booted foot in the stirrup and swung his leg over the great beast's back.

Fuming, Althea expected him to spur the horse and gallop

away. But he steadied the animal, pressing his thighs into the flanks, and bent down. He caught hold of her around the waist and lifted her on to his lap just as he had outside the stables. His arm held her as the horse shifted beneath her.

She twisted around and Yannick leaned forward. He kissed her. Masterfully. Hungrily. Until his fiery kiss left her dizzy and she had to hold tight to his arms. With his lips locked to hers, he urged the horse into a canter. Her rear bumped painfully on the saddle. She had rarely ridden and had no sense of horses. They were large, unpredictable, and scared her.

"Relax," he whispered, "It's instinct."

Somehow his hot kiss did make her relax and Althea found she could match his rhythm, lifting slightly on the saddle to avoid a pounding. Once she moved gracefully in unison with him, Yannick released her lips. He sped them into a gallop, the rain pelting at her from beneath her sagging bonnet brim. She had to close her eyes and trust completely in Yannick.

As they thundered over the field, he pressed his mouth against her ear. "Goddamn it, sweet angel, do what I say tonight. I couldn't bear to lose you."

"You aren't afraid, are you?" Yannick pushed the wet branch back to allow Althea to follow. A shower of droplets rained down on him. Above, rain pattered into the canopy of leaves. Ahead he saw an opening in the denser woods and a stretch of untended lawn, grass bent down by the storm. Between interwoven branches and rambling shrubs, he spotted the porticoed roof, white columns, and quiet solidity of the mausoleum.

"I cannot begin to count the number of mausoleums I've entered in the middle of the night." Althea ducked for another low branch, but once she cleared it, she stood absolutely straight, her spine stiff with courage.

Even with her hair plastered against her face, her bonnet flopping, and rain dripping from her point of a chin—which made him wince with worry that she would catch cold—she sparkled with beauty. And strength. An inner strength that, oddly, he'd encountered more often in jades and courtesans than in women of the *ton*. Certainly, his gentle, timid mother never had it.

He'd been raised as a gentleman. Possessiveness, protective-ness had been bred into him. Qualities he believed to be the measure of the man. But never had his instincts to cosset and protect screamed so loud. He'd shielded his mother from the slaps, the blows, the insults, and been whipped brutally for his audacity. With Althea, his need to take care of her burned in him like a raging fire. He was determined to protect her from evil. And she was equally determined to face it.

Althea seemed to have no qualms in standing up to him—and he was a far more dangerous man than his father had been. He was bigger in build, but also immortal and possessed preter-natural strength.

But he wasn't his father and would never use that strength against a woman. Never against Althea. Her stubborn streak sorely tried his patience, but, God in heaven, he'd never raise his hand against her.

"Are you coming?" she asked. "You aren't afraid, are you?"

Yannick frowned and stalked toward her. Branches slapped at him but he refused to duck. One branch, as thick as his wrist, strained, resisted, and broke with a snap against his chest.

She gasped at that and her eyes widened, but as he reached her side, cheeky mischief gleamed in her eyes and he knew she'd only intended to goad him with her question. He wished she would show a trace of fear, just so he could be sure that she took this seriously. This wasn't a lark or a game or a dare.

"I'm afraid only for you, sweet," he admitted and let her make of that what she would.

It was the bloody truth. Bringing her here was a mistake, but he didn't doubt she would have made her own way here. And worse, he had the nightmarish suspicion she would have done so alone. He knew she would. Not because she was foolhardy. She was an intelligent woman with experience in realms that no sweet innocent should have but she would have been concerned about protecting him from her father's "vampire hunters."

He held aside more branches for Althea, although thorns snagged at her sleeves and skirts. He reached down to help her tug.

"Couldn't Zayan have engaged a gardener?" she muttered as together they wrenched the sodden wool free.

"It's entirely possible Zayan did but drank the poor sod's blood."

"I suppose he would do that to his servants, wouldn't he?" She frowned and worried her lip as she hoisted her skirts out of the mud. "Though I've heard no gossip about disappearing servants."

She gripped two fistfuls of her skirts, still carrying the handle of her valise.

He reached for it. "Allow me."

Althea jerked her head up, grave concern in her eyes. "What of you? You still live at your estates. Do *you* bite your servants?"

"I expect Zayan feeds far from home—he has the ability to travel great distances when he changes shape. I merely try to be discreet."

She paused at the edge of the woods. Beyond the screen of trees, rain slashed down. "I know nothing about you. The way you live. How you survive as a vampire."

He grasped her hand, threading his fingers between hers to hold securely. A low, slippery hill marked the start of the unkempt lawns. "Watch your step."

But she gamely sprinted down, pulling him along. His boot soles slipped and slid, as did hers, but she scrambled down with surprising grace. He blinked away the water dripping from his eyelashes.

She tipped her face up to him and droplets danced on her curving cheeks. Her wet lips tempted as she innocently licked the rain away. "I've been so caught up in those dreams and in being seduced by you and Bastien, I haven't asked the questions I should."

But then she turned without asking him another question and began stalking across the sloping lawn to the quiet white mausoleum. He turned and followed. Never in his existence, both mortal and immortal, had he found himself spun in so many circles by a woman.

She twisted back as she skidded over the grass. "I want to know how you escaped imprisonment. We racked our brains to understand how you broke Zayan's controlling spell. Which, of course, we knew you did, since the Earl of Brookshire was known to be rusticating at his estate in the country. And since no one spoke of a long, mysterious absence, you must have escaped soon after you were imprisoned. Did someone help you? Someone who knew the incantation?"

Yannick caught up and took hold of her elbow as they reached the wide stone steps, dotted with large puddles. Soaked and heavy with the rain, her red hair finally tumbled free of her hastily jabbed-in pins and spilled from beneath her bonnet.

"Bother," she groaned.

He caught his breath as she shook out the waist-length mass. He couldn't answer her questions, so he threw out some of his own. "Your father must have planned to approach me once he had resurrected my brother. Did he hope to coerce me to help him destroy Zayan?"

"Yes, and then Father planned to capture you. I didn't—couldn't—I wouldn't have done that." She blushed. "But who helped you escape?" she persisted, perhaps to change the subject. "Another vampire?" She grabbed the door handle and pulled, but the door didn't budge. As hard as she could, she shook it.

He leaned over her, bracing his hand against the door. "He planned to stake my brother and me, didn't he?"

"Well, he planned that of course. But we—he—wouldn't do that now."

"How very considerate of you, my dear." He laid his other hand on her shoulder and felt her body tense and jump slightly.

"I can open that door," she promised stubbornly. "I have a lock pick in my valise."

"Bolted from the inside, I expect. Allow me." He drew her back and sent a bolt of white fire through the crack between the oak door and the stone wall. A light clang sounded as the blast of power sheared the drawn bolt. He pulled the enormous door open.

"Impressive," she said grudgingly and he laughed. "But what about Bastien?"

"In there."

"No, why did you not free your brother once you were free?"

A cold, brutal memory rose: *because my brother had stuck a knife up under my ribs and made me a vampire?* No, it hadn't been anger or resentment that kept him from freeing Bastien. He gave his jaded shrug. "I did not have the ability to free him. Just as you did, I had to search for that bloody incantation. And I didn't want you to release him, Althea. I knew your father wouldn't be able to control him."

The black interior of the mausoleum stretched before him. Marble tombs stood in neat rows. Much sooner than he'd expected he saw the smooth surface of the wall—then the faint crack of a door. There was another room, and from whatever lay beyond its door, he detected voices.

Althea's hands gripped his hips through his sodden trousers. How could even her lightest touch act with such magic?

"How did you escape, then, if you did not use the spell?"

"I made a bargain with a devil and the devil always exacts a price. But I didn't have a soul to barter with." He shouldn't have revealed even that much, Yannick realized, but Althea's touch seemed to bring the truth to his lips. He stepped over the threshold and reached back for her.

"And now the adventure truly begins," he promised.

12

Opium

Althea stood in a mausoleum in the pitch dark. Despite her claim to courage, she felt a cold chill shoot up her spine—she'd never been completely without light in a crypt before. Suddenly her imagination conjured monsters in the shadows.

She normally felt fear when hunting the undead. The key was never to give in to it. And Yannick's arm about her waist gave her a flood of reassuring intimacy.

With no moonlight, she couldn't see. Fathomless black stretched around her and she had no sense of the size of the room or even of what stood directly in front of her. She didn't dare take a step. Only the fact she stood on her two feet let her know which direction was up and which was down. The eerie blindness left her disoriented and she found herself stumbling even as she stood still.

What do you see? She spoke in his mind, afraid Zayan would detect even the faintest whisper.

You will see soon, love. Do you smell the smoke?

Yes. The memory of Bastien's tomb rose in her mind. Of the sarcophagi filled with ash. Of the chiseled letters that forever preserved the name of the eight-year-old vampire. *Oh, God, is he burning Bastien?*

You'd have tossed up your dinner if he was, Althea. No, it is just a fire to warm. Which will give light.

But where is the fire? She moved out away from his arm and turned a full circle. Shouldn't she see some hint of light? Yannick had drawn the door closed behind them and she couldn't even detect the position of the double heavy oak doors, even though she'd walked through them just moments before.

"There is a room beyond this one. Well-sealed, it appears," he murmured behind her.

Without his touch, she was at a complete loss and she turned toward the sound of his voice, the only landmark she had. The scent of the smoke, rich and cloying, set her head spinning. She groped for him. Her heart dropped to her toes as she felt only air. *Don't move from where you stand,* urged an inner voice—or was it his voice in her head? But panic gripped her and she did take a step. Then another. Her boot collided into solid stone and her hands bumped the smooth, cool surface of a tomb.

She bit down to swallow a scream. *What is wrong with you,* she chided herself. *How can you be afraid of a sarcophagus? How many hundreds of tombs have you seen?*

She swallowed more of that sweet smoke and felt her heart thud even faster. It must be incense and it appeared to affect the beating of her heart.

Don't go stumbling about in the dark. Yannick's hands settled on her waist. *Now we will go forward, toward the door. Just move as I direct with my hands.*

He propelled her forward and she allowed herself to move at his direction. Once again she was putting all her trust in Yannick—in a vampire.

She couldn't smell the usual stale odors of a crypt. Instead, that thick, heavy smoke filled her senses. Now she could see the door because curling fingers of smoke slithered out from minute cracks.

Are you still able to speak in Bastien's mind? she asked him.

Do you know that when you speak in my thoughts you have the most delectable, sensual voice I've ever heard?

That startled. *What?*

Pressed tight against her, he shifted his hips, drawing the hard ridge in his trousers across her skirted bottom. *Every time you speak in my mind like that, I want you so much it hurts.*

He rocked forward, his rhythm unmistakable.

This— His brother was at risk. They were in the mausoleum of the most powerful vampire she'd ever encountered. Hardly the time to feel lust. But she did. Like a live thing, desire uncoiled deep in her belly with twinges of agonizing weakness. His hard cock jutting into her was a delight.

No, she repeated with conviction, *this really isn't the time.*

But her words had no effect as his hands slid up her ribcage toward her breasts. She was sodden and still chilled, dripping like a drowned rat. They both carried the wretched aroma of wet wool and even the exotic, spicy smell of the wafting smoke couldn't obliterate that entirely.

She took a deep breath. He smelled wet. Wet hair. Wet skin. All musky and male. *Bastien*—

She forced her traitorous thoughts to endangered Bastien. *Can you speak to him? Hear him?*

Not since we reached the start of the woods behind the house. Hot, demanding lips attached to her neck, above the sodden ribbons of her bonnet.

For heaven's sake, Yannick! Can you tell if he is . . . is still alive?

He is definitely alive. I just heard him moan.

Moan! He must be in pain? She reached forward. *Where is that bloody door?*

I can assure you he is in agony. And here, my sweet, is the door.

An undercurrent ran beneath his words, one as dangerous as the undertow of surging tides. He knew something she did not, and, of course, he would not deign to share it with her.

He left her to attend to the door, and she wrapped her arms around herself. Zayan could have stood at her side and she wouldn't have been the wiser. How she hated this . . . this blindness. This weakness.

Surrounded by the dark, she listened for the creak of a door, the groan of hinges, but the door swung open without sound. A golden glow spilled out, along with billows of the intense smoke. Drawing it into her lungs, Althea felt a spurt of wetness between her thighs. A burning heat ignited in her quim.

Her fingers strayed down and began to press through her skirts at the vee between her thighs.

Are you ready?

No, she was mad with lust and shouldn't move an inch until she conquered this ridiculous need. She had to force her fingers away from her nether regions.

Accustomed to the light now, she saw Yannick by the side of the door, an amused smile playing on his handsome face. Plastered down by the rain, his pale, silvery hair looked dark, which made him look almost a stranger. His wet trousers molded to his thighs and outlined his large, obvious erection. She swallowed to ease her tight throat. Almost transparent, his shirt cradled the broad muscles of his chest and stuck to the ripples of his abdomen. His dark, erect nipples poked against the fabric.

You may as well be shirtless, she observed in shock. But her body wasn't the least startled, and that extra heartbeat in her quim pounded urgently.

I should have insisted you wore white, sweet maiden.

She glanced down and realized her pelisse clung to her just

as suggestively. But it was serviceable brown wool and not at all enticing.

At least warmth swept out through the open door.

Will they see us? Hear us? Vampires had such enhanced senses. *S—smell us?*

For the moment, I believe they are too . . . distracted to sense even the alluring perfume of an aroused virgin. He pulled her to him, until her body pressed as tightly to his as his wet clothes.

Oh yes. She yearned for this. Arching up on tiptoe, she pushed her cunny against his bulge.

She caught hold of his shirt and tried to draw him back . . . to where? There must be a coffin somewhere . . . and they could lie back against that while she tugged those wet trousers off—

Sex against a coffin?

What was happening to her?

It was Yannick. He possessed the power to turn her into a sex-mad creature with no control.

She ached to stay draped around him. Her right leg was wrapped about his booted calves and her arms clenched tight around his back, but she forced herself to let go.

Before I go in, I am arming myself. She unfastened the ties of her bonnet and wrenched the wet thing off her head. It would only hamper her aim. Then she lowered to the ground and, on her knees, opened and searched her valise. Two stakes she tucked into her bodice, the sharp ends poking between her breasts. She spread her hinged bow on the floor, pulling the arms until they clicked into place. The bow might be small but it used levers to provide advantage. There wasn't much light, and loading the bolt into the crossbow by feel proved a challenge. The tip of the bolt pricked her fingertip and she sucked it. No blood at least. No fresh scent to alert a vampire.

She prayed the bow would fire correctly when the time

came. And hated being left with only one bolt. Only one chance.

Are you ready now, my huntress? Gentle amusement reached her through the dark.

True, a crossbow and a stake couldn't match his powers, but she took pride in looking after herself.

Yes.

Then come—he hesitated on the word—*come with me.*

Tombs. Althea had expected more of them—the white marble boxes to contain mortal remains. But the room proved to be another small chamber and it contained only one coffin. An elaborate, not-so-final resting place carved of oak and inlaid with rich, gleaming gold. Candles flickered in tall iron stands, flames wavering. The heady, spiced scent seemed to pour off them like the thick smoke. She'd never seen so much smoke come from a candle, not even cheap ones or dipped rushes. But the scent wasn't choking. It was drugging, enchanting, and she took deep breaths to drink in as much as she could.

Sex can be addictive as opium . . .

The scent of these candles was addictive. The more she took in, the more she craved it . . . And the white smoke hanging in the air lent a dreamlike quality to the room.

Velvet in jewel tones hung about the walls, like draperies, but there were no windows behind, only smooth, tooled stone. Rich, bright carpets bearing intricate oriental patterns covered the floor.

This wasn't a cold crypt. It wasn't what she'd expected. She had never walked into such a . . . a sensual den. Exotic. Dazzling. She almost wanted to run her fingertips along the polished surface of the coffin. Two other doorways led off—giving the sensation that they could travel deeper into sin by going through. Golden doors guarded both, though both doors stood open and more light reflected from within.

She'd never seen such an elaborate mausoleum. *Which way do we choose?*

The right. But you must stay behind me, and follow everything I do. There should be some place for us to hide just beyond the door.

Hide? Aren't we going to confront Zayan?

There is something I think you will be most interested to watch first.

And what is that?

Silence. Trust me, sweet.

But she couldn't bear just to sit and wait while he spied around the open righthand door. More smoke spilled from in there and she wished to inhale the stronger scent. She squirmed between Yannick's solid body and the wall and peeked into the room.

This room, a large, rectangular room, had also been transformed. On the wall directly opposite, a fire blazed in an enormous marble fireplace, giving warmth and light. Enough light to see the most remarkable things.

What is that?

Shh, he warned. *Don't speak, even in my thoughts, until I do first.*

She squinted. Indeed, it was a cage, just as she first thought. An oversized bird cage—large enough to keep a man inside. It was closest to the door. Formed of sturdy iron, the cage stretched as tall as the ceiling of the crypt and was suspended off the floor. Tasseled cushions of vivid silk surrounded it, piled in decadent splendor. A large door and a padlock faced them. Bars formed the floor, spaced apart so a person inside would have to balance precariously. Chains dangled from several bars and at the ends of the chains . . . shackles.

Where was Bastien? Zayan?

A low, throaty groan came from . . . from somewhere.

But on the way to finding the source of the hoarse sound, Althea's gaze fell upon a wall hung in crimson velvet.

Whips of every sort hung on the wall. A solid-handled bull-whip. A cat-o'-nine-tails. A long-handled creation with a thin, evil-looking leather strap attached. At least two riding crops. And goodness—a mace with frightening spikes. Along with coils of rough rope and lengths of what appeared to be thick black velvet ropes.

And then she saw the bed.

Draped entirely in black silk and velvet, it looked like a bed in which Satan might lie. Eight glossy black columns, two at each corner, supported a black silk canopy. Heavy black tassels hung around it and the thick black silk ropes held the drapes open.

Another moan came from the center of the bed. Now she spied a shape there, lifting the raven sheets.

Why did Yannick not do something? What was he waiting for? He cuddled her back against him, arm wrapped around her. The warmth of the room seeped in through her wet clothes and his body lent a heat of its own.

You may speak now, Althea, if you wish. I've shielded us from their senses.

How could you do that?

"Because men focus on sex even to the risk of their own deaths," he murmured.

Sex? She wanted to speak in his thoughts—it was so intimate.

Do you see that trunk there? The one with the pile of furs on top of it? We can slip behind that, I believe. You need to be warmed, angel, and the furs will help.

She dropped close to the floor and crept toward the large trunk strapped with beaten gold bands. Only a yard separated the door from the massive box, but her heart lodged in her throat the entire way. Crawling in sodden skirts made covering just three meager feet seem almost impossible.

Triumph flared when she reached their hiding place.

Take off your clothes.

She spun around to Yannick as he crouched beside her. *I will not.*

You are drenched. Shadows hung over his features but his eyes gleamed, silver discs in the dark. She could sense his expression. Concern and displeasure. He stroked along the lapels of her pelisse and even through the layers of wet clothing, his touch set her damp skin afire. A shiver leapt through her.

I refuse to face the enemy naked. But she did fumble with the buttons of her pelisse. No reason to wear two sodden layers.

Yannick peeled it from her with expert ease. *Don't be foolishly stubborn, angel. You can hide amongst the furs here. I refuse to let you develop lung fever—*

Then feed me your blood.

He stilled, holding her wet pelisse. *It would protect, Althea, in a small quantity. But are you prepared to do such a thing?*

Fear and excitement burned in her. What would it taste like? What would it be like? Would she understand him more?

Yes.

His smile was pure rogue. *Very well, love. To protect your health.*

At the first welling drop on his wrist, she began to doubt her courage. Rich and dark red, the drop beaded, then ran down his pale wrist. *Don't waste it, sweet. And it will tempt Zayan if too much flows.*

What was there to fear? She'd licked her own cuts. She knew the taste of blood. With her tongue sticking out, she bent to his wrist and caught the drip. Others followed, and the taste slammed into her like potent brandy. The coppery taste tantalized, intoxicated, made her hunger for more. It heated like fine spirits, burning down her throat. Fiery warmth uncoiled inside her. Like delectable wine, a sip wasn't enough.

She pressed her lips to his warm, smooth skin and drank.

"Enough, sweet," he murmured but she scrambled to hold his wrist in place. She could understand why he craved the taste, the intimacy, the sensuality of this. She had taken his cock into her mouth but suckling his blood was every bit as deliciously intimate.

His low, deep, agonized moan startled her into stopping. Eyes half-closed, he smiled. *It is very erotic for me, Althea.*

She became so much more aware. Of the lush, teasing scent of the candles. Of the fine texture of his skin, the soft hairs on the back of his forearm. The thrumming of her blood. The patter of her heart.

With a nudge of his palm, he stopped her suckling. *I can't risk giving you more.*

Of course, it would weaken him. She gave one last sensuous lick—

The bed creaked.

"Did you keep me imprisoned just because you wanted to fuck me again?" The deep, hoarse voice unmistakably belonged to Bastien. Definitely alive.

Althea's heart soared with joy and she peered over the top of the trunk.

From here, she had a much better view of the massive bed.

Bastien sat up in the middle of it, bare-chested, with the sheets in a dark band across his hips. His golden hair was a tangle about his face, his eyes heavy lidded and glowing.

The word he'd used slowly sank in. *Fuck.* She knew what it meant. The sex act.

And she saw Bastien wasn't alone in bed. Another long shape lifted the black sheets. A shape that stirred, leaving the impression of a shadow as it moved. No, not a shadow. A man in dark clothes, a man levered up on his arms.

Bastien had told her, without an ounce of shame or shyness, that he'd been Zayan's lover. But to actually see two men in bed stunned her.

Zayan—the gruesome monster who had grabbed her in Father's room. But the cold malevolence she sensed when he attacked her father was no longer there. His face was turned away from her, his body shrouded in shadow, but he exuded power. A frightening power.

She took her first good look at him. Firelight cast a red glow to midnight-black hair that poured over his shoulders and hung almost to his waist. It was thick and wavy, in the style of Charles II. A dark blue silk robe covered him from shoulder to foot and he possessed shoulders broader than any she'd ever seen—even wider than Yannick's or Bastien's.

Zayan half-turned, throwing light up his profile. The fiery glow made his sharp-planed face both handsome and demonic. She couldn't draw her gaze away.

Could staring at him make him aware she was there? Even a mortal could sense a stare. Was Yannick able to screen it?

She swallowed a gasp as Zayan cradled Bastien's chin. His touch was gentle. A lover's touch.

She'd never expected such tenderness in the way a man touched another man, and certainly not in the way a brutal demon touched a vampire. But Zayan's long fingers stroked and Bastien's half-closed eyes betrayed his pleasure.

Althea held her breath as she heard Bastien's low, encouraging moan. Suddenly softness brushed her skin. Warmth and heaviness settled around her. Furs. Yannick had piled the furs around her, burying her almost up to her breasts. While watching Bastien and Zayan, she hadn't even noticed.

She met Yannick's hot, suggestive eyes. With a start, she saw he was now bare-chested. Her throat dried as her gaze slid lower, to the pile of black, white, and brown furs scattered around him. A stretch of trousers showed.

"Why don't you take off your gown, sweet, beneath the furs?"

Lust, she guessed, made his voice thick and low. Concern for her health had nothing to do with his request.

You are still wearing your trousers and boots, she chided into his mind.

With a roguish grin, he parted the furs. She caught a glimpse of dusky pink. His falls were unfastened and his cock free. Imagining the feel of the luxurious furs skimming over his sensitive shaft, the swollen head, she shivered. As she drank in air—and that drugging, seductive scent—her nipples tightened against her bodice until they stood up like thimbles.

His cock sprang out of the furry nest. But she heard a low, rumbling growl from the bed and she swung around to see what was happening.

Zayan no longer cradled Bastien's face like a gentle lover. He caught hold of the golden locks and dragged Bastien forward. She winced, empathizing with Bastien against the brutal treatment. Until Bastien pinched Zayan's chest through his silken robe. His finger and thumb must be clamping Zayan's nipple. In return, Zayan wrapped his hand around Bastien's shaft and jerked it hard.

Bastien's harsh moan made her body clench in agony.

Goodness . . . Bastien liked it.

Bastien's lips collided hard with Zayan's. Heads tilted to allow the kiss to deepen. Their mouths opened, and they devoured each other. They kissed with the hunger and longing of a man and woman, but far more aggressively. They were competitive males, dueling for superiority even as they pleasured each other, but there was no mistaking the passion in their joining.

"So you like to watch, sweet angel." Yannick's soft, teasing tone rippled down her tense spine.

Heaven help her, she did. Yannick's erection nudged her

thigh, and his hand settled over her left breast, but she couldn't turn away from the two men on the bed. Large male hands gripped nipples and tweaked and tugged. Their hands ran over each other's broad backs—one cloaked in fine silk, the other only in perfect skin that gleamed with sweat.

Oh, she did like to watch, but she didn't dare admit it to Yannick.

Do you like to see a man's hand on another's cock?

He must know she did. Against his palm, her heart raced. And her chest was swelling with each panting, shallow breath.

Tell me if it excites you to watch. Even in her thoughts, Yannick's voice was deep and compelling.

Why does it excite you to hear me tell you?

Because fantasy and the forbidden enhance the pleasure for men.

Does it excite you, Yannick, to see two men touch each other's—? She broke off as Bastien and Zayan began fondling each other. They weren't merely touching each other's ramrod-straight cocks. Both Zayan and Bastien clutched the other's member and manipulated it with long, tight strokes. Zayan's strokes were obvious, with Bastien's cock naked and exposed. Bastien gripped the demon's through his blue silk robe. Bastien's cock looked almost red, reflecting the firelight and the crimson silk on the walls. She gulped as Zayan jerked his hand down to Bastien's balls. He toyed with them roughly and she'd always believed they were delicate and must be treated with care. But men must know more about pleasuring each other than she did. They obviously knew secrets she did not.

Mesmerized, she watched Zayan play with Bastien. Pressure varied, and speed, and the lengths of the strokes.

Finally, Bastien's head dropped forward, hair spilling over his agonized face like a golden curtain. "God . . . God . . . God . . ." Bastien groaned. "Don't make me come. Not yet. Not until

I've pounded my cock into your arse until you scream for mercy."

Into his—! And he was so crude about it. *Men—*

Yes, sweet? Yannick bent close to her neck. He pushed aside the damp weight of her hair. *What have you discovered about men?*

What hadn't she discovered about men? A great deal, she feared. How could she be falling in love with such dangerous, unfathomable creatures as vampire males? As Yannick?

As Bastien?

She licked her dry lips. *With each other they are much more . . . more crude than when they are with women.*

It is how they show their affection.

Affection? It hardly seemed to be affection as Zayan shoved Bastien back on the bed and pressed his fangs against Bastien's chest. The ancient vampire gripped Bastien's rounded balls in one large, powerful hand and squeezed them. But instead of yelling or fighting, Bastien tipped his head back. "Yes," he moaned.

Men, then, definitely enjoyed rough contact.

But she could understand why. She couldn't deny the thrill she felt just watching. The strange arousal and fear in her that made her feel tight and wound up and ready to burst.

Yannick licked her neck at the exact instant Zayan bent his head to Bastien's neck. She had to bite down into her lip to strangle her cry. Suddenly she was almost living the scene on the bed and Yannick's hot tongue mimicked the caresses that Bastien received.

She expected biting and blood, but she couldn't see anything but the back of Zayan's head and his long, gleaming raven hair, and the fierce agony on Bastien's face.

"Who is Zayan?" she whispered. "What is he?"

But Yannick was tugging up her damp skirt from behind.

She saw her calves revealed, scandalously bare, as she hadn't bothered with stockings.

"What is Zayan?" she repeated, but again she received no answer. Instead Yannick bent between her now-naked legs and dragged the furs over them both.

Tell me what you see, he directed.

Describe it for him? *But—*

Her protest stopped abruptly as Yannick buried his face between her thighs. She parted her thighs but he drew them back in and shifted so her legs lay over his back. The back of her bare legs rested on his strong shoulders and her feet, in half-boots, were on either side of his slim waist. His chin rasped against her sticky inner thighs. His hands gripped her bottom.

At the first flick of his tongue, she feared she'd cry out. *You mustn't. Won't a scream give us away?*

No, sweeting. You are free to scream. But if you want to stay quiet, I know you are a woman of admirable willpower.

Flattering, but Althea was beginning to understand his technique. He professed his respect for her stellar qualities to seduce her into giving him exactly what he wanted.

His fingers opened her nether lips wide and she moaned, as quietly as she could, at the gentle tug.

While I what, angel?

The wretch. He wouldn't rest until he made her say scandalous things.

While you suck my quim. Even though she only said the words in her head, she blushed. *And why do you wish to hear what is happening on the bed? Do you wish to be there?*

Another cock is interesting, but I much prefer your wet, delicious pussy. I do crave hearing what you are watching, in your own enticing words. You do know, sweeting, that you have the power to make me come with just your words.

Althea gazed down at his wide, muscled back, at his powerful arms bent around her thighs. He was playfully nibbling her nether lips. Teasing and toying with her and determined not to drive her to ecstasy, she realized, until she played his game.

You have incredible power over me, Althea, he promised.

She drank in the scent of the candles and looked toward the bed where two male bodies tangled in an erotic dance that stole her very breath.

Tonight, she wanted to explore her power.

13

Rescued

"Zayan," she whispered, "is ripping off his robe."

It took Zayan only a moment to do so and he tore the beautiful silk in his haste. The ancient vampire lifted from Bastien's chest to discard the robe, and Althea gazed at the whole of the demon she'd come to destroy. Lying on the bed, he had appeared impossibly long. He must be far above six feet in height. Closer to seven feet. In the Carpathians, she had seen such giants. And like those magnificent men, Zayan possessed the build of a bull. Big shoulders that flexed as he bent down to Bastien's—

"Oh!"

A cry of surprise? Yannick asked, buried between her thighs. *For what, sweet?*

*He's kissed—kissing the tip of Bastien's—*She struggled to say the words—*Bastien's cock. His mouth is open, his fangs on either side of the shaft. He . . . he's running his tongue around it. Just as I—*

As you did to me?

He's put it into his mouth!

Is Bastien enjoying it?

He's taken hold of Zayan's hair—I think he means to pull Zayan away.

Yannick chuckled. A sudden surge of wetness filled her quim. Yannick's tongue, sliding in and out. She watched . . . watched the suckling of Bastien's cock while Yannick thrust . . .

She was hopelessly sinful.

She might as well toss away that controlling collar. She was hardly an innocent anymore. And what Zayan did shocked her. *He's taken Bastien's cock all the way into his mouth. How could he do that? Wouldn't the cock have to go down his throat? Wouldn't he choke?*

It's tricky, sweet, but it can be done.

Breathless, Althea watched Bastien's hands caress Zayan's head. Zayan lavished such loving delight to Bastien's cock, she was astonished. Zayan licked it all over, swirling his tongue about the head and stroking the shaft. Bastien's cock seemed to swell bigger and bigger. His hips began to rock upward. Suddenly—so quickly she gasped—Zayan plunged his mouth down, swallowing the member whole, and began to bob up and down. His cheeks sucked in as he drew back, revealing the broad, veined shaft inch by inch. Then he plunged down again.

Bastien panted and gripped the vampire's head. Zayan sucked harder, faster, and he seemed to be moaning around Bastien's cock.

What's happening, angel?

I think—I think Bastien is going to reach his release. She shut her eyes and turned away. *This is wrong. It's private. I can't watch. I want to, I'm ashamed to admit I truly do, but I shouldn't.*

Yannick's tongue reached deep within her, as deep as she believed it could go, then slid back, teasing the walls of her passage. The pleasure weakened her. *Bastien has always performed for an audience.*

But this is intimate. The room reeked of sensual lust—the candles' aroma only seemed to heighten the smell of male sweat, male juices. This was more than mere sex, she sensed. The slaps and rough grabs between the men spoke of anger and violence—no, of power.

She couldn't quite understand why Bastien would allow Zayan to even touch him unless it was the price of his life. But Bastien had not seemed unwilling. And Zayan appeared determined to give his former lover pleasure.

Yannick's tongue slid upward and curled around her clit. "Ooh!"

"I'm coming!" Bastien cried out and, heaven help her, she looked.

To see Zayan's long throat moving as he swallowed. Bastien's head was arched forward, his shoulders lifted off the bed. Climaxing still. Her quim snapped tight around Yannick's lazily thrusting tongue as she watched Bastien come. His muscles thrashed with his orgasm, his legs jerked, and his hips surged up, hard against Zayan's mouth.

Her hips moved to, rocking wildly against Yannick's mouth. He gripped her thighs to control her.

Bastien was yelling. Cursing even as wave after wave of pleasure swept over him. His lush, firm lips were parted. Half-hidden by his lids, shrouded by thick amber lashes, his eyes glowed like embers.

And Yannick was suckling her clit. Suckling harder and harder. Shifting to change his angle, to rasp her—

Ooh—

She was panting—or Bastien was—she couldn't be sure. Hoarse, ragged pants. Hers, scratchy and ragged in her throat.

Yes, yes.

La petite mort. How she understood now. She must have looked like Bastien the very first time she'd come for Yannick. Only last night! And Yannick's eyes had burned like silver stars, like comets, watching her. She'd loved watching Yannick tumble into the maelstrom, and she loved watching Bastien come too. He climaxed just like Yannick, with a grimace of agony as shudders racked him. She loved how vulnerable he appeared as he bucked with his climax. Loved watching him explode.

Yannick's finger invaded, plunging deep into her quim. One finger for several wonderful thrusts. She arched with each one, reveling in the wet sound as he withdrew it. She wanted to make Yannick come too. Come for her . . .

Sweet Althea.

"Do you . . . do you want to know . . ." She struggled to speak, to find words to describe Bastien finding his pleasure.

Two long fingers slid inside her, stretching her wide. She gasped at pressure against the entrance to her bottom. His finger, delving in enough to make her muscles clench. He circled her anus until she moaned incoherently, half-mad, "Yes, yes. Oh please. Yes, in there."

She shut her eyes tight as his wet finger slid into her bottom.

She opened her eyes wide as he penetrated her rear with one more finger, as he worked until he had all his fingers in her drenched pussy.

On the bed, Bastien slumped back, eyes shut, as though he was utterly spent and exhausted. She choked on a moan. Was it over? Zayan climbed back over Bastien's slack body. Would he bite now that Bastien was sated and weakened?

Instead the ancient vampire claimed a kiss from Bastien. Zayan's cock protruded, as large as a stallion's and rigid, as he showered Bastien's body with kisses and love-nips and licks from his long, pointed tongue. The affection and the love she saw on Zayan's handsome face stole her breath.

Zayan urged Bastien over onto his stomach and Bastien obeyed, stretched naked the length of the bed.

Yannick thrust faster and her eyelids flickered down over

her eyes as the pleasure built. She glimpsed the long line of Bastien's pale shoulders. Let her gaze trace the beautiful curve of his back to the taut round muscles of his derrière.

Zayan's large hand settled on the bunched muscles of Bastien's rear.

What was he doing?

But she realized as Zayan pressed his erection between Bastien's solid cheeks. The head disappeared between.

He's going inside his rear!

She watched, stunned, as Zayan thrust his hips forward. The long length sank in. Withdrew and sank in again.

Braced over Bastien's broad, muscular back, Zayan pumped himself inside.

Yannick's fingers slid in and out of her quim and her bottom.

Zayan's long muscles bunched as he pumped harder and harder. As he pumped deeper, until he invaded Bastien to the hilt, until his groin slapped Bastien's tight cheeks. And Bastien lifted his ass to meet each hard, deep thrust. Sweat gleamed on Bastien's back, reflecting the firelight, and he appeared to be forged of gold. Zayan's hair flailed wildly, and sweat drenched his broad back.

Both men moaned, their deep, gravelly voices blending. Zayan bent forward and Bastien, willingly, arched back. Fangs grazed Bastien's neck. Toes linked. Hands gripped, fingers entwined.

Being a voyeur to this scene, charged with desire but also with love, was unbearably erotic.

Althea gripped Yannick's head through his hair, urging to meet the rhythm of Zayan's thrusts. Urging him to go faster. His fingers pounded her. His tongue lashed her. Lashed like the flick of a whip—

She shattered.

Lights exploded before her eyes—bolts of blue and red and white.

Zayan's howl echoed in the room.

Surrounded by fur, by the rich aroma of Althea's pleasure and the cloying candles, Yannick fell back and dragged Althea on top of him. Fire and need shot through him as her wet lips puckered sweetly and touched his. Her heart pounded against his.

Blast this wet, appalling dress! He'd love to tear it off her and drape her naked curves in these sumptuous furs.

If he were going to live beyond the next full moon, he would burn every one of Althea's drab dresses and purchase her dozens of beautiful gowns.

But did Bastien intend to destroy Zayan—the demon he was fucking?

Althea wrapped her arms around his neck and pressed her womanly warmth against him to kiss him deeply. Yannick cursed inwardly. He must link quickly with Bastien.

But Althea's warmth and comfort mattered more. Her chest rose and fell adorably with her quick breaths. He tossed a length of sable over her, then kissed her deeply, covering her lips with the exotic flavor of her quim.

Her hand fluttered up and brushed his cheek. *That was so wonderful. I'm flying still.*

This was madness. Making love to her in this mausoleum, with danger so close at hand. But danger appeared to heat her blood. As he tumbled her down into the pile of furs and arranged the sable over her again, her nubile leg hooked around his. He flicked back her waist-length hair, almost dry now.

Her eyes sparkled in the firelight. *They made love to each other. I'd no idea what men did. How exciting it was—*

Did you find it arousing to watch?

Yes. I'm horrified to admit it, but I did.

She feathered kisses along his jaw. Damnation, but he hungered to make love to her. His lungs were filled with that thick smoke—an aphrodisiac, he was sure. His prick was as hard as the stone that formed this place. Every breath he took made his cock hurt.

Zayan made love to Bastien from behind. I thought it would be . . . but it was so . . . so sensual. So exciting. Intense and hard, but after, it was the way Zayan touched him. Not like a demon. Not like evil. It was the way I would touch you. It was with such love—

Love? The last emotion he expected Bastien to show to Zayan. To anyone, in fact.

Althea was no longer innocent. Not after witnessing that.

Her hands skimmed down his throat, down to his nipples. She caught hold of both and twisted. Pain shot from his poor, squeezed tips like a bolt of magic and exploded in his loins. His cock, in turn, almost shot off like a cannon. She was so brave, his sweet huntress. And she was an apt pupil of sensual arts.

Yannick fought for control and barely recovered before her hand ceased its torment on his hard nipples and squirmed down between their bodies to his cock, hard as a cricket bat and nestled against her soft, rounded belly.

Her delicate touch was gone. She gripped him like he would when he was mad with frustrated lust and wanted to wank off with speed.

"I want you." Her husky voice was more alluring than a room full of demonesses and desire-inducing candles. "I want to do everything we did in my dreams. I realize now the dreams were the most tempting fantasies and I want to experience every one."

Love-nips rained over his neck and shoulders as she flicked his hard nipple and tugged on his cock. A little of his juice bubbled out, dampening both her hand and his stomach. Her other leg hooked around him too and clamped around his hamstrings.

A beautiful virgin was begging to explore all her fantasies. Despite knowing he could be shot through the back with a searing bolt of magic, he hungered to oblige.

Hell and perdition, he couldn't. Yannick shut his eyes to focus, but without sight, his other senses heightened. Smell, most certainly. Althea's scent bewitched him and her touch tormented. She arched her hips up, trying to surround his cock.

Wait, please, love.

Her fetching moan of frustration made him question his sanity. But he had no choice. He shut out everything—her lovely face, her tempting body, her soft sighs, the wicked magic of the candles—and focused on the dark. On reaching into Bastien's mind.

Anger struck him first. A turbulent blend of fury and sexual arousal. Bastien's emotions warred inside him, a kaleidoscope of the most base and brutal of human emotions. Revenge and hatred. Passion and fury at feeling so much need. And beneath them all ran a longing—a love so bound up with pain that Yannick flinched and felt his blood turn to ice as he experienced it.

He severed the connection, sagging slightly on his outstretched arms.

Would Bastien be willing to attack Zayan with him? Hunger for revenge was the dominant emotion he'd sensed.

Althea moaned, hooked her arm around his neck and dragged him down to her.

He opened his eyes. *Althea, sweet, I won't make love to you here.*

Her eyes pleaded with his. *It's too dangerous but I want you so much,* she whispered in his thoughts.

The damn candles.

What are they doing? she asked. *Are they resting?*

Oh, they aren't finished, sweet. I believe Zayan is tying Bastien's wrists to the bed.

Tying him up?

For erotic purposes. I believe Zayan is fetching a whip.

Shouldn't we attack?

The whip is also for sexual pleasure.

Oh God, Bastien spoke of that. Of craving the flick of a whip against his . . . his bare bottom. Do you also enjoy being whipped?

Regret surged up in Yannick's heart. Althea's innocence had been a precious thing and he'd chipped away at it, piece by piece. A gentleman's duty was to protect a woman, to protect a young lady's starry-eyed view of the world.

No, I don't enjoy whippings. I received too many of them at my father's hand and I never developed an addiction for the crack of a whip on my arse.

Althea's arms slid around him and she held him tenderly. Concern and sorrow and shock—all the emotions he hated to evoke—glittered in her emerald eyes. *Your father whipped you? Why?*

For disobedience. For breaking rules. For protecting my mother. To pass the time on a winter's afternoon.

That's horrible.

He eased off her. His cock, he could see, now drooped a bit. Instead of standing proud between his thighs, it listed to the left and the head arced down. Damn his father.

Crack!

The first blow had landed across Bastien's buttocks. Now would be the time to attack, while Bastien was caught up in punishment, while his emotions were raw and engaged, while he was caught in the cusp of subservience and defiance.

I am going to attack Zayan, Yannick warned. *You must stay here.*

Althea felt the excitement of battle surge as she caught up her crossbow and defiantly followed Yannick out of the shadows. Though he didn't turn, he issued a command in her head.

Stay back, Althea.

By the bed, Zayan stood with his back to them. Sweat gleamed on his back with each powerful stroke of the whip. Splayed across the black sheets, Bastien whimpered and moaned. The velvet ropes binding him to the bedposts went taut as each blow struck, then Bastien would relax and the ropes would go slack before the next flail over his skin.

Even she could smell the coppery tang of his blood.

How could that be pleasurable?

Althea caught her breath as Zayan ceased to crack the whip and instead bent over his victim. He licked each of the wounds, murmuring gentle words.

And suddenly the unthinkable, the horrifying, became erotic.

Now was not the time to contemplate that. She dropped behind another trunk, one with a direct line of sight—and line of fire—to the bed. At least she had her spectacles, though they were streaked with dried raindrops. When Zayan turned, she could fire the bolt at his heart. And she had better bloody well not miss.

Get back and hide, Althea.

And what would be the point of that?

Her heart leapt to her throat as Yannick, barechested, approached the bed. Without his shirt, he appeared too vulnerable.

He stopped several yards away, legs slightly spread, hands up in front of his chest. Shielding his heart.

Her fingers hovered over the bow, ready to launch the bolt.

The next slash of Zayan's whip was arrested in mid-flight and the tail fell limp over Bastien's body. At the same instant, two white bolts shot from Yannick and struck the ropes binding his brother's feet to the bedpost.

With a roar, Zayan spun around. His hair whipped about him like a black cape. Glowing hellish red, his eyes riveted on Yannick. A deep, evil chuckle echoed around the room.

Zayan's blast sent Yannick hurtling back. Horrified, she watched, helpless, as his backside struck the bare floor with a crunch and his head followed with a bang. Despite the punishment, Yannick leapt back onto his feet so fast he blurred before her eyes. In mid-jump, he sent a stream of brilliant white light that drilled against Zayan's naked, wide chest.

Triumph shot through Althea as she saw Zayan stagger. But he took only two steps back before regaining his balance. In that instant, she saw the uneven match between Yannick and the ancient demon. She had never felt so afraid of a foe before, and her fear was all for Yannick.

Zayan could blast him off the face of the earth.

Instinct guided her finger to the bow's triggering mechanism. Steady breaths. She drew them in. Refused to let emotion guide her. Wait . . . wait . . .

Zayan howled like a wolf and lifted his hands—

Now.

The bolt flew true and sliced into Zayan's naked chest. The force drove him back, slamming the back of his legs against the bed's footboard. His enormous hand wrapped around the carved bedpost. His fleshy lips curved into a smile as he looked down at the shaft protruding from his chest.

Damn. She'd missed. The bolt pierced him two inches too high.

Althea tensed, ducked back behind the trunk, knowing Zayan's next bolt would blow right through the trunk and tear her apart—

Fire exploded in front of her and the flame shot around her like an embrace. Screams rang in the chamber—her own horrified screams. She could see the fire, centered in a world of black.

Then nothing.

"Do you want her? She is yours for the taking."

Dazed, Althea opened her eyes. She was falling—

No, she was on the bed. The bed where Bastien and Zayan had made love. Where Bastien had been whipped. Above her, the black canopy was large and fathomless, like the night sky, but she saw blurry forms on it. Female forms, nude and voluptuous. Frolicking against the black silk in a tangle of limbs. She squinted to see. Her spectacles were gone.

Pushing with weak arms, Althea sat up. Her dress was half ripped apart, gaping indecently over her left breast, and her skirts hung in tatters around her legs. Zayan lounged at the foot of the bed and flashed her an evil smile. His fingertips lightly brushed the sole of her foot.

She scrambled back. Beyond the foot of the bed, Bastien and Yannick stood several yards apart, facing each other, but watching her. Yannick's face appeared carved of stone, his eyes flashing firelight like mirrors, but she knew that he hid intense protectiveness behind that impassive, cold gaze. She squinted again to focus on Bastien. His eyes set her heart racing. They held such longing. Such fear.

"I am not standing in your way to claim her," Zayan said to Bastien. "You may keep her as your plaything if you wish." Zayan pointed carelessly toward Yannick. "It is your privileged brother who is preventing you from claiming what you want. If you destroy me, what will you achieve? Domination by your brother? Destruction, perhaps."

Deep and controlling, Zayan's heavily accented voice filled her mind. She wished she'd forced Father to tell her more about

Zayan. Yannick and Bastien must know everything about him, but she did not, and now she saw how impetuous she'd been to chase after a foe she didn't truly understand.

Zayan sprawled across the mattress like an indulgent Roman emperor. "I cannot destroy him, Bastien. He is protected. But you, as his twin, have power that I do not. The choice, my lover, is yours."

With a gasp, she realized that was true. The choice rested entirely in Bastien's hands. Destroy his lover or destroy his brother.

Althea realized that once Zayan had caught her, neither Yannick nor Bastien had tried to combat him out of fear for her safety.

Holding her breath, she sent a pleading look to Bastien. But his expression darkened, his lashes dropped to hide his eyes. He crossed his arms over his naked chest. A sneer curled his perfectly formed lips. "*You* want me to kill my brother." He turned to Yannick. "And you wish me to destroy the vampire who embraced me. For once in my life—or rather my after-life—I hold the balance of power." Bastien licked his lips, as though savoring a new taste, large silvery-blue eyes brimming with wicked mischief.

Zayan flicked the whip. The tail of it struck the floor near Bastien's feet. For his part, Bastien didn't flinch, even though the strap nicked his toes. He took on an expression of mulish stubbornness. For a full-grown, naked vampire, he appeared startlingly boyish and vulnerable. "You whipped me because I allowed it. Once again, in that circumstance, the power is in my hands."

Zayan laughed, low and cruel, and grabbed her ankle. Before she could launch a kick, he dragged her down the bed. Already bunched high above her knees, her torn skirt pulled higher, revealing her naked inner thighs. Those red eyes bored into her soul as Zayan stroked the length of her left leg, halfway up her inner thigh. His touch set her quaking, igniting fear she'd never known before, even when at grave risk.

Zayan held her gaze but released her leg. He inclined his head with eerie politeness. "I will not desecrate her. So, my young lover, what then is your choice?"

"I choose to kill neither of you."

But Bastien's hand shot up and fire leapt from it. A white bolt struck Zayan's shoulder. At the same instant, Yannick hurtled an equal weapon. The spear of white light struck Zayan on his other side, just above his heart. The twins sent bolt after bolt. They drove Zayan from the bed, drove him to cower on the floor, and to scramble back like a wounded animal.

A red flash raced from Zayan's right hand. It exploded against Yannick's stomach. For an instant, Althea's heart ceased to beat. But the light vanished and Yannick was still standing and thankfully unhurt. Absorbing the onslaught of power from the twins must have drained Zayan of his strength. Both Yannick and Bastien glowed with new power and their eyes burned with an eerie blue-white glow. Combining their powers had strengthened them—they seemed to be feeding off each other's magic.

She should feel safe, triumphant, but the sight chilled her. It reminded her of what these men were. She was a mortal amongst demons.

Althea searched the bed and floor for her stakes. They were gone—found by Zayan and tossed aside. She hated to be without a weapon but she could see the twins didn't need her help. They drove Zayan back toward the fireplace. Each time he tried to dart to one side or the other, the twins combined their powers and sent fiery blasts to keep forcing him back. Did they mean to force him into the flames?

Zayan's bare back was almost at the fire now. The flames danced behind him and with his mane of raven hair, his wild, fiery eyes, he looked like Satan at the portal to hell.

Bastien threw a triumphant, cocky grin to Yannick, who returned the smile. Their hands lifted.

Whoosh.

The fire vanished, and a fierce wind swept through the room from the doors to the fireplace. The candles extinguished, plunging the room into inky blackness. The air rushed by Althea's cheeks. It was as though the fire had flown up the chimney and dragged the air in the room in its wake. Zayan's red eyes no longer glowed by the wall.

Althea strained to see, but dots danced before her eyes. A loud rustle approached the bed, the swirl of turbulent air.

Wings. Something swooped past her, so close that her hair flew back as it passed.

She swung out, blind, determined to defend herself. Hit a warm chest.

It's all right, love. He's gone. Flown away. Bastien.

How amazed she was by Bastien. She would not have had the courage to spare Zayan's life. She would have killed him out of fear.

Bastien's arms slid around her; his lips brushed a kiss on the top of her head. She tumbled happily against his strong, reassuring body, embarrassed to lose her strength and courage.

She hugged him tight. They had saved her life, the Demon Twins. They had fought together for her. Tears threatened, tears of relief, and joy, and thanks.

Yannick rested his hand gently on her shoulders. He kissed her neck and she shivered at the sensation of being caught between the two powerful men.

Now, sweet, Yannick whispered into her mind, *about your fantasies . . .*

14

Shared

"A fitting place for an angel to lose her innocence to two demons."

Althea gasped as Bastien scooped her up to carry her across the threshold into one of Zayan's bedchambers. Yannick followed, carrying a bottle of Zayan's wine, three glasses, and a candelabrum with three long white tapers.

Bastien's golden brows waggled playfully. "Not Zayan's candles, alas."

"Zayan's candles?" she asked.

"Desire-inducing. They inflame lust."

She caught the play on words and groaned as Bastien nudged the door open with his bare foot. He crossed to the bed in two long strides. She found herself spinning, then dropping through the air. She bounced upon an enormous bed. Beneath her a cream and ivory silk counterpane bunched where she landed. This bed was the antithesis of Zayan's black one in his mausoleum. Cream drapery was roped to gilt columns and white silk roses in bunches decorated the gold ropes.

Astonished, she stared at the feminine touches in the room.

A white and gilt escritoire and a dainty chair with cream silk upholstery. A chaise of pure white, and white feathers in tall white vases.

Who could this room have been for? Bastien had told her about the submissive courtesans whom Zayan used. Was this lavish room intended for them? Had it been left by the previous family?

"Let us take that sodden dress off you." Yannick placed the candles on the escritoire.

Althea took an unsteady breath. "Are you certain Zayan won't return until dawn?"

"A little danger adds spice," Bastien teased.

"Zayan will be feeding to regain his strength and to heal," Yannick assured.

Which meant innocent village folk would be prey to him. She scrambled to sit up. Zayan's house must be filled with secrets, with knowledge she could use to defeat him—

Bastien kissed her, a hot, claiming kiss, and began to work at the buttons on her dress. Heat flooded her as his knuckles brushed her damp skin beneath the torn wool. She was a huntress . . . she couldn't give in to her desires, she should search Zayan's house . . . .

But as though the drugging smoke filled her lungs, she gave a languorous sigh of pleasure into Bastien's mouth. He kissed so beautifully he stole her will to move.

"You are perfect," he murmured. "A goddess."

"Exquisite," Yannick agreed in a soft, coaxing tone.

She blushed at the blatant appreciation in both men's eyes as her naked breasts came into view. Yannick helped her to her feet on the carpeted floor and her dress fell to her ankles. How wonderful to be free of its cold weight. How suddenly self-conscious she felt in the midst of her dream come to life. At least both men were naked now too, but they were exquisitely perfect. But truly, they did look at her as though she were too.

Both men sat down onto the bed and patted their laps with matching devilish smiles. But she couldn't choose. Simply couldn't. Yannick watched her with intense silvery eyes, a vulnerable look on his gorgeous face. He had rescued her father, saved her life, made love to her in her dreams, had wanted to protect her. A demon and a hero—two things she'd never believed could coexist.

And naughty Bastien. The wild, wicked rogue who had refused to kill Zayan but had attacked the more powerful vampire to save her. Her heart thumped just as loudly for Bastien as it did for Yannick. Her heart and her nipples and her quim were blissfully unaware it was utterly wrong to fall in love with two men.

She sat on the bed between them and they laughed, throaty, gravelly laughs that vibrated in her aching quim. Yannick reached for the bottle, poured a glass and handed it to her. A sip for courage, she decided, but Bastien flopped back, pulling her with him, and before she could catch herself, she sprawled against him. To her relief, she balanced the glass, but wine sloshed over her breasts and droplets sprayed them both.

A delicious treat. Bastien licked the wine running down her naked breasts. *Zayan has other bedchambers filled with many toys we could use on you.*

"I will not be whipped," she declared, but not as forcefully as she should. Bastien's tongue played such magic on her nipples, he left her breathless.

Yannick's hand coasted over the small of her back as he drank. "Drink your wine, love. You must thirst." His palm followed the curves of her bottom. Cupped. Squeezed. Parted the cheeks and made her quiver. She had to grasp Bastien's shoulder to steady herself.

She didn't thirst. She hungered. Hungered for sin.

And as though they could read her mind, the Demon Twins delivered her into temptation. To her shock, Bastien dipped his fingers into her wine, then delved between her thighs and rubbed wine over her hard clit. She laughed, filled with a wild madness.

Intense spikes of pleasure washed over her from behind. She half-turned to watch Yannick. He coasted his tongue all over her plump bottom, teasing and tickling, and his finger gently stroked her puckered entrance until her feet tingled. He must have known, the rogue, for he skimmed his bare toes along them. She squealed. Wine spilled. They didn't care, the demons; they thrust and sawed their fingers and licked until she screamed. Until she dropped her wine glass and it hit the floor. Until her back arched and her head fell back and she tensed like a drawn bow.

Twang!

It hit her like that. Screamed through her like a crossbow bolt. She bucked so wildly with her orgasm, she hit them both, and they both hugged her tight.

I do love watching her come. Bastien kissed her damp forehead.

Yannick merely gave a lusty laugh, stroked her sensitive bottom, and bent to suckle her neck.

Her lids cracked open and she hazily saw Bastien's mirror-like eyes. *I would love to taste your blood, sweeting, and it would enhance the pleasure for you.*

"No." Yannick's simple statement held the sharp authority of a warning.

Bastien merely smiled and retrieved her glass. He poured her more wine. Yannick stretched out along the bed behind her and teased her feet with his as she took a gulp of the fine French wine. The rich, deep red of blood, of course.

She stroked Yannick's soles with her toes to tease him. His feet were rougher than hers and his toes very long. Her feet were soft and smooth, his were bony, crisscrossed with veins, so different. Men, she decided, had the most beautiful feet.

They aroused her—but everything about these men aroused her.

"I like that," Yannick murmured. He guided her hand between his legs. At her touch, he grew harder, longer, and she stroked his length.

God, but it is wonderful torture to have you make me hard again.

Althea stilled. He had been erect at least twice before and had been on the brink of making love to her. His cock appeared even larger this time and harder, which she hadn't believed possible, and his ballocks had mysteriously vanished. Instead of dangling between his legs, the sack was a tight bulge and she could only feel one of the delicate eggs.

"My turn," Bastien whispered and rolled her to him. Warmth engulfed her from behind as Yannick pressed close and his hot length slid between her thighs. Instinctively, she parted them and moaned as the thickness of Yannick's cock pushed against her nether lips. She was slick, ready, and he used the tip to spread her fluid over her. But the thought of taking him in from behind as she kissed Bastien's mouth—

But Yannick only let his member rest between her legs. Bastien released her from the kiss, reluctantly, and Yannick took his turn. His lips slid over her with confidence, almost with arrogance. He kissed her until heat rushed down to her toes and she soared in heaven, moaning with desire. She heard Yannick's throaty chuckle. He was showing off in front of his brother! At least, in this infantile competition, she was the true victor, she decided.

Bastien covered her bare shoulder with kisses. Althea felt hot, teased, tickled, as though she were still beneath one of the furs. She gave a sumptuous sigh and arched in pleasure. In her dream, she'd been a brazen bit of goods and had taken hold of each man's cock at the same time. She knew they would delight in it, but shyness kept her hands in more innocent places.

Barely innocent. Each of her hands was caught in the middle of a broad, naked chest.

Bastien's mouth enveloped her nipple. The tug of his lips, the heat of his tongue, the tingle radiating from her nipple and spiraling down to her quim were familiar now, but no less enthralling.

She brushed kisses down Yannick's throat. Eyes closed, she dipped her tongue into the hollow at the base of his neck, trailed her tongue across his collarbones. She loved the sweetness of his skin, the tang of his sweat. She moved lower and Bastien shifted to accommodate, his tongue twined around her hard nipple.

Opening her mouth wide, she took Yannick's nipple into her mouth, delighting in his moan. But to tease, she pushed Bastien away, forced him to stop suckling.

"Your turn," she whispered and kissed Bastien's nipple. She laved first the right then the left, pressing her lips over his heart.

"Sweet dove," he whispered.

But would Yannick be hurt because she'd kissed both of Bastien's nipples but only one of his? That wouldn't do. She returned to him and snuggled in to reach his right nipple. Pressure of hands increased. Kneading her buttocks, stroking her breasts, drawing up the insides of her thighs. Fingers delved between her legs, and she should care whose, but she no longer could. Fingers, sticky with her juices, caressed her bottom, her thighs, her navel, her breasts. Both men growled, low in their throats like dangerous wolves, as her potent scent filled the room.

Bastien gently tugged her away from Yannick's nipple.

Voice husky, she chided, "I can't ensure each man receives equal treatment! You must learn generosity of spirit and put aside competition and comparisons. You will have to be satisfied with what I choose to do."

"Will I indeed?"

Which man had posed that challenge?

Yannick, she realized, as he rolled her onto her back. In his fire-bright eyes, she knew exactly what he meant to do. "Do you want this, angel?"

"Yes," she urged. And she did. Desire overpowered nerves. "Now."

Braced on his strong arms, Yannick lowered his hips between her legs. She spread them wide, knowing it was the position she should take, but with no idea of whether her legs should be parted just a little, or as wide as she could stretch.

But the instant the tip of his cock slid between her lips, she knew where she wanted her legs. Wrapped around his hips.

"Patience, sweet angel," Yannick admonished. "We will take our time."

He lowered his mouth to her breast. To her surprise, Bastien took her other nipple in his mouth, lavishing loving caresses on it. He touched her everywhere Yannick did not, and she burned with need. She was so slippery, so wet, Yannick easily slid in further. Spreading her. Filling her.

She moved to arch up to take him deeper, but hands stilled her hips.

"Let him do it, sweeting," Bastien urged. "There will be some pain."

"Try to relax," Yannick murmured.

"You're best to break the barrier in one plunge," Bastien advised. Yannick lifted his head and glared. She glanced over at Bastien and caught his smile as he said, "I know you've no experience with virgins."

"Thank you for sharing your vast wealth of knowledge, brother."

She giggled. So inappropriate but she couldn't help it. Yannick gave her a rueful smile before capturing her lips. His hips thrust forward.

One plunge.

Pain radiated. Althea tensed until her teeth ground together. Her fingers clenched and her nails dug into Yannick's broad back. She sobbed, struggling to pull back. With nowhere to go, she could only jam her bottom down into the bed. Yannick held himself above her, head bowed, his tongue licking her lips. She shut her eyes tight and thought only of his warm tongue tracing the curve of her lower lip.

Warmth and wetness surrounded her nipple again. Bastien's lips. It could only be, for Yannick's mouth was still pressed to hers. Fingers rasped across her clit and she jolted in shock. Yannick's fingers, between their bodies. He brushed more soothing kisses on her mouth.

"Relax. It's easing already, isn't it?" Bastien whispered, and he drew more lazy spirals around her nipple with his tongue.

She nodded. To Bastien. Yannick. Both. Yes, he spoke the truth. The pain receded and a delicious fullness remained. "I think," she whispered with a tentative squirm, "I am ready for more." Arching her hips, she linked her hands behind Yannick's neck and gazed into his shining eyes. Inch by exquisite inch, his length slid into her. Gently, slowly, he slid out, withdrawing to the tip.

Bastien teased her nipple and Yannick thrust back in until his groin pressed against his hand and drove his finger hard against her clit.

Lightning bolts seemed to dart across the canopy above at the contact.

She clung tight to his shoulders. He looked so agonized. Sweat beaded on his brow. Salty droplets fell and struck her lips, cool when they hit. One landed in her lashes. As she turned to blink it away, she saw Bastien's golden head at her breast.

Oh, the intimacy of this was frightening. Thrilling. With a sob, she ran her hands down, down the deep curve of Yannick's spine to the hollow of his back. He thrust again, invading deeper, harder, his hand rubbing mercilessly at her clit all the while.

He moved his hand. Her poor button throbbed with thwarted need. Desperate, she reached out to catch his wrist, to drag it back. Even though he had the experience and he knew best, she wanted his hand just where it was.

But he did know how to please in ways Althea couldn't imagine. He splayed his massive hand beneath her rump, lifted her hips, and, as his hips collided with hers and ground against her swollen nub, she knew to trust.

To trust him.

Yannick held her up, open and welcoming as his strokes grew faster, harder. With each plunge, he drove his hips forward, driving in to the hilt. His ballocks bounced against her rear. He shifted his hips and slid in higher. His thick shaft sawed across her clit.

Yes. Oh yes.

The rhythm commanded and she gave in to it. She had no idea how to dance, she'd never learned the steps, but instinct drove her to move to him and meet each thrust. Their slick bodies slapped, joined, slid apart. To her delight, she took him in deeper. Too deep once and she gasped at the shocking penetration, the push against her womb.

But she couldn't quite match him; she dropped back and he fell out. With a desperate groan, he pushed back in. She tried not to make the same mistake, but did, and couldn't concentrate on the pleasure at all for trying to time him.

He moaned and stroked her tangled hair back. "It is good, sweeting?"

"Good?" she breathed. "It is heaven and sin and the most wonderful, amazing thing I've ever experienced."

Bastien laughed. "If she can tell you that much, you aren't thrusting hard enough." He turned her chin and captured her mouth.

"Lie still," Yannick urged, "Let me take command, love."

She tried. But her hips moved of their own volition, propelled by need, moving to join his.

Bastien kissed, Yannick thrust. She hooked both legs about Yannick's thighs. Her heels bumped and bounced on his clenched buttocks as he pumped and pumped. And her hands—one slid up Yannick's sweaty back, the other bumped Bastien's erection.

There were no drugging candles to blame for her wanton wildness. This was no dream.

She didn't care. She wanted. Wanted it so.

15

Shattered

Poised over Althea's beautiful, flushed, nude body, Yannick moaned from deep inside his heart as his rigid cock slid again into her fiery core. He had no soul, but he'd never known such an intense yearning while making love. He gazed down on Althea's fey green eyes and his heart tightened and pounded from more than exertion.

Strands of her wine-red hair dusted her lips. Her plump cheeks glowed pink. With his every thrust, her head arched back in answer, and a throaty moan spilled from her lips. He wanted to drive into her until she screamed.

But a virgin should be treated with care. Yannick fought for control, struggled to rein his need to bury his considerable length to the hilt. She grabbed at his buttocks to pull him deeper, driving her nails in.

"Oh yes," she cried, and his restraint snapped.

He spread her supple thighs wide and rode high and hard to kiss her clit with the length of his shaft.

Thump, thump went the legs of the bed on the floor. Above,

the canopy swayed with rhythmic groans. And the wanton angel beneath him urged him on with her hammering heels.

She was silk and cream, scorching as boiled sugar. Tight and snug, and each time he pulled back, her velvet passage closed behind him, so he had to nudge it wide all over again.

Through the haze of his vision, he saw Bastien get up on his knees. Saw his brother's hand wrap around his thick, curving shaft. To his shock, Bastien tapped the taut, shiny head of his cock against Althea's moist, parted lips. She turned, gave a tremulous smile, then opened her mouth wide.

"Don't."

Bastien, demon that he was, ignored him and took up the invitation. The head of his cock slid in. Stunned, Yannick saw purplish-blue skin—Bastien's swollen head—and Althea's soft, pink tongue merge in wet splendor.

Bastien threw back his head and howled. Althea smiled saucily around the rod filling her mouth and put her fingers around it, just above Bastien's hand. Her fist joined Bastien's in pumping his prick.

Yannick's balls sucked tight and his cock swelled and pulsed. *Wait*, he told himself. *Hold off. What is a dozen years of experience if you can't hang on to a bloody orgasm?*

But as Bastien's cock slid further between those pretty pink lips, Yannick knew he'd never last. At least Bastien was respectful of her innocence, allowing Althea to take control—

She grasped Bastien's arse and pulled him to suckle his cock deep. Yannick groaned in surprise and desire. His sweet angel had shocked him to his core. She feasted on Bastien's prick as though it was a tasty delight. Her tongue laved and swirled and he could not believe his eyes.

But she took Bastien in too deep, Yannick guessed, because she gagged and pulled back. Coughing, she brushed at tears and a fetching blush rose on her cheeks. She gulped, blinked, and swallowed, and then took his brother's cock in her mouth once more.

His balls tightened more and he knew he had to make her come because he couldn't last any longer. He rode hard and fast and high, rubbing her slippery clit.

She drove up to him and their hips slapped hard. She dropped Bastien's cock out to pant and moan around it.

Incoherent words tumbled. "Yes . . . oh yes . . . I'm going . . . I'm going—"

Her scream rang up to the canopy. Yannick thanked heaven above, drove deep into her climaxing quim, and let the first spasm take him.

His brain ignited in flame. His spine dissolved into sweet, warm fluid and shot down through his balls, exploding out of his cock. The orgasm he'd flirted with all night released with the force of cannon fire, ripping him asunder. He gave in to it, lost and vulnerable and blind, rocking deep into Althea.

"Sweetheart, you bit me," Bastien said.

"She needs her rest."

The commanding tone of his brother's voice ignited Bastien's usual flare of defiance. He ignored the warning and kissed Althea. Her lashes fluttered and she wore a sweetly dreamy expression. How he wished he'd been the one to put it there. The scrapes on his cock from her teeth still stung—even as they healed—but a dip in her molten honey would soon cure that. The healing was slow, which meant dawn was close.

True, he didn't want to hurt Althea, but he had so little time. And her embrace welcomed.

"I fear it is too scandalous," she whispered, "to make love to two men in the same night."

"Nothing is scandalous, little dove." Bastien opened her with his fingers, releasing a flood of juice.

"Are you too sore?"

"A little sore, but I also ache to have you." She gave a soft giggle. "I am incorrigible."

The head of his prick lodged in her fiery quim, cradled by the walls and the soft, plump lips. "You are wonderful." But before he pushed forward, he cupped her chin. "You do want me?"

She didn't speak but she nodded and trapped her lower lip with her teeth in a beguiling gesture. Her body spoke for her, arching to take more of him, and she clasped her hands about his neck and slung her leg over his. But he was not a demon for nothing and he had no desire to ride her in the same bland fashion as his brother.

With a teasing wink, he begged for her trust and caught hold of her ankles.

"You can do that while you enter me?" she asked, astonished. So Yannick had lifted her legs this way, obviously to display her pussy and rear for oral play.

Two slow thrusts and Bastien forgot about being second. He bent to her neck and nestled his face there as he held her legs wide, but not splayed enough to hurt. She worked up to him, bouncing with avid enthusiasm and he loved her for it.

Daylight was coming. He felt it in his blood. Felt it in his slowing heart.

Damn, he'd hoped for slow and languorous, not rushed and speedy. He moved fluidly to his knees without unseating his cock, and lifted her ankles to his neck.

"Goodness!"

His first long thrust elicited a delighted cry. "It makes you go so deep!"

Pride caused his cock to swell more—he couldn't help it—and he pleasured her this way. Deep and slow. Until she shattered with kitten-like squeals and a squirm. Pulsing around him, her cunny ignited him like a match to a fuse and he exploded.

* * *

"How did your father learn about Zayan?"

Althea sipped the excellent wine. Was this still her second glass or now her third? Or very possibly her fourth? The buzzing in her head grew a little louder. She tried to focus on Yannick's question—and on the questions it raised in her mind. "What intrigues me more, my lord, is how you learned about my father."

Sprawled across the tousled, luxurious, ivory sheets, Yannick lifted her foot into his naked lap and sensuously stroked her sole. Tickling pleasure raced up her leg and she almost sloshed wine in her own lap. Her foot gave a little jolt and her heel grazed his now slumbering member.

He smiled, giving a glimpse of his white fangs, and massaged more firmly. "The Royal Society for the Investigation of Mysterious Phenomena. Your father is ostensibly not a member, but all there know of his outstanding reputation."

She was wrapped in the counterpane with Bastien lying by her other side. Snuggled up to her left side, just as in her dream. His eyes were shut and she thought him sleeping. Until he reached up to lazily tap the underside of her breast beneath her cover.

She really must try to think.

"Once I learned he was planning a trip to Maidensby," Yannick continued, "and that by all accounts he was in a state of great excitement, I suspected he had learned of Bastien and planned to resurrect him. I guessed at once he planned to keep Bastien under control and coerce me to destroy Zayan."

She nodded. "He hasn't shared all of his plans with me. I did know he has been trying to discover the origin of vampires. We'd learned that Zayan's existence shows in records prior to the Middle Ages. There are Roman and Celtic accounts of a creature that my father believed to be a description of Zayan. Is Zayan the oldest vampire? Is he the sire of all vampires?"

Bastien stirred at her words but, to her frustration, he didn't respond other than to trace his fingertip in the fold between her breast and her ribcage.

"No, Zayan is not," Yannick said, giving each toe a squeeze. "If that is what your father seeks, he's in error."

"Is Zayan as evil as it is claimed he is? He didn't kill the girl in the field—"

"Only because he knew I would sense death," Bastien interrupted with a yawn. "He used her as bait for me, and knew I would only be drawn to a living victim." Like a warm, sated lion, he stretched and gave a rumbling purr. "Enough talk, little dove. It is almost dawn. I would like to ensure you are safely returned to the Inn before the sun is up."

Bastien plucked the glass from her hand and drained it. Licked his lips. "Delicious. Smooth wine, the taste of a delightful woman, and even the flavor of my own flesh."

"Time for home," Yannick said.

Home! How could she go home after this night? What would she say? Surely someone had noticed her missing?

Had Father? Or was he still hunting? Dear heaven, she hadn't spared him a thought when he was putting himself in danger. Had he encountered Zayan after the vampire had escaped? At least Zayan was weak.

So many secrets must be locked in this house. Zayan had to be stopped, and if Bastien would not do it, she and Father must. During daylight she could explore in safety. She put her thoughts, her plan, into words. "I could learn much about Zayan."

Yannick shook his head as he moved her foot off his lap.

She put her hands on her hips, intending to argue. But she didn't. It wouldn't be necessary. She would merely return with Father.

She swung her legs around the side of the bed and jumped off. In the day, Yannick and Bastien would be safe—

"But wait. Where will you sleep, Bastien?"

"Are you daring me to return to that room you locked me in at the Inn?" He grinned cheekily, flashing fangs.

"You could. I can assure you that no harm will come to you."

"Perhaps I will then, little dove. I would sleep a happy demon knowing that you watched over me." He yawned. "We have an hour or more before dawn. Enough time to make love again."

Without further ado, Bastien dropped to his knees in front of her and buried his face in her cunny. It was so quick! Pleasure rushed through her and she clung to his broad, beautiful shoulders. Her legs buckled but he held her thighs, held her wide as he licked her burning clit.

She was going to explode.

Yannick watched her as though mesmerized, his molten silver gaze fastened on her face as though he were entranced. She must look wanton, dishevelled. A flush bloomed over her cheeks. Her lips parted as she panted. Her hair was a mass of tangled curls, dancing around her as Bastien rocked her over his mouth. Rocked her hard against his hot, slightly rough tongue.

Her eyes shut tight. Her juices flowed like a spring river bursting a dam.

"Lord, she soaked me," Bastien rasped. "With a flood of sweet honey."

She heard, from somewhere close, Yannick's hoarse groan in response.

All she could think of was the wonderful explosion building between her legs. Just a little more and—

Hands took hold of her ass cheeks. Startled, she looked down to see Yannick on his knees at her rear. He'd done this before, kissed her this way, but in combination with his brother's caress, it seemed too shocking for words.

"No," she gasped.

Oh yes, they chorused.

Yannick touched the tip of his tongue to her puckered entrance and she sobbed. Althea wanted it so. Just as she'd wanted everything else. To her shame, she realized all she wanted was to come. She was so close, so tantalizingly close, and she knew—simply knew—that both men would take her to the most incredible ecstasy. To hell with rules, with emotion, with proper behavior.

She wanted. And they offered. And if she loved both and was caught up in this unbelievable dilemma, she didn't care. Not now.

Yannick's tongue circled and coaxed. Heat seared and his wetness made her slick and accommodating. His tongue filled while Bastien's rasped and sawed and drove her mad.

Say my name, they both urged at exactly the same moment.

Yannick's tongue plunged deep, and her sensitive rim throbbed as his tongue spread it wide open. Bastien suckled hard, as though he sought to suck her aching nub right off her body.

Oh, you truly are demons, she cried in her head. *Oh, oh, oh!*

They shared a very demonic laugh. Plunged, suckled, teased her thighs. Faster and faster.

She shattered, like fragile glass. A thousand pieces spinning through the air. She cried out, lost her legs completely, and they supported her as each lush spasm racked her.

Just as she toppled over the peak, they took her there again. Another orgasm on the heels of the first. She sobbed and sobbed. Thrashed and bucked with it as fireworks, worthy of a Vauxhall extravaganza, exploded before her eyes.

She was coming and it was primitive and wonderful and wild. And her twin vampires held her tight as she rode upon their faces.

16

Morning

Yannick held Althea close, possessively, as he spurred the gelding along the rough lane as fast as he dared. He stifled a groan as her lush bottom bounced upon his cock. Clamped tight in his trousers, it tried to stretch toward the two plump cheeks subjecting it to sensual torture.

The sleeping village lay before them and a break in the trees at a stretch of black field gave a glimpse of the horizon. Deep black melted into dark purple and midnight blue.

Yannick squeezed his thighs against Ares' flanks, urging the beast into a faster pace. Dawn was close. Bastien followed, in the shape of a bat, swooping about them. Determined not to leave Althea alone with him, he realized ruefully.

He took the reins in one hand and wrapped his arms around Althea's waist. She fit beautifully against him, an intoxicating mix of opposites—soft, abundant curves paired with indomitable courage, shown through her straight spine and the confident tilt of her head. She was a unique woman. Stubborn and sensuous, intelligent and fiery. Brave but not foolhardy.

I am trying to understand exactly why Bastien refused to slay Zayan.

Of all the things he thought she might be thinking, that was not on the list. He'd hoped she was reliving their more sensual moments. He'd hoped she was thinking what a wonderful lover he was.

He would prefer to discuss his prowess in bed.

I don't know, sweet. And he didn't. He could guess that Bastien somehow knew of the terms of Yannick's release from imprisonment and had decided to wait until the next full moon. In mere days, if Zayan wasn't destroyed, he would be—and that left Bastien to claim everything. Title, wealth, estate—for as long as he was willing to keep his nature hidden.

And Althea. The most precious treasure of all.

I can't see a clear way to convince Bastien to kill the man he has shown such love toward, he said. *They were lovers and it seems that there is still . . . feeling.*

She twisted in his arms, and her cheek pressed against his chest—where his shirt was unbuttoned. The bumping contact of her satin skin set his on fire. *Yes, that is true, isn't it? I saw the way they touched. They were aggressive and combative sometimes but every touch was . . . was charged with love. There was tenderness underneath.*

So she'd understood that.

But if he wasn't willing to destroy Zayan out of revenge, she continued, moving gracefully with him as they trotted, *what other possible motivation could there be?*

I don't know, angel, he admitted once more.

And there is no other way to kill Zayan? What if you were to weaken him and then I stake him?

No, it needs both Bastien and me.

Her chin tipped up a notch and her hair tickled him, driving him mad. He wanted to kiss her again on the horse. Hell and damnation, he wanted to make love to her on the galloping horse.

I refuse to believe it's hopeless, she insisted.

As much as her stubborn streak drove him mad, he admired it.

What was Zayan in his mortal life? Father wouldn't tell me much about Zayan and I couldn't find anything written about him that told me.

Her bottom bounced on his cock again and Yannick struggled to think.

Zayan is an ancient one so he must possess a very bloody past, she mused.

Althea was a single-minded wench. Sex with her had rocked him to his core, yet she seemed to be completely matter-of-fact about a passionate interlude with two men, as though it was not of great import.

He groaned into her wild hair. *Zayan does have a bloody past, sweet.* He spurred the horse to greater speed here, where the track was good. *As a mortal, he was a general, so he waged war. I believe his mortal name was Marius Praetonius and he conquered much of Europe—before the birth of Christ. He killed for glory, for necessity, but also for pleasure. Reputedly Zayan drank the blood of his victims, even as a mortal, and developed an unholy thirst for blood. Eventually, to satisfy his craving, and take the blood of more pure men, he began to sacrifice his own commanding men. Then he craved the blood of innocents—*

"Virgins," she supplied aloud and her bottom rocked maddeningly over his prick.

"And children," he added hoarsely. "As Zayan aged, he sought the blood of the young to give him life."

She nodded in understanding. "Like Countess Elizabeth Bathory, drinking the blood of young women to keep her young."

Even just talking about Zayan, Yannick found his grip on Althea tightening protectively. Damn, he didn't want her to hunt Zayan, but he knew that trying to keep Althea ignorant would not work. She was too stubborn. So he told her what he knew about his foe.

"But as happens to many brutal generals who become insane," he explained, "Zayan was betrayed and his closest confidant, a general jealous of Zayan's strength and success, attempted to murder him. Zayan escaped but was taken prisoner by the people he was attempting to destroy. They tortured him, yet he endured. He claims he made a pact with Lucifer to survive. He bargained to walk as a devil among the human world, to enter into the service of Satan for eternity, and in return, he would turn living, breathing people into the undead, delivering their souls to the dark lord who craved them. But he began to believe himself stronger than the devil he served. He began to believe he could defeat his master. And so, when Zayan became obsessed with Bastien, my wild brother became the tool of Lucifer to destroy his monster. And then Bastien, under Lucifer's control, turned me. Created me. To share the power, so no one demon would possess too much."

"The tool of *Lucifer*?" Althea lifted up in her surprise and her derrière banged down hard on his cock. He soaked his trousers with desire.

"Do you—do you converse with Lucifer?" she asked, twisting again in his arms.

Why? he drawled in her mind. *Would you care to meet him?* The last thing he needed was courageous Althea hunting Lucifer. *But you can't stake him and destroy the devil, love.*

Bastien was the tool of Lucifer? Althea could hardly believe it. And what did it import? What would the devil demand of Bastien once Zayan was destroyed?

Cold fear raced down her spine and she felt sick with horror.

If the twins were truly in service to the devil, would she be obligated to destroy them?

"But are you in Lucifer's service?" she persisted to Yannick.

"I have never made a bargain with the devil."

"You said you did," she reminded him.

"I mean that I never made one directly with Old Nick himself. And there are ways to free yourself of a deal with the devil, if you are careful."

"So Bastien could be freed?"

"I don't know, love, and I am growing too tired to think."

She understood why. At the horizon, the deep indigo sky was lightening, and she saw the faintest glow of pink, the promise of sunrise. Yannick spurred his mount. With one arm and his powerful thighs, Yannick held her tight as they galloped into Maidensby.

And you, too, sweeting, need to rest.

Were all women generally coddled when they surrendered their virginity? She had no idea. She was so unknowing about women's concerns. She'd spent so much of her life with just Father.

But Bastien had treated her like an invalid, had carried her to Yannick's horse. "Tender treatment for an injured former maiden," he'd said.

They thundered up to the lane to the church and the churchyard where Bastien had been imprisoned. Yannick suddenly reined in. Above lay the gray stone church and the manse by its side. But ahead, bobbing lights were moving toward them on the road, coming up the hill.

Yannick brought Ares to a stop and she heard the beat of wings. This time Althea saw the shadow of a large bat swoop against the pre-dawn sky.

Bastien materialized in front of them. "Jesus," he muttered. "Men with torches. Never a welcome sight to a vampire."

"Lanterns, not torches," Yannick corrected. He spoke in his jaded drawl, which she now realized he used to hide any sign of fear or weakness.

"It must be Father, returning from his hunt." His hunt of the two men she had spent the night with! Guilt washed up like a wave. "Leave me here and escape. Please. I'll take your horse back to the stables. I'll claim that I took it alone to come out here."

They were silent for a moment, a long, precious moment.

"Please," she repeated, "Let me protect you."

"They'll guess you're lying." Yannick frowned as Bastien held out his strong, naked arms and helped her down. He brushed a kiss to her cheek as he set her firmly on her feet. "I don't like leaving you alone to face their possible anger," Yannick added.

"What other choice do you have?" she asked.

Althea's father will want to believe her story, Bastien added.

Finally Yannick nodded. He bent and murmured in the huge horse's ear before dismounting himself. The black carriage horse stood, calm and docile as Yannick handed her the reins. It was an immense creature and she had no familiarity with horses.

She felt a surge of joy that Yannick trusted her with his horse—she saw how much he loved his beasts.

"You both must be careful," she urged. She felt foolish, but she couldn't help stating the obvious. For Zayan to ensure his safety, he had to destroy at least one twin.

They both stood in the shadow of a large oak, a stretch of protective darkness against the oncoming dawn. She didn't see them change, but they flew by her face as though trying to blow one last kiss to her.

And then she was alone, holding the reins in her hands. The horse, Ares, gently bumped her back, as though urging her forward to meet her fate.

To face Father, and the workmen with weapons and lanterns.

Her father, who was five and sixty, charged up the hill, ahead of the lamplight. Before Althea could admonish him to stop, to slow down at least, he pulled her into an embrace and wrapped his arms tight around her. The smell of wet wool swamped her and she couldn't catch her breath.

"Thank heaven, you're alive! Oh, lass, you're not to do that to me again."

Only as she crumpled against Father's greatcoat did Althea realize she no longer felt the unconditional comfort she'd always known in his arms. Tonight, in one mere night, she had betrayed every moral dictate he had taught her. Guilt warred with practicality. She couldn't reveal what she'd done with Yannick and Bastien, but she couldn't back down from the obligation to tell Father about the manor house and the mausoleum.

But how to explain where she'd come by the knowledge? Could she do it without admitting she had been with the twins?

She had found the courage to break into Zayan's lair armed with only a stake and crossbow but one look at Father's anguished blue eyes behind his spectacles had her tongue-tied.

"What in blazes did they do to you?" he cried, then he groaned, "Oh, sweet Jesus," and raked her hair back from her neck.

None too gently, he inspected, then tipped her head the other way to look on the other side.

He thought she had been lured out by the twins. "No, Father, I haven't been bitten."

She pushed back gently. Father's hat was gone and his wiry white hair was soaked and slicked down against his head. Splatters of dried droplets and fingerprints made his spectacles a hazy mask over his eyes. Mud was streaked across his forehead and cheeks. Deep lines were etched around his mouth and his lips trembled.

His chest heaved with his breaths. Shallow, rasping breaths.

By the light of the lantern held by a soaked young man, Father's face appeared vivid red.

"Heavens, Father, what happened to you?" Had he encountered Zayan?

"What happened?" he roared, but then he succumbed to coughing. Panicked, she wrapped her arm across his shoulders and almost fell as his weight sagged heavily into her. "You vanish into the night and you ask me what happened? I've been combing every inch of this blasted village looking for you. I feared—I feared you were lost to me already, Althea, lovey."

Mr. O'Leary appeared behind Father, took hold of his arm. Those dark Irish eyes cast a look of condemnation on her. "He's exhausted, lass. We must get him warm and dry."

She could see the truth of that. "Well, let us not tarry then—"

"No, I'm not moving from this spot until I find out what's happened to my little lass."

"That's foolish talk, sir, and that's a fact," O'Leary forced Father to take a step down the hill. She clung to Father's hand.

"It's true, Father. I'm safe and sound, but I fear you aren't. Please, let us get you warm and dry and then we can talk. You need to sleep."

Father turned and she flinched at the penetrating fire in his blue eyes. "You've not slept either, have you, lass? And you are soaked through as well, though I'd like to know where you came by that cloak."

Her hands strayed to it. Bastien had wrapped one of Zayan's cloaks around her. She gulped nervously. But there was no urgency to tell Father of her night. Tomorrow, in daylight, would be soon enough and then they could search Zayan's house. In perfect safety, during the day. And when she'd had time to concoct a good story.

"I'll tell you all in the morning," she promised.

But, for the first time in her life, she would have to tell Father a pack of lies. And she realized there was now a far greater distance between them than there would have been had she obeyed and gone to London.

Halfway down the hill, with pink splashing over the brightening sky, Father stumbled. She couldn't support him. O'Leary must have been taken by surprise, for he dropped down too.

Father clamped his hand over his heart. His face contorted in agony.

His heart! She had no idea what to do.

He gasped desperately for breath.

Get him air. Let him breathe, a voice screamed in her head.

Fearing her efforts futile, Althea pushed open his greatcoat and tore at his cravat. Father kept his hand pressed tightly over his chest. His face became gray, and sweat poured from his brow. She mopped at it with the trailing ends of the loose cravat.

"Please breathe, Father. Try to breathe." She had no idea what one said to a victim of a heart attack. The men standing helplessly around her seemed to have no idea either. One shoved a flask of spirits forward.

Would that help or make things worse?

O'Leary seemed to think the idea sound; he held it to Father's mouth. But the wine or brandy or gin just spilled over Father's lips.

"Please, please, Father," she begged. "Please hold on." *Yannick, Yannick, I wish you could come. You could save him. I know it.*

She glanced around the sky, but of course, Yannick wouldn't—couldn't—come to help now.

Father's hand fluttered on his chest. His breathing deepened. Grew slowly steadier.

"The pain's . . . pain's going. . . ." he wheezed.

She tried to warn him not to speak.

"Pet . . . oh, pet, it was like lightning striking me chest. Pins and needles down me arm. Couldn't even feel me fingers." He slumped back, against Mick O'Leary's strong arms.

Tears burned her eyes, began to blur. No, she couldn't give in to hysterics right now.

"Lift him, Mr. O'Leary," she directed. "With haste, but gently."

It took two men, the strapping Mr. O'Leary and a brawny man named Creedly, to carry Father. She held Father's cold hand on the entire procession back to the Inn, and kept her fingertips on his wrist. Now and again she felt the pulse. Not strong, but it grew steadier.

It was worry over her that had almost killed him. And no amount of holding his hand or brushing her hand over his cool, drenched brow would make up for what she'd done.

Yannick's blood might help, but what was she to do? She had to ensure she didn't give Father another bad shock. She had to ensure he never learned the truth of what she had done.

She stood at the top of a flight of stone steps. Beneath the moonlight, the stairs gleamed white. Sweeping in a curve, they vanished into shadow where masses of blooming lilacs dripped over them. Directly before her, the moon sat high and blue-white in the sky, almost full, entrancing and magical. Softness teased her skin and she discovered, as though she hadn't known before, that she was naked beneath a sable wrap.

Whose garden did she stand in? Pale statues frolicked amidst the stretch of lawns and bushes of pale purple lilac and budding white roses. She spied the satyr Pan. Diana with bow and hounds. Bare-breasted nymphs bent over a small pool. A water sprite caught one in a forbidden kiss, the damsel desperately attempting to pull away.

Strangely, although they were stone, sightless and soulless, the kissing pair stirred her desire. Which was mad, for the idea of being forced truly horrified her.

Well, a statue could not come to life and pursue her, but where was she?

Not Zayan's gardens, surely, for this one was well tended, groomed to orderly beauty.

There should be a house behind her. She began to turn, although it seemed difficult to do so, her feet sluggish and unwilling to obey.

Sweet angel, come with us. *Yannick and Bastien raced up from the shadows. Bastien's long, gold hair streamed out behind him, glinting in the moonlight. His thighs bunched beneath trousers of robin's-egg blue as he took the steps two at a time. The tails of his deep blue coat bounced against his buttocks. She'd never before seen him dressed. His taste was . . . flamboyant, to say the least. Yannick smiled and held out his hand, his hair burnished silver. He wore simple clothes—the attire of a young, affluent country gentleman. A tailored coat, white cravat at his throat, leather breeches that outlined his muscular thighs, gleaming boots. More subdued, but he shone just as brightly.*

Yannick caught hold of her right hand; Bastien clasped her left. They laughed, fey and wicked, like schoolboys about to announce they planned to steal a pie from the kitchen. As they tugged, the wrap fell, leaving her naked.

They exchanged a glance and before she could gasp, they drew her down to the steps and smothered her with kisses to her lips and nipples. They cuddled her and tore one-handed at waistcoats, shirts and breeches, exposing broad chests and large, bronze-pink erections.

We can't make love on the stairs, *she thought shyly.*

We can, if I cushion you from behind, *Bastien promised.* Do you want this, now, little dove? Yannick's cock buried to the hilt in your hot quim and mine . . . mine thrusting in your ass? We want to cram you full of cock.

She gasped at his shocking words.

Do you want that? To be filled with cock?

Wantoness surged. She did. Her quim ached for it, her bottom tingled. She moaned and arched back to lick his neck as Bastien pressed the head of his thick staff between her cheeks—

"Miss Yates? Are ye up, miss? I must speak with ye, if ye please."

The high-pitched voice invaded her dream at the critical point. Althea flinched, blinked and tried to blot it from her thoughts. She tried to envision Yannick parting her legs but the dream was lost and it was her imagination supplying the image—

"Miss Yates!"

Althea's eyes shot open. Fragile sunlight filled her room. Her curtains were still wide open and it was obviously long past dawn. The hustle and bustle of the Inn sounded from below and the cries and scents of the village poured in her open window.

Had Father had another attack?

Jolted awake, she pushed back the sheet and thin blanket. Her naked breasts greeted her. She dropped the sheet. She'd been so exhausted, she mustn't have bothered with her nightgown, but what a foolish thing.

"What is it, Sarah?" she called as she leapt from bed and grabbed her shift from her chair. She recognized the voice of the maid who tended her and did her rooms, though for once the girl's speech didn't contain mostly giggles. "Is it Sir Edmund? Is he unwell?"

"No, indeed, Miss, though as 'e's 'aving a rest, Mr. O'Leary told me I must come to you."

With her shift over her head and her arms tangled in it in her haste, Althea called out a muffled answer, "Well, then, whatever is so urgent, Sarah?"

"I was bit by a vampire, Miss."

By a miracle, her tangled shift dropped at Sarah's announcement and floated over her hips, the hem settling around her thighs. Not decent but at least not nude.

"You had best come in then, Sarah, and tell me your story."

So, after Father's search last night, all of Maidensby must now know them to be vampire hunters.

Which put Bastien and Yannick at even graver risk—being hunted by a torch-bearing mob.

As she crossed to the door in quick strides, she realized how much her father was changing. Aging. In his younger years, Father never would have been so careless. He was always so discreet. Not so much in the Carpathians, where legends of vampires ran deep, but in England he took care. Best to let people believe such things to be myths, he claimed.

Scooping up the key from the floor, Althea inserted it and unlocked the door.

Sarah all but tumbled in, blond corkscrew curls in a wild tangle beneath her cap and her wide, blue eyes filled with excitement, not fear. She brushed her hair, the gold of guineas, back to expose her neck. "Look at the marks of 'is teeth, Miss."

Two tiny puncture wounds marred the creamy white throat. But Sarah's cheeks were flushed a healthy pink and she appeared no worse for wear. The wounds were clean.

She took Sarah by the elbow and steered her to the chair. "What happened to you?"

"Well, it weren't a bad experience, Miss Yates, and it didn't hurt none. In truth, it were right exciting."

"Oh, Sarah. You must tell me exactly what happened. What was this vampire like?"

"Tall. And, gawd bless me, but 'e was the most devilish 'andsome man I've seen. Just afore dawn, I laid the fires and I took out the pail wi' the ash. It were still dark and I just stepped out the door when this gent caught me about the waist and dragged me wi' 'im. Oo, but I were right scared. Then I thought it were 'is lordship, 'as 'e was tall and 'ad fair hair."

"His lordship," Althea echoed. She'd thought the vampire was Zayan, not Yannick. Of course Yannick must feed, but why did he have to choose a voluptuous maid?

Well, one look at Sarah made the answer obvious. Althea's heart gave a twinge of pain. The girl was perhaps eighteen and a bonny thing. She wore a simple dress with a low bodice and her breasts spilled over the top. Her shift covered the plump mounds but it was laundered to translucence and was barely decent. The dress tucked in to a neat little waist, then swelled once more about generous hips.

Althea found it impossible not to stare at Sarah's lush figure. Her breasts wobbled in a captivating way as Sarah told her story with expansive waving of her small hands. Bastien's naughty stories about women dallying with other women tormented Althea as she tried to listen.

Look at the poor girl's face, she chided herself. And she tried, valiantly.

Sarah didn't seem to notice her wandering gaze, thank goodness. The girl leaned forward. "But it weren't."

"Weren't?" She'd lost the thread.

"'Is lordship. 'E was a gent though. And 'e was nude. Starkers. In 'is full naked glory, and a broader chest I never did see. Me arms sort of flew about his waist when I were caught all surprised and I got ahold of his arse. 'Is cheeks were so snug and small and tight in me hands, like a couple of firm apples."

It wasn't his lordship? Not only were her cheeks on fire but her blood was almost boiling, and she was pacing about. Sarah's colorful description matched Yannick, but also—

"'E has lovely, long, golden hair," Sarah continued. "And when he put 'is lips to my neck, I caught a hank of it to steady meself."

"Bastien."

"I beg your pardon, Miss?" Sarah's eyes narrowed and her tongue made a light clucking noise. Disapproval.

A hysterical giggle hovered on Althea's lips. Apparently the maid thought she'd muttered the word *bastard*.

Which she had every right to do, for Bastien had professed his love and then went around snatching innocent maids. Of course, not once had Bastien promised to be faithful—

This time the giggle broke free. Faithful! Was she mad? She'd made love to both twins; she could hardly expect both men to pledge fidelity to her, could she? And she'd made love to Bastien after watching—oh, she still flushed with shock to think of it—him enjoy sexual pleasures with another man. She'd known perfectly well that Bastien didn't intend to forsake all others for her.

"Do you wish to 'ear the rest of me story, Miss?" Sarah interrupted.

Althea realized she'd stalked to the window and now stood with her back to the girl. She turned. "Do go on," she urged.

"Well, I thought he meant to swive me, though most coves don't strip to the altogether to force themselves on a lass. He had quite the broadsword—"

"He was armed?" As soon as she spoke, she realized what the maid had meant.

"No, Miss." Sarah flushed. "'Is prick, I meant. Ye know, 'is Member for Cockshire."

Althea put the flat of her hand against the aging wardrobe. The maids certainly possessed a varied vocabulary for male private parts, but she wasn't sure if she wanted to hear more.

She was becoming quite a perverted individual. She must call a stop to this—

"But 'e just bit me." Sarah stroked her neck. "'E promised it wouldn't hurt and 'e had this husky, deep voice that sort of mesmerized me. I couldn't move me own two feet. There was a bit o' pain. Just a wee bit. And then this wonderful feeling came over me. It were like tupping, but so much better. And even though he didn't touch me melons or me quim, I exploded. Oh, but of course ye wouldn't know, Miss."

Startled, Althea only gaped at the girl. Quick thinking had her demurely agreeing, "Err . . . no." Once she would have reproved the girl for her vulgar speech, but now she found her tongue tripping about in her mouth. Straightening it, she managed, "We needn't have improper descriptions, Sarah. But please continue."

"No, Miss. I didn't mean to be crude. But that was the way of it. I were gasping and heaving and 'e laughed. 'E gave me neck a lick and then just seemed to vanish into the air. I saw a great big bat and so I raced inside—me feet could move all of a sudden, though I almost fell headlong into the pantry."

Althea began to understand Yannick's attitude toward his twin. Bastien was incorrigible. To bite Sarah in a place he might easily be caught was foolish enough, but to neglect to heal her wound or erase her memory of the incident was completely . . . well, insane.

Given his nature, Bastien no doubt enjoyed spreading panic and fear by not being circumspect about his hungers. After all, he enjoyed whippings . . . which of society's rules would really matter to him?

As she mulled over Bastien's brazen behavior, she realized her heart was completely confused. She had much more in common with Yannick, despite his status as earl, but she couldn't resist the charming scoundrel that was Bastien. He promised the forbidden, the dangerous, the sinful, and she hungered for a taste.

"Do yer think 'e'll come after me again?" Sarah asked.

"No, he most definitely will not. I will make certain of that."

"Oo, 'ow will you do that, Miss?"

Sarah's question brought her up short. She'd spoken without thinking.

"Do you 'unt vampires, then?" Sarah's eyes were wide with astonishment and respect. For a moment, Althea preened beneath the girl's awe.

"Coo, I'd love to 'unt vampires."

Althea realized Sarah assumed she hunted gorgeous, naked men about the countryside. Which she did, at times, but not all vampires were handsome and charming men. Some were hideous beasts, white and grotesque. Others were mindless demons, driven only by the thirst for blood. The undead came in many guises.

"It is a very dangerous profession and—" Althea broke off. The words *and not suitable for a young woman* died upon her lips. She'd felt a distinct sisterly urge to deter the younger, naïve woman from danger, but that was the reasoning that all men used around her—now, even Father.

"You could hunt vampires, if you wish, but there are many skills you would have to learn first. You would have to train with an experienced hunter and read . . . yes, lots of reading. About legends and history and ancient civilizations."

"Could you teach me?"

"I don't think so, Sarah. Now, you don't feel unwell, do you? Not weak or dizzy?"

"Oh, no, Miss. I'm right as rain."

"I think you should rest before you go down to work—"

"Crenshaw won't abide with that."

"Then I will speak with Mr. Crenshaw. As for you, Sarah, don't tell anyone else your story."

The girl's blue eyes lowered, her gaze riveted to the floor. Which meant the girl had already shared her tale—likely with every servant she'd encountered.

Blast.

As Sarah stood up, her pretty face turned serious. "If 'e does come back, Miss, I'll tell ye about it," she vowed.

"Don't go seeking danger, Sarah," Althea warned. "Not all

vampires are as charming and . . . considerate as the one you encountered." She didn't want Sarah trolling for another encounter with Bastien—and not just because of the jealousy spearing her heart. The image of that girl on the field, drenched with rain and covered with blood, would be forever seared in her mind. What if Sarah encountered Zayan? She caught hold of Sarah's hand. "There is a vampire prowling the village who is neither gentle nor charming. He's a vicious monster and if he bit you, he would kill you."

"Ooh, I'd not want that!"

"No, of course not. You must take care after dark, Sarah. And so must other girls." The way Sarah described Bastien, what young maiden wouldn't hope to meet a vampire? Althea gave as vivid a description of Zayan as she could, enhancing the details of fangs and red eyes and brutal strength, until Sarah was quaking.

Wide-eyed, Sarah promised she would warn every young woman or child that she saw.

Then, Althea propelled the girl toward the door. She really must see how Father was feeling. But she couldn't stop wondering. Would Bastien return? Or now that he was free, would he return to his wild life with Zayan—the one he was once addicted to? Would the twins return that night for her?

17

Sapphic Pleasures

Althea stared in astonishment at the tray Mick O'Leary held. "Sausages! I really don't think he's strong enough for sausages."

Mr. O'Leary gave a shrug, twinkled his eyes at her, and nodded toward Father's closed door. "He smelled them cooking and told me to fetch him some."

She rolled her eyes. "Take them back down and have the cook make beef tea." But she did retrieve the teapot and cup from the tray before Mr. O'Leary turned away with it.

No matter what she might see, she promised herself to put on a cheerful face. After all, they'd weathered Father's injuries during battles with vampires. Once, after a fierce fight, they'd had to spend months at an abbey while Father's broken limbs healed.

Balancing the tray, Althea opened the door and strode into Father's room.

But her steps faltered. He looked so small, as though he'd shrunk overnight. His face was ashen. The hands lying on his quilt were white and his skin appeared thin as parchment, crisscrossed with blue veins. His lids flickered as she approached the bed, then opened slowly. A weak smile touched his lips as he saw her.

She'd not expected him to still look quite so ill. Her hands wobbled. The tray made a clatter as she placed it on his bedside table. Steam wafted up from the tea as she filled a cup.

"How are you feeling?"

His hand shook as he reached out for the tea. "Improving, lass, and the sight of you alive and well does much to make me better."

She clasped his other hand. Once again she choked on her guilt. "I spoke to Mr. Crenshaw, Father. There's a doctor in Stropshire Downs, only an hour by carriage. I've sent for him."

He lifted his cup and it bumped against his lips as he trembled. "I've no need of a doctor."

"You do, Father." *And all this was my fault.*

"What happened to you last night, lovey? And I want the truth."

Even though his spectacles sat on the table, and he surely couldn't focus properly on her, she flinched at his gaze.

"Bastien . . . Bastien de Wynter came to my room last night, Father." She had to give him some truth—but not enough to give him another attack.

Tea sloshed from the cup.

She half rose over him.

"No," he waved his hand. "What did Bastien de Wynter do to you?"

"Nothing . . . he just talked to me." Which was true, but she wouldn't ever divulge what Bastien had talked about. Now, that admission could very well kill Father.

"Did he?" Father's eyes narrowed.

She nodded with a guilty swallow. "I don't know if he intended to bite me; he did not try. But then Y—the earl came to . . . to protect me."

"So the Demon Twins are fighting over you, lass." He sank back. "I feared this. That one day a vampire would fall in love with you, would do anything to possess you."

"In love with me!" Althea colored. She felt the burn all over her face.

"Lass, please, I couldn't bear to lose you to a vampire, for the only way either of the de Wynters could claim you is to turn you."

She jerked with shock, rocking the bed enough that his tea spilled again. "How clumsy," she cried, "Let me—"

"What else happened, pet? Did they lure you outside?"

"I wasn't bitten, Father, I swear it. And Bastien left, you see. But the earl was able to make a mental connection with his twin and saw him in danger with Zayan—"

"So you went in pursuit of bloody Zayan!" He tried to straighten. His saucer hit the floor with a crash. Slivers of crockery flew.

"With his lordship. And he was most reluctant to take me. I insisted, but he kept me from harm. And we rescued Bastien." Her story was tumbling out in a confusing mess. "From what the earl saw, I realized where Zayan is."

She expected Father to pounce upon that. To demand to know where Zayan was. Instead he pressed his free hand to his heart. "And you went there. In the company of a vampire earl!"

"Is your heart—?"

"A wee pain. And not important compared to this! God in heaven, Althea, they could have killed you."

"No, Father, I trust Yannick."

She might as well have prodded him with a hot poker. "Yannick!" he roared at her use of the earl's Christian name. His cheeks flamed bright red, and the flush raced up to his forehead. "And you trust him, you say! A vampire! You never— *never*—trust a vampire."

"But I can," she insisted, launching up from the bed. "Never once has he bitten me or hurt me." But she sank back down. Protesting was only making him more upset.

He sighed, groaned, and sank back against the mound of pillows. "Oh, lass. You're clever and brave. I've never doubted that for a moment. But you are too much of a temptation for a vampire."

That startled her. Temptation in what way?

"Where is he, then?" He was angry still, even as he took another drink of his tea.

"Chatham House. The one for let—Zayan has rented it. And he keeps his coffin in the mausoleum." How much to reveal? She faltered at the thought of explaining about the big bed, the whips upon the walls.

To hide her nerves, she took Father's cup and dutifully poured more tea. A rap at the door announced the return of the tray. Sarah carried it and gave her a little bobbed curtsy. This was much better for an invalid. A large dish held steaming beef tea, and a plate was piled with biscuits. A small plate held a pat of butter.

He groaned as he saw it. "If you really want me to feel better, lass, you'll agree to go to London. For I'm sending you today, whether you want it or not. I want to know you're safe."

Althea took his teacup and replaced it with the bowl of steaming broth. What was she to do? Leave the twins? Leave the mission that would be the start of her career as a vampire hunter? Or stay and risk losing Father? Worry over her could overwhelm his weakening heart.

"I'd rather stay and watch over you."

"I've lived a long life, Althea. And I'm stronger than you might think. But the Demon Twins want you and the best way I know to protect you is to send you away." He took a shaky spoonful of soup. "God in heaven, I'd rather have sausages."

"Eat all your broth, Father."

He groaned again.

"Father, I understand why you are so determined to stop Zayan, but I can't let you pursue this. You are much too weak. Once the physician—"

"I've no intention of seeing a physician. And as for Zayan, I won't be stopping him. I can't. Only the twins can do that. And now, it may come down merely to their thirst for revenge."

"Do you mean you won't hunt him?"

"Turn my back on him and let him continue to kill? No, lass, I can't do that. I have to try to find the twins. Try to at least protect people from Zayan."

"More broth," she encouraged. Her heart hurt, aching with pride for her father. He was willing to pursue the impossible, even if he saved only one person.

Father took another spoonful and grimaced. "In the crypt, I found some journals. Buried there. Preserved there. Protected. That told of Lord Devars' pursuit of Zayan. Did you see the sarcophagus in the crypt? The one that held the child?"

Heart in her throat, she nodded.

"Zayan turned the child of that hunter. Out of spite. And left the father with no choice but to put a stake through the heart of his own young son, just to allow the boy to find peace. That is what I am afraid of, lass, that Zayan will try to turn you to stop me."

Zayan had the chance last night, she realized, but hadn't turned her because he had used her as bait for Bastien. But next time . . .

She could see Father was crippled with worry, and pain was etched upon his face. A confrontation with Zayan, in his weakened state, would no doubt lead to his death. To save her, he would be more than willing to risk his own life.

She didn't have a choice.

"If I go to London, will you come with me? Would you leave this pursuit to the Demon Twins? Please Father, I'm begging you. I will go to London if you agree to give up your battle."

Father scooped up more of the beef broth. "And will you look for a husband?"

"A husband!"

But to protest might lead to the truth. She couldn't even imagine her father's shock, anger, and horror if she admitted she'd given her virginity to two vampires.

Well, one, technically, but she truly felt she'd lost her innocence with them both and—

It didn't matter about the technicalities. It would kill him for sure.

Guiltily, Althea met her father's eyes. He was waiting, stirring his broth, and the look of hope in his eyes made her heart lurch.

She would have to lie and pretend she would search for a husband, just as he wanted. Lie for now, worry about the truth later.

Her heart ached as she nodded her acquiescence to Father.

She would be leaving Yannick and Bastien, and that hurt as much as the fear of losing her father.

"Coo, London! However can I thank ye, Miss Yates?"

Eyes agog, Sarah leaned forward and stared out the window of the carriage, as though a mere three hours of travel had already brought them to London.

Althea settled back against the swaying seat. The carriage, as Father had directed, was making all possible haste, though the road was rutted from spring rains and the team could not be driven too hard.

For three hours, Sarah had been full of bright chatter and excitement. Althea had answered with grunts and murmurs and had twice pleaded the need to nap, though she couldn't sleep.

Lunch, at least, had given her another reason to be quiet. While Sarah had tackled her kidney pie with delight, Althea had noticed every man's eyes alight on Sarah, with interest and hot desire.

Her reasons in choosing Sarah as a travelling companion hadn't been completely altruistic.

Though she had the coachman and several of Father's men as outriders, Father had insisted she have another companion. A chaperon. She'd decided on Sarah. And Sarah had been pleased to leave behind Maidensby and go to London to act as lady's maid, which kept her away from Yannick and Bastien.

"Will we meet vampires in London, do ye think, Miss? Are ye to have me 'elp you 'unt the beggars?"

With a wry smile, Althea shook her head. "I've promised my father I will hunt husbands, not vampires." A dreary thought, since she certainly couldn't marry now. She would be dragged to balls and routs and musicales—things she'd only heard about— by Father's matchmaker, Lady Peters. The thought of having to pretend to be a marriage-obsessed innocent for weeks on end filled her with despair.

But Sarah beamed. "How glorious! Oo, I'd love to go to a ball and meet 'andsome gentlemen."

"And I would love to send you in my place," Althea muttered.

"Beg pardon, Miss?" Sarah appeared to be waving out of the carriage window. She turned around, cheeks flushed pink. "The most 'andsome man on a great black gelding just passed at a good gallop, but 'e waved at me."

Althea sighed. Sarah unleashed on London would certainly keep her distracted. She pressed her hand to her temple, which throbbed. She'd never suffered a headache before in her life.

Sarah sat on the seat across from Althea, facing opposite to the direction of travel, as a servant was wont to do. She tugged off her shawl and with a dreamy smile, she snuggled into the corner of the seat. Her eyes closed, golden lashes brushing her cheeks. She gave a soft little giggle.

Althea reached for a book. Watching Sarah made her strangely tense. The girl's little wiggles and jiggles made her perspire into her gown and pelisse. And Bastien's naughty story kept tantalizing her. The one about young women touching each other's breasts and quims.

Sarah's eyes opened and the most wicked smile curved her plump, pink lips. "I were thinking about me vampire, Miss."

He's not your vampire! Her head throbbed more and she felt ready to snap, like a weakened bow strung too tightly. A madness took control of her and she crooked her finger at Sarah, who was squirming on the soft seat. The girl was a saucy piece and she could see why Bastien wanted to have a suckle at the smooth, lovely neck.

As Sarah settled beside her, fluffing gray skirts, a mad compulsion directed Althea's fingers to cup the girl's pointed chin. To tip her face. Those moist lips tempted and she licked her own. She could almost hear Bastien's deep, seductive voice urging her onward.

She gave a small peck to Sarah's lips. The girl squealed, and she expected Sarah to leap back. To scream for help. To slap her. Instead Sarah giggled and kissed her back. Althea tasted the wine from lunch on the pretty pink mouth. She felt wild, hot with a daring desire. She felt like Bastien, a master of seduction cleverly charming an innocent girl.

"Cor, Miss," Sarah gasped as she kissed the girl's delicious neck, "Do ye drink blood, too?"

"No, no," she murmured, terribly shocked at her behavior but too fiery hot to stop.

Sarah's skin, soft as warmed satin, tasted of simple soap and tantalizing perspiration. Althea licked Sarah's wounds, now only light dimples in her smooth flesh. This was wrong. Erotic, but oh so wrong! Only in Bastien's dark, wicked world did women do things like this.

But Althea couldn't seem to stop.

Before she could think, she cupped her hand against Sarah's bodice and touched the full breasts that every man they'd encountered had glanced at with admiration and lust. Sarah moaned and wriggled and a large, hard nipple poked into Althea's palm through the taut gown.

No wonder men delighted in women's breasts! No wonder Bastien and Yannick enjoyed suckling hers. All she yearned for was to explore that thick nipple with her mouth.

Some force seemed to drive her and she hurriedly undid the buttons at the front of the gown. Once it loosened, she tugged it down, feeling very much like Yannick or Bastien. But she wasn't being quite as seductive, though she couldn't help but admire Sarah's bared breasts.

"Beautiful," she whispered with awe.

Sarah gave a demure smile, but Althea read the confidence there. Sarah was accustomed to receiving compliments about her bosom. They were round and plump, pale white touched with a blush of peach and faint blue veins. Althea's heart beat like a drum as she bent and kissed the lush, abundant flesh, her lips sinking into the softness. Feminine skin had a more delicate taste.

Somehow, she didn't think Bastien or Yannick would disapprove of her behavior.

"Might I 'ave a grope of yours, Miss?" Sarah whispered. "Would ye like that?"

"Oh yes, I would, Sarah," she breathed. Sarah's nimble fingers pushed hers from her pelisse and she licked and laved Sarah's nipples as her clothes were pulled open. The pliant nipple swelled against her tongue. She had no idea of skilled technique but she tried to mimic what the twins had done. Pure pleasure took over and she suckled merely for the joy of it.

"Cor Miss, let me kiss you," Sarah whispered. "Would ye touch me under me skirt? I've an itch there now."

Sarah fell back against the seat. Althea dragged up the girl's skirts, trembling at the sight of smooth, ivory legs clad in sturdy stockings and plain garters. She was nervous but so excited she thought she might explode into a thousand pieces. Crisp curls teased her fingertips.

"Althea, you mustn't," she whispered to herself. But she could picture Bastien, silver eyes burning with lust as he watched them. She could imagine Yannick, a little shocked but growing excited regardless. She parted Sarah's nether lips and a river of warmth spilled onto her fingers. Goodness!

This was madness. How could she have Sarah as a lady's maid after this? What if Sarah talked of it! What was she thinking? But she wanted more. She wanted to touch that silky heat. Wanted to watch Sarah squirm in pleasure.

Find a husband in London! She almost laughed. She was debauched. She truly did belong in Bastien's wicked world.

She touched Sarah's sensitive nub, amazed, strangely, to find it felt like her own. Sarah squealed.

Althea could hardly breathe. Sarah arched up to her teasing fingers in the most delightful, sensuous way. Althea knew she had none of the skill of the twins, but Sarah shut her eyes, moaned with pleasure, and ground hard against her fingers. The girl fractured in an instant.

"Ooh, Miss!" she cried as she clutched her ample breasts and rocked with her orgasm.

Stunned, enthralled, Althea burst too. She hadn't expected it . . . hadn't thought just by touching . . . watching—

Her anguished cries joined Sarah's to fill the small carriage. They both moaned desperately, until their climaxes slowly faded away, then sated, soaked with dewy sweat, Althea slumped beside Sarah. Sarah giggled and did up her gown as though she were suddenly shy. Althea felt like the experienced one, the tutor in sin, but still she couldn't think of a word to say. What did one say afterward?

Somewhat repaired, Sarah snuggled against her with a coy giggle. And soon the rhythmic breathing and gentle snores announced the girl was sleeping.

Althea sighed in relief as she struggled the fix her own dress. What a mess she'd made of things. And all for a bit of pleasure.

At least the windows were open—to allow the spring air to blow out the scandalous smells of their pleasure.

And out the window she spied a carriage in the ditch and a woman at the roadside trying to flag down a passing carriage.

She'd just shared a shocking interlude with her maid. The last thing she should do was invite a traveler, a stranger, inside. But she saw the woman's face as they passed. Well-dressed in silk pelisse and elaborate bonnet, the woman seemed so lost, so imploring, so upset, that Althea's heart went out to the stranger. She doubted Sarah would speak of what they'd done, certainly not in front of a stranger.

The carriage slowed, showing the concern of the coachman. She rapped the ceiling, signaling the man to stop.

18

The Queen

"A sound sleeper, is she not?" Crimson lips curved into a smile as the stranded traveler studied Sarah, who looked delectable in slumber.

Althea flushed with embarrassment. True, it surprised her that Sarah had dozed through the stop, the subsequent introductions and discussions, but she didn't wish to talk about why the pretty blonde was so exhausted.

The woman had introduced herself as Madame Roi when she accepted Althea's offer of a ride on to the next village where a bed could be found. Madame spoke with an accent that was decidedly not French. She had the look of a gypsy—thick, raven-black hair pinned beneath an elaborate bonnet adorned with peacock feathers, golden-bronze skin, a lush, vivid red mouth. Her manner was much older than her appearance, though the long fringe of feathers shielded her eyes.

Madame brushed back the feathers. Heavy-lidded almond-shaped eyes assessed Althea. The black lashes appeared several inches long.

At first, Althea had presumed Madame Roi to be an actress.

A choker of small sapphires ringed her neck, sapphires dripped from her earlobes, and her fanciful clothes suggested a besotted gentleman willing to spend a fortune on her. Her form-fitting pelisse of turquoise silk was trimmed in sable at the neck and cuffs. The skirt of the pelisse fell open to reveal a gown with sheer ivory skirts.

If not an actress, a courtesan. Overdressed for traveling. Now, she saw Madame was something much more sinister. Her smile was careful, but not quite careful enough to hide the long canine teeth. Not all immortals were hurt by sunlight; that she wasn't meant that Madame Roi was a very powerful being.

"Do not worry, Miss Yates, she will not waken. And you and I have much to discuss."

Althea frowned. Much to discuss with a strange vampiress? Her hand curled around the stake hidden in the deep pocket of her pelisse. The cross on the chain around her neck bumped with the jolts of the carriage.

The woman tapped a long finger, clad in a turquoise leather glove, thoughtfully against her chin. "I can see at once why Zayan chose you." The smile turned wicked. "I assume you were exploring sapphic pleasures with that pretty young miss."

Zayan? Sapphic pleasures? "Who are you, truly?" Althea demanded.

"Queen of the vampires, my darling." She held out her hand with a regal air, obviously expecting Althea to bow before it, moving coach or not. In the vampiric world, as in the mortal, a hierarchy had developed. A political structure, where the more ancient, stronger vampires claimed power and control. She had read of vampire queens, heard rumors of their existence from the thirteenth century onward. But she'd never been in the presence of one. And this woman, despite her bold, arrogant claim, could not be queen of *all* vampires. Such a being did not exist.

Or did she? After all, if Lucifer could conscript a vampire to do his bidding, was anything beyond possibility?

Althea should be frightened, but instead a hundred questions bubbled out of her. She held tight to her weapon. Vampire or no, the woman held herself as royalty, and exuded the arrogance of one entitled to privilege and authority. Like Yannick, Althea realized.

Though she was still blushing at the woman's accusation (and a true one) of sapphic activities, Althea tried to keep her voice steady. "How do you know of Zayan?"

"You may address me as Your Highness." The dark, arching brows rose haughtily and the silvery-black eyes flashed in the sunlight.

"What do you mean about Zayan choosing me . . . Your Highness?" She used the title to flatter.

"To seduce and divide the twins, of course. Very clever of Zayan," the queen purred, "since he is prevented from destroying Yannick."

For one moment Althea felt relief—Zayan couldn't hurt Yannick—but then the import of the other words sank in. *To seduce and divide the twins.* Icy dread shivered down her spine. "But Zayan didn't have anything to do with—" The dreams!

"Zayan controlled my dreams?" she cried. The dreams were no premonition at all. Not a sign of her destiny. She'd been manipulated by an evil vampire.

"Yes, Zayan sent you into their dreams."

"To come between them? But why?"

"Zayan cannot destroy Yannick," the queen repeated, exasperated.

Althea bristled at the dismissive tone. "How is he prevented from destroying Yannick, Your Highness?"

The queen leaned back against the velvet squabs with a fluid, sensual grace. "Because the delightful boy carries my protection—and the protection of one even more powerful than I."

"Your protection . . . so *you* released Yannick." She remembered his words. A bargain with the devil. This woman was the devil Yannick had meant.

"He agreed to my price for his freedom." The almond-shaped eyes narrowed to slits. "He agreed to find his brother and destroy Zayan for me. Yannick called to me, so I could come to him, but Bastien was too immersed in anger and betrayal and hatred even to bargain for his life. He would not even call to his own brother. Once Zayan learned of Yannick's release, he knew he must destroy Bastien to ensure his own safety. And that, as you have seen, he will not do."

How did the queen know about the night in the mausoleum? Once more, Althea felt a blush creep to her cheeks. "That is why he tried to goad Bastien to kill Yannick."

"Yes, the twins may destroy each other—they are linked in a special way. With the magic of the *Geminiani*—vampires who are made from twins or even triplets. In mortal life, their souls and essences are linked, are part of one whole. The magic bestowed upon them in immortal life is even more powerful."

The crimson lips smiled evilly again. "And so, Zayan sent you into their dreams. To tempt them, to give them pleasure, and to give them love. Neither twin has ever truly known love. They had a brutal father, a weak mother, and both died before finding true love from mortal women. Zayan realized that despite their link, despite their bond, each man would be willing to kill the other to claim love for himself."

But was what she felt for both of them—the pain and joy and quickening of her heart when she merely thought of them—was that truly love or was it just created by Zayan? Was she just being controlled like a puppet?

Damnation, that made her mad. She refused to let that monster control her heart.

"Delicious little thing." With a shock, she realized the queen was assessing Sarah and licking her fangs.

Althea began to lift her stake from her pocket.

"Not to worry, my dear, I never feed during daylight." The queen looked so amused, Althea shivered apprehensively.

"I am sure your pleasurable activities with the sweet little thing were more of Zayan's mischief."

Humiliated, Althea gasped, "Why?" But now she understood why she'd felt such a mad compulsion to do those things.

"He seeks to make you more accepting of your natural sensual nature. He wants to make you more of a temptation to Bastien. A sweet, naïve, charming young lady who delights in bedding more than one man or even other women? Dear Bastien would be unable to resist."

"But I'm not dreaming. And this is daytime—"

"And Zayan is a powerful being. But I sense you only needed a slight push in the right direction." The queen's forefinger slid over her full, red lips in a very suggestive way.

"Well, Zayan will lose, because I won't allow the twins to fight over me."

The queen smiled, and her condescension grated.

As enlightening as Althea found this tale, suspicions lurked. "Why are you revealing this to me?"

The long fingers toyed with the sparkling sapphire choker. "To thwart Zayan. And the twins were once my lovers." Madame Roi gave a wistful sigh. "Wonderful lovers. But Yannick will be destroyed at the next full moon—in mere days—unless he destroys Zayan. He knew, of course, I could not make a bargain and give him eternity to fulfill it."

"What do you mean, destroyed?"

"At dawn, on the night of the full moon, he disintegrates into dust."

"If he is out in the light."

"No, my dear. Wherever he is."

Althea's heart missed a beat. Fear swamped her and she fought it, fought to stay calm. "But that's a monstrous price!"

The queen gave a dismissive wave. "But one he accepted."

With the only other choice being eternal imprisonment! "And what about Bastien? Will he disintegrate also?"

"The twist in the bargain is that Bastien will risk death only if he attacks Zayan with Yannick. Though the twins can defeat Zayan if they combine their powers, Bastien will be vulnerable."

"Does Bastien know about this? Does he know Yannick would die?"

"He will. It is essential that he knows when he makes his choice."

The elegant hand strayed toward Sarah's thigh. "Lovely creature."

"Don't touch her!"

The queen stroked the valley between Sarah's thighs. "She won't remember what happened, Miss Yates. However, I believe Bastien and Yannick will have witnessed your uninhibited behavior in their dreams."

That made her blush even harder and her head throbbed with the heat and embarrassment. But she feared for the twins far more. "Bastien has always felt he is secondary to Yannick; I sense that in him. He might be willing to let Yannick die to claim everything his brother has."

Wasn't the queen worried about Yannick? Both men had been her lovers—a thought that curdled Althea's blood. The vampiress was ravishing—how could she hope to compete with such beauty and power?

The queen cocked her head so the peacock feathers shivered. She didn't look in the least sympathetic about Yannick's plight. "I understand the nature of twins. I was one myself. But that is the choice he has to make. Yannick searched for a decade to find the incantation to free his brother—the incantation your Father found. But once he had it, he was not sure if he wished to use it."

That surprised her. "Why? When it would mean his death if he didn't?"

"Bastien enjoys being immortal—he revels in the power, the sensuality. But Yannick was raised with responsibilities. He despised being a vampire and destruction represented escape."

Stunned by this, Althea moved to rap on the ceiling to stop the coachman. "I'm returning. I must ensure that Yannick doesn't die. That Bastien doesn't allow it."

To her astonishment, the queen clasped her hand between hers, the leather warm. "No, Miss Yates, you must continue to London. Zayan will go there to hunt tonight and he will not return to Maidensby. Bastien and Yannick will follow him there."

A sly look in the dark, flashing eyes made her wonder. Was Zayan going to London because he knew she would be there? How could he know? He could control her dreams—could he see into her thoughts?

"I must leave you now, my dear," the queen said, "But remember, Zayan believes you will cause the destruction of the twins."

"You must tell me how I can prevent that."

The queen glared down her straight nose. "You must discover that yourself, mortal."

Althea realized the queen had come to her to protect Yannick. Perhaps the queen wasn't allowed to interfere any more than she had. The rules of immortals and magic and the netherworld were complex, confusing. Like never-ending riddles. Was there some way she could cleverly get the answer?

The vampiress—and her lovely clothing—vanished in a flurry of turquoise light.

Too late.

"Where the hell is she?" Yannick strode into the bedchamber of Zayan's mausoleum and shouted his demand at

Althea's father. He knew he would find Sir Edmund here—he knew Althea had told her father about this place.

"Good evening, my lord." Sir Edmund leaned over to peer closely at an open book lying on top of Zayan's closed coffin.

Yannick gaped, irritated, as Sir Edmund all but ignored him and continued to read the book.

Behind him, a whip sliced through the air with a hiss, followed by a slap as the tip struck the floor. Something else, the mace, no doubt, hit the floor with a clang. He heard ribald laughs amongst the men as they explored Zayan's treasure-trove of bondage and sex toys. He focused on Sir Edmund, but he kept the half-dozen well-built laborers in his peripheral vision.

" 'Ere lads, look over there, it's the vampire 'imself!"

Hell and perdition. Yannick groaned—he had no time to battle six men armed with whips, picks, and crossbows.

Sir Edmund looked up and held up a quelling hand. "Rest easy, men," he called, "His lordship is no threat." He then adjusted his spectacles on the bridge of his nose and pointed to the book. "Might I trouble you to look at this, my lord? Zayan's journal—kept over one hundred years. Infrequent entries but I expect this journal to illuminate much—"

Exasperated, Yannick stalked over toward Sir Edmund. "Forget the bloody journal. Where is Althea? Why in hell did you send her away alone?"

He heard the men shift restlessly, knew they were just awaiting an order to attack, but he damn well didn't care. "I expect an answer, Sir Edmund. Now."

Sir Edmund let out a low whistle of appreciation as he turned a page of the book. Suddenly Yannick was struck by the sense that Sir Edmund was playing a role. Acting as a barmy scholar. Putting him off guard. Any second now, he'd probably get a bolt through his heart.

Sir Edmund flipped another page. "Althea is not alone, my lord, I can assure you."

Yannick fumed. How could he be stuck in a stalemate with a man far beneath his rank? He had to make the man see sense.

"Whoever she is with cannot protect her as I can," he snapped. "Tell me where she is—in return, I'll tell you anything you need to know about Zayan."

Sir Edmund slammed the book and surged up. "You think I would betray my daughter to catch Zayan?" he barked. "You insult me, my lord. An unwise thing to do, when I have enough weapons trained on you to destroy you. Not even a vampire can survive being hacked limb from limb. Or being decapitated."

True. Yannick detected a scent he had been too distracted to notice over the strong odor of garlic flowers. Though faint, it was pungent. It swept through his lungs and already he felt his muscles weaken. Flower of solange—a plant long thought extinct, though it was rumored that a Dutch vampire hunter grew it in a protected greenhouse. Garlic had no effect, but solange— breathe in enough of this light smoke and he would be captured in a trance-like state. Oil gathered from the plant, and burned, acted as a mind-destroying opiate for vampires but had no effect, remarkably, on mortals.

So he had no time for pleasantries. "I know from Crenshaw that she traveled to London. Where is she there?"

Sir Edmund shook his head. He took a small notebook from his pocket and a graphite pencil and scribbled down a line of notes.

"Damnation, I only wish to protect her from Zayan."

"Then help me destroy Zayan tonight."

Yannick's control over his rage snapped. "You don't understand, do you?" He slammed his fist down on the coffin. As a crack shot through the gleaming cover with an explosive bang, Sir Edmund jumped back. "Goddamn it, old man, I thought you were more intelligent. Zayan won't return here. He needs to destroy either Bastien or myself, and he knows damn bloody well that Althea is the way to accomplish that."

He felt the tension ratcheting up amongst the workmen. Saw picks and shovels raised to shoulder height, ready to swing, and crossbows aimed. Saw the men move forward, slowly encircling him and Sir Edmund. Sir Edmund gave a slight shake of his head. Telling the men to wait, he guessed.

"Althea is with someone who won't let that happen," Sir Edmund stated.

"No one you entrust Althea to could protect her from Zayan!" he shouted again. "Only I can do that—I'm the only one whom Zayan can't kill."

Suddenly he realized how pale, how weak, Sir Edmund appeared. The man pointed a finger at him and it quavered. "You brought her out here—"

"I brought her to protect her. Don't you realize that she would have come alone? She would have armed herself with her stake and her crossbow and followed me, thinking herself completely able to take care of herself."

"She would not have done something so—" But Sir Edmund broke off. He seemed to sink down, looking old and deflated, and he braced his arm on the coffin as though to keep himself from collapsing.

"You're the one who taught her to hunt bloody vampires!" Hell, the man was sick. Yannick could see it, could sense it. Sir Edmund's heart was laboring, and the blood was flowing weakly. "The attack by Zayan?" he asked. "Are you in need of more blood?"

Sir Edmund shook his head. The man was paler than a vampire, his breathing shallow. "An attack of the heart, and I'm afraid I have to let nature take her course." His hoarse voice came out with a strain.

Althea's father hung his head, as though cowed by a great

weight. "Althea would have gone alone. I know she would—even though it was dangerous. She would have done it to protect you, I expect, my lord, and done it to try to stop Zayan. Althea is a noble, courageous lass—with stronger will than most men I've encountered, but she's still . . . innocent."

Yannick tried not to choke on that statement. Not anymore, thanks to him. Though he didn't think sexual innocence was exactly what Sir Edmund meant.

"She's determined to hunt vampires, to follow in my footsteps."

"I know; she made that plain to me."

"You are correct that it's my fault, my lord. I dragged her around the Continent. She's lived longer in the Carpathians than in England—is more at home in Buda-Pesth than London. I was a bloody selfish man, never once thinking of how I was molding her future. And now, I want her to wed. I want to see her married, happy, mistress of a home, raising children of her own." Sir Edmund took several breaths and rubbed his chest. "Not the heart this time, I don't think. More likely that kidney pie."

"Where is she in London?" Yannick repeated.

Sir Edmund rallied his strength and shook his fist. "I should shoot a bolt through your heart on the spot for visiting her last night. You've captured her with your charm and your handsome looks and blinded her to what you truly are—"

"And what do you think I want from her, Sir Edmund. Why do you think I went to her?" What in hell was he doing, goading her father? He'd *seduced* her. Only a lunatic would challenge a man who had six armed men ready to attack him.

But goddamn, he wanted Sir Edmund to understand—

"I know what you want. Her blood. She's young and beautiful and you want to destroy her."

"God in heaven, no, that's not what I want! I . . . I think . . . I am in love with her—"

"Then you want to change her into a vampire and I won't allow that to happen."

To Yannick's surprise, Sir Edmund's eyes grew sad, and the anger and strength faded. "She deserves to live and be happy, my lord. She's seen horrors that no lass should see—I understand that now. Strong enough to endure it, she was, but it has forever marked her."

Yannick understood. "And you want to try to turn back time? You want her to marry and be happy and forget there is evil in the world."

"It's too late, I know. Too late for a selfish man to right his wrongs." Sir Edmund took hold of a cane lying on the cracked coffin and put it to use. He shuffled across the floor, back to the anteroom. Yannick followed and the armed men followed him.

He found Sir Edmund amongst the sarcophagi, leaning heavily on the walking stick. "You there, Bowman, would you open that coffin?"

With a shudder, Bowman set to the task. Yannick didn't know why he lingered to watch. He should make haste to London, and set about finding Althea.

Bowman shoved the prying bar beneath the heavy lid. Yannick was tempted to display his strength, to move the lid alone, which he could do easily. But he also knew it to be unwise to reveal too much before his enemy—they both might love Althea, but Sir Edmund would never see him as anything other than the enemy.

As Yannick expected, when the lid slid open, it was not an old skeleton inside. A young boy, perhaps twelve, lay within, eyes open but glassy. Undead at first glance, but Yannick smelled the life in him. Zayan had not yet completely drained this one, and was keeping him controlled and imprisoned. The faint, tenuous life was trying desperately to hang on.

Just as he was. Within days—five, to be exact—if he didn't destroy Zayan, he would be dead himself. Burnt to mere ash.

And he would not be able to protect Althea then. Neither could Bastien—not alone.

For Althea, he must convince Bastien to help him destroy the man he knew his brother had once loved.

"Let me give the boy my blood, Sir Edmund," Yannick said. "I can save him."

"Go ahead, my lord." Althea's father wiped at a tear and stepped aside.

19

The Ball

She prayed she didn't fall down the stairs.

Gloved hand trailing along the curving oak banister, Althea took tentative steps down the sweeping stairs to the marble-tiled foyer, where the rest of the party—Sir Randolph, Lady Peters, their son David, two giggling female cousins, and a tartar-tongued aunt—stood waiting. A fringe of gold beads swirled about her ankles as she lifted the hem and negotiated another step.

She wasn't accustomed to finery. Worse, she feared that if she didn't hold herself perfectly straight, the bodice might drop to her waist. Or her curls, piled high on her head and threaded with a ribbon studded with emeralds and gold, would tumble free. But she risked one brief glance, a squint without her spectacles, just to make certain she wasn't stepping on her hem.

She could see her pink areolas rising above the low, square-cut gown. True, a band of ivory lace disguised them but a gentleman with the advantage of height—

"Miss Yates, you look magnificent."

She rounded the sweep and stopped, ostensibly to display

the finished product, but mainly to regroup. Her Norwich silk shawl, draped over her arm, was dragging again, and she'd snagged the foot-long fringe with her heel.

Sir Randolph, quizzing glass to his eye, turned to his wife. "Marvelous work, my dear."

Althea couldn't help a wry smile. The undertone to his words was obvious. *We'll find a suitor quickly and have her off our hands.*

Lady Peters, a lovely woman of forty with ash-blond hair, a voluptuous figure, and dramatic dark eyes, patted Sir Randolph's arm. "The credit most certainly goes entirely to Miss Yates. She is a true gem with fine taste."

Althea flushed. She hated to feel like a display at the British Museum. She clutched a hand full of ivory silk skirts and fragile emerald-green net, and tried one more step. Her first interview with Lady Peters hadn't been successful at all, so she could sense her patroness's relief that she at least dressed up well. She remembered that first afternoon.

Radiating kindness and gentility, her ladyship had propelled her into a magnificent drawing room, a room the size of the entire second floor of the Maidensby Arms. It spoke of fabulous wealth to Althea's eyes. Carpets of exotic patterns covered the floor. All the furnishings lushly created in spare, elegant Grecian lines or sumptuous oriental splendor. Gleaming wood, rich silks and velvets, delicate plasterwork, flocked wallpaper. Much of the wealth came from Lady Peter's substantial dowry—she was second cousin to a duke. Althea couldn't imagine how beautiful Yannick's house must be.

Here and there stood curios that caught her fascination. A sheelagh-na-gig—a Celtic fertility symbol. She couldn't stop a blush at the sight of that stone figurine of a grinning woman who held her nether lips wide open. A display of tall, thin stones, the ends rounded off. Staring at those, she realized they were phallic symbols.

"Have you spent much time in London, Miss Yates?"

Althea had started guiltily. She had—heaven help her—been thinking of which of the long, thick stone cocks were closest to Yannick and Bastien.

"Have you formed an opinion on London, Miss Yates?" Lady Peters had probed again with a pleasant but appraising smile.

Althea's teacup had rattled on its saucer. She must concentrate. Lady Peters was judging her ability to banter and flirt with gentlemen. The protracted silence would be ringing alarm bells in her ladyship's head. She didn't want Father to learn she was not even trying.

Was the lady already crossing potential suitors off the list? Mentally searching to the bottom for those most desperate for a wife? Althea could imagine the thoughts whirling behind her ladyship's stoic expression: *Old knock-kneed Lord So-and-So—he'd take her. Or Lord Such-a-Body is as deaf as a post—he'd never notice the silences.*

The gentle tick of the clock had marked her poor showing as she'd searched her brain for a redeeming answer. Father had warned her not to speak her mind in polite London society, so she knew it wouldn't do to tell the truth.

"I've not even spent a month in London in my life. I don't wish to form an opinion too hastily, my lady."

"Hmm. I detect disappointment," her ladyship had teased, blue eyes twinkling.

"Homesickness," she'd lied.

Genuine surprise showed on her ladyship's lovely face. "You don't consider England to be your home?"

"I barely remember it, my lady." And all the memories Althea had were of her mother, more so than of England. Her mother's pink cheeks touched by a winter wind. Her mother's warm embrace, comforting even on a hot summer's day. Then Mother was gone and Father left England for the Carpathian Mountains . . .

She furtively brushed a tear. Her father's warnings came to mind. *Don't harp on about your foreign travels, pet. And don't speak of vampire hunting. A woman adept at the use of a crossbow would make a man nervous.*

"Shopping!"

Althea only realized then that she'd been staring at the cooling tea in her cup. Shopping?

"That is the true delight of being in London, Miss Yates."

"Yes," Althea had hedged, "I am looking forward to London's bookstores—"

"Books! Edmund did warn that you were something of a bluestocking, my dear. I'm speaking of gowns."

"But I could not afford—"

"But I can."

"I couldn't accept—"

"Yes, you can. Dear Edmund saved Randolph's life on more than one occasion. Turning you out in some fine plumage would barely begin to repay him. Now, come along, Miss Yates, we have much work to do!"

And so Althea found herself swathed in rich ivory silk that barely encased her bosom and swept over her hips in a way that showcased their sway as she walked. At first, with Yannick's and Bastien's lives at risk and Zayan on the loose in London, she'd chafed at standing while a modiste's seamstress poked her with pins. She'd fumed and fretted while shopping for frivolous bonnets. What did it matter if she looked lovely when she had to warn the twins to keep away from her! And as for trying on a hundred pairs of slippers—!

But the glowing smiles of Sir Randolph and Lady Peters, and the stunned look of David—who was a mere twenty and the object of Sarah's dreamy sighs—told her she was transformed. In front of her own cheval mirror, as she'd twirled and sent her fringed hem spinning, she'd felt beautiful.

Struck by a whim, she had held her miniature of her mother up to the mirror. She wanted to believe her mother could see her.

She hoped, foolishly so, that Yannick and Bastien would somehow find her at the Fortesques' ball. She wanted to dazzle them. And after three nights of celibacy, she hungered to make love.

"Damnation, I hate these things."

Bastien took a champagne flute from a passing tray and drained the fine, bubbly wine in one gulp. He grinned at his brother. "Only because every maiden and matron here is targeting you for marriage. What a joke—can you imagine the reaction if you did marry one of these chits? Once the sweet little virgin realized that her eccentric husband who sleeps until dusk is truly a big, bad vampire?"

God almighty, you really don't belong in polite society.

Bastien laughed at his brother's comment, then groaned as a warm female body pressed close to him from behind. A lush, rounded female body. The Fortesques' foyer was so crowded that people couldn't avoid collisions. Spicy perfume wrapped around him. The pumping of her heart was a more entrancing melody than the one drifting out of the ballroom. He smelled her rushing blood and his fangs pounded forth, shooting out from his gums. Perhaps he could lead the lovely matron off into the dark and indulge in a little supper—

"There she is."

Bastien's heart surged with an excitement he'd never known. He strained to catch a glimpse, swiveling in the direction Yannick faced. Althea. Where was she? Damn, he wanted to see her again. Needed to see her. He'd never craved being with a woman as much before.

"She's ravishing," he whispered, as he spied her.

She far outshone every woman there. Even the duchesses, the countesses, the heiresses could not compare. Althea's rich, gleaming burgundy-red hair shimmered, unique and breathtaking beneath the chandeliers. One long curl tumbled down to bounce seductively against her slim back. She half-turned and his mouth dried. Tiny emeralds glittered in those thick tresses, but her sparkling eyes put them in the shade. A pink blush touched her cheeks. It was a crush of a ball, hot, overcrowded, and tedious, but Althea radiated excitement and joy. Althea made enduring this event worthwhile.

Bastien had come here only in hope of finding her. He didn't dare present his card at Sir Randolph's to visit. As a friend of Althea's father, the baron likely knew exactly what he was.

He couldn't wait to be with her again.

During his day sleep, he'd been visited by a scorching dream— Althea and a pretty blonde exploring each other's delights, reaching ecstasy together. He'd slept with a raging erection and was bone-hard again, harder than he could remember being. His eager cock was pushing the buttons on the falls of his trousers to their limits.

He started to head toward Althea, but Yannick grabbed his shoulder. "Wait."

He moved to shrug off Yannick's hand, then noticed that a blond woman and a tall, distinguished gentleman accompanied Althea. A dark-haired youth walked at her other side, and the boy's gloved hand looked to be hovering close to Althea's silk-clad bottom.

"Mr. de Wynter! How delightful to see you returned from the Continent."

Hell and the devil, Lady Somebody-or-Other was advancing on him, daughters in tow.

"Is that where I was?" He turned to shoot a glance at

Yannick, only to see his brother trying to flee into the crowd. He bowed to Lady Somebody and to her starstruck daughters. Angular and plain, they curtsied, and he couldn't avoid promising them both a dance. Anything to get them to move away so he could chase after Althea.

"I accompanied my brother, Lord Brookshire," he remarked as casually as he could. He almost laughed as Lady Somebody, obviously trolling for marriage candidates, set off in pursuit of Yannick. Served his bloody titled brother right. With the advantage of height, he could see over the crowd. Yannick was fending off an assault by two matrons—a plump woman in purple, armed with a cane, and a doe-eyed beauty who was hanging on his arm and obviously hoped to snare him for some bedsport.

With his brother otherwise occupied, Bastien searched the crowd for Althea.

Gone.

He raced up to the ballroom door, possessed with the need to find her.

For the first time in his life, Yannick shuddered as a large, soft breast pressed against his arm. Its owner, the voluptuous, beautiful Lady Aubrey tapped her closed fan against full lips. She snapped it open and flapped with savage strokes. "I fear I may perish in this heat. The gardens are lovely and delightfully cool . . . and private. . . ." Her lashes batted as she awaited his invitation to escort her. Her hip rubbed seductively against his thigh. Up his arm, her fingers danced until they reached his biceps and boldly stroked.

Yannick gritted his teeth. Why should this irritate him so much tonight?

Coming to the first large ball of the Season was madness. To polite society, he was an available earl—a prime quarry in the marriage mart. And he since he rarely appeared in Society, he was elusive prey—the matrons knew they had few chances to snare him.

Being squashed amidst several hundred warm bodies—more than half belonging to attractive females—was playing havoc on his self-control. His fangs had long since exploded out of his jaw and he had to watch his every move to ensure they didn't show. Stabbing pain shot from his teeth through his entire body as he breathed in the tormenting scent of the blood of five hundred people.

Since becoming a vampire, he hadn't risked attending a ball.

Lady Aubrey inclined her head, revealing the white length of her neck.

Just one bite—

So easy. Lure the lovely lady out into the dark and have a taste of all that delicious blood. . . .

No. And not because he feared exposure. No, tonight he had come for Althea. And he was damned and determined to control his vampire nature.

He removed her ladyship's hand from his arm. Kissed her satin-covered fingertips. "We can't have you swooning on us, my dear. Pray don't let me prevent you from seeking the restoring breezes out on the terrace."

Lady Aubrey dipped the fan. Frustration flamed in her eyes. "Would you join me, Lord Brookshire?"

"I must decline, my dear. I'm searching for one particular young lady. The lady I hope will grant me the first waltz."

"Really?" Her dark eyes gleamed at the prospect of gossip. "And who might this fortunate young woman be?"

God, he hated this. The gossip, the games, the rules. All he wanted was to claim Althea. To have tonight with her.

"An angel," Yannick answered shortly. With that, he left Lady Aubrey abruptly, not caring if his behavior was rude.

He wanted Althea—he wasn't pursuing her only because

she was in danger, and he hated himself for that. He was bred to be a gentleman, and he should possess enough honor to let her find a husband. Her father spoke the truth. She deserved a devoted husband; she deserved children.

He'd been a selfish bastard even to consider capturing her heart, even to think of making her a vampire. He couldn't steal her away from a happy mortal life. That was the future she was destined to live, not one with him.

But right now, he had to protect her.

"Save me a waltz, Miss Yates. I must dance with you at least once tonight."

Althea trembled as Bastien murmured by her ear. The brush of his hot breath set her tingling. She turned on her heel, heart soaring as she met his darkly intense gaze. His silver eyes shimmered beneath the twinkling candlelight. His hair, elegantly snared at the nape of his neck, glowed like pure gold. One strand fell free, following the sharp curve of his high cheekbones. As in her dream, he wore beautiful dress clothes. A black tailcoat topped a gold satin waistcoat and black trousers. He moved closer, leaning over her, capturing her against the wall, his stance blatantly intimate.

She glanced about for prying eyes, but in the pack of bodies, she couldn't tell if anyone had a gaze—or a quizzing glass—trained on them. Not that she expected anyone but Lady Peters to be watching *her*, but many eyes must be following golden-haired, gorgeous Mr. de Wynter.

Playfully, Althea reminded him, "If you dance with me more than twice, society will rumor that we are engaged."

"Then let us dance every dance, for I belong to you, my sweet, even though I have no soul to give to you."

Her breath caught. She met Bastien's gaze, knowing she shouldn't flirt. Relief had flooded her when he'd first spoken to her—relief that he was here and safe. Yannick might be here, too. But as much as she wished to melt into Bastien's arms, hold him tight, kiss him, and touch him, she couldn't. Not just because they were in the middle of a ballroom, but because she represented risk to him and Yannick. She was Zayan's tool and she had to warn him.

She caught hold of his sleeve. "Would you come out onto the terrace with me? I must speak to you about what I've learned."

Bastien winked. "Slip out into the dark with you?" He gave a slow smile that ignited a fire in her quim. "Should I worry about my virtue?"

This was going to prove terribly difficult. She wanted him so much she wished she could rip his clothes off immediately, in the midst of polite society. But she couldn't give in to the desire, not when it could destroy the men she loved.

"I *wish* you should," she murmured. Damn Zayan.

Instantly he responded to her sad tone, to the soft regret there. The sorrow. He caught her elbow. "Let us make haste and talk, then, little dove."

The crowd parted for him, to her surprise. He had presence, an aura—a power that emanated from him. Even men who far outranked him instinctively allowed him through. Some greeted him, but he propelled her quickly.

The night was balmy, and the terrace doors thrown open to let the warm gentle breezes in. Other couples strolled toward the open doors.

Come with me, Althea.

Hand in hand with Bastien, she walked with him down the steps at the far end of the terrace. Soon they passed a series of statues, half hidden by lilacs in full bloom. Pan amongst pretty water nymphs. So similar to her dream—her heart set up a fervent patter.

No, she couldn't make love to Bastien, because if she did,

she was helping Zayan. She didn't understand how much her desires—and theirs—were controlled by Zayan.

Here, we'll be safe enough here. Lust crackled through his voice as he spoke in her mind. But something deeper also. She sensed it.

In the shadows here, behind a wild growth of lilac at the very end of the garden, Althea could see little. Only the sculpted planes of his cheeks, his shining eyes, the glitter of satin and the shimmer of fine wool.

And his grin of delight. She could see his white, curved fangs.

Bastien caught her in his arms. She slammed her palms into his chest to break free. She knew exactly what he wanted.

"No," she pleaded, "Let me tell you what I've learned first."

"No, little dove, let me give you an orgasm or two first."

He was so incorrigible she laughed despite the tension that made her muscles ache. "Do be silent or . . . or I'll whip you."

His body went rigid against hers; his erection, pressing against her thigh, seemed to buck in response.

"Well, then, I'm hardly going to want to be silent now, am I?"

"Oh!" she groaned in frustration.

He broke away and studied the lilacs.

"What are you doing?" she whispered.

"Looking for a suitable branch to use for my punishment."

Was he teasing? Or not? His nonchalance—no, his *enthusiasm*—over punishment made her nervous. She could hardly picture wielding a whip and striking him, whether he liked it or not!

How did he do this to her? She'd brought him here to discuss Zayan, to save his life, and now all she could think of was naughty, sinful, sexual acts.

"Bastien." She spoke his name as a command.

With a long, swaying lilac branch in hand, he turned.

She couldn't draw her gaze from the bobbing blooms as she told her the story, everything she'd learned from the vampire queen.

He frowned. "You believe Zayan alone is responsible for our dreams and desires?"

"Yes. To destroy you—or Yannick. You both must stay away from me. For your safety! I refuse to be used as the weapon to hurt you!"

"Noble little dove," he whispered, with a soft smile. He shook his head, a few loose strands of his hair dancing in the light breeze, reflecting gold like fireflies. "The dreams may have been planted by Zayan, but our desires are real."

"But—"

"Everything that happened in those dreams came of the true desire in your heart and soul, little love. Zayan cannot plant emotions; he can only try to manipulate those that really exist."

"You mean . . . I wanted to do . . . truly what happened was what I wanted?"

"Sorry, love."

But she was already breathing the words, "Thank goodness." She'd wanted her feelings, as improper as they were, to be real. But suddenly she clapped a hand to her mouth. "Even—"

"Even your dalliance with the little blond maid." His voice was throaty, his eyes twinkling.

Suspicion rose. "Are you just making this up so I will make love with you?"

"I couldn't lie to you, sweeting, even if I wanted to. You possess my heart and it would be impossible for me to deceive you."

Althea frowned, "You are magically forced to be honest to me?"

He nodded and turned away. He moved to break off another lilac branch.

She crept up behind him and slipped her arms around his narrow waist. He didn't speak. He only acknowledged her by moving back against her, and she answered by pressing her cheek to his back.

"I wish I could make love to you," she whispered. A foolish thing to do, to goad a man she knew she mustn't have. Even if the desires were real—

"Has my brother made love to you yet tonight?"

"No." she said, uncertain at his cold tone. "I wish I could make love to you . . . first."

"Oh you do, do you?"

She flinched at Bastien's curt, hard words. This wasn't the reaction she'd expected. He tried to draw away but she clasped her hands together. Her arms couldn't make much of a prison. He could easily force her hands apart if he wished, but she took it as hopeful that he didn't try.

Was he still hurt and angry that she had chosen Yannick? Her feelings were so different now.

"Don't pity me, Althea."

"Pity you! You think I want you out of pity?"

"No, I think you are asking me to be first out of pity. You fear for my poor broken heart, knowing I'll always be second fiddle to Yannick."

"It's not true. Not with me it isn't."

"You made a choice—"

"Yes, and I made love to both of you! I gave my virginity to both of you! Don't you realize what that meant to me?"

He eased her arms apart and stepped out of her embrace.

"You gave your virginity to—"

"Stop it!" she cried. "I've never known love before. And now, I find myself in love with the two of you. I can hardly credit such a thing. And for all you both insist you are quite willing to share, you both keep forcing me to make a choice. In these little, irritating ways."

"We irritate you, do we?" he grinned and slapped the ground with the broken lilac branch. "No better sign of true love than that. But you aren't in love with me, little dove. You just lust for me."

Why was he so determined to punish himself? To refuse to believe she loved him? "Why shouldn't I be in love with you?" Althea demanded. "Why would you find it so hard to believe? What of all the women you—?"

"They weren't in love with me," Bastien interrupted. "They were tempted by the promise of real sin. That's all they wanted from me. Wickedness and sin, and they knew I'd give it to them without censure. But all too often a woman—especially a good one—needs to justify her lusts and so she fancies herself in love. You aren't in love with me."

"Well, I fear that I am. And I know my own feelings."

"If you loved me, sweetheart, you'd never be able to admit it to my face."

The depth of that statement left her speechless. But in truth, even though she was so easily saying "I love you," her heart was in turmoil.

"But I will be happy," he continued, cupping her chin with the hand that did not hold his makeshift whip, "to fuck you."

Her quim clenched at the forbidden word, even as she wanted to sink into the earth out of embarrassment. She'd admitted she loved him, she had laid her heart open, and all he did was insist she didn't. What a fool she'd been! Obviously he didn't love her.

His voice was a dark sinful whisper carried on the breeze. "I suspect you would enjoy a good, sweaty, sticky, legs-hooked-around-my-neck fuck."

She'd meant to turn and escape. She'd embarrassed herself

so much, but what he said rooted her to the spot. "Legs around your neck!"

"For supreme depth of penetration."

"You . . . you couldn't possibly go deeper than . . . than you did."

"A challenge. You do know me, don't you? I can't resist a challenge."

"That's what I was to you?" Anger overcame the humiliation. "A challenge?"

A sad smile played on his lips. "I told you I loved you," Bastien promised. "That was the truth, sweetheart."

"If you do . . ." Althea began, heart thumping madly, knowing she was about to ask for something he might refuse to give. "Then you'll promise to me, in all honesty, that you won't let Yannick die. You know he will turn to dust if you don't help him destroy Zayan."

"Yannick, of course." He groaned and turned away.

"Bastien, please. He's your brother and I know that you love him. You wouldn't destroy him in Zayan's chambers—which must mean—"

His smiled became wicked. "Without Yannick, though, you will be all mine. That is a great temptation."

She shoved on his broad chest. "And that is exactly what Zayan wants you to think. But I promise you, Sebastien de Wynter, that if you let Yannick die to claim me, I . . . I will never love you. Not truly. Ever."

"An enormous price," he said as he stepped back. But his tone was jaded, nonchalant, and told her nothing.

Footsteps crunched on the path behind them and she jumped in surprise.

"My brother has arrived."

20

Brazen

Bastien watched Althea's lovely green eyes, expecting to see a brighter fire now that she knew Yannick was there. Damnation, but she must love his brother deeply. Pleading for his life with such fear etched on her pretty face.

Jealousy burned through Bastien, like destructive fire, as Yannick lifted her gloved fingers to his lips.

Like all the other women he'd been with, Althea wanted him sexually—but he needed her heart, not just her lust.

And what had he done to try to win it? Where were his romantic promises? Where was his seductive nature? He'd thrown her promise of love back in her face because he didn't believe it. With any other woman, he would have charmed and dazzled. Why had he just lashed out at Althea?

He saw the pain flash across Yannick's face as Althea pleaded, "Both of you must stay away from me until you kill Zayan. He believes that I will be the instrument to destroy you."

To Bastien's surprise, Yannick leveled his gaze at him. "Bastien only risks destruction if he actually attacks Zayan with me."

"That is what this vampire queen says," Althea pointed out. "But she might have lied."

"No, she speaks the truth." Yannick sighed. "It was the deal I had to make to be freed. I might be protected but, amongst demons, protection always comes at a particularly twisted price."

Yannick looked back to Althea and Bastien saw the longing in his brother's expression. And the resignation.

Yannick believed his destruction to be a certainty. His brother believed he would let him die. He met his brother's gaze and Yannick gave him a wry grin. It shocked him—he was accustomed to the cool arrogance in his brother's expression. He was also accustomed to having Yannick look at him as though he was a half-witted child. In truth, he'd given Yannick a lot of reason to doubt his sanity when they'd been mortals. He'd gambled hard, developed a taste for whippings and flailings, and had found himself on the dueling field at the crack of almost every dawn.

"I know, brother," Yannick said softly, "you won't kill Zayan."

For once Bastien held the upper hand, and unexpectedly he had no idea what he wanted to do with it. He gave a jaded shrug. "I didn't know about your bargain, Yannick. Nor did I know that I risked death if I did try to kill Zayan. Apparently, if we fail, I also evaporate into dust."

Althea, standing between them, looked back and forth, curls bobbing as she did. A shaft of moonlight caressed her face and he saw teardrops shine at the corners of her eyes.

His heart clenched as she laid her hand delicately on his sleeve. "Please, Bastien, you musn't let Yannick die—"

Yannick, Yannick, bloody Yannick.

"But I don't want you to die." Two tears broke free and

dribbled down her cheeks, diamond bright. "You must take care, you must protect yourself."

She whirled onto Yannick. "You must take care of him, too!"

Yannick inclined his head. "I always have."

The exchange between Althea, with tears flowing, and his brother left Bastien stunned. Althea hadn't shed one fearful tear in Zayan's chambers—she wasn't the sort of woman to give in to hysterics. For her to cry now—

For her to make demands of his brother, the earl—

She truly must care for him.

His heart leapt as Althea grasped his hand, twining her fingers, in fragile ivory silk gloves, with his. She took hold of Yannick's hand too. Her message was obvious. She wanted to join them, link them, bring them together.

No one had ever cared enough to do that. Their father had driven them apart. Punishing the twin who refused to betray the other's transgressions. Punishing the one who lost to the other—at card games, chess, or sports. Their father had used their naturally competitive natures to drive them, and it made them hate—both each other and their father.

As for their mother, she pitted them against each other unintentionally. Yannick was her stalwart one, the one she poured out her pain to. Bastien was her passionate one, the one she bestowed cuddles and kisses to, until she tired of it and sent him away.

Only Althea cared enough about them to want to heal their rift.

Bastien held Althea's hand tight and bent to kiss her perfumed hair.

She smiled up at him, hope shining through the tears. "You two do love each other! You've endured so much together—"

"I don't know about love," he drawled, grinning evilly at

Yannick, "but I've always had to keep in his good graces so he'd loan me the money for my gaming debts."

But Yannick didn't smile in return. "Althea is right," he said. "Goddamn, I always wanted to protect you from Father's whip—"

"And how did you expect to do that?"

"I was the eldest."

"By fifteen bloody minutes. And getting thoroughly whipped yourself."

"But you got it the most." Yannick spoke almost guiltily. "And the worst."

Bastien bowed his head. "I apologize for turning you, Yannick. I know you hated to become a vampire. I know you hesitated to free me because you thought it would be nobler to let yourself be destroyed, even though you have always been downright gentlemanly about the way you feed. And I have to admit, I turned you out of spite."

Yannick shook his head. "In truth, Lucifer controlled you— he played on your anger and forced you to turn me."

"But it was a desire I already had—to destroy your life."

"Because you were afraid. Afraid to face being a vampire alone."

Bastien hated to admit that was likely true. He didn't want to relive those gut-churning days, or the last whipping from his father that had broken his spirit and sent him to the gutter where Zayan had found him. He'd been twenty-five and his father, enraged, had struck while he slept. He'd lain there, bound and shocked, while the blows rained down. . . .

Hell, he should have been able to fight his father. Physically, he could have done . . .

"I don't want to talk about our bloody father, may he rot in hell. Or about the past," Bastien growled. "I want to make love to Althea."

*   *   *

Althea gasped as she was kissed and shared, like a plaything, between the brothers. Dizzily, she knew the rogues were tormenting her deliberately. First Bastien kissed her breathless, then he took hold of her shoulders and turned her gently. As Yannick took his turn, playing magic upon her swollen, moist mouth, Bastien's hands caressed her bottom through her skirts.

Bastien's lips danced over the nape of her neck. His hands kneaded on her derrière, then parted her cheeks through the thick silk. The most irresistible caress of her anus made her moan into Yannick's mouth. Her nipples tightened as Yannick gently stroked the backs of his hands over them. Leather gliding over silk.

She reached out to explore both men, touching a wide shoulder here, a solid, silk-covered chest there, a lean hipbone, a stretch of hard thigh.

It was scandalous and enthralling and exciting not to know which man she touched. Yet, she could now tell . . . some inner sense guided her.

The warm flesh that seared through her thin gloves—that was Yannick's strong neck. The rasp of stubble against the silk—Bastien's jawline. Hot mouths explored her neck, the points of fangs drew lines that tingled and tickled, but she felt no fear.

She let them run their lips over her neck. Her heart pumped wildly and she knew they could hear the thrumming sound, knew they could smell her blood. But she trusted—

"I would love to make you ours," Bastien whispered.

Fear rose so quickly it left her immobilized. Althea stood, frozen, as Bastien gently pricked her neck with the tips of his canines.

No, don't touch her. Yannick shoved Bastien back.

Eyes hot with fury, Bastien pushed Yannick.

"No, stop this ridiculous fighting! I will not become a vampire!"

Breathing hard, hands fisted, Bastien and Yannick paced around each other.

"If one of you strikes the other, I will leave this minute. And as for biting me, I've got a stake hidden under my dress. Try it and you get that through the heart!"

Bastien stared at her, then laughed. He stepped away from his brother, moving to her side, then moving behind her to embrace her around her waist. "I won't do it," he whispered, "I only mean that I wish you could be mine—ours—for all time. Which means quite a lot coming from a man who never thought beyond the night at hand."

She turned to him. His hands slid over her breasts. He kissed the hollow of her throat, then delved his tongue into her cleavage, thrust up by her corset in a scandalous display. She gave a squeal as the wetness traced the valley, teasing her skin. She felt as hot as she had under the thousands of candles in the ballroom.

Yannick lifted her skirts. The froth of petticoats slid up her thighs as the weight of the silk skimmed upward. "Blast," he groaned. "Drawers."

"Terribly fast, I'm told," she whispered, remembering Lady Peter's shock at the garment. "But I am not a proper young woman any more, am I?"

"And improper young women should definitely eschew drawers," Yannick teased. His long fingers found the lace-trimmed slit. She knew the lace was drenched, sticky, perhaps even ruined by the thick fluid—the honey, they called it—dripping from her.

Bastien nibbled the upper curve of her breast at the exact instant Yannick slid two fingers inside her. She feared she might dissolve onto the ground. The ballroom had been horribly hot and she'd sweated into her exquisite clothes, but the heat had been nothing like this.

She felt ready to burst into flames.

The twins were both so handsome in evening dress. Moonlight caught their profiles and highlighted the bulges tenting their trousers. They made no move to undress her, but she ached to take their clothes off.

Fingers trembling, she opened Bastien's gold silk waistcoat. An embroidered pattern of dragons decorated it. She was acquiring much more experience undressing men. The waistcoat fell open and she made short work of the buttons of his shirt. Spreading the fine linen wide, she exposed his beautiful chest to the night.

We shouldn't undress completely, Althea. We will have to return you to the ball. And without a hair out of place.

She hadn't even thought of that, but of course it was true.

Yannick tossed his tailcoat beside Bastien's on the end of the stone bench. Almost hidden beneath the tumbling bushes, and polished smooth, the seat appeared designed for trysting.

But with two men?

Althea found herself seated on it, the twins standing before her.

Perfect, she decided as she set to opening the falls of Yannick's trousers. As soon as the first button gave, she motioned Bastien to take a step closer. He did with a flourishing bow.

"Straighten, please," she admonished in a whisper. "How else will I unfasten yours?"

And with Bastien, too, she released only one button. One button at a time, she undid them both, moving back and forth. Heads bowed, arms folded across magnificent chests, they watched her.

She should free Yannick's cock first—she'd started with his trousers, after all—but after a brief hesitation, she turned to Bastien. Though lust burned in his expression, so did a sweet uncertainty, as though he still wasn't certain she truly loved him.

His cock had no doubts. Released from his small clothes, it stood proud, reaching for the stars. She couldn't resist one lick, from the thick base and the soft golden curls to the quivering head. With the tip of her tongue, she traced the column along its back. Already slick, the head tasted tangy and rich, and his fingers slid into her hair as her tongue dallied there.

"Don't muss her hair," Yannick teased in a raspy voice.

"That will be bloody impossible," Bastien groaned.

She laughed at that—powerful vampires made weak by desire—by desire for her. She felt a surge of womanly power she was only just beginning to understand.

Filled with courage, she freed Yannick's prick from his trousers. His breathtaking cock gleamed in the moonlight. A little tear bubbled at the eye. She guessed he expected a long lick too, so she surprised him by sucking him suddenly deep, so deep the head pressed to the back of her throat. Tears sparkled in her eyes as she slid him in and out, keeping tight pressure on the shaft, taking him in as far as she could.

She loved his taste, and the satiny feel of him against her tongue.

Angel, you are enslaving me.

Althea looked up and saw Yannick drop his head back and moan to the sky. *God, you are a treasure, sweet angel.*

Boldly, she released Yannick's cock and took Bastien's in her mouth. She fondled Yannick's ballocks, still snuggled in his linens, while she suckled Bastien's cock. They both gasped in surprise. Back and forth she went, bestowing a lick, a suck, and a quick fondle to each man's cock in turn. Their moans grew into a sensual chorus. They panted harshly as though nearing the brink. Their hips began to move, even when she wasn't sucking. As she pleasured Bastien, Yannick's hips rocked and jerked, apparently impatient for his turn.

Her jaws began to ache and she had to slow her strokes, treating Bastien to a slow, loving caress with her mouth. He tasted every bit as earthy and rich and sweet as Yannick. She slid her hand around to his buttocks to hold his hips tight to her mouth. She lavished little kisses to the head, then swirled her tongue lovingly around it.

"God, God, God," he groaned.

She knew Yannick was watching her suck Bastien, his reflective eyes burning with need and lust. She saw how watching each other excited them more. She moved back to Yannick, and tried for a delightful show, exaggerating her caresses and her motions.

Bastien was panting wildly. Yannick was groaning.

The most scandalous idea took root. Something shocking and naughty and irresistible. Quelling nerves, she took hold of their cocks, one in each hand. They stood side by side and she held the two pricks on either side of her mouth, each just an inch from her lips.

"Yes, sweetheart," Bastien urged.

"Angel, you are unbelievably sensual," Yannick whispered, and she heard the awe.

She licked Yannick's beautiful prick first, then turned, saucily gazed up at Bastien. A dazzling drop of his come glistened on the tip and she licked it up. Under her lashes, she watched the agony contort their beautiful faces.

Bastien howled up to the sky as she bobbed her head on him. Yannick joined the cry and they howled up to the moon like wild wolves.

"I'm going to come—now." Bastien tried to pull back but she held his buttocks. She wanted this, wanted to taste his fluid.

"I can't hold it—" He yelled and his buttocks clenched tight beneath her grasp. His hips lurched forward and suddenly her mouth was filled. Filled with wet fire, tangy and tart, swampy and rich. She swallowed, drinking it down, and Bastien shuddered as she did.

"Sweet, no, I'm too sensitive—"

Feeling devilish, she suckled him, drawing out more drops of his slightly sour semen. She flicked each drop with her tongue and he moaned and trembled at the touch. His head arched forward as though all his strength had poured into her along with his come.

He cradled her cheek. "Sweet Althea."

Yannick, she realized, had dropped to his knees. His silver eyes glowed, hot and hungry. He lifted her by her stocking-clad calves, arranging her over the smooth bench with her thighs parted. But as he stood at her side, obviously ready to mount, she took him into her mouth.

"Yes . . ." he groaned. Then, "No." A distinct plea. "No, angel. You must be tired. Let me make love to you."

Ignoring him, earl or no, she sucked him in. She loved to do this. Liked the taste of him, the feel of his flesh against her questing tongue.

But though she teased and suckled and licked and he moaned in delight, she couldn't bring him to the edge. He had remarkable control.

Bastien had sank down to the bench at her back. *If you want to make him come for you, there's a little trick you must know. He's developed impressive stamina, but if you do this, he will surely explode.*

Goodness, it was naughty to have a private conversation with Bastien while sucking Yannick, but she wanted to know the trick. *What do I do?*

You must slide your finger into his arse.

She knew how much she loved being teased there with a tongue, remembered from Zayan's chamber how much pleasure Bastien found from being penetrated that way.

But lick your finger first. Do it subtly, so he doesn't suspect.

Althea obeyed, then pressed her fingertip to Yannick's puckered entrance. Snug, tight, it refused to yield. Yannick's

cock swelled in her mouth, leapt upward. His legs almost buckled but he caught himself.

*Find the trigger with your finger, sweeting, and send him off
like a Vauxhall rocket.*

Trigger? What did he mean? She wriggled her finger into his
fire-hot passage. Velvety soft, it gripped her finger tight and she
could barely slide it in.

His groan startled.

Am I hurting him?

No, Bastien reassured, *he's enjoying this very much.*

Yannick's deep moan floated on the spring breeze. Gently,
she withdrew her finger to the tip and slid it in again. The way
they did to her with their cocks. A slow, long thrust. He swallowed her finger up. She crooked her finger, searching for this
mysterious trigger.

And by sheer luck she found it.

"Angel!" Yannick's cock swelled enormous in her mouth,
then pulsed wildly, shooting his thick come into her mouth.
She felt him restrain himself, felt him fight to control his jerk-
ing hips as he died away for her.

He panted for breath.

Afterward, Yannick dropped to his knees. She gasped at the
sight of his elegant trousers ground into the dirt.

Sweet angel. His mouth slanted over hers, kissing her deep.
A hand took hold of hers.

Bastien's, she realized, and he drew her to stand up. *Turn
around and bend over. Hold the bench.*

"Bastien—" Yannick issued a low warning.

But her skirts bunched up at her back and Bastien's fingers
parted the slit in her drawers. She squealed at the brush of cool
air on her thighs, bare above her stockings. Two fingers slid
deep, opening her. Bastien rested his hand on her hip.

"I do enjoy sex al fresco," Bastien whispered.

Sex in the outdoors. Like her dream. Clutching the smooth

surface of the bench, Althea steadied herself. To her astonishment, he tugged her drawers down. The fancy embroidered silk dangled around her knees and the breeze blew up her tumbled skirts and skimmed her naked bottom.

His hand clapped against her cheek. The pressure excited her and she arched back against it, presenting her bottom to him. She was so wet, his cock slid in easily as he pushed it into her. On the first thrust, his hips collided with her derrière. She loved it, loved the way her cheeks jiggled, loved the tingling sensation.

He drove deep and his hips slammed into her again and again. His balls slapped against her wetness and the sound echoed into the quiet night, heightening their moans.

Yannick stroked her breasts and teased her lower lip with his tongue.

Wicked. She felt wicked and wild. Unfettered. Arching her back, she drove hard against Bastien and he pounded into her. She half-turned, her breath catching at the sight of him behind her, her legs splayed, Bastien's bent and tensed. His hands were splayed on her hip and the small of her back. His hair flying forward as he . . . he fucked her from—

Aah!

The orgasm tore through her. Took her. Consumed her in a lush fire. Her legs collapsed, and only Bastien's hands held her up.

Yannick and Bastien wrapped their arms around her, holding her tenderly, kissing her as the spasms faded. It was heaven. Wonderful.

Yannick brushed back the free strands of her hair.

Oh no.

She broke free, and, in a panic, she reached up. Her fingers brushed a loose curl . . . then several more. Her hair had fallen into a tangled mess. Bastien worked to smooth her skirts, but silk showed every crumple and crush.

How would she explain herself to Lady Peters?

"We'll think of an alibi," Yannick promised.

Bastien kissed her fingertips. "I vow we will always protect you, little dove."

"Even from the matrons in the ballroom." Yannick slid his arm around her shoulders and she let him draw her into his embrace. He was warm, strong. She let her arms slide around him. Oh, it had been pure delight to make love, to have wild sex, to forget all the fears, and tension, and uncertainties.

Yannick kissed her disordered hair. "We will not stay away, sweeting; we will always protect you. From Zayan. From anything."

21

The Choice

He couldn't believe an innocent woman could invent such wicked sexual games.

As dawn rose and the day sleep began to claim him, Yannick sank back against the silk lining of his coffin. He could not resist reliving the stunning sight of Althea licking first his swollen cock and then Bastien's, even though he was rewarded with a brick-hard erection that would haunt him painfully until dusk.

What amazed was how much she enjoyed playing the vixen. How much she enjoyed pleasuring both him and Bastien.

He was normally too jaded, too experienced, to reach orgasm from even the most skilled cock-sucking. With Althea, he'd almost burst blood vessels trying to restrain himself.

And then . . .

Hades, his cock throbbed just to think about it, and the rim of his arse tightened with a sensual jolt . . .

Yannick couldn't believe she had stroked inside his ass and sent him shooting off like a cannon.

Every memory of the night flooded through him, teasing and torturing him—

The silkiness of her tumbled hair as he'd pinned it up again. The sparkling trust in her eyes—the hope. She wanted to believe he, and Bastien, could survive.

Damn, his palms tingled, still feeling her satiny smooth skin.

And then he'd waltzed with her—tame compared to threesome sex in the garden—but it had been magical, and he'd loved holding her in his arms in front of society, loved making it known she was his.

He felt his heartbeat slow. His legs weakened; his arms, crossed over his chest, grew heavy.

Two nights until the full moon.

Bastien was climbing into the other coffin, which he had brought into this secret room. A decade ago Yannick had had it built into Brookshire House, erasing the memories of the workmen and the staff after its construction. A secret passage led back to his bedchamber, and when he rose at dusk, he would return there, and lie in his bed to muss up it up. Night after night.

While Yannick believed he could sleep in a bed, if he ensured that no light could enter his room, he still used the coffin, which immersed him in the complete dark. At least he did not sleep in the earth, as so many of the undead did in the Carpathian Mountains.

Bastien levered up into the box, then swung his legs in. His brother sat upright for a while, obviously thinking.

Yannick felt the sleep tug at him, fog his brain. When Bastien spoke, he couldn't make out the words.

"Brother," Bastien repeated. "If the price of Althea's love is living in peace with you, I have no choice but to do it."

He had to make Bastien understand, even as his mind grew more tired. *We have to destroy Zayan. I know you are thinking that you could let me die and claim everything I have, but then you wouldn't be able to protect Althea from Zayan.*

Bastien lay back. *Thank you for the comfortable coffin, brother. I realize I hadn't shown my appreciation.*

Damn Bastien's irreverence, his refusal to be serious about anything. *Do you understand that you have to help me fight Zayan?*

And risk my own bloody arse?

For Althea's sake, yes. I'll accept nothing less from you, Bastien. If you don't, I swear I'll destroy you myself—

Leaving no one to protect Althea? Tell me, Yannick, why would Zayan go after Althea? He told me that if I let him live, he would give her to me.

And you believe a demon who tried to renege on his deal with the devil? Yannick felt his brain grow more sluggish. Concentrate. Fight the sleep for just a little longer. . . . *He will kill Althea because if he doesn't, you will find love with her and he would lose you for eternity. He's not going to accept that. His bond with you is too deep.*

Yannick felt a blackness steal around his heart. A pain that he'd never known before. He remembered watching women he cared about look at Bastien. Surreptitious glances they thought no one else saw—but they gazed at him with eyes sparkling, lashes fluttering, lips parted in breathless adoration. He saw the longing in their eyes. They loved Bastien, all those women. They chased him for his wealth and title, but Bastien was the one they truly wanted. He was too cold, too reserved. He had always distanced himself with women. Except Althea. No, with Althea, he didn't care about getting his heart broken. It was madness, but he wanted her too badly to worry about pain.

Two nights left—

Did Althea love Bastien the most, just as the others had done? What if they did conquer Zayan? Was he willing to walk away if Althea loved Bastien more than him? Could they share her and make that work? But what about the happy mortal future Althea deserved? What of her determination not to be turned into a vampire?

He only wanted Althea to be happy. Hell, he was willing to condemn himself to an eternity of pain to ensure that she was.

Bastien had to admit Yannick had a point. Zayan had made a deal with Lucifer and had then tried to destroy the devil himself. An impossible task, but Zayan had been Marius Praetonius in his mortal life, a Roman general who defeated impossible odds. Arrogant enough to believe he possessed the intellect to outstrategize Satan, Zayan had nearly won in their battles.

Bastien closed the lid, enveloping himself in safe darkness, and remembered.

Zayan had turned him into an immortal, but Lucifer had been the one to give him the power he craved. . . .

The whip flailed his back. Jolting him awake with a scream, the lash parted his skin. A fresh welt across healed scars.

Bastien tried to raise his head but the whip landed again, and he fell back on the mattress against the onslaught of pain.

He slept nude, and the sheets were tangled around his hips, leaving his back bare and vulnerable. He felt a warm trickle of blood, felt it run beside the bumps of his spine.

He heard his father's voice. Condemning him for some transgression or other. He couldn't listen. The angry, lacerating voice flayed him along with the whip. He gritted his teeth, and moved to roll over, only to find his father had bound his blasted wrists to the bed posts. He wrapped his hands tight around the ropes and willed himself not to show any emotion at all. Not anger. Not despair. Not shock or fear. And damnation, he wouldn't allow himself to cry.

Father, he knew, had lost badly at hazard, and Bastien had made a mistake—he'd impregnated a young dairymaid. Since his father had left a trail of bastards across England—he usually

planted one or two at hunting parties and house parties—
Bastien couldn't see that his was worth a whipping.

The whip struck again. Eyes shut, he strained at the ropes,
choking back a cry. His head arched back with the force of the
blow, the goddamned pain of it.

Goddamn him, he was five and twenty. Too old to let his fa-
ther whip him—and even though he was tied up and couldn't
move, he still felt he was allowing the beating. What in hell was
wrong with him? Why would he submit to this? Why in the
name of Jesus had he come home at all?

He lay there, immobilized by guilt and shame and an anger
he was too afraid to give in to, and he submitted like a weakling.

Some of his father's words began to penetrate.

"Damnation, I can't believe I've raised such a pervert. To
touch another man in that way—makes me sick."

And the whip rose again. So somehow his father had found
out about Zayan and knew about Bastien's forays into clubs
where pleasures between men were the norm.

His father had indulged in orgies, was a well-known patron
at most London brothels, beat his sons mercilessly—but called
him a pervert.

And for some mad reason, Bastien lay face down on his bed
and cowed to his father's opinion.

Bile and hatred rose. But at himself . . .

By that night he'd returned to London. He went to Drury
Lane, charmed the drawers off of the Duke of Ormston's mistress, the pretty little actress Maria, and fucked her in her dressing room. He still remembered the feel of her derrière slapping
wet and hard against his groin and the horror in her eyes as she
saw, reflected in her mirror, Ormston opening the door.

The old goat had looked a lot like his father, far too old for a
saucy little nineteen-year-old vixen like Maria. His explosion,
deep in Maria's snug cunny, had been the greatest of his life.

Imminent death had that effect. He was so soused with brandy he could barely stand, much less shoot straight. Still, he'd accepted Ormston's challenge to pistols at dawn, named his second, and with the matter of his death settled, he had strutted out into the night.

He never reached the dueling field. Never made it more than a block from the theater—never even reached his carriage. Two footpads held him while the third carved him up with a knife. Dimly, he remembered likening himself to the Christmas goose.

Then he'd fallen face first in the muck and the horse dung. He'd planned to die with some dignity on the field, not in the gutter.

Zayan had been less than pleased at his revolting state. Apparently, he'd vomited in the ditch he was lying in and also on himself.

Even as his last drops of blood had leached into the dirt, Bastien had known humiliation. Deep, cold, bitter shame.

But then Zayan had cradled his head. He'd thought his lover was caressing him one last time before he died. He'd shamed himself further as tears pricked his eyes. Not even his mother had ever cradled his head, had ever lovingly stroked his cheek.

Before his fading sight, Zayan's pointed teeth had lengthened, had grown into long, curving fangs. He'd thought it a hallucination—because he was dying. He'd closed his eyes. He was ice cold, wet, and filthy. The hot wetness on his lips had taken him by surprise. As the tinny taste hit his tongue, as the fluid filled his mouth, he drank. Weak as he was, he gulped at the stuff, not even understanding what it was.

"Drink," Zayan had urged, stroking his hair. Feebly, his eyes had opened and he saw Zayan's bared arm, realized his mouth was at Zayan's wrist and he was suckling like a babe. Suckling blood.

Revulsion hit and Bastien had fought to stop. But Zayan's

powerful arm held him in place, and he drank and drank, until Zayan had ripped his wrist away from his questing mouth.

"Do you understand what you are now?" Zayan had asked.

Amazed by the strength he felt flooding back to his frozen, numb limbs, he hadn't cared. Hadn't given a damn what he now was because it appeared he was alive.

Suddenly, he'd heard Zayan's voice in his head. *You are now Nosferatu.*

By stealing death from his grasp, Zayan had prevented him from finding the escape he'd craved, and at first Bastien had hated Zayan for that. But it had been a pleasure to find Ormston and drink his blood. Not that Ormston hadn't owed him death. He'd poached the man's mistress, after all, and he would have been glad to accept death had it been dealt in an honorable manner. But being cut down by surprise in a filthy alley behind Drury Lane had been an insult.

On his second night as an immortal, he'd run wild throughout London. Crazed and furious, he'd gloried in his newly found power and strength. But damn, he still hated Zayan for forcing him to live an eternity condemning himself for letting his father whip him.

And he hated himself for giving in to tears when he admitted to Zayan how he had submitted to his father's beating. Zayan had seen the evidence, the fresh, swollen slashes on his back. Wounds that had miraculously disappeared after he drank Zayan's blood.

God, he remembered the first taste of blood. How much he'd hungered for it. Craved it. And he would never forget the sheer pleasure of the first time he'd sunk his fangs into a human neck. His cock had gone rock-hard at the pressure of flesh against the tips of his fangs. The warmth, the tang of sweat, the first rich tantalizing droplets as his teeth cleaved through skin.

Then the rubbery feel of the artery, the moment of resistance, the pop as he punctured. The ecstasy of blood flowing into him, a hot, coppery river into his waiting mouth.

He only wished his father could have witnessed him drinking another man's blood.

Yes, indeed, he was a pervert.

But the third night after his transformation, his father had died. An attack of the heart in his bed. Bastien had wondered afterward if Zayan had paid his father a visit.

On the night of his father's death, Yannick became the new lord. Yannick took all—title, wealth, power. And his father, while whipping him, had told him Yannick had been the one to tattle about Zayan.

Blinded by jealousy and rage, he'd killed Yannick. With a knife.

But he didn't let Yannick die. He turned his brother, while Yannick lay bleeding to death, shocked at his twin's betrayal.

As he forced his brother to take that first swallow of his blood, he'd thought he wanted to take everything from Yannick. How could Yannick be the lord now?

But deep in his heart Bastien had suspected his father had lied—he knew his valet had always been his father's spy. He'd turned Yannick because he'd been scared and angry and was afraid to be forever parted from the brother who condemned him but also loved him.

He hadn't realized that Lucifer had manipulated his anger, his jealousy, his fear. He thought he'd willingly murdered his brother.

And killing a brother—even to resurrect him—was a sin. A mortal sin.

Which made him the perfect candidate to do the devil's bidding.

* * *

"A Mr. Zayan?" Lady Peters rested her knife and fork by her plate as she considered. "No, my dear, I don't believe I have heard of any member of society by that name."

Althea sighed, and speared a slice of roast without enthusiasm. She had not expected success from Lady Peters. At breakfast she had asked Sir Randolph about Zayan—it was her only chance to speak to him before nightfall, since he normally took lunch at his club.

They had been alone in the dining room. "You needn't fear Zayan," he had said, in a highly patronizing tone. He was a handsome, austere man, and after giving her that reassurance, he had returned to his newsheet.

"No," Althea had replied, pouring coffee. "I want to hunt Zayan."

Her host had exploded at that—decreeing that she wasn't going to do any such foolhardy thing—and she knew she would be kept on a tight leash.

She took a sip of her wine. At Lady Montrose's musicale tonight, she would ask the ladies of society about Zayan. He existed openly, and he lived well, and she suspected he didn't preclude debutantes from his choice of victims, so he probably ensured he had entry to the fashionable world, to the *ton*. She suspected he was like Bastien. He enjoyed walking amongst the mortals as a demon—it was his private joke.

But while Bastien hid a gentle, loving nature behind his joke, Zayan hid evil. Althea reached for her glass of wine, but as she took a sip, Ridgeway, the butler, entered.

"Sir Edmund Yates has arrived, my lady."

Father! She pushed her chair back and stood. He must have received her letter, in which she explained her meeting with the so-called queen of the vampires.

Lady Peters smiled. "Do bring him in, Ridgeway."

And there was Father, looking weak still, but so familiar, in breeches and tweeds, a wide smile on his weatherbeaten face. Beneath his hat, his wiry white hair was in its usual disarray, and his spectacles were smeared with fingerprints. He clutched a leatherbound book under his arm.

And how overjoyed she was to see him.

"Oh, Althea, lass, I'm so glad to be with you again." He held her tight to him and stroked her hair. "And you're looking a fetching beauty, I might add."

She was just so happy to see him safe and well, even as he beamed with pride and approval at her new clothes and her elegantly dressed hair.

There was no chance to speak of any personal matters—not in front of Lady Peters, David, the female cousins, and the aunt.

But when David, with a twinkling eye, remarked that Althea in her fine gown had set the *ton* on its ear, the aunt, a Mrs. Horatio Thomas, had harumphed. "Seems she's settled on the Demon Twins—though I hadn't seen hide nor hair of them for years. Running wild on the Continent, I've heard, though it appears to agree with them. They don't look a day older than the last time they graced society with their presence. Though there's rumor that Lord Brookshire has been in England for years, living as a recluse. Too lofty, still, to pick for husband material, even with his eccentric behavior."

"Mrs. Thomas, I wouldn't dream of aspiring so high," Althea responded, heart pounding.

She noticed her father, who'd joined them for supper, about to protest, but he stuffed a piece of potato in his mouth instead—no doubt realizing he'd been about to defend his daughter's suitability to wed a vampire.

"Good. Even a second son would be a coup, gel. Though a life with Bastien de Wynter would not be an easy one. Wild as they come, that one. Remember the rumors that he'd been knifed in the stews, dead drunk before an upcoming duel with the Duke of Ormston? Some scandalous business with Ormston's actress mistress—"

A sharp intake of breath by Lady Peters at that. Apparently, Mrs. Thomas' conversation was decidedly improper. But the elderly lady, who was half deaf, continued in the loud voice used by those who didn't hear well. "Some thought he'd died there, but others insisted he'd fled to the Continent. Can see why—Ormston was a notoriously good shot, even at his age." Mrs. Thomas' small eyes narrowed even further. "Now Mr. Fenwick would make a good match for you—"

A milquetoast. Dull, moon-faced, but in truth, in the eyes of the haute *ton*, Miss Althea Yates should be delighted to receive an offer from a man with a solid income and good family.

Mr. Fenwick had shown interest at the Fortesques' so she'd promptly told him about vampire hunting. He'd gone a shade whiter and had looked distinctly ill.

Her father, she noted, also looked distinctly ill as Mrs. Thomas and Lady Peters launched into a lively debate about the merits of potential suitors. Maybe he now realized what he'd thrown her into.

"I'm sorry, lass. They're like dogs on a scent, aren't they?" Her father spoke in hushed tones, in the quiet of Sir Randolph's library.

"You did seek a good matchmaker, Father," Althea replied, knowing that she would best make her point by "allowing" Father to come to the conclusion himself.

"But you are lovely, lass." Father slid his arm across her shoulders and hugged her. "I wish—" his voice caught. "I wish Anne could have lived to see you grow up."

Althea swallowed hard around the sudden tightness in her throat.

"Ah," he sighed. "But she would have had my head for letting you hunt vampires."

He had said that before, but she wasn't convinced it was true.

Father let his arm drop from her shoulders. "Lord Brookshire came to see me, while I was searching Zayan's crypt, and demanded to know where you were. The madman walked in on me while I was surrounded by armed men."

Even though she knew Yannick had survived—she'd seen him last night—she still felt her heart thump erratically.

"His lordship claimed to love you," he continued. "And I expect he does."

With that, as she stared at him in astonishment, Father bent over and retrieved a book from the seat of a chair. The leather book he'd brought with him. He laid it on the table. "Zayan's journal. Kept it for a century, he has. Thought you might wish to read it for me—search it for clues."

She caught his sleeve. Tugged. "Are you telling me that Y— the earl came to you to tell you that he loves me?"

He gave a deep, sad sigh. "I can see it in your eyes, lass. You love him too, don't you?"

"Yes." Her heart soared the instant she admitted it. Nerves and happiness and shock and delight tumbled around inside.

"Lass—"

She held up a quelling hand. Though it surprised her when he stopped. "I know, Father. He's a vampire. I still love him, but I understand that we can never be together. But to save his life, I have to find Zayan."

She opened the leather bound cover of Zayan's journal. "I know he's in London, I just haven't the resources to find out where. And I've only two nights to do it in." Her voice rose in panic. Calm, she must stay calm. Panic wouldn't help her find Zayan. Panic wouldn't save Yannick. Or Bastien. Even after Mrs. Thomas' attempts to show how inappropriate Bastien was, she still loved him. Loved him more perhaps, because she sensed his bad ways concealed an aching, lonely heart.

"There must be deaths—Bow Street might know about that," she reasoned. "I'm assuming he will go out in society—and I hope to interview ladies and gentlemen at the musicale and balls tonight."

One musicale and two balls were on her night's itinerary. If it wasn't for the opportunity to hunt for Zayan, to see Bastien and Yannick, she'd faint at the thought.

"What I fear, lass, is that Zayan will find you."

Althea had set society on its ear. Tongues wagged, fans pointed, discreet and not-so-discreet whispers flitted around the Benthlams' ballroom. Not only had the Demon Twins attended a musicale where they had promptly attached themselves to a Miss Althea Yates, a nobody, they had apparently followed her to the Benthlams' ball.

The earl had waltzed with Miss Yates three times, the matrons clucked, which clearly meant a partiality. More than two dances signaled an engagement in the offing. But then the earl's brother, Mr. de Wynter, had claimed her for one more waltz and two country dances.

At the twins' obvious interest, Miss Yates' stock in the marriage mart had soared. Young men—viscounts, barons, earls, even a handsome duke—all sought a place on her dance card. What was it about this seemingly ordinary young woman with the dark red hair that had tamed the Demon Twins?

Listening to Mrs. Thomas relay the gossip to Lady Peters, Althea groaned. Why were the twins being so conspicuous? For protection? She feared that all this attention would keep Zayan away and they only had two nights left.

But the twins were instinctively possessive, she realized. They couldn't stand idly by and watch other men converse with her, flirt with her, dance with her. Her heart leapt in joy, knowing they cared so much.

She asked the group of matrons about Zayan.

"A Mr. Zayan? Indeed, I believe a Mr. Zayan has recently come to town, Miss Yates." Lady Rawlstone frowned. Obviously Zayan had a dark enough reputation that her question evoked curiosity. "And how did you say you were acquainted with him?"

Because he is the embodiment of evil. "A distant relative of a close friend."

Lady Rawlstone was a contemporary of Mrs. Thomas, and Althea had learned much about the Demon Twins. She'd heard many scandalous rumors about Bastien. And about Yannick's failed engagement—which he had never mentioned.

"Mr. Zayan is not the sort of gentleman that you should acknowledge, I fear," said Lady Rawlstone, "I believe he favors gaming hells to good society, though alas, so many gentlemen do—oh goodness, here is Mr. de Wynter."

Althea caught her breath as Bastien bowed before her. Another dance would surely shock society.

Lady Rawlstone smiled. "Your ears must be burning, Mr. de Wynter."

Althea gaped. She hadn't expected her ladyship to be so blunt.

Bastien only laughed. "They always are, dear lady. Always." He gave her a courtly bow.

Althea stifled a soft whimper as he turned and bestowed a wicked smile upon her. Despite being surrounded by hundreds of watchful eyes, she felt her nipples tighten, threatening to pop forth from the scandalous neckline of the clinging apricot silk dress she wore. Creamy, hot, yearning, her cunny ached for him. For she knew exactly what he had come to her to do.

Follow me, love. I've come to lead you astray.

Yannick drew her into a scorching kiss the instant she stepped behind the potted palm at the end of the terrace.

God, I've hungered all night to do this.

She sank into his heat and fire, hooked her arms around his neck as he swept her literally off her feet and into his embrace. The instant he released her, Bastien claimed his kiss. Together they kissed her into dizziness. The moon, a large white globe, almost full, watched over them with blue shadowed eyes.

Or so it seemed.

Bastien began lifting her skirts from behind.

"On the terrace!" she squealed. "We don't dare."

"I dare anything," Bastien promised.

"So I've heard," she muttered. For some mad reason, jealousy prickled. Why should it? She'd already watched—witnessed with her own eyes—Bastien make love to another man. Why should decade-old scandals bother her? But she heard the snippiness in her voice as she demanded, "Speaking of hunger, have you two fed?"

Bastien nodded, blond hair fluttering in the soft breeze, free of the black ribbon that had held it back.

She crossed her arms beneath her breasts and looked from Bastien to Yannick. "Voluptuous maids, I assume?"

"A frisky widow interested in a liaison," Bastien admitted.

"Goodness, did you give her one?"

"No, my love. I have pledged my fidelity to you."

"And my prey was male—a footpad," Yannick said. "I enjoy turning the tables on some brute who thinks I'm a soft toff easy to rob."

She glanced at Bastien, to see his reaction to the word *footpad*, but his eyes were a swirling blend of reflected moonlight and black shadow.

I want to make love to you from behind, Bastien said in her thoughts. *It is perfectly safe here. I will lift up your skirts and stand behind you here in the shadows. I will press you to the railing and no one would ever guess what we are doing—never guess I am pleasuring you in your bottom.*

"What?" she gasped, startled. Her skirts were at mid-thigh at the back and she heard the men's harsh, hungry breathing.

In an instant her cheeks were bared to the night air. She hadn't bothered with drawers.

"Damn." Her skirts fell with a swish and Bastien broke away quickly.

"So here you are, pet," came Father's cheerful voice, just at the instant her hems danced around her ankles.

"Why the devil were you out there with both of them?" Father demanded in the foyer of Sir Randolph's townhouse. "They're both in love with you, aren't they? Fighting over you?"

Althea was so tired and all she wanted to do was collapse in bed. Apparently debutantes also never went to bed before dawn. "Not fighting exactly—well, yes, I guess they are competing for me." She couldn't admit they were sharing her! "It was Zayan's plan to lure them to fight over me."

She regretted revealing even that much because she didn't dare speak of the dreams. In the last few nights, she hadn't had any dreams at all.

"And you love the earl."

"I—"

"Oh blast, you're not in love with both of them, are you?"

A telltale blush swept over her cheeks with the heat of wildfire and she turned to the stair to hide it.

Behind her, Father groaned. "Oh lass, you can't be."

She'd expected him to be horrified. But she suddenly understood—he wasn't thinking of them sharing her. The shocking idea had not occurred to him at all.

And she thanked heaven for that. But if he learned the truth, she could imagine the damage it would do to his fragile heart.

"Bastien de Wynter is not the sort of man any woman should fall in love with—even if he were a mortal, which he bloody well isn't. You can't be in love with two vampires, lass. Please, please, Althea, I'm begging you—"

She leaned against the railing and turned to face him. "Father, I understand."

She couldn't even hope for a future with the twins. It would destroy her father.

Father held her hand as they climbed the stairs. He gave her a hesitant smile and she blinked away tears.

She'd force herself to wake early and read the rest of Zayan's journal. There must be a clue there.

All she had to do was ensure Zayan was destroyed and neither Bastien nor Yannick died in the attempt.

And then she would have to say goodbye to the twins. Forever.

22

The Brothel

"We shouldn't have brought you here," Yannick insisted.

"I was not about to stay away!" Masked, Althea stepped across the threshold of Madame Roi's elegant brothel, on both Yannick's and Bastien's arms.

After all, she had been the one to find the reference in the last diary entry, in Zayan's neat, perfect handwriting: *I have been to one of Madame Roi's establishments. A mortal's brothel. Deep play, mesmerizing jades, an excellent selection of restraints, most assuredly the finest establishment in London . . .*

No, she was not going to miss adventure just because it would take place in a house of ill repute owned by a vampire queen. And since she had shared two vampires in bed—how could she be shocked by what went on in a London stew? Certainly nothing about Madame Roi's foyer shocked her. The flocked wallpaper, a glittering chandelier, a jewel-toned carpet looked suitable for a gentleman's home. Statues of nude females stood about, but they were hardly scandalous.

The twins led her forward and Althea instinctively checked

her disguise. Soft and supple, her black leather mask clung to her face from hairline to the upper curve of her lips. Large openings at her eyes let her see as well as she could without spectacles. Yannick had given her the lovely mask and had fastened it behind her head while they'd traveled through London in his luxurious carriage. She'd worn a gown of emerald green with her most revealing neckline—a woman who would come to a brothel wouldn't be shy, after all. Yannick had given her one other gift—the beautiful necklace of emeralds and one heart-shaped diamond that now hung around her neck.

They stepped inside the salon and Althea gasped. The entire atmosphere changed—currents of sexual desire sizzled throughout the room. Handsome gentlemen attired in fashionable evening dress prowled Madame Roi's salon. It appeared that only the most gorgeous of males were allowed admittance to Madame Roi's. A rather interesting quirk for a woman who sought to make a living. Aging men losing their looks might be more likely to pay well for dalliances with lovely courtesans.

So, obviously, the vampire queen did not run a brothel for financial concerns.

Madame Roi's women were lovely, each and every one. Possessing excellent manners and gentle voices, the girls smiled and bantered with the men with the charm of well-bred debutantes. For several moments, Althea stared at a dozen pairs of breasts, all but naked beneath transparent, gauzy bodices. Then she remembered her playful interlude with Sarah and looked away in embarrassment.

Which turned her attention to one couple bartering services. Right before her eyes, the gentleman lifted the woman's skirt to inspect her quim, which was shaved completely bare. Apparently pleased by what he saw, he immediately slid one long, gloved finger inside.

The public nature of the display made her realize she was

still innocent after all. She flushed behind her mask as she watched various couples and threesomes strike up erotic bargains.

Shocking to think she was in a threesome herself—and she was certain her back must be scorched from the burning, envious glances thrown at her by several women. One courtesan approached and asked if they were seeking another lady to make a fourth. She suggested it as though they were seeking another person for a game of whist.

Bastien politely declined the offer from the blond prostitute and the woman flashed a look of disappointment. With a coy smile, she strummed her erect, scarlet nipples through the filmy ivory lace of her bodice.

Althea's quim pulsed at the gesture. The woman's breasts were the size of melons, the hard nipples long and pliant. Althea couldn't even begin to imagine how much the sight must be arousing the twins.

"I would love a night with the Demon Twins, my lords," the woman simpered.

"And with our demoness," Bastien remarked. Althea almost squealed in protest. He meant her!

"But not right now, love," he continued. "Perhaps later."

Later! Since he knew of her dalliance with Sarah, she whirled on him, afraid at what she might see in his expression.

Bastien bent close. "Lovely tits, weren't they? I'm rather tempted by the thought of both you and I suckling them together—"

"Bastien, bloody hell," Yannick snapped. "Tonight is not about titillation, brother; it is about protecting . . . Miss Carstairs."

They'd agreed to call her by a false name, to protect her reputation.

"Personally, I've never enjoyed an evening in a brothel more. There's an intriguing novelty about seeing it afresh, through a novice's eyes." Bastien gave her bottom an illicit squeeze through her skirts. "I believe there are several tableaux in the next rooms. That might be where we'll find Zayan."

"Tableaux, hmm?"

"What are tableaux?" She turned to Yannick, then to Bastien. Though neither man answered, she was soon to find out. They joined several couples—handsome gentlemen and voluptuous jades—moving into the room through an opened double door.

Althea received her next lesson in her enlightening education the instant she crossed the threshold. A raised dais, draped in crimson velvet, stood near the entrance. In the center of the stage, a nude man reclined on a chaise. He placed his fist at the base of his cock to push his member upright. It was . . . enormous.

"Big, isn't he?" Bastien whispered against her ear. "Must be at least fourteen inches long."

Fourteen inches? She quivered uncomfortably at the thought. "Could a woman truly fit that inside?"

"I believe we are about to find out," Yannick pointed out.

Two women stood on the dais in Grecian-style gowns of pure white. They'd been dressed as statues, with hair powdered white, and white paint or powder on their faces and skin. The reclining man recited a bit of poetry—Althea was too startled to really grasp its meaning, but she caught a line where he pleaded to the nymphs to come to life to pleasure him. When he complained that he'd been cursed with equipment that would make a stallion jealous and that terrified mortal women, all the men in the audience laughed.

One woman gave a performance of being brought to life. Slowly moving her limbs, she conveyed astonishment, delight, then began to explore her breasts and quim. Her dress fluttered to the ground, exposing her lithe form. Small, high breasts with rouged nipples, and child-like, slender hips.

The jade dropped to her knees, approached the man on the chaise, and made a plea for gentleness. He urged her up and she gracefully moved to straddle him.

Althea moaned as his fingers slid inside the woman. First one, then two, then three. The jade's juices apparently flowed liberally; his fingers made a sucking sound on each thrust.

As he worked his entire hand inside, Althea's toes curled. Did it hurt? It must. But the "statue" moaned in agonized pleasure. Beads of sweat gleamed on her brow and across her bare breasts as she began bouncing up and down on his hand.

And then he withdrew his hand, and held his cock upright. His "statue" impaled herself with a scream.

Althea bit back a shriek of sympathy.

"Do you sense Zayan?" Yannick asked.

She tore her gaze from the bouncing woman and grunting man. How could Yannick not be enraptured by the display? Every scream from the woman as she took that monstrous cock inside made Althea ache.

"No," Bastien shrugged. "Too distracted."

Althea felt his fingertips stroke her wrist. An innocent gesture, but it made her burn.

"Ignore the fucking."

Fucking. Even the word, on Yannick's lips, made her throb and grow wet.

"No, too distracted by the fair Miss Carstairs. She seems to flood all my senses until I can think of nothing else but her." Bastien lifted her fingers for a quick kiss. "Shall we continue our search?"

"Of course," Althea said, pretending to be completely unaffected by the shrieks and moans. But Bastien grinned, and she knew he guessed how excited she was.

No, she vowed she would "ignore the fucking" as Yannick had said. But the next tableau dissolved her vow in a heartbeat. The very large-breasted blond courtesan stood upon it, completely nude. She called out to the audience, "Two gentlemen, if you please. Would two gentlemen care for a most satisfying pleasure?"

Several offered their services—gentlemen Althea had danced with in her brief forays into society.

The woman, who one man called Ruby, made her selections.

Althea gaped as David Peters sprinted up the steps onto the stage. She fiddled with her mask, praying it was good enough to hide her. But a greater shock awaited.

The second man was Zayan. He strode up to the stage with a fierce, sensual energy that made every woman who watched whimper. Althea found herself gasping too.

"It appears we have found him," Bastien murmured.

"Indeed," Yannick agreed.

Standing on the stage, David Peters pulled the jade to him. He kissed her lips and then licked the swells of her massive breasts. Cheering erupted as he drew one of the long nipples into his mouth. For a young man, he obviously possessed skill. As he toyed with the nipple, he stroked Ruby's smooth inner thighs and rounded bottom.

As Zayan undid the falls of his trousers, Althea felt a shudder of fear, apprehension, excitement. Should they attack now? She looked between the twins.

"Not yet." Yannick shook his head. His arm slid possessively around her waist.

"Enjoy the show," Bastien added. He bent to nuzzle her neck.

Enjoy it! Pleasure swamped her at both men's touches but she was fearful for Ruby's life. Would Zayan dare bite the woman in front of so many witnesses? Or was his intention just to have sex?

Zayan's long, dusky cock sprang free. He paced around to the woman's backside and slapped the lush rump.

Bastien's tongue tickled her earlobe. She wished she could read his expression—was he jealous, angry, or only aroused?

"Bend her over," Zayan instructed Mr. Peters, who obliged immediately, holding her hands to support her. Silence gripped the audience as Zayan's cock pressed between the ivory cheeks. The woman gasped—it must be pushing against her entrance. Mr. Peters held her as she squirmed back against Zayan.

"Please be gentle, sir," she begged.

"Of course," Zayan growled. Althea expected him to renege on his promise, but he did not. Inch by excruciating inch he drove his cock into her bottom, moving his hips with a slow, languorous, circular motion.

Althea heard Bastien's low laugh and Yannick's hand tightened on her waist. She could hear both men's heavy breathing as Zayan stopped and the courtesan pleaded, "No, no, please sir, I must get used to you."

Gently Zayan stroked Ruby's spine until she rocked against him and demanded, "More. Oh yes, now, I want more."

All the while, the audience watched, enthralled.

Zayan exuded a power that held one captive, Althea couldn't deny that.

Bastien cuddled up beside her and nestled his erection against the right cheek of her bottom. She half-turned. *What are you doing?* Suddenly she was afraid he might pull up her skirts—

Tormenting myself. He gave her an angelic look. *Look, sweetheart, he's buried completely inside.*

She couldn't resist looking. Zayan's hips were pressed tight to Ruby's derrière, the cock inside as deep as it could go. Ruby's face was red and she was gasping. Moaning, and whimpering, and taking short, desperate breaths.

Yannick moved his arm from Althea's waist as he pressed against her from the left side. His cock, as rigid as Bastien's, jutted against her hip. He teased her neck with his fingertips.

"Stretched you to the limit, has he Ruby?" called out a

gentleman from the audience. As though a spell had broken, ribald laughter followed.

"Ooh, I'm right stuffed," Ruby moaned.

"Touch her clit," Zayan instructed Peters. "It eases the pain."

Mr. Peters, handsome in evening dress, with his mahogany hair in disarray around his face, obeyed.

Ruby squealed. "Oh, do play with me wee bud, sir."

"I'll make it blossom," David promised. He'd freed himself from his trousers.

Althea had sat at the breakfast table with this man and now she was seeing him—

Goodness.

Zayan moved back, drawing Ruby away from Mr. Peters and toward the chaise that sat upon their dais. Somehow he managed to keep himself embedded in the woman the entire time, though she was on tiptoe to move with him. Holding the full-bosomed jade with one arm, he lowered himself onto the chaise.

"Oh no!" Ruby cried, and sobbed as his cock twanged free.

With a muttered curse, Zayan embedded himself once more, then arranged her legs across his, wide open.

Mr. Peters approached, cock in hand.

Althea gasped as shock and excitement tightened her chest. She was going to witness a woman penetrated by two men. She was going to find out what Yannick and Bastien wished to do to her.

Nervous anticipation swirled in the pit of her stomach. Already her drawers were soaked and clung to her wet nether lips. Bastien's hand massaged her bottom, the sensation thrilling and mind-numbing. She leaned back against him. At her side, Yannick bent and kissed her shoulder, tickling the bare skin at the neckline of her dress.

She met Yannick's bright gaze for a moment. He smiled

wickedly and nodded toward the performance. Of course, he wanted her to watch. And learn . . .

The jade, Ruby, appeared eager and willing. Candlelight showed her cunny to be wet and swollen and glistening. Her nipples stood upright. Zayan's hips moved slowly, sensuously, beneath her.

"Oh, please," Rudy begged, and she reached down to part her nether lips wide. "Oh, please, sir."

Mr. Peters mounted the chaise and knelt between Ruby's— and Zayan's—outstretched legs. Ruby's shapely, bare legs straddled Zayan's long, muscular ones, his every lean muscle outlined by the tight-fitting trousers.

Althea's throat dried as Mr. Peters touched his tip—taut and purplish—against Ruby's quim. But she couldn't see the actual act of penetration as Mr. Peters surged forward and his trouser-clad buttocks hid the view.

But there was no doubt he'd sunk deep. Ruby screamed at the top of her lungs.

"Can you . . . can you feel his cock inside her too?" A man with glazed-over eyes fired the question at Mr. Peters, his hand rubbing his own swollen crotch.

David Peters panted and grunted as he began to thrust. "Yes, God in heaven, I can feel him. And she's so blasted tight—"

Althea imagined the weight on top of Zayan must be crushing but the demon appeared not to mind. He thrust his hips hard at the woman's arse despite the disadvantage of being on the bottom.

Ruby moaned and sobbed. "Have mercy. You're both so huge inside me."

But the audience did not have sympathy, it appeared, for a third man unleashed himself as he climbed up. A man Althea didn't know, he was as dazzlingly handsome and as dark as Zayan. He offered his member to Ruby's lips and she took it into her mouth with a saucy wink.

Althea looked helplessly to Yannick.

"In an orgy, men enjoy joining in, finding release in whatever way they can." Though he spoke so calmly, his deep, throaty voice set her heart pounding.

She could not believe she was watching a woman pleasure and be pleasured in every possible way. She knew her mouth was wide open, and she knew that Yannick was now kissing her ear. It tickled and teased, but it felt distant too. She was so absorbed in the scene. She thought she'd seen the most shocking thing ever—even more so than Bastien and Zayan making love—until Ruby let the cock in her mouth slide out.

"I've two hands," the courtesan called out, "And if any of ye gents are excited and wish a little groping—"

Immediately two other men climbed up. Transfixed, Althea watched Mr. Peters pump and the raven-haired man thrust his hips at Ruby's mouth while she rubbed up the pricks of the last two men to join in.

Somehow the tangle of bodies all managed to move together. Faster and faster. More and more urgently.

"Oh god, I'm coming!" Ruby cried. She screamed as the orgasm took her, thrashing between the two men who sandwiched her tight. Her hands clutched the cocks so hard it must hurt the men.

At Ruby's cry, Mr. Peters went utterly rigid. His face contorted, his eyes shut, and he bucked forward. He didn't moan or groan, as though he was holding himself in great control.

And as Mr. Peters succumbed, the one of the last two men to join erupted, and his white, molten come poured over Ruby's hand. Like dominoes, the men fell to pleasure—the second squirted into Ruby's palm and the one in her mouth pulled free and sprayed his seed over her throat. The droplets clung there, white and pearlescent, like a pearl necklace.

"But he's not come," Ruby moaned. "The one up me arse. 'e's got stamina, this one."

"If you want to make me come, you'll have to work at it, wench," Zayan growled. "Sit up on me."

Mr. Peters moved off her and the other men stepped back so Ruby could sit up. She bounced frantically upon the cock impaling her. Her large breasts swung up and down with her motion. In a half-dozen bounces, Ruby came again.

"Get off me, lass."

Weak, with half-closed eyes, Ruby whispered, "But I've not finished you, sir."

"I doubt you could. But I'll wash and perhaps return, if you wish."

Ruby lifted off him with a sated sigh. "Oh I would want you to return. You're a blooming challenge, you are."

Althea almost cried out as Bastien licked her neck. "Little Ruby has no bloody idea," he groaned. "And I'm so aroused I'm about to explode."

And so was she. She could barely breathe, her body burned with need.

Zayan gave a deep chuckle and got up from the chaise. The other men were dismounting the stage, presumably also to wash, but as Zayan stepped down he was greeted with an ovation from the audience. He didn't bother to fasten his trousers, and moved off with his erection jutting ahead.

"I think it's time," Yannick said.

Bastien should have guessed his final confrontation with Zayan would occur in a brothel's bechamber. By the light of one candle, his maker was washing his privates in a washbasin mounted on a table.

It didn't seem sporting to attack a vampire with his trousers down. But, then, in his mortal life, had he ever truly been an honorable gentleman?

He stood on more than just the threshold to the lavishly appointed room—he stood the cusp of the choice that might mean his final destruction. He could risk his own life and destroy the man he once loved. Or lose his brother and risk Althea's life—because once one of the Demon Twins died, Zayan would be unstoppable.

But Zayan could have easily let him die in the gutter, and it was hard to betray the man who'd saved him from that. Hard to destroy the man he suspected had taken revenge on his father.

Time to choose.

Bastien lifted his hands. A mild blast shot from his raised palm and exploded in the center of Zayan's back. It singed fine wool, no doubt from London's foremost tailor, but it wasn't intended to wound.

His maker swung around, bellowing a howl of fury that sent a quiver of excitement up Bastien's spine. A vivid green bolt shot from Zayan's hand. The stream of light punched through the oak column at the foot of the bed and missed his shoulder by inches, exploding instead into the wall. Chunks of plaster flew and dust rose up in the air.

"So you have made your choice." Zayan inclined his head, eyes glowing with fire. But on his face was sadness and Bastien reeled at the sharp jolt of guilt.

"I couldn't let my brother die." He glanced to Yannick who had joined him in the room.

"So, of course, you would not be willing to kill him, would you?" Zayan smiled. He crossed his arms in front of his massive chest, a chest Bastien had explored and kissed.

Bastien had loved this man once, with a fierce need that had consumed him, but now, he knew, he loved Althea more. And he loved one other person . . .

"No. I might envy my brother," he said, "but I love him more than that. Even if he does upstage me with emerald necklaces."

Bastien could sense Althea's rapidly beating heart. She was standing behind him and he could taste her tension. *Rest easy, sweet dove.* Her pulsing blood sang to him.

He remained calm, weighing up options and watching Zayan, who watched him with the same motionless appraisal.

It was like this before a duel.

He sensed Zayan would not strike until he did. Lucifer had given him the power to destroy Zayan because the ancient vampire was too powerful, but he knew Zayan wasn't entirely without mercy.

We should take him down now. Yannick's voice in his head was curt, abrupt. A man ready to commence battle.

Wait. Give me just a moment more.

"Zayan," Bastien called, "I'd lay down my life in place of my brother's if you would promise not to hurt Althea."

Zayan's dark brows rose in surprise.

"But even if you promised it, I am not confident I could trust you." Bastien shouted out in the gloom. "Come to me, Your Highness, Elizabeth, Queen of Vampires. I've a bargain to strike with you."

She appeared in a flash of golden light. He almost laughed at the sight of her. Elizabeth—Madame Roi—looked exactly like a successful madam—bedecked in rubies, heavily made-up, squeezed into a provocative gown, and ravishingly beautiful. She looked a dewy-faced twenty-five—yet she'd walked the earth for a millennium.

"Ah, the Demon Twins. And pretty Miss Yates." Painted lips curved into a bewitching smile. "A bargain, dear Bastien?" she asked. "And what sort of bargain do you wish to make? If you back down from combat with Zayan now, you will be destroyed. This is as Lucifer has commanded."

He knew that now.

He shrugged. "Lucifer strikes deals all the time—he might give me a new one."

Her Highness laughed. She waved her bejeweled hand and Zayan appeared to slip into a trance. "It will not last long, Bastien. So make haste. What do you want?"

Bastien felt a tug at his sleeve and glanced back. Althea stood behind him, her hand at his elbow. "What are you doing?" she whispered.

"Gambling." He grinned.

"So, what is your offer?" Elizabeth asked, tapping her chin. "If it is sexual in nature, I am intrigued, but it won't be enough, I'm afraid."

Bastien winked. "I wish it were, my dear queen, but alas, I am now a tamed man. I plea for safety for the woman I love, for the safety of my brother, and for the life of the vampire who made me. In return, I offer *my* life."

"Bastien, no." Althea's fierce whisper touched his heart.

But he couldn't back out now. Not even for her love—this was the only way to protect everyone he loved.

"You offer your life in place of Zayan's?" Elizabeth repeated in disbelief.

Did everyone assume he was a selfish scoundrel? "Yes," he said, fighting impatience. "I can't destroy Zayan, nor can I bring myself to betray him. But that would mean that Yannick dies, leaving Althea at risk of great harm, which I could not stop. By failing to destroy Zayan, I die anyway. But I know that you can imprison vampires, in the same way that Zayan imprisoned me. And I offer you anything you ask of me in return for imprisoning Zayan."

"And you believe that will satisfy Lucifer?"

"I believe you could convince him to accept it."

Once more, Her Highness' mouth curved in a feline smile. "Perhaps I could. But why give such clemency to Zayan?"

"He never hurt me. Other than Yannick, he is the only person to show me only love, not pain. He is capable of love. Of humanity. He attacks out of anger; his need for power comes from once being powerless. I don't understand his past entirely, but I know it was brutal. As a general, he knew that the penalty for failure was death. And he had everything taken from him—

he told me how his wife and children were slaughtered. Not by the enemy, but by ambitious men he believed were his friends. Could he not be freed to rejoin his family? Not destroyed, but released from immortality?"

Elizabeth crossed her arms beneath her generous breasts. "And the payment for such a favor is your death? But if I wished to have your death, I would have it anyway in just a few hours, so that does not tempt me."

Bastien held his hands out, palms up. "There must be something I have that would tempt you."

"There might be . . . but it is too early to request it. It would be more interesting to wait—"

Hell and perdition, ancient vampires always tended to speak in riddles.

"Anything you want from me," he repeated.

"It would interest me to try to bend Lucifer to my wishes," she mused. "He is a stubborn old goat. And it would intrigue me to control Zayan—to have his power under my command. Not that I intend to free him, but merely to . . . use him for my pleasures. Lucifer has forbidden me from interfering but now that you—the assassin he created—have come to me to request that I give Zayan clemency, Lucifer's wishes no longer govern me."

She gave a regal nod. "Then it will be done."

Zayan, still standing motionless, with his cock still exposed and upright, vanished.

Bastien stared. He hadn't expected her to agree. "Where the hell did you send him?"

"Oh, not to hell. He's been imprisoned in a place that pleases me. A dimension between life and death. A place that possesses all the beauty of earth in its most primal state. A place I do enjoy visiting with a male worthy of existence there."

"You've sent him to Eden?" Bastien asked, trying to understand this dimension, this world he'd never heard of.

"I have imprisoned him in paradise. And now—"

"No, wait." Althea surged forward, pushing past him. "What of Yannick? What of Bastien? They will be safe, won't they? Even though Zayan wasn't destroyed?"

"The bargain was that they destroy Zayan."

"But Zayan has been stopped," Althea shouted. "Isn't that good enough?"

"And what if it is not?"

"Do you mean that they will die anyway? That isn't fair."

"We are demons, my dear," Elizabeth answered. "We are not *fair*."

"No, please, you can't let this happen. Let me bargain with you. Take my soul in place of their lives. Please."

"Your soul? How intriguing. I wondered if you would offer to sacrifice it, my dear." Before Bastien's horrified eyes, Elizabeth reached out to Althea.

Terror gripped his heart. God, not that price. No, he wanted Althea for eternity, but dear God, he knew he couldn't let her give up her soul. Yannick was right—she deserved life and happiness.

"No!"

Bastien saw Yannick launch forward and haul Althea back. "You are not getting her soul."

With his preternatural speed, Bastien moved between Althea and the queen. Elizabeth laughed, a soft melody that spoke of demonic evil. She sashayed forward until her fingertips touched his chest. He glared down at her as she walked her fingertips up to the base of his neck.

"I have no intention of taking her soul, gentlemen, but if she can help you find yours, perhaps you will live to see another moonrise."

Bloody cryptic demonesses. "We have no souls," Bastien snapped, "What do you—?"

But Elizabeth vanished.

23

Discovery

"If we are to die with the dawn, I want one last night of pleasure." Yannick kissed Althea's hand. She was lovely, the siren who had seduced him in his dreams. Behind the mask, her eyes widened. Around her neck, his gift glittered, emeralds that couldn't compare with the vivid green of her eyes.

His carriage rumbled up to the door of Madame Roi's, passing the long line of elegant coaches that waited outside the brothel.

Strange to think he hadn't known of this club, though since he had escaped Zayan's imprisonment he'd spent little time in London. The less the better, to help preserve his secret.

None of that mattered now. Not his care in protecting the family name by keeping his secret. Not his conviction that the most honorable option would be to let himself be destroyed. Damnation, he didn't want to die now.

Tears glittered at the corners of Althea's eyes. One spilled over the mask, leaving a trail that glinted beneath the light of the street flare. "I am praying that neither of you will die," she whispered.

His carriage stopped, horses snorting.

"I doubt praying will help Bastien and me," he said ruefully. He took hold of her hand, small and delicate in white satin gloves, and handed her up into his carriage. He stroked her hip, ran his hand down her thigh as she moved up.

God, he wanted to touch her as much as he could.

Only a few hours to make love to Althea in every way he'd fantasized about.

Yannick could barely swallow as she disappeared into his coach.

Bastien grinned. "Tell your coachman to race home. We have a lot to do in just a few hours." Then his expression sobered. "I'm sorry Yannick, I should have destroyed him. Then we wouldn't be facing destruction—"

"I think I understand."

Yannick looked up inside the coach to watch Althea settle her skirts around her, every inch a beautiful lady. She'd cried for him and no one had ever done that before.

"It's for the best, Bastien. How could we ever have claimed her for eternity? We'd have to turn her and we have no right to do that." Hoisting on the door's handle, he jumped up into the carriage. He sat at Althea's side and nuzzled her cheek as Bastien took the seat opposite. The carriage moved on, making all possible haste through the crowded London streets.

"Would you take off my mask?" Althea asked.

Yannick reached for the ties.

"No, don't," Bastien protested. "You are lovely and mysterious when masked. All you need is a whip. . . ." He gave a lusty sigh.

Yannick couldn't help but grin himself. Bastien was determined not to give in to emotion, to play the scoundrel right to the end.

On impulse, Yannick drew Althea into a hot kiss and lifted her onto his lap. Her rounded bottom settled across his thighs, sweetly cuddling his erect cock. When she'd offered her soul in return for his life, he'd known terror like he'd never felt, even more than on the night he'd died. His blood had run ice cold. Althea's soul could not be claimed unless she were dead or undead and he'd expected the demoness to trick Althea into sacrificing herself in some way so she was lost to them forever. Thank the devil that Elizabeth had refused the offer.

Yannick broke the kiss and brushed his fingertip along Althea's bow-shaped upper lip. The mask made Althea mysterious and enticing, her deep green eyes and tumbling burgundy curls a lovely contrast to the black.

He lifted her chin and, holding her gaze, kissed her again. He groaned as her tongue slid into his mouth, toyed with his fangs, and tangled with his tongue. She kissed expertly now but this kiss was more . . . more intense. It was raw and needy, poignant and sad. Her fingers slid into his hair, clutching, holding him tight to her as she devoured his mouth.

Yes, angel, kiss me hard. His cock swelled and pressed eagerly upward toward her bottom. She wriggled on him, deliberately teasing.

Bastien made no move to join them. In truth, Yannick thought he deserved some private delights with Althea. He wasn't the bloody idiot who had condemned them to destruction over a point of honor toward a demon who'd tried to imprison them for eternity. But he did understand why Bastien had done it. His brother was soft-hearted—weak, their father had complained. For all Bastien had fought in dozens of duels, he always deliberately ensured he never killed anyone. Bastien was sensitive, like the poets. He wounded deep, but refused to show it.

Yannick could understand why Bastien felt he owed a life to the vampire who'd saved him from a humiliating death, but it didn't stop him from wanting one night to make love to Althea in private and express his love for her.

He wanted it, but could not do it. What was the point in laying his heart bare, in trying to coax Althea to fall in love with him, when he was only going to die? He couldn't risk hurting her.

Bastien had the right idea.

Tonight, it was time to introduce Althea to all the delights a threesome could offer.

"Welcome to our home, sweet angel."

Still masked, Althea waited as Bastien removed her cloak and handed it to the impassive, white-haired butler who had opened the door.

"That is all," Yannick commanded. The man bowed and left.

"Very correct," Bastien commented, "but we shock him. He's been here since Father's day and has never approved of us." His handsome face lit up with his cheeky grin. "None of the servants approved of us—except the young maids. Our valets even used to spy on us, providing Father with regular reports of our scandalous behavior."

"Was he very moral then, your father?" she asked tentatively.

"No. And let us not discuss him." Bastien led her to the sweeping stairs. "Let us get to bed."

As she'd suspected, Brookshire House far outshone Sir Randolph's townhouse. Yannick's home was an enormous manor on Park Lane, overlooking the verdant stretch of Hyde Park. Over the generations, the most exquisite art and furnishings had been acquired, she could see. Portraits and other oils covered every inch of the paneled walls. Chairs and tables in every imaginable style filled the foyer, all beautiful, priceless. Overhead, the foyer ceiling was a painted dome, richly detailed with gilt and elaborate moldings. It was breathtaking. Althea felt foolish gawking, but couldn't help it as she let them lead her upstairs.

And finally she was in Yannick's bedchamber. But she realized he didn't use it, of course—he slept in his coffin. Curious, she whispered, "Where do you keep your coffin?"

"In a secret room, accessed through a panel by the fireplace."

She nodded. "We had searched for you at the Inn during the day, Father and I, but couldn't find where you had hidden."

"That was a huge undertaking." He grimaced. "First I had the box hidden in one of the old stables no longer used by the Inn, and then I had to erase the memory of every servant who'd helped to place it there."

He lifted her hand and tugged at her satin gloves. "But tonight, angel, we are just a man and a woman." A smile curved his seductive mouth. "*Two* men and a woman."

A shiver raced down her spine as Bastien began to undo the buttons along her back. Bastien was far more adept with fine gowns than Sarah. Her dress gaped in no time, and his hands, warm and strong, slid in to capture her breasts.

"Bloody corset ties," he cursed.

But suddenly she felt them give, felt the tight garment slacken, even as his hands cupped her breasts. He'd cut the ties with his fangs.

Being undressed by two men was the most delicious delight. Yannick slid her gloves off, nibbling her fingers after he did. Her gown dropped to the floor, displaying her curves, still molded by the corset and hidden by her gauzy shift. In a heartbeat, her corset sailed over into the corner. Bastien drew up her shift and lifted it over her head.

Yannick left, then, and returned with a full-length cheval mirror from his dressing room. It reflected the most scandalous image: a red-haired woman, nude but for garters and stockings and a black mask, and two men in impeccable evening dress.

She wanted this. Wanted to watch what it looked like. Wanted to be both voyeur and delighted participant.

Neither twin moved to remove his clothing. Instead, fully dressed, they bent their heads to her nipples. Sensation exploded through her from her breasts at the exact instant she saw the reflection. One golden head and one white-blond head suckling at her, their pale hair a startling contrast to the midnight black of their clothes.

Four hands skimmed up her naked thighs and stroked amongst the dark red curls at the juncture. She was already sopping wet, already so aroused, so ready for them.

Bastien moved around to her rear and turned her. Stubble scratched over the sensitive curves of her bottom. She squealed as the whiskers abraded between her cheeks. Moaned in anticipation as Bastien's tongue massaged her puckered entrance.

"Look behind you at the mirror," Yannick urged, his voice thick and husky.

She did. Gasped. Her curves reflected back to her—the indent at the small of her back and the flare of her bottom. With his hands on her cheeks, Bastien was buried between the plump globes of her derrière.

All the tension inside her snapped with the force of a lashing whip. The climax hit her hard, and she screamed with it.

"God, she's coming already," Bastien said. Yannick's hand was between her legs, his hand catching honey that poured out of her. She blushed as it spilled over his fingers. There was so much of it.

She knew they could wait no longer and neither could she.

Yannick carried her to the bed as Bastien tore off his clothing. Buttons popped off his gorgeous satin waistcoat. He trampled his starched cravat after he removed it. His linen shirt flew and almost landed in the fire.

"Bloody boots," Bastien cursed, as he jumped around to tug them off.

Althea dissolved into helpless giggles. Which stopped the instant he was naked and he pushed her down onto the bed. He kissed her senseless, but she still peeked around him to watch Yannick undress. Yannick merely shifted shape for a moment. His clothes fell to the floor as he changed to bat form and then he changed back.

He flashed a triumphant grin.

She couldn't resist giggling. It was wrong to laugh, knowing what would happen at dawn, but she wanted just a few hours of happiness . . .

And she wanted to try to understand the queen's words. How could she help them find their souls? What could that mean?

But her wits scattered to the winds as Bastien pinned her arms above her head. His large hands wrapped tight around her wrists. Pointing upward, her breasts, tipped by swollen, hard nipples, poked his naked chest. His long, strong leg clamped across hers. Being captured was exhilarating. A little frightening, but terribly thrilling. She struggled playfully, but he had her imprisoned, utterly at his mercy.

She licked her lips, breathless with anticipation. Soft fabric brushed her arm. Bastien's cravat, looped around his right hand.

"Hand me your cravat," he called back to Yannick.

"What in blazes are you doing?" Yannick demanded.

"Tying me up, I believe," she said, as calmly as she could. But the very words sent another rush of molten fluid pouring from her cunny.

Bastien whispered hotly by her ear, "Sometimes, being absolved from control allows one to be the most daring."

"I want to try," she whispered. The linen looped around her wrists to bind her hands. Bastien's scent, sandalwood soap and the tantalizing hint of sweat, was imbued in the fabric. Snug, it bit into her skin.

"Too tight?" Bastien asked.

A little, but that made it more exciting, so she shook her head.

With Yannick's cravat, he secured her bound hands to the corner post of the bed. She was stretched diagonally across the large mattress. A not-so-innocent captive of gorgeous vampires. Spread upon an altar for their pleasures . . .

Fear struck suddenly. "You aren't going to whip me, are you?"

"No, little dove. Only torment you." And with that threat, Bastien licked the rim of her ear and made her feet tingle.

Powerful, stronger than mortal men, the twins touched her with gentle caresses that inflamed her heart. They touched her swollen, aching breasts and she gasped at the relief. Skimmed their palms over her smooth belly. Slid their fingers between her thighs. Yannick's fingers stirred her into a moaning, sticky frenzy.

Althea squirmed on the bed. It drove her mad that she couldn't touch them too. It was torture not to stroke the muscles of their shoulders and backs, or squeeze their taut, delectable asses, or play with their hard, wobbling cocks.

She yearned and wanted and needed and couldn't bear it anymore. She wanted to join with them as intimately as possible. In a soft voice raspy from her sighs, she begged, "Make love to me, please. I want you both. Both at the same time."

She dredged up her courage and met Bastien's gaze. "You wanted to cram me full."

At her naughty words, both men gave deep, throaty groans, and their need crackled in the room like magic, like sparkling lights and spinning stars.

Bastien spread her thighs wide and, despite her eagerness to try, she tensed. She remembered Ruby's screams from Madame Roi's.

"Relax, sweeting, just relax," he urged. "We will make it

beautiful for you." He licked his finger, then slid the wet tip over her clit.

Jolts of dizzying pleasure raced up from her nub and she could barely think. She looked from Bastien to Yannick. Their eyes were gold discs, reflecting candlelight—hiding their hearts. Hiding their deepest emotions.

She knew they had so much pain in their hearts from their pasts. Even though they were vampires, they still knew pain, they still ached for love.

Was this what the queen had meant about their souls? That they still possessed souls because they were capable of love?

"But first . . ." Althea gulped. Here she was, tied up, and about to coerce two vampires to reveal their hearts. She took a long breath to steady her nerves. She wanted to see inside their hearts—she loved them and she needed to know who they truly were. "How did you die, Bastien? What happened to you?"

"Not now." He bent to her breasts.

"No," she protested. "I must know. I need to know before I can make love to you, Bastien." Her legs were free and she skimmed her feet up his long legs. She pressed her heels into his taut buttocks. "Please."

Like a springtime river over a dam, his story spilled out—so quickly she had to struggle to follow. About his father's whippings over Zayan. About his rage and humiliation; his death in the gutter. About a bastard child. He spoke without emotion, but she knew the pain churned underneath.

"What of your . . . your child?" she asked around the lump in her throat.

"It didn't live. Nor did the mother, a maid. I wanted to provide for the child, I did, but I never had the chance. . . ."

Two tears dripped down his cheeks, falling off the prominent ridges of his cheekbones. She'd never seen him give in to emotion. No, these men had souls. She believed it.

"How is it that you are my prisoner, Althea," Bastien whispered, "but you have forced me to reveal my heart to you?"

Once again she wished she were free so she could hold him tight. "I suspect because I did not force you. You needed to talk about those things."

"I'm sorry for the child, and for its mother, who was a saucy dairymaid. If I could have turned her . . . I don't know . . . I might have done. But there was nothing I could do for the babe."

Althea's heart lurched at his story, and skipped a beat as Yannick rubbed his brother's shoulder, consolingly. She felt her tears roll from the corners of her eyes into her hair. "I'm so sorry."

Bastien kissed her tears away, his damp cheek brushing hers. She saw Yannick watch them, lashes lowered. He looked troubled. "And what about your fiancée?" she asked him.

"I think we should have gagged her," Yannick said. And he put his fingers to her lips. "Shh. Tonight is not the time for pain."

"I stole his fiancée," Bastien admitted. He rolled off her and lay at her side—her left side, the way he had done in dreams. "I took anything that was his. But, of course, her family refused to allow her to marry a second son. Her father then lost his fortune at hazard and the family shoved her into a duty match with a wealthy viscount."

Yannick sat up and shrugged. "I've never been fortunate enough to capture a woman's heart."

"Nonsense!" Althea cried. "You are gorgeous, charming, titled—"

"And women wanted to marry me, but not one loved me."

"You were cold and cautious," Bastien said. "Women never believed you loved them. Even your pretty little fiancée. You never gave her passion."

"I gave them respect—which was what I believed a woman

wanted. Blast, I don't want to waste the night talking about my failings." Yannick skimmed his fingertips along her arms, from her underarms to her wrists. She never would have guessed that a touch there would make her cunny throb. But it did. "The truth is that I never did love them. I was waiting for you, Althea. And, Hades, none of those women would have hunted a demon for me or offered her soul for me. I love you so much, angel." He ripped through Bastien's knots, freeing her.

"Get on top of me, sweeting." Bastien massaged her numbed wrists.

"On top?"

"You on top is what I crave right now, love."

But on top? "I have no idea what to do," she admitted. "How to . . . to—"

"To ride me? Like a stallion, love."

"I don't ride. Not well, at least."

"This is instinctive. Trust me."

She straddled Bastien's hips, poised over his cock, which curved over his flat, muscular stomach. Suddenly she felt powerful. In charge. In control. Exciting but nerve-wracking. But she wanted to do this properly, wanted to please him.

Instinctive, he'd promised.

She remembered the courtesan at Madame Roi's climbing aboard that enormous cock. Bastien didn't hold himself upright, so she did, sliding her hand around the thick, hot flesh. His smell flooded her senses. Moist, rich, and ripe.

Holding herself up on her knees, she brushed his cock against her sticky nether lips, prying them apart. She sank down on him slowly and his cock filled her, making her gasp. She was down to the hilt, and ground her hips down against him to take him in as much as she could. Her clit hit his groin. Stinging pleasure rocketed through her.

"Oh lord!"

"Move up and down on me," he urged. "Ride me."

Awkwardly she did. Should she ride fast, gallop on him, or ride slowly, the way genteel ladies trotted their mounts? She rose up slowly, then sank down and slapped his ballocks with her bottom. He groaned and so did she. The slapping was rather fun. She gave another bounce, faster. His girth teased the ridges inside her, the impact rasped her clit, and once again she squashed his balls with her arse.

Althea liked riding hard like this, so she did, hammering on him. With bang after bang, her clit hit against his flesh until she was dazed, dizzy, and pounding on him like a crazed wanton, her hair lashing her breasts. Bastien pulled her forward, arched up, and took her right nipple into his mouth. Framed by his fangs, her pink nipple disappeared between his lips. His hips bucked up to hers and he rubbed himself hard against her throbbing, abraded clit.

Yes, yes, yes.

More of this . . . just a little more . . . the climax was mounting with delicious insistence.

He moved.

Her clit lost contact and she groaned in frustration. Blindly, she tried to reseat herself in the same place. But as he lowered she had to shift position, lifting her derrière. Suddenly she knew why he'd done that. Her bottom was now up and ready for Yannick.

Dear heaven. There was no turning back now.

But her anus seemed to tingle in anticipation and she thrust her rear back as she moved up and down on Bastien's long, rigid pole. Something wet and warm teased her. Yannick's tongue.

Something pressed against her entrance. Not big enough to be his cock. His wetted finger. Slowly, he worked it inside with short, gentle thrusts, filling her to the brim.

"Ooh!"

Her cry froze both men. But she rocked tentatively back against Yannick. A stronger, more compelling pleasure than

she'd ever known spiraled through her. Truly addictive pleasure. She thrust back harder.

Her arse was so sensitive—it felt as good to be filled there as
in her quim.

Yannick kissed her spine, thrusting his finger in deep.
Heavenly pleasure washed over her. But she wanted . . . something bigger. Something that would fill her more.

Yannick pressed the head of his cock—thicker and bigger
than he'd ever seen it—between Althea's plump, flushed cheeks.
Her taut little hole still resisted his entrance, and he pushed
gently. God, he didn't want to hurt her, but he yearned to be
buried in her.

Her soft, sweet moans filled his bedchamber as he rubbed and
pushed his cock against the puckered rim. Suddenly she opened
for him and his head popped inside. Her muscles instantly
clamped tight around him, gripping him in their fiery bite.

With Bastien inside her, she was extra tight and he was
sheathed in burning velvet.

Damn, it was good. So good.

Slowly, he thrust in, a little deeper each time.

She cried out and he retreated.

"Oh, I can't—" she gasped and he withdrew completely.
Gave her time to breathe. She could, he knew she could. He
just had to fight for control and give her time.

Bastien nuzzled her right ear, and he licked the rim of her
left one, soothing her.

"Try again," she begged. "Please."

She would be looser now, open for him. Yannick took it
slowly, and this time, inch by inch, he filled her. Suddenly she
took him all the way in, and his groin slid forward to press tight
against her voluptuous cheeks.

Engulfed in her vicelike grip, he was on the brink. He felt
Bastien move, felt the fullness of Bastien's cock in her quim.
And then he couldn't think.

He pumped into her, loving her, trying to hang on to his climax. All he could see was the back of her head, her wild tumble of dark red hair flying about as he and Bastien fucked her. He could see his brother's face was contorted in agony, and knew he looked as much of a slave to the incredible pleasure.

He'd expected Althea to stay still and let them fuck her. But she didn't. She moved with them, wild and unfettered.

"Oh God," she wailed, and he realized that Bastien was stroking her hard clit between their bodies. He tried to match Bastien's pace until she cried, "Harder. And deeper. I do like it deep."

The blend of wanton and innocent drove him wild. And he was lost. Thrusting wildly. Sweat poured into his eyes, off his face.

"I'm going to . . . going to . . . Oh!"

Yannick surrendered control at her desperate announcement. His orgasm surged through him like pounding waves. A bolt of magic fire shot from his balls, down the length of his cock, and exploded deep into her tight arse. His brain dissolved, his spine melted, and he collapsed against her. Inside the maelstrom, he heard Althea's sobs and cries of pleasure. He heard Bastien yell as he climaxed. And against Althea's ear, Yannick gave her the only promise he could.

"I love you, angel. If I had eternity, I'd love you for it."

Bastien joined in. "I love you too, little dove." Then Bastien groaned. "Damn, Yannick, I think she might have fainted."

Althea floated in a velvety black void. She was flying in heavenly, sated exhaustion.

Two wonderful orgasms.

She had done the most scandalous thing. She had made love to two men—two men she adored—at the same time and it had been exquisite. Earth-shattering.

Strangely, this no longer felt wrong or forbidden or bad.

Perhaps she was as sensual as Yannick and Bastien had told her she was.

Strong hands skimmed over her body.

"Are you all right?" Yannick's voice, soft and filled with concern.

Strength returned—and with it desire. If they were to have only one night, she intended to enjoy it thoroughly. "Do you think you could do it again?" she asked.

"Did you hear what we said?" Bastien asked, "After you came?"

She nodded. Smiled up at his silvery eyes. "I believe you said you loved me."

"Do you have anything to say to us?" he asked.

Althea caught her breath at the naked uncertainty in his expression. And Yannick, the arrogant earl, looked vulnerable, awaiting her answer. "Well," she said slowly, "I have always wondered what color your eyes were."

"Blue—" Yannick's voice caught. "Our eyes were both blue. Mine were a greenish blue, and Bastien's were light, gray-blue."

She'd teased and a twinge of guilt hurt her tight throat. She reached up and touched both Yannick and Bastien's rough-hewn, stubbly cheeks. "I love you both. I love you so much. I would give my soul to save you both."

Her heart soared at the beautiful, loving smiles that lightened their serious, cautious expressions.

As though in response, a bright, golden light flooded the room. Brighter than fire, pouring in from the doorway. She shut her eyes, almost blinded by it.

"Well, my dear, do you truly mean that?"

Althea almost screamed. Madame Roi, the vampire queen, dressed in a turquoise gown and cloaked in rich furs, suddenly stood at the foot of the bed, drumming her elegant fingers against one of the carved columns.

24

Turning

She was caught naked, sandwiched between two nude men! Althea's cheeks flamed as the vampire queen smirked down upon them.

Yannick and Bastien weren't embarrassed in the least. They blatantly stroked her body in front of the queen. Naked, they were pressed tight against her, Yannick to her derrière and Bastien to her quim. Their cocks were growing hard again, prodding her hips. The vampire queen must know exactly what had happened between them.

And with the three of them sprawled on the forest-green counterpane, she couldn't even pull a sheet over herself. She covered her breasts with her hands to preserve some modesty—

Then Althea realized the queen had asked her a question—did she truly mean it?

Before she could answer, Yannick snapped, "No, she doesn't." His commanding tone brooked no argument.

"No, I do. I truly do." She didn't want the queen to leave. And she did mean it.

"What a delightful tangle," the queen observed. "I do wish I had been invited. I miss being shared by the Demon Twins—the most handsome vampires in London. And the most skillful lovers."

As the queen leered at Yannick and Bastien's naked bodies, jealousy burned like acid in Althea's stomach. What price would the vampire queen ask? Perhaps the queen might demand they become her lovers again.

She knew, in her soul, that if they agreed to it, it would be to save her. But could she give them up to save their lives? She must.

The queen arranged her skirts and sat on the end of Yannick's luxurious bed. She waved her hand elegantly at the men.

"You have found a most intriguing mortal. Surely you would want to bargain to live and keep her for eternity."

Althea's breath caught as Yannick tightened his protective embrace. If she gave up her soul, would she be a vampire like Yannick and Bastien? The twins were not like other vampires—they weren't evil, deadly predators who had no mercy and no capacity to love. What if she became a brutal demon instead?

"I wish we could, Your Highness," Yannick said. "But Althea deserves to live, to marry, to be a huntress, to have children."

They weren't going to transform her . . . the twins were not going to make her undead . . .

"But as a vampire, she can still marry," the queen pointed out, "And give you both children."

"Vampires can have children?" Althea gasped.

The queen fixed her with a pointed stare. "I would be willing to spare their lives for you."

Should she curtsy? It hardly seemed right to get off the bed and do it naked. But she knew she must be effusive, she must be grateful. She must behave like a proper serf. "Thank you, thank you so very much, Your . . . Your Highness."

"But there is a condition—"

Althea swallowed hard, waiting for the price. It would be high, but she could pay it.

"You must agree to be changed," the queen continued. "As I told you, they are linked by the magic of the *Geminiani*. If you divide them, you drain their powers. So you must pledge yourself as their shared mate. For eternity."

Althea gaped. The cost was to become their shared mate? There must be a catch. A twist.

"Too easy?" the queen smiled. "But you will be sacrificing your mortal life. It will devastate your father, I am sure. But an existence as a vampire is so much more fulfilling than a human life. And so much more pleasurable."

She must do it, must do it to save Yannick and Bastien. It meant leaving everything she knew, the father she loved, the goals she wanted to achieve. Her heart pounded at the enormity of what she was about to do. In England, it was illegal for a widow to marry her late husband's brother, yet she was about to pledge herself to two brothers.

"What kind of vampire will I be?" she asked, hearing the shake in her voice.

"If you are making the choice with a pure heart . . ." The smile turned evil. "You will have to wait and see."

She *must* do it. Love was worth the risk. Her mother had believed that and had married a man who hunted vampires because she loved him.

If she were a vampire like Yannick and Bastien, who were noble and loving, she could give them the love they both needed. Yes, it was truly worth the risk.

And if she became a good vampire, she could still protect mortals from the evil ones.

Bastien kissed her lips. "I would be honored if you were to pledge as my mate. As both our mates."

Yannick lifted her fingers to his lips, between his fangs. He kissed them. "Will you marry us, Althea?"

A nervous giggle almost escaped. She'd never expected a proposal of marriage at all, certainly not one like this. Not naked on a bed in front of . . . an audience. Not from two men. She couldn't help but smile as the queen winked at her. She realized the vampire queen had given her the perfect reason to give in to her wildest desires and claim both twins.

"Your Highness," she asked nervously, "Will you ensure they live?"

The queen nodded and stood up from the bed. "Well, my dear, aren't you going to give an answer?"

"Yes," she gasped. "Heavens, yes."

"Our shared mate, for eternity?" Yannick asked.

"Yes." Tears welled as the twins hugged her tight and rained kisses on her cheeks.

To Althea's astonishment, the queen dabbed at her eyes with a turquoise silk handkerchief. "Congratulations, gentlemen. I am sure you will endeavor to keep her very happy. And now, I have an appointment with Lucifer."

Before Althea could blink, the golden light swirled around Elizabeth and she vanished inside its vortex. The light faded to twinkles. The queen, and her sumptuous furs, had disappeared.

Althea looked from Yannick to Bastien. "Now what do we do?"

Their fangs lengthened before her eyes. She'd never seen their canines grow so long and they appeared wickedly sharp.

Their eyes glittered, unreadable mirrors.

"Now we give you eternity," Bastien promised.

She tensed and closed her eyes, waiting for the bite. She caught hold of the strands of hair covering her neck and brushed them back. "I am ready," she announced.

It wouldn't hurt too much . . . surely, it wouldn't.

"I'm ready," she repeated. Why wouldn't they bite now, while her courage was strongest? Hot, moist lips trailed over the swell of her breasts. They kissed so differently. Yannick liked to use the tip of his tongue, Bastien the raspier flat.

"Please . . ." she murmured.

Or were they having second thoughts? They might love her, but they were both strong, arrogant vampires. Dominant men. Could they truly share forever?

They shared her breasts, swirling their tongues around her nipples in perfect unison. Pleasure flooded through her. Opening her eyes, she saw Yannick's pale hands on her hips, his signet ring glinting. He lifted her, settled her on top of his body so she lay on her back over him. She splayed her legs to balance herself.

His cock was hard again, hot and thick and rigid, jutting against her bottom.

Bastien poured a stream of viscous fluid onto Yannick's hand. Her body blossomed in anticipation and his slippery finger slid easily into her as he spread the fluid on her. She sobbed at the mind-numbing delight, whimpered as he withdrew, until she felt a bigger, harder pressure against her rim and her muscles resisted opening for something so big.

With a throaty growl, Yannick pushed his cock inside. With a jolt of pleasure and pain, her entrance gave around him, then snapped closed.

He cradled her beneath her breasts once more. Against her ear, his gravelly voice tickled. "God, I love to feel the head pop in past your tight muscles, to have you grip me so hard . . ."

She moaned at his words.

"It's such torture to hold back . . ."

"Then don't," she whispered, "Don't hold back." What had she just asked for?

She rocked on him, savoring the way his thick shaft stretched her as he slowly pushed deeper inside. Coarse curls rubbed her derrière when he reached the hilt. At that instant, she turned her face to him and he covered her lips with his own.

He held still, kissing her, as Bastien mounted her from above. Golden hair trailed across her face, as Bastien pressed the head of his prick to her sticky folds. Like an artist with a brush, he stroked her wetness, nudged her lips apart.

The moment of shock as Bastien filled her too. Impossibly full. Instinct made her tense—it would be too much. Once again, they soothed with kisses and caresses, until she relaxed and knew nothing but pleasure and the urge to come. They both thrust together, the two shafts withdrawing and then surging forth.

"My bite will be gentle, little dove." Bastien kissed her cheek, nibbled her ear, put his mouth to her throat.

She knew he would take care, knew she could trust him—

They thrust hard, another deep double thrust. She was being pleasured in every way possible, in cunny and rear, her nipples caressed, her neck suckled, Bastien's shaft kissing her clit with every long stroke.

Her skin stretched as his fangs pressed. She was so dizzy with pleasure that the touch of his canines sent a jolt of delight through her.

A pinch. A prick. A push. The sharp pain vanished in a heartbeat or two. But another twinge came as the tips of teeth found the wall of—

No, don't think. Don't think about it ... Heavens! Her blood was flowing. She felt it being drawn from her.

They were supposed to feed her their blood but only at the point of death, she knew. Which meant they must take hers until—

Yannick's fangs plunged in. She was growing weaker as they pumped their cocks in and drank her blood. Their thrusts grew harder, more frenzied. Every stroke became magnified. It was as though they could stroke her very soul.

Yes, yes, it was worth dying for this.

Her climax crashed through her. She couldn't cry out—she was too weak. All she could do was whimper and moan and gulp for air.

Now. Althea heard Yannick's soft, deep voice in her mind. Dimly, as though she was floating away from him. Her orgasm kept pulsing in beautiful, powerful waves, as though she would never stop coming. Never.

Yannick's wrist touched her lips. His blood dripped into her mouth, struck her tongue with its coppery heat. She put her lips to his flesh but was too drained to suck.

Yannick's blood filled her mouth in a choking stream. She forced her throat to swallow.

Bastien's wrist replaced Yannick's. A different taste—more tart, almost spicy. She found the strength to drink and suckled at his wrist. He timed each stroke of his cock with her suckling, riding so high that his cock must be painfully bent.

But she was still coming . . . still coming with long, wonderful pulses, and—

One hard, slippery stroke ignited her. She exploded with the force of gunpowder. Oh God, she was coming apart. Shattering.

Drinking made the pleasure last, so she grabbed Yannick's wrist and drank greedily. Yannick had to pry her off so Bastien could give her more. She must be draining them of their blood, but each gulp gave her strength, heightened every sensation, until she sobbed with the racking spasms of her never-ending climax.

Beneath her, Yannick cried out. His hips pushed up, hard and demanding. She felt him come. Felt the hot rush inside her. An instant later, Bastien joined them both in ecstasy.

Althea's chest rose and fell fervently, trying to draw in air.

Bastien, still buried inside her, lay on top of her, his head snuggled against her neck. He'd licked both wounds and miraculously they no longer hurt.

Did she feel different? Did she feel . . . dead?

She didn't feel crushed by Bastien's weight, though her skin felt especially sensitive, as though she could feel the tickle of each golden hair sprinkling Bastien's beautiful body. She felt the ridges and planes of Yannick's muscular body beneath her more acutely than she had before.

The candles seemed to glow brighter.

Everything surrounding her—the bed, the paintings on the walls—was clear, in focus, even without her spectacles. The air held a different scent. Her nose filled with the rich, ripe aroma of blood. She drank it in as though it was the finest perfume. A rhythm drummed through her head. She could hear all three of their heartbeats.

Tentatively, she ran her tongue over her teeth.

"Fangs don't appear until the night after you've changed," Yannick murmured. His cock was still in her, soft now, but thick enough to leave her breathless. Shifting his hips, he withdrew. Bastien rolled off and moved from the bed.

She closed her eyes. How close was it to dawn?

Cool water dribbled onto her inner thigh. Surprised, she snapped open her lids. With a wet washcloth, Bastien bathed her, his touch loving and gentle as he rinsed her sticky quim.

"Roll over, little dove," he instructed. She did so, but her limbs felt strangely weak now, as though they were going numb. She lay upon the wrinkled counterpane as he washed her derrière. "A hot bath will have to wait."

Yannick yawned. "God, I feel weak. Drained. It's almost dawn."

She yawned too. "I feel so tired . . ."

"It's the change. And dawn. We have to sleep—"

"But it's worked hasn't it? She didn't lie? You two aren't going to die?"

"We won't know until the sun rises, love." Yannick stretched and sat up. "Tonight I think I will sleep nude." He held out his hand to her. "Sleep with me tonight, angel—if we survive."

"No." Bastien dropped the cloth in the basin lying on the bed. "Sleep with me, Althea." Then he laughed. "Hell, you can have her tonight, brother, because you're the eldest. But tomorrow, she sleeps with me."

Sleep? In a coffin? But in Yannick's arms, she could do it—she knew she could.

Yannick pressed a panel in the wall and a section of the wall swung open with a click. Beyond was darkness, although she could distinguish two gleaming coffins on the floor. Bastien extinguished the candles in Yannick's bedchamber and plunged them into the dark. But in moments, her sight adjusted and she could see. It was like her first dream in which the twins had shared her. Even though Bastien stood in the darkness, she could see his golden hair, his bronze-red mouth, golden curls on his chest, and the thick nest of gold between his thighs. Yannick was silver and shadow, pale shining hair and silver eyes beneath black lashes.

"With the drapes closed, we can wait a little longer—we have a few minutes after the sun rises before we must go to sleep."

Her heart thumped, each beat a countdown to learning the truth. The men were moving away from her, possibly to protect her, but she grasped Yannick's hand, then Bastien's. They would meet this fate together.

The twins broke free of her grip. "We have to keep you safe, love."

They stepped into the secret room. "You stay there," Yannick commanded.

She was so tired she had to lean against the wall to stand up. Only a few minutes . . . it must be only a few minutes . . .

Once she'd never believed it possible to fall in love with a vampire. Once she'd thought it unforgivably sinful to have two lovers.

How would she survive now if she lost them? How could she endure eternity with a broken heart?

Althea spun around to watch at Yannick's crimson velvet drapes. At the top, there was a small gap. Gray light showed there, revealing the brightening sky. The sun must be up.

She was tempted to race to the drapes, to peek outside, to see, but she feared what would happen. And she couldn't will her feet to move.

She leaned heavily against the doorframe. Yannick moved unsteadily toward her, as though his legs were turning to water beneath him.

"It is dawn, angel. We aren't going to be destroyed. Now we have to get inside the coffins. Quickly."

Dawn.

Tears welled, broke free. The queen had not lied. Dawn had come and they were still alive—undead, rather.

Yannick's hand was outstretched, concern etched on his face. How clearly she could see now. She could even see the stark emotions in his eyes. Worry. And love. He might have died, yet all he felt was concern for her.

She tried to meet him halfway but her legs wouldn't obey. She tried to force them into a step but they crumpled. Yannick caught her. How he found the strength to scoop her into his arms, she couldn't imagine.

Bastien gave her a soft kiss as Yannick stopped beside one of the coffins. "I love you, little dove. And tomorrow night you are mine."

Finally she could see the color of Bastien's eyes—a hint of

the iris around the large, shiny black pupils. Gray-blue, the color of stormy seas.

Thank you, Althea, for believing in me. For seeing beyond the demon, Bastien murmured in her thoughts as he kissed her lips.

Love flooded through her at his kiss, his love, and it warmed her heart like a flame. A flame which would burn for eternity. She didn't feel as though she had given up her soul. How could she have no soul and feel such wonderful, delirious happiness inside?

Tomorrow at dusk she would awaken and hold both Yannick and Bastien in her arms again. At night they would explore pleasure once more . . .

And there are many more combinations that can be tried with three in the bed, Bastien promised in her head.

Exhausted, but happy, she giggled.

Yannick cuddled her close. "You don't regret your choice, do you?"

She glanced up and saw a hint of sparkling sea green in his eyes. Her throat tightened at the tenderness, the admiration, the joy she saw.

"How could I? I love you. Both of you. And I've learned love is far more powerful when shared among three."

Epilogue

"I just felt a kick!" Althea cried happily.

At her announcement, Yannick sat up so quickly to place his hand on her rounded belly, water sloshed out of the bath onto his polished floor. She couldn't help but laugh at his enthusiasm.

Resting against the other end of the enormous porcelain tub, Bastien grinned. "Push gently, brother."

Yannick did and to her delight and his, the baby kicked out in response. Even though she was immersed in hot water up to her fuller breasts, Althea saw a little bump push out and move. The bulge actually swung across her stomach before disappearing. She giggled again, knowing she was beaming. It was so amazing. Such a miracle.

"He's got a strong kick," Yannick crowed with obvious pride.

"Perhaps *she* has a strong kick," Bastien suggested, lifting his leg to soap it.

Althea glared indignantly at Yannick—he continually called the baby "he."

"After all," Bastien continued with a wink, "*her* mother is strong and courageous."

And her father was . . .

Well, in truth, she couldn't be sure. And though she'd been afraid that the twins would bicker and fight endlessly over the baby's paternity, they hadn't fought once. They spent every night coddling her instead. And making love to her.

Bastien stood, water sluicing off his chest, his slim hips, rolling down his lean legs. Steam swirled around him and her heightened senses inhaled his sensual scent. Sandalwood soap, clean skin, and rich blood.

His silver eyes glittered and she knew what he had in mind. She stroked her belly.

Sex isn't harmful for the baby, little dove, Bastien promised, his expression appealing and hopeful.

I fear your opinion might be biased, she teased. But she knew it to be true. Elizabeth, the vampire queen, had told her many facts about being an *enceinte* vampire.

His look of sudden worry lightened at her smile. She'd been astonished when Bastien had promised that at the end of her pregnancy, when she was tired and eager to deliver, sex was one of the time-honored methods to start the labor along. How did he come by such knowledge? He was so genuinely delighted to be a part of this baby's life. She knew he still grieved a little for his first, lost child.

And Yannick, too, spent every moment talking of being an expectant father.

Yannick bent and nibbled her bare breast. *Your breasts were utterly luscious before, but now they are irresistible.*

Althea sighed. The Demon Twins could not leave her plumper, rounder breasts alone. She had to admit her new, generous curves fascinated her too.

Yannick stood and swung out of the tub, sending water

cascading to the floor. She loved watching the way he attended to drying himself with a thick white towel. He dusted the towel over his body with spare movements. Rubbed his hair. Then tossed his towel aside, took another. *But we must help her dry and dress. Her father will be arriving soon.*

Yannick held out his hand. Bastien steadied her hips as Yannick lifted her from the tub. Thick warmth wrapped around her. Both men helped her dry, rubbing every inch of her through the towels. Bastien toweled off in haste. He flung the towel onto the heap of discarded ones.

And now to bed. Bastien nipped her throat.

No time. Yannick sighed.

This would be their last dinner with her father before he left for the Continent. The three of them would follow in a few weeks. The four of them, actually. Yannick, Bastien, their child, and herself. Yannick had purchased an estate—an old castle—near the Carpathians. They could not stay in England, for it would soon become blatantly apparent that the twins never aged.

Father had decided to return to the Carpathians as soon as he selected a young apprentice or two to help him hunt. Now he didn't destroy vampires. He was studying their culture and existence. Only when a vampire was rogue, evil, and uncontrollable, did he resort to destruction.

She was so grateful for Father's unconditional love. He'd been shocked by her decision to become a vampire. And by her unorthodox marriage—to two men! She'd feared he might collapse, but he was so happy to know she was safe, he'd survived her stunning news. And eventually he'd accepted it.

She remembered his kiss to her cheek. His soft words. "I love you far more than I care for society's rules, and if you are happy, then I am willing to welcome two demon sons-in-law."

And she was happy. She doubted any woman could be happier. And she knew their love grew stronger—her telepathic connection with both men became more powerful each day.

Lift your arms, sweeting. Yannick broke into her thoughts, holding out her gossamer-fine shift.

Sarah rarely had the chance to dress or undress her. The twins were so eager to make love that she was usually assisted in or out of her clothes by one of them. Not that she minded at all.

He slipped it over her head. The wispy fabric settled over her, but the hem sat up across the bulge of her belly. Bastien kissed her there, before tugging down her shift. "For you, little one inside. I cannot wait to meet you."

"You'll have to wait a few months," she reminded him.

"It will seem like eternity."

Can you imagine both our mouths on you, love?

Althea moaned as Yannick's hot breath whispered over her neck. Pregnant vampires were very sensitive, she'd discovered. And very responsive.

The dreams. Yannick still remembered the dreams. Dreams that still came to her—though they were no longer planted by Zayan. And they were no longer a glimpse of her destiny. Now they were erotic memories of all the wonderful pleasures she, Yannick, and Bastien shared.

Althea reached for Bastien's hand on her belly, twining her fingers in his. She clasped Yannick's hand and moved his palm to the small bulge too.

A threesome, soon to be a family of four. Tears threatened to spill as she smiled at both Yannick and Bastien, the wonderfully demonic twins.

I can't imagine anything I could ever want more.

Sink your teeth into BLOOD ROSE.
Coming in August 2007
from Aphrodisia . . .

1

---

*L*ondon, *October 18, 1818*

Sex. She wanted sex. But she wanted this anticipation, too.
Serena Lark stirred sensually on the bed, enjoying the feel of
silky sheets beneath her bare skin.

A candle lit the room—it could only be one, for the light
was weak and the candle must be close to guttering. Golden
light wavered on the wall and danced with the reflections of silvery blue moonlight.

Serena's hands skimmed her tummy and touched—boldly
stroked—her cunny, which ached in delightful agony.

Shadows swept over her. She saw the sudden darkness cross
her belly and she looked up. Her heart hammered but she
smiled a greeting at the two masked men who strolled arro-
gantly into her bedchamber. Lord Sommersby and Drake
Swift—the Royal Society's two most famous and daring vampire hunters. Both men were dressed for the hunt, though
masked, and they swept off their greatcoats as they crossed her
threshold.

A gold mask framed Swift's glittering green eyes and a deep royal purple mask clung to Lord Sommersby's face. Swift threw his hat aside, revealing his unfashionably long white-blond hair. He dropped a crossbow on the floor, followed by a sharpened wooden stake. He lifted a heavy silver cross from around his neck, letting the chain pool on the floor and the cross fall with a clunk.

As dark as Swift was fair, his lordship gave a courtly bow and doffed his hat. Thick, glossy, and dark brown, his hair tumbled over his brow. Her breath caught at the heat in his eyes—the dark, delicious brown of chocolate.

Serena crooked her finger and both men came to her, tugging their cravats loose as they prowled to her bed. They tore at their waistcoats and shirts, and stripped to the waist. She could barely breathe as she drank in the sight of two wide chests. Swift's skin was bronzed to a scandalous shade, which brought the gold curls on his sculpted muscles into stark relief. The earl was massive, possessing a barrel chest and biceps as big as her thighs. He looked like a giant, one with a body honed by battle with the strongest creatures on Earth.

She was dreaming. Even lost in it, she knew somehow. And in this dream, Serena had no idea what to say—what did one say when two men came to one's bed for the first time? Everything seemed inane. She was most terribly shy. And as a governess, she'd been well trained to be a silent servant. But she gave a welcoming moan—the prettiest, most feminine one she could muster.

Tension ratcheted in her. Desire flared as the men approached. They would touch her. Her heart tightened with each long, slow step they took. *Yes. Yes!*

Laudanum. Even here, in her dream, she remembered the laudanum. A few swallows in her cup of tea because she couldn't sleep.

Mr. Swift paused to yank off his trousers, and he flung them aside as he stalked toward her, his ridged abdomen rippling. He wore no small clothes. His magnificent legs were formed of powerful muscle, lean and hard.

And his cock. Serena looked at it and couldn't turn away. It curved toward his navel, thick and erect and surrounded by white-blond curls. She knew it would fill her completely, stretch her impossibly, and she knew it would be perfect inside.

Mr. Swift reached the bed first. He smiled, his teeth a white gleam in the darkened room. His hand reached—she followed the arc of his fingers with breath held—and he touched her bare leg. *Oh!*

"Miss Lark." He dropped to one knee. "Let us dispense with the pleasantries and begin with the delights." And with that he parted her thighs and dove to her wet cunny.

Candlelight played over his broad, tanned shoulders and the large muscles of his arms. His tongue snaked out and slicked over her. Serena arched her head back to scream to the ceiling.

So good!

Boot soles sharply rapped on the floor. Leather-clad knuckles gently brushed her cheek. Lord Sommersby. She flicked her eyelids open as Mr. Swift splayed his hands over her bottom, lifted her to his face, and slid his tongue in to taste her intimate honey.

Lord Sommersby looked so serious, and he never smiled. He required encouragement, so she held out her hand to him, but her smile vanished in a cry of shock and delight as Mr. Swift nudged her thighs wider, until her muscles tugged, and feasted on her. His lips touched her clit, the lightest brush, and pleasure arced through her. She tore the sheets with her fisted hands, heard silken seams rip.

Then, she squealed in frustration as Lord Sommersby lay his strong hand on his partner's shoulder and wrenched Drake Swift from his work.

"She is a woman beyond your ken, Swift. A woman to be both pleasured and treasured."

Pleasured and treasured. Serena could not believe she'd heard those words from the cool, autocratic Earl of Sommersby's lips. He thoroughly disapproved of everything about her, didn't he?

And then the earl was gloriously nude. The hair on his chest was lush and dark, and the curls arrowed down his stomach into a thick black nest between his thighs. His cock was straight and hard and remarkably fat, and it pointed downward, as though too heavy to stand upright. It swayed as he walked.

A sweep of his lordship's arm and his rich purple mask flew aside, revealing dark brown eyes narrowed with lust and a predatory determination in his expression that made his fine features harsh. "Out of my way, Swift."

"I think the lady wants *me* to finish, Sommersby." With an insolent grin, Swift rolled back onto his lean stomach and lowered to her sex once more. She lost all her breath in a whoosh.

To have two such beautiful, naked men argue over which would lick her to ecstasy . . .

It was almost too much to bear.

Lord Sommersby bent and licked her nipples. Of course this was a dream, for she lifted her breasts saucily to the earl and spread her legs wider for Mr. Swift. His lordship sucked her nipple at the exact instant devilish Mr. Swift slid fingers in her cunny and—dear heaven—her rump.

Her heart pounded; her nerves were as taut as a harp's strings. "I will let you bed me," she gasped, "If you let me hunt with you."

Drake Swift laughed, and thrust *two* fingers in her quim and ass. "You were made for this, lass. For naughty fucking. Not for hunting vampires."

How illicit and wonderful it was to be filled, to feel invaded with each thrust of his fingers. Serena looked to Lord Sommersby. "I would never risk your life."

"But you know it is what I want most of all," she whispered.

"Is it?" Drake gave a roguish wink that set her heart spiraling in her chest.

In the blink of her dreaming imagination, both men were kneeling on the bed at her sides, looking down on her, their smiles hot and wild.

How had—?

Mr. Swift's cock approached her mouth from the right, his lordship's from the left. The two huge, engorged heads met in the middle, touching right over her mouth.

Serena had never seen anything so erotic. So wildly arousing that she forgot about decorum, about bargaining, about hunting vampires.

What would if feel like to run her tongue around and between the two heads?

Their fluid was leaking together, making them deliciously wet and shiny—

What on earth was she doing? This was scandalous!

Her mouth opened to protest.

They moved to push their cocks in, parrying for position. Serena lost herself to the moment and stuck out her tongue . . .